"What exactly does Westman have?" Bolan demanded

"He has it all—tapes, disks, files that prove there's a major paramilitary force hard at work executing criminals. If you can believe my client, it's a national conspiracy."

The Executioner put a grim stare on the lawyer. It took a few moments to form the question, but he had to know.

"Point-blank—are they policemen?"

Abrams hesitated, broke Bolan's stare and swallowed hard. "Yes."

The Executioner had once vowed never to fire on a warrior on the same side, dirty or not. But any personal code he'd honored before had evaporated.

He was in it for the long haul, no matter who got stepped on along the way.

D0976494

DON PENDLETON's
MACK BOLAN.®

RENEGADE FORCE

A GOLD EAGLE BOOK FROM
WORLDWIDE.®

TORONTO • NEW YORK • LONDON
AMSTERDAM • PARIS • SYDNEY • HAMBURG
STOCKHOLM • ATHENS • TOKYO • MILAN
MADRID • WARSAW • BUDAPEST • AUCKLAND

First edition October 1998

ISBN 0-373-61462-4

Special thanks and acknowledgment to
Dan Schmidt for his contribution to this work.

RENEGADE FORCE

Wherever Law ends, Tyranny begins.

—John Locke
1632-1704

Any man, anywhere, who strives to do what is right, deserves to live in peace, respect and dignity. It's a simple philosophy, but without some code of honor, without respect for life, then life itself becomes meaningless. Without the law, we are no better than animals.

—Mack Bolan

CHAPTER ONE

Mack Bolan walked into the restaurant and pegged two men as stone-cold killers. He assessed the situation and knew that his rendezvous with the New York lawyer was poised to erupt into sudden violence.

Even still, taking out the two hardmen might prove his only way in if Bolan was to get a handle on this lawyer who had contacted the Justice Department with a very ugly tale about a rogue force of bad cops.

Policemen and other law-enforcement officers, either on active duty, retired or washed off their respective force, were possibly on a killing spree in cities across the country. And Hal Brognola had put together enough jagged pieces of an ominous puzzle to turn the Executioner loose. Factor in two weeks of major headlines about the mysterious, execution-style murders of mostly minority criminals from New York to Los Angeles, and it all smacked of a deadly riddle Bolan intended to solve. If nothing else, the allegations were insidious enough for him to launch a hard probe, take whatever came his way and run with it.

Bolan set his grim sights on the two hardmen for a moment, then let his surveillance wander around the place. He decided to stretch his luck that the goons hadn't come in with backup. Outside could prove different, if it even got that far.

The Executioner sized up the opposition. They were big men with hard faces and ice in their eyes. One wore a black leather trench coat, while the other guy had donned a thick corduroy jacket. Even from forty feet, Bolan spotted the bulges of holstered side arms beneath their coats. The two thugs had already slid in on Maury Abrams, the lawyer, pinching him in the booth from his flanks. Judging from the shock and fear on his contact's face, the soldier knew the lawyer wasn't acting. All that meant was a possible setup wasn't in the cards.

Corduroy said something to Abrams, then indicated the bulge under his coat. As the lawyer looked down and froze with eyes widening in panic, the Executioner knew it would be hit-or-miss from there on. If Abrams made a rabbit run out of terror, all hell was sure to break loose.

Bolan melted into the congestion of the crowd scene, on the far side of his potential quarry. It was a Greenbelt hot spot for the after-work players. Music was blaring, couples out on the dance floor, shaking and baking. Everyone was too caught up in the frenzy of potential night games to give Bolan more than a passing glance as he made his way around the circular bar, looking for partial cover from the two goons and Abrams in the booth. Luckily the bartenders were too busy slinging drinks to pay Bolan any immediate attention.

Just as well, he thought. He was there on deadly serious business with the potential to ruin everyone's fun. Beneath his long overcoat, he had the Beretta 93-R in shoulder holster, with the .44 Magnum Desert

Eagle riding quick-draw leather on his hip. A shoot-out in a public watering hole, though, wasn't in his plan. He needed to get Abrams away from the two goons, and would do whatever it took. If the slivers of information the lawyer had thrown Hal Brognola's way were part of some nationwide conspiracy among those sworn to protect and to serve, then Bolan was determined to keep the lawyer breathing.

Two hard questions flared into the Executioner's mind: How had the lawyer been trailed all the way from New York to Maryland, cornered now by potential enemies at the exact place and time Brognola had arranged? And were the lawyer's two unwanted escorts legitimate law-enforcement officers? He had no clue on the first question, but Bolan judged that the menace, the glint of something sadistic in the goons' eyes suggested they weren't simply cops on official business.

No, they wanted something—or someone—from the lawyer, and they meant to get it from him. And Bolan already knew the "someone" they were hunting. According to Brognola, a former Brooklyn homicide detective kicked off the force for misconduct was being brought in by Maury Abrams. Bolan wanted hard intel from the lawyer before rounding up his rogue-cop client. From there, the soldier knew, it was anybody's guess where it would all lead. But Bolan had a strong hunch the former homicide detective wanted immunity, planned to use Abrams to cut himself a sweetheart deal and have the Justice Department reel him in for protection from his former wolf pack of cutthroat lawmen.

As far as the Executioner was concerned, all bets

were off. He would take the action as it showed, make no promises.

Moments later, the goons presented him with an option. Abrams threw some bills on the table. They allowed the lawyer the final gulp of his drink, then they forced a grim casualness in ushering Abrams out of the booth. Out of the corner of his eye, Bolan spotted the bartender making his way toward him. But the Executioner was already en route, sliding farther down the bar, angling out of sight from the threesome.

At the instant the hardmen decided to check their surroundings, Bolan was blessed with a good several moments of cover behind a group hogging the end of the counter. When the goons marched Abrams toward the door, the soldier fell in behind them.

They were a dozen yards ahead, forging into the sprawling parking lot of the shopping center beyond the club. It was then Bolan heard enough to confirm his suspicions that he was dealing with a life-or-death situation. No doubt, there would only be one option.

"Who are you?" Abrams cried. "FBI? Justice?"

"Shut your mouth. Who we are isn't important. Like we already told you, if you give up your boy, you have my word you'll go home safely to your pretty Anglo wife and mongrel kids. You lie to us or resist in any way, we'll put a 9 mm hole between your eyes. I hope we're clear on that, Counselor."

Corduroy, with a slight New Jersey accent, was laying it out, hard and angry, loud enough for Bolan to catch every word.

Bolan gave them a little more lead, watched as the hardmen checked their flanks and front. For some reason, they opted not to inspect their rear. That oversight gave the Executioner a critical edge. Swift and silent, he moved away from the club, giving the parking lot a hard search. Because of the time of night and the brisk chill in the air, only a few vehicles were in the lot. No one was driving in; there were no bystanders, no watching eyes. It was as perfect a killing ground as Bolan would get.

He cut the gap to their rear when they veered for a row of parked vehicles. It struck Bolan right then that he might be forced to breach a personal code of ethics he had maintained with steely determination over the years. The Executioner had always kept sacred a code of honor about killing, even wounding a law-enforcement officer, no matter how dirty the cop was. That was yesterday, though. If these men were indeed lawmen, retired or otherwise, engaged in selecting and executing citizens for their own reasons, then any man's principles needed to be altered if he was to survive. Still, Bolan decided to give them a choice, just in case. He pulled out his Justice Department ID, his other hand grasping the holstered Beretta just as the two hardmen reached the rear of a gray Cutlass Supreme with New York plates. They started to turn Bolan's way, as if suddenly sensing a threatening presence from behind.

"Freeze, get your hands up. I'm with the Department of Justice—"

They made their play, but Bolan beat them to the draw. His Beretta was already clearing leather and barking its lethal message. For a heartbeat, the soldier thought he might miss his mark as the two hardmen split up, bringing handguns into view. They were quick and they were good, but they weren't fast enough. If nothing else, their decision to use deadly force on a man identifying himself as a Justice Department agent told Bolan all he needed to know. They were the enemy, regardless of what they were or ever had been.

Trench-coat was reaching for Abrams, prepared to use the lawyer as a human shield when Bolan's trio of 9 mm parabellum slugs ripped through leather. Punched back behind streams of blood jetting from his chest, Trench-coat was slammed into the side of a white van, the vehicle rocking under the hammering force.

Corduroy proved the more ominous concern for Bolan. As the second goon sidled up the driver's side of the Cutlass, a hand cannon Bolan recognized right away as a .44 Magnum Smith & Wesson shredded the night with thunder. A running gun battle was the last thing Bolan wanted, and a standoff was out of the question. As the back window of a Toyota exploded in a cloud of glass shards, Bolan launched himself over the vehicle's trunk, determined to cut the gap to the enemy, end it hard and quick. There was another peal of thunder, and the soldier felt the slipstream of the .44 slug graze his face.

Trench-coat was convulsing, struggling to stay up, then did a slow topple but not before he triggered two rounds from a 9 mm Glock in the dying instinct of a man desperately wanting to cling to life. No such luck, as Trench-coat crumpled. Still, the dead man's wild rounds whined off the metal above Bolan's head as he went to ground. Then the soldier popped up, but was forced to duck as Corduroy loosed another round that drilled a hole in metal just above Bolan's head.

The Executioner made an instant but risky decision

to gain the upper hand in one movement. He threw his shoulder into the vehicle, hoping that Corduroy believed he was down. In the next eye blink, Bolan darted up the side of the vehicle, came up and saw that Corduroy had his .44 Magnum trained on the spot the soldier had just vacated.

Before Corduroy could correct his error in judgment, Bolan drilled three holes into the man's face. No sooner was Corduroy's face evaporating in a scarlet halo than Bolan was moving to intercept the lawyer, who had come out of his shock and was in flight.

Abrams looked at the surging shadow of Bolan, then stumbled into a nosedive.

"Who are you? Are you with them?" Abrams cried.

"I'm with me. I'm the one who was sent to take care of your problem."

He hauled Abrams to his feet, marching him away from the scene. A slew of questions swirled through Bolan's head, but he needed to put distance between them and the killing zone, quick.

ABRAMS WAS on the verge of coming apart with the postbattle hysteria of a noncombatant who had just witnessed violent death up close and for the first time. For the moment, Bolan bit down his impatience, giving the man some time to compose himself before interrogating him.

Eye to eye now, Bolan scoured the lawyer's face, more for any signs of treachery and hidden intent than anything else: a head of dark, tight curls, most likely from a monthly perm job; neatly trimmed salt-and-pepper mustache; features large but soft; a slight frame going pudgy around the middle, all indicating the good life of a high-priced mouthpiece. Gauging the degree of fear in the lawyer's dark eyes, Bolan decided the man hadn't walked him into a setup. Given what little he knew so far about Abrams and his ex-cop client gone bad, though, the Executioner wasn't about to take anything at face value.

"Which way?" Bolan asked, hands tight on the wheel of his older model black Plymouth Fury, his gaze searching Greenbelt Road in all directions for either an enemy tail or flashing lights. So far so good, but they were only two minutes out of the lot. During the lingering pause, as the lawyer breathed hard, wiped sweat off his brow and licked dry lips, the easy rumble of the Plymouth's big-block engine filled Bolan's ears. For this mission, a couple of Stony Man engineers had installed a custom-built engine with enough horses under the hood to maybe push the speedometer to 160. Of course, the Plymouth would gobble up fuel like a man-eating shark in a feeding frenzy, but speed and power were what Bolan had asked for. Due to the possible nationwide network, from what little information Brognola had been able to put together, the Executioner had suspected he would be on the road, perhaps hopping from one urban war zone to the next.

If necessary, he had enough muscle under the hood to outrun any police cruiser, but he hoped it didn't come to that. Of course, Brognola could always bail him out, get him back in motion, if Bolan was detained by the police. But time was critical. Convicted and suspected criminals were being murdered, and there were rumblings in the media that cops were doing the killing. Already poverty-stricken areas, such as Liberty City in Miami and Harlem in New York, were set to blow in full-scale riots. Bolan had to find out who these killers were and why they had seemingly knighted themselves as righteous vigilante avengers out to rid society of criminals. At this point, it didn't matter if they were lawmen or ex-cops. The law was the law. In fact if it turned out the killers were lawmen using their badges and oaths of office to execute those they deemed criminals or unfit or unworthy to breathe, then that made them worse than the common thug, armed and dangerous. Make no mistake, the Executioner would take on any and all cannibals, badge or no badge.

Locked in the vehicle's trunk were an M-16 with an M-203 grenade launcher, two dozen fragmentation and incendiary grenades, and plenty of spare clips and rounds for his personal hardware. Zipped up in a large duffel on the back seat floor was a 6-shot Mossberg 500 pump-action 12-gauge shotgun, his close-engagement, take-no-prisoners piece. Another duffel in the trunk held combat webbing, pouches and his skintight blacksuit for midnight hits.

The Executioner had the heavy firepower, all right, if his mission roared into all-out battle. If nothing else, all the signs were there—indeed, had already shown themselves just minutes ago.

"What?"

"Your client. Where is he?"

The lawyer sucked in a deep breath, his eyes wide with fear and paranoia as he finally pried his stare off the side-view mirror. With a trembling hand, he dug out a piece of paper from his overcoat. "Find Route 1. I believe it's at the end of Greenbelt Road. North. He's at a motel in Laurel. Look, before we go any further, there's a few things we need to talk about, Mr...."

"Belasko. Special Agent Mike Belasko," Bolan said, giving the lawyer an alias he often used. "You're right. We've got a lot to get squared away."

"I need a smoke."

"In the glove compartment."

Bolan waited as the lawyer fired up his cigarette. A few deep drags seemed to calm him.

"If you don't mind, why don't we stop somewhere to talk? I could use a drink."

Bolan pinned the lawyer with a steely gaze. "Don't push it. You smoke and talk, I drive. After I round up your so-called client, you can have all the martinis you want."

The lawyer seemed on the verge of lapsing into despair. "God, I didn't bargain for any of this. I wasn't looking to be an accessory to anything, much less get myself in the line of fire in a full-scale gunfight. I'm an attorney. I've got a wife and kids to think about."

Bolan wasn't about to cut the guy any slack for family values. "Life is tough, Counselor. Do you have any idea who those men were back there and how they managed to follow you to our contact site?"

"I don't know who they were, and I can't imagine how they found me. All I know is that myself and my client have been under surveillance this past week. I've been tailed, and I've gotten anonymous threatening messages left on my answering machine. I've been jumping every time the phone even rings. It's been the same with my client. It's the reason I had to move my family out of Long Island. I told him the only way was to get in touch with the Justice

Department to work this out. The only thing I can figure is that my client got cold feet about this group, and they smelled him out. Unfortunately he came to me and brought the wolves with him. If I led them to our contact site back there, then I did so unknowingly,'' Abrams added, putting a cold eye on Bolan but showing the Executioner for the first time some hint of resolve and complete honesty.

"One thing you can be sure of, Counselor. Where you find one cockroach, you'll find another and then another.''

"Meaning?''

"Meaning those two I left back there more than likely didn't come down from New York by themselves.''

"Look, I'm not a lawman. I've never even fired a gun in my life. If you're asking me to keep dodging bullets, that's out of the question.''

"You're involved, for better or worse. It's up to you and your client how it falls. Let's start by defining 'them.' We can begin by putting a name on your client and filling in the blanks on his problem.''

Abrams sighed, smoked, rubbed his face. "His name is Ron Westman, a homicide detective who worked Brooklyn. Less than a year from having put in his twenty and retiring, he was kicked off the force for misconduct, alleged brutality. Nothing was ever proved in a court of law, but internal affairs had enough to take his badge and gun, or so they thought. No police chief or commander anywhere likes to see one of their own go down dirty. It tarnishes the image of an entire department. When a cop goes bad and the public finds out, well, it sort of feeds a lot of the public perception about rogue cops, police brutality, so forth. More distrust and suspicion of authority and those we're supposed to trust.''

The guy was sidetracking, so Bolan put some steel into his voice. ''I know how all that plays, Counselor. That just comes with the territory of being a policeman. You're not telling me what I need to know.''

''If you'll let me finish. Anyway, I worked a deal between IA and the district attorney for Westman that left him a choice—quit or go to jail. This was a little more than a year ago. Ron resurfaced with his problem, as you put it, one month ago to this day.''

''What is it exactly that he has to sell?''

''He has it all, Agent Belasko. Tape recordings, disks, files that prove there's a major paramilitary force hard at work executing criminals. In New York City for certain, that I know of. And if you've read the papers or listened to the news the past two weeks, it could be a national conspiracy. That is, if you believe my client. I've gotten a glimpse of what he has. I believe he's on to something that up to now I believed only happened in countries like Iraq or Iran.''

Bolan put a grim stare on the lawyer. It took a few moments for him to get the next question out of his mouth, but he had to know. There was no other way.

''Point-blank—are they policemen?''

The lawyer hesitated, broke Bolan's gaze and swallowed hard. ''Yes.''

A ball of ice-cold anger lodged in Bolan's gut. More often than not, the truth was downright ugly. In this case, the truth was on the verge of becoming the Executioner's worst-case scenario. Any personal code he'd honored before then about law-enforcement officers gone bad had evaporated.

Not only had the truth turned ugly, but it was also

poised to explode in lethal engagement with the law of the land.

Bolan was in for the long run, no matter what. No matter where the ugly truth took him.

CHAPTER TWO

It was tough knowledge to swallow, some of the most bitter truth ever revealed to Bolan. His hands gripping the wheel so hard his knuckles were stark white, the soldier guided the Plymouth Fury onto Route 1, proceeding northbound through College Park. The Executioner took a few hard moments of silence to let this dreaded worst-case scenario sink in.

Killer cops. An organization of secret police with its own code of vigilantism, hiding behind badges and sworn oaths, taking the law into its own hands. The lawyer was right on one count. It was something that happened in other countries where dictators were spawned as the result of senseless mass violence. Brutal military regimes in foreign nations where roving squads of gun-wielding thugs butchered anyone judged unfit, unworthy or suspected of posing some real or imagined threat to state security. It was only supposed to happen in countries such as North Korea, or Iran; countries like Afghanistan with its secret police called Khad, who had unlimited authority to maim and murder; little-heard-of places in Central and South America where megalomaniacal leaders used vicious death squads to subdue and keep the masses oppressed in order to fist the reins of power.

Bolan expected tyrannical governments such as these to create their own laws in order to unleash torture and murder on their peoples. After all, instilling fear was how the tyrants maintained their power, inflicting savagery how they furthered their twisted aims. Tyranny, the encroaching shadow of a brutal police state, wasn't anywhere close to being a viable option for the United States of America, even in the worst of times under the clouds of rampant crime and senseless violence. In the greatest democracy the world had ever known, a secret organization of assassins, hiding and operating behind the law of the land, could well mean the beginning of the end of freedom for all. Of course, it all depended on how far the conspiracy went, who exactly was involved.

Bolan took in his surroundings, poised to hit the accelerator at the first sign of flashing lights on his rear. What he found in his rearview instead was an older-model white Pontiac Grand Prix. He was observing the posted speed limit, and other vehicles were flying past him as if he were standing still. But the Grand Prix kept a steady pace on his rear, four car lengths behind. Instinct warned Bolan he was being followed. Less than a quarter mile off Greenbelt Road, he was certain the Grand Prix had turned onto Route 1 behind him. He was passing shopping centers, bars, fast-food joints, but the lighting in the area wasn't good enough for Bolan to make out either the faces in the vehicle or the plates. Still, he counted five shadows, two up front, three in back.

With a warrior's judgment honed from years of surviving, Bolan figured the Grand Prix for an intercept vehicle, a backup team if the front-line troops failed at the bar. Bolan was ready to unleather the Desert

Eagle if they roared up on his side. For the moment, he decided against warning the nervous lawyer about a possible tail and the potential for sudden violence. He still needed more answers from Maury Abrams.

"Actually, Agent Belasko, I should correct my answer some. It's yes and no. There are and there aren't policemen in this secret vigilante organization."

Now Bolan pinned the lawyer with angry eyes. "Don't jerk me around. Which is it?"

The lawyer fumbled for another cigarette. "Before I answer any more questions, I need to know for my benefit and the benefit of my client exactly where it is we stand. In other words, what is it the Justice Department is prepared to offer?"

"You two stand in a world of hurt. That's a fact. Here's some more facts the way I see it. You've been tailed here by the enemy who made an attempt to snatch you. Had they been successful, both you and Westman would be dead before the night was over. What I'm offering is real simple. Life over certain death. Your peace of mind is the last thing I'm worried about."

"Is that supposed to be a threat, Agent Belasko?"

"It's reality. I'm the only thing that's certain to keep you alive from whoever it is wants you and Westman dead. It won't be me who steals all you hold near and dear. As for your client, it's all up to him."

The lawyer tried to sound tough, but he didn't wear it well. "I want your guarantee of immunity, that my client will be placed in the Witness Protection Program, that myself and my family will likewise be relocated until this situation is resolved."

"I can't guarantee that."

"You mean you won't."

"It's not my call. It's something you'll have to work out with the man who sent me. Right now, you need to think about surviving the night, giving me some answers. How is it you came to be of such special interest to Westman?"

Abrams blew smoke. "Actually I was close to his father, who was also a policeman, and my father knew his father, like that. When they refer to a law officer as the city's or the state's finest, Ron's father definitely filled the tab. Enough commendations, citations and awards—well, the man had problems. If he hadn't shot himself to death, he would have drank himself to death. Anyway, before that happened, Ron's father bailed me out of a bad situation that could have ruined me when I was a young lawyer. I'll skip the details, but it involved a mistress and narcotics. There was a bust, an undercover cop...how the old man nipped that fiasco in the bud, I'll never know. I didn't ask. He only told me I owed him. Said that one day I would know when my marker was being called in. I suppose this is the moment of truth he was referring to."

"So, this is pro bono work for the kid."

"I resent the insinuation, Agent Belasko. I have money. My main concern is keeping my family alive. If my client is looking to enter the Witness Protection Program, maybe land himself a sweetheart deal, well, sir, you better believe I will do everything I can to see he gets that."

Suddenly Bolan found himself stopping at a red light. Luckily the lawyer was too busy working on his cigarette, nursing his hard feelings and sucking on his fear to pay the soldier any attention. Bolan glanced into the rearview mirror. The Grand Prix had anticipated the light, slowed to a crawl that kept it several car lengths from the Plymouth's rear. No, it didn't feel right to Bolan at all. Suspicion mounting, his warrior's combat instincts flared to life. Any second he was braced to snake free the big .44 Magnum Desert Eagle, burst out the door.

"Tell me exactly what you know about this group of alleged killer cops," Bolan said as the light turned green and he eased the Plymouth through the intersection. "Start at the beginning, and cover it from A to Z. Who they are, Westman's involvement, what he has on them."

The lawyer seemed to think about something, staring out the passenger's window at the passing blocks of suburban enclaves.

While he waited for the lawyer to start talking, Bolan kept one eye on the side-view mirror, his gaze fixed on the trailing Grand Prix through hooded eyelids. He had a fleeting impulse to stomp on the accelerator, find out one hundred percent if the vehicle held enemy guns. But not just yet. First he wanted concrete answers. Action could wait, unless the shadows in the Grand Prix made the call for him.

Bolan listened intently to Abrams. The immediate conspiracy Abrams was aware of was entrenched in New York City. Enclaves of ex-cops had banded together to search out, stake out and execute suspected criminals, all of them black or Hispanic to date. Some of the targets had been out on bond, awaiting trial. Some were known criminals, armed robbers, drug and gun dealers, gang members who always seemed to elude the long arm of the law.

The self-appointed justice squad took care of business the courts couldn't or wouldn't handle. They used cop talk, seemed to have cop contacts and used former street informants. They had handheld radios, police scanners, even had access to NCIC files. They were heavily armed with the latest in military hardware, and they were protected by their own code of honor and a code of silence that, if breached, meant certain violent death for the offending member.

Their basic philosophy came complete with hardcore antigovernment racist views. Crime in society? Blame it on minorities. A country hinging on the verge of anarchy? Lay it on the liberal politicians and media. Bolan knew the hate spiel, the angry rhetoric of disgust and discontent with contemporary American society that seemed to be sweeping the land lately. Only this time out, the enemy wasn't a bunch of good old boys in the boondocks playing weekend warrior.

Apparently, Abrams went on, not all of the conspirators were former lawmen. A number of the assassins were wanna-be cops who had washed out of the academy, simply couldn't cut it, either physically or psychologically. Others in this ring of conspirators were members of various right-wing extremist groups. Exactly how the right-wing fanatics linked up with former cops, what their connection was, Abrams didn't have a clue. From what he could gather from Westman, Abrams believed the New York cell was part of a larger organization. Who ran the organization, where the group's main headquarters was located, he didn't know. Nor did Abrams have names or exact working locations where the rogue force operated in New York.

Bolan asked why Westman decided to roll. Abrams claimed that when Westman saw how serious his colleagues were, how far they would go, risk their own lives to stalk and murder during what the group called "their watch" Westman bailed. According to Abrams, Westman didn't mind the idea of getting killed in the line of duty. No, it was landing in Attica and having to deal with men he had sent there that terrified him more than dying. Bolan could understand that. A cop in prison was a constant target for the general population to vent more than just an impulse to commit murder. Among the savages, there were fates worse than death.

"These men use standard police procedures," Abrams said. "Only their suspects go out in body bags instead of handcuffs. That they seem to operate with impunity, can disappear without a trace, with no witnesses to identify them—well, it would indicate this thing reaches beyond them, quite possibly into elements of the New York police force."

"Unfortunately, Counselor, those are likewise my own instincts. What else?"

"Well, it seems this group my client was involved with would take 'roll call' to get themselves up to speed for their 'watch.' These roll calls were taped by their 'watch commander.' Not too smart on their part, as it now turns out. When Westman decided he couldn't stomach it any longer, he confiscated entire files detailing to some extent, according to him, their operation. Unfortunately for me, Ron jealously guards what he has. He says he won't turn it over until a deal is struck with the Justice Department."

"How many murders has this rogue force committed that you're aware of? Or did you bother to ask Westman?"

"I bothered, Agent Belasko, believe me. To his

knowledge, he tells me they have committed at least a dozen executions.''

''Westman an eyewitness to any of these executions?''

''Yes.''

''Did he pull a trigger?''

Abrams hesitated, ground out his cigarette in the ashtray. ''I asked, but he wouldn't answer. I'm assuming he has.''

''Is he armed right now?''

''I'm assuming he is. We came down in separate vehicles. I met with him at the motel just before our rendezvous. Whatever else you need to know, Westman can fill you in. To tell you the truth, I've grown tired of him baiting me along. If I'm to be of any further help to him, then I need to know what it is precisely he's going to turn over. But he definitely wants to play ball with the Justice Department, which brings me to another matter.

''He believes the FBI could be involved in this conspiracy. A safehouse in D.C. is out of the question. Hauling him downtown, anywhere near the J. Edgar Hoover Building, well, he seems to believe it could cause a stir, a leak, especially if Justice and the FBI haggle over who gets him. I don't know if he's just being overly paranoid or cautious, but he thinks it would be best if he's kept under watch somewhere in the Baltimore area. If nothing else, I would kindly ask that you at least honor that request.''

Bolan figured it was a small concession. He nodded. From the point of view of Abrams and Westman, it made sense, in their paranoid way. Given what had happened already, a safehouse in Baltimore might be the best course of action until the Executioner knew exactly who and what he was dealing with. Bolan knew Brognola could make the arrangements, though exactly what Bolan would do and where he would take Westman would all depend on just how cooperative the former detective proved.

The Executioner drove in grim silence. For the time being, he had heard enough. It was best to bring Westman in, beneath the umbrella of the Justice Department, and get him to hand over what he had on the conspiracy. Brognola could iron out the logistics, separate fact from fabrication. From there, Bolan intended to run with whatever intel he could dig out of Westman.

Checking the rearview mirror, the soldier found the Grand Prix was still following, stuck to his rear even when Abrams finally indicated Bolan turn onto a road branching off from Route 1. Just as Abrams informed him the motel was on the left, right before the Baltimore-Washington Parkway, Bolan decided to push it.

Swinging onto the shoulder of the road, the soldier told Abrams, "When I tell you to hit the floor, do it. Don't ask questions."

Bolan slowed the Plymouth Fury, the Grand Prix rolling closer. Abrams started to look behind, but Bolan growled, "Don't look back, just face front."

The Grand Prix closing, the Executioner drew the Desert Eagle, his stare locked on the side-view glass. The Grand Prix loomed in the mirror, and Bolan was certain the passenger's window would roll down and guns would start flaming any second. If that happened, he would whip the Plymouth in reverse, race up on the Grand Prix's rear and unload the hand cannon on the driver.

It didn't go down like that. Instead, the Grand Prix rolled by. Out of the corner of his eye, Bolan watched the five shadows. The fact that none of the silhouettes in the vehicle even bothered to look his way further stoked a fire of instinct in the warrior's belly. From the light spilling from the shopping center directly across the road, Bolan caught a glimpse of the Grand Prix's plates—New York. It was enough to have him believe he needed to be prepared for the worst.

"We were being followed and you didn't even see fit to tell me," Abrams snapped.

"Everything was under control, Counselor. It will stay that way as long as you do exactly what I tell you."

Waiting until the Grand Prix vanished down the road, Bolan killed the engine and took the keys. Ignoring Abrams's insistence on wanting to know what the hell was going on, Bolan went to the trunk and unlocked it. Quickly he pulled a fragmentation grenade from a duffel and shoved it in the pocket of his overcoat. Behind the wheel again, he reached over the seat to dig out the riot gun. The Mossberg flesh-shredder was fully loaded. When Bolan racked a live round into the chamber, Abrams flinched, his eyes wide with fresh fear at the sight of the ominous-looking shotgun. Bolan placed the shotgun against the seat, next to the lawyer, barrel up.

"You don't think...you're not assuming—"

Bolan cut the lawyer off, firing up the engine and peeling out onto the road. "I have to assume the worst."

As he drove, Bolan found no sign of the Grand Prix. It seemed to have just vanished. But there were enough side roads branching off, winding by the shopping center and apartment complexes that the vehicle could have cut a quick turn. Waiting to circle back, come up from behind. Bolan could feel the danger, out there, somewhere in the dark.

With a shaking finger, Abrams indicated the motel, up ahead, to Bolan's left. It was a sleepy two-story structure, the parking lot half-full. Abrams gave him the room number, second floor, east wing, toward the back. How Westman greeted him when Bolan hauled the lawyer to his door, the soldier didn't know, but he damn well cared. He needed Westman alive. And if his hunch was right, the Grand Prix was a potential rolling death machine of hardmen, come to put their rogue colleague on ice, take back what he had stolen from them.

Glancing from the rearview, with still no sign of the Grand Prix, Bolan slowly drove into the lot. Toward the end of the building, Abrams indicated the brand-new Mercury Sable that belonged to Westman. Moments later, Bolan slid in beside the vehicle. It felt more wrong than ever all of a sudden. Too quiet, too still.

Shutting down the engine, slipping the keys into his pocket, Bolan gave the lawyer a steely look. "Stick right beside me. Don't run, don't panic if there's a problem. When I tell you what to do, just do it. Whatever happens, don't let your bad nerves get the best of you."

Bolan was reaching for the door handle when it happened. Out of nowhere, the Grand Prix was roaring down the lot. Inside the vehicle, Bolan saw four of the five shadows digging at their chests, no doubt going for hardware. A moment later, he glimpsed the barrel of an assault rifle, jutting up from behind the driver, in the hands of number five. The Grand Prix slid to a stop on a squeal of smoking rubber, less than a dozen yards from Bolan's door.

"Get down and stay down!" Bolan shouted at Abrams.

As the Executioner snatched up the Mossberg and burst out the door, the first of two hardmen was out of the Grand Prix, weapon in hand, flaming and barking. Once again the night was shattered with screaming death. Only this time the enemy seized the initiative, gained a potentially lethal edge.

CHAPTER THREE

A split second and lightning-fast reflexes proved the difference between life and death for Bolan. Surging to his left, away from the opening rounds of enemy slugs peppering the driver's side of the Plymouth, Bolan cannoned off a rapid-fire peal of Mossberg thunder. Downrange the wheelman's pistol stopped flaming as the shotgun blast took him full in the chest after it vaporized the driver's-side window. No sooner was that hardman kicked back and lost in a cloud of glass and blood than Bolan was tracking on.

With the soldier's first victim hammering the lot and sliding back in showering gore, the Mossberg's second blast blew in the windshield. It was a hasty shot, but it bought Bolan a precious few heartbeats. The goon crouched behind the passenger's door was driven to cover, razoring glass shards and slivers washing over him with hurricane force, threatening to blind or rearrange his face forever.

From beside the Sable's trunk, the Executioner racked and fired, holding his ground. Due to their decision to pile into a two-door, the three in the back seat were destined to have serious problems disgorging.

It proved a fatal mistake in choice of wheels for at

least one hardman clambering with wild desperation to get out the driver's side. Mossberg thunder-hell number three all but removed the side of that goon's face and head in cleaverlike shearing. The guy went down, hard and final, as if he'd been dropped by a wrecking ball.

A slight shift in aim and the fourth earsplitting roar blew out the Grand Prix's back window. From there the two hardmen in the back seat were diving for quick exit through the shards, rolling onto the trunk. Both of them were armed with assault rifles, sure to stack the odds even more in the enemy's favor. Worse, something Bolan had feared all along then happened.

He glimpsed a shadow streaking from his left flank. It was a look he threw the fleeing figure that was long enough to divert his attention, give the enemy a critical heartbeat to come roaring back. Ducking an eye blink before a line of automatic-weapons fire started cranking from behind the Grand Prix, tattooing Westman's new wheels, Bolan saw Abrams beating a panicked retreat, across the lot, for the road.

The lawyer never made it.

A quick look at the enemy revealed the passenger's-side gunner tracking the lawyer's flight with deadly precision. It happened so fast the Executioner had no time to even attempt to save Abrams. That hardman unloaded at least three slugs from his barking pistol that cored through Abrams's head. The lawyer was dead before he hit the ground.

The Mossberg jacked, Bolan popped up and triggered a round, one-handed. His unsteady fire tore apart the cushion of the Grand Prix's front seat, spewing stuffing, the storm of steel pellets blasting out a hanging shard of glass in the back window. When the trio of gunmen ducked that Mossberg explosion, Bolan pitched the grenade, which he'd already primed. Three seconds to detonation and counting.

The Executioner jacked the last round into place, surged in a crouch up the walk in front of the motel. With this close an engagement it was risky to opt for blasting the enemy all over the lot. But Bolan needed to end it quick, and evacuate. Not to mention rounding up Westman—provided, of course, the renegade former detective wasn't spooked already into a desperate flight.

The grenade hit the pavement and rolled under the Grand Prix's chassis. Bolan couldn't have delivered a more perfect toss, and he hoped the explosion went up and away from his position and spared the Plymouth Fury of disabling flying debris.

Lady Luck smiled on the warrior.

Bolan went to ground behind the front end of a Ford Taurus. Just as the three gunmen came up, weapons blazing, the steel egg blew. The initial blast lifted the Grand Prix several feet off the lot before searing flames ignited the gas tank. With the night ripped apart by a saffron fireball that shredded man and metal, Bolan unleathered the Desert Eagle, came up, fanning the flaming bed of wreckage. Just in case someone survived that blast.

Nothing moved from the slaughter bed. Twisted, smoking metal banged off the pavement, wreckage still pounding vehicles, slicing through windows to Bolan's right flank.

Suddenly Bolan spotted a figure dropping from the sky, pounding feetfirst onto the roof of the Sable. Darting with pantherlike speed, Bolan made it to the shadow just as the big figure in a black leather bomber jacket and clutching a large duffel bag spun his way. With the stainless-steel pistol in the man's fist poised to blow Bolan's face apart, the Executioner reacted.

One-handed he hurled the Mossberg, driving the barrel through the man's ankles for a vicious takedown. The gun went flying from the man's hand. Bolan assumed he had just introduced himself to Ron Westman as the big shadow hammered the Sable's roof, tumbled and flopped to the pavement at the Executioner's feet. Bolan found a grizzled bulldog face with blue eyes full of rage staring up at him.

Point-blank, Bolan stuck the barrel of the Mossberg in the man's face. "Westman?"

"Who the fuck are you?"

"The last real law you'll ever see if you don't do as I say. On your belly."

The guy hesitated, but rolled over. Bolan leathered the Desert Eagle. The crackle of flames from the shattered ruins of the Grand Prix in his ears, the shadows of bystanders peeking out the doorways of the motel rooms in the corner of his eye, Bolan pulled out the pair of handcuffs he'd brought along just for this occasion. There wasn't much time. He needed to put quick distance to this new hellzone.

Slapping the cuffs on Westman, Bolan hauled the ex-cop to his feet, relieved the guy of his duffel bag, then slid the former detective's stainless-steel .45 Colt into his waistband.

"You and I need to talk," the Executioner said before he tossed Westman into the Plymouth with all the thought and ease he might give to throwing out the garbage. Make no mistake, the ex-cop was dirty, with no telling how much blood on his hands. The Executioner would treat him like he would any savage who preyed on innocent or even not so innocent life.

Whipping the Plymouth in reverse, Bolan rolled out of there on screaming rubber.

A TIME BOMB of tension ticked down hard in Bolan's gut. Ahead he saw a swarm of flashing lights, strobing the night, above the overpass to the parkway. An eternal moment later those lights faded, then vanished, cruisers, southbound for Greenbelt. One roadblock, and Bolan knew his problems had only just begun. The night would come to a screeching halt, Justice Department special agent or not. Two crime scenes and eight dead men needed explaining, no matter what. Detainment and going through the normal booking procedure was out of the question. Time wasn't on the Executioner's side.

Feeling Westman's angry gaze boring into the side of his head, Bolan checked his rear. Flames danced in the mirror, with shadows of onlookers sliding out onto the parking lot. No doubt, someone would make the Plymouth Fury. Top priority would be getting to a pay phone and bringing Brognola onto the scene. The big Fed would get Westman under wraps in a safehouse, flex whatever muscle necessary to iron out the night's carnage and get the soldier back on track. Luckily the firefight and ensuing obliteration by grenade of the enemy's vehicle had left the Plymouth Fury with nothing more than a few bullet holes, scratches and dents on the driver's side. The downside was that the damage was clear evidence pointing to Bolan as the suspect at large in eight homicides.

Hitting the overpass, Bolan swung onto the exit and

down the ramp, giving the big-block engine some gas. The Plymouth Fury's muscle put some thunder in Bolan's ears when he streaked onto the parkway, northbound for Baltimore. In the opposite lane, he watched as a Maryland state trooper raced his cruiser past the Laurel exit.

When it looked like they were clear and free for the moment, Westman decided to strike up a conversation.

"You sure don't strike me as typical JD. You got a name, cowboy?"

Bolan turned his head a little. Up close, he read a simmering hatred in Westman's eyes. There was something feral, not to be trusted about the ex-cop. Bolan knew the look. The only interest Westman had in any of this was Ron Westman. Without the cuffs, if he turned his back on the guy, Westman would sucker punch him. No mistake, the ex-cop was dangerous.

A sardonic grin cut Bolan's lips. "Lawnmower. And your ass is grass. Let's skip the intros, cut the small talk. I don't like what I see. Meaning you and I won't be getting chummy. You came to us with a problem. Your lawyer's dead, and right now I'm your only solution. You play ball or you strike out."

"Screw Abrams, and you can kiss my ass. I was always on my own anyway. The only thing that guy probably saw was a movie deal in all this. All he ever wanted was to keep the good life he made off other people's problems. Especially the problems of righteous police officers. Typical defense-lawyer bloodsucker. All I needed him for was to smooth out the details with you Justice flunkies. The world won't miss another lawyer anyway."

"I can tell gratitude isn't one of your virtues. According to your lawyer, your father bailed him out of an ugly mess. He was helping you as a favor owed to, and I pretty much quote your late attorney here, 'New York's finest.' Your father."

"Just because my old man got a few medals and was a good cop didn't make him any hero. My old man was a mean drunk who never thought twice about taking his frustrations out on me or my late mother. And like most of New York's finest, I can be sure he wasn't above taking a few 'gratuities,' maybe even indulging in an opportunistic theft here and there. So, spare me the flattery, cowboy."

"I can see we're going to have a classic failure to communicate."

Westman grunted, then scowled, obviously in some serious discomfort with his hands cuffed behind his back. "All we need to get clear, cowboy, is I want full immunity, relocation, new identity and some decent dollars in my pocket. Without me, what I've got in that bag won't mean jack-shit to you Justice boys. You could be weeks, maybe even months figuring out what's in there, since it's coded for the most part."

"You want to tell me what it is you seem to think will land you the sweetheart deal of the century?"

"What I've got is a conspiracy among current and former lawmen that, if the general public knew about, could well turn this country into a police state out of sheer necessity for survival. There would be war in the streets. There would be riots that could damn well burn down entire major cities. That's what I've got."

"Specifics. I got that much from Abrams."

"Oh, I read you. You want answers without giving me any guarantees. Let's understand something here.

I'm your Judas goat with all the pieces of the puzzle to a Sphinx riddle. Why don't you show me a badge first, hotshot, do this by the book?''

Bolan pulled out his Justice Department ID and put it in Westman's face. Then he tucked the ID away and pinned Westman with a steely gaze. ''One last time. Specifics.''

''Okay. Here's some specifics. This society is on the verge of total self-destruction because no one has had the balls to do something about the scumbags out there who have this country in a stranglehold. If they're not whining on the talk shows, playing the victim and bellyaching about how unfair life is, they get out there and sell dope. They rob, or they murder good people, or get on a subway at rush hour and start shooting white people or Asians because they can't have or earn what good people have. They laugh at the justice system because gutless lawyers and soft, fish-belly judges and spineless juries of a scumbag's peers don't have the character to make the right call. So they turn them in and out of the courts and jail like it's a revolving door.

''Maybe you haven't taken a walk down an inner-city street lately. Maybe you haven't noticed that the perpetrators of nearly all crime are either black or Hispanic. The prisons are chock-full of Tyrones and Pedros. You've got those people who can't cut it on their own merits, so they hustle, blame the system for their perceived plight and injustice because they don't have what it takes to be a real man. Crack, guns, sell their women because a minority scumbag is interested in two things—money and his dick. The men I was running with are heroes. They're the last line of defense for a democracy that's on the verge of complete collapse due to thirty years of liberal whining and laws that have allowed the so-called disenfranchised to get an undeserved handout and an upper hand.''

Bolan kept his eyes on the road. He let Westman ramble on, figuring if he let the guy vent his hate, spew his twisted venom he might let down his defenses, slide himself into the information Bolan wanted. Westman raved on about affirmative action, how welfare had ruined the country because half of the people on welfare were drug abusers anyway.

''You're a white man,'' Westman growled. ''What's more, you're supposedly a law-enforcement officer. Surely you've got to see something extreme has to be done in order to turn the tide—hell, in order to save this country. Look around. The scumbags have even discovered the suburbs. You want your neighborhood contaminated by animals? You open the lid on a sewer, what comes out? Besides the smell of feces, you get overrun by rodents.''

Bolan had neither the time, patience nor desire to get dragged in or down by Westman's diatribe about society's ills or perceived wrongs. Life was whatever it was, wherever it was. Evil didn't confine itself to one race, one culture, one social class. Right was right, and wrong was wrong to Bolan. It always had been, always would be. Deal with it. Like money, honor and respect were earned. Any man anywhere who strove to do what was right deserved to live in peace, respect and dignity. Simple enough, right, but without some code of honor, without respect for life, then life itself became meaningless. And without the law, man was no better than an animal. As far as Bolan was concerned, Westman was far out there, as off base as any savage he'd ever encountered. If noth-

ing else, though, at least the soldier knew what sort
of warped mind-set he was up against.

"Sounds like you're still a believer in your boys,"
Bolan said. "So, why are you rolling on them?"

"Because they've gotten too big for their own
good. The cause is righteous, but I could see the end
coming. Twenty-to-life in a cell block full of gorillas
doesn't have me sleeping too well at night. It's a
wake-up call to America. It's only the beginning.
Even if they go down, someone will pick up the fight.
Maybe even these worms in the White House and on
Capitol Hill will start toughening up the laws. Maybe
we'll even see the death penalty back in New York.
Maybe it will take a few more Oklahoma-type bomb-
ings or another Amtrak derailment to shake up the
ranks of decent white people everywhere. Who
knows? Maybe the next place gets blown to kingdom
come might be the NAACP headquarters." Westman
showed Bolan an ugly grin. "I get the feeling I've
trampled on some politically correct, tender sensitiv-
ities here."

"The only thing you've done, pal, is confirm my
worst suspicions about you. All you've done is harden
my resolve to put your buddies out of business. Either
that cell block full of what you hate and fear the most,
or six feet under, it doesn't matter to me. But it will
get done."

"Is that right? The way I'm reading you is you're
just another citizen who thinks everyone deserves a
fair shake just because they're breathing the same
air."

"What I believe is a little more complicated than
that. It's all cut-and-dried. The law is the law, and no
one is above it. A person makes a choice—to go left

or right, and I'm not talking politics. Something you seem not to be too concerned about. Your people came down here to hunt you down like an animal and take back what you have on them. Somehow they found you, and they would have executed you just as easily as they have butchered anybody else. And you still sit there and defend them, even after what's happened."

The mention of his cold reality melted some of the defiance from Westman's stare, but the guy still held hard. "It was a tough choice, but I'm interested in saving my own neck right now. I breached our code of silence. I knew the consequences. It doesn't mean I still can't admire what they're all about. And what you don't seem to understand is that what they're all about is saving your way of life before it all goes to hell."

"That's where you're wrong," Bolan said with ice in his voice. "Beyond the way we look, I'm not a thing like you or your self-appointed genocide squad. When you start deciding who's not good enough to live, let me ask you, who's next on your list of those you feel unworthy to live in the same world as you, Westman? Senior citizens who want to hold on to Medicare?"

Westman chuckled. "You know, more than once some black or Hispanic would tell me I wouldn't be such a tough guy if it wasn't for my badge and gun. Know what I would do? Take off the gun, put down my badge. Hold my hands out. Punks were so stunned I called their bluff, it wouldn't take but a sweet right cross to the jaw or a foot to their balls to lay them out. Then, if nobody was around, I'd drag the assholes into the nearest alley and get in some serious stick time until their faces were pulpy mush. Just to let them know who was in charge.''

Bolan had had enough. It was time to make Westman a believer.

"You're telling me you're not convinced I'm serious?'' Bolan said.

"That's right. Why don't you pull off somewhere and convince me, cowboy.''

So be it. Bolan found the next exit and swung off. He wasn't sure what road he was on, but he passed a convenience store and gas station and spotted a pay phone. A few minutes more before calling Brognola wouldn't hurt, he decided, might even make the future for the big Fed a little easier when he had to deal with Westman. He searched the strip that cut a long way through a brightly lit road of shopping centers and fast-food restaurants. Too public. Finally Bolan found a side road that ran dark and isolated past a large field.

"Can I ask you one thing first?'' Bolan said. "Did you recognize any of those men who came to kill you?''

"All five of them. All you did was kill five good white men and made the world a little sadder place. End of discussion.''

Ahead, Bolan focused on a tree on the shoulder of the road. Without warning, he floored the gas and aimed the Plymouth for the tree.

"What the hell?'' Westman cried.

Gauging the distance before collision, Bolan stomped on the brakes. The wheel tried to rip itself from his hands, but Bolan let the momentum and slide carry the vehicle with all the expert skill of an Indy 500 race driver. As the tree rushed for the front end, outlined as a potential beacon of sudden death in the headlights, Westman's face bounced off the windshield. A cloud of dust spumed in the headlights. Bolan had played it close. The tree was almost right on top of the front bumper.

Before Westman's shock wore off, Bolan opened the door and hauled the guy out by a hand full of leather. Outside, the soldier slung the man against the front end. Silently Bolan took out the Beretta, the .44 Magnum Desert Eagle and the confiscated .45 and laid them out on the roof. A cold grin started to cut Westman's lips when Bolan took the keys and uncuffed him.

Westman was quick, but Bolan was ready, pumped on his own anger and righteous convictions that he was onto a cancer that needed cutting out. The ex-cop twisted slightly, then spun, throwing a short right uppercut that would have caught most men off guard and put them on their backs.

Mack Bolan was no ordinary man.

Stepping back, the soldier felt Westman's knuckles graze his chin. The guy had put everything into going for a quick knockout punch. Off balance, Westman stumbled a half step past Bolan, who sledgehammered a fist deep in the ex-cop's gut. Air belched from Westman's vented mouth, and Bolan cracked an uppercut off the guy's jaw that snapped his head up. Following up with a straight right to the ex-cop's mouth, Bolan slammed his adversary off the Plymouth.

Somehow Westman held on. The left came out of nowhere and caught Bolan on the blindside. Smacked on the jaw, the Executioner staggered back a step. There was enough distance now for Westman to launch a high roundhouse kick for Bolan's face that would have ended the fight.

Only Westman didn't connect. Throwing out his arm, Bolan blocked the kick. Still there was enough brute force behind the blow to jar Bolan to the bone. It was another all-out assault that left Westman open for a counterattack. With his free hand, the Executioner came up under the leg, a sweeping windmill motion that put his opponent down, hard on his back. Before the grunt of pain fully left Westman's mouth, the soldier drove his foot into the guy's testicles. Bolan stepped back as Westman grabbed himself, squirmed and gagged on bile that was suddenly pouring from his mouth. The ex-cop made no move to try his luck again.

Quickly Bolan resnapped the cuffs on Westman, jacked him to his feet and tossed him back in the Plymouth. Taking back his weapons, the soldier hopped in behind the wheel.

"Now, can we talk?" Bolan rasped.

Westman coughed and glared at Bolan, but there was a look of newfound respect in his eyes. Funny how that could happen, Bolan thought.

"Sure...whatever, cowboy. Just be warned. That was only round one."

A few minutes later, Bolan backtracked to the convenience store and gas station. Inside, he got the clerk to tell him where he was, then went out to the pay phone to place a call. He knew Brognola would be at his office, waiting for word. Bolan dialed the big Fed's twenty-four-hour emergency number.

When the man came on, Bolan said, "It's Striker. I've got him. But there are problems. You might want to get here and handle this personally."

CHAPTER FOUR

For John Stanton, formerly Queens' finest, narcotics division, it was a twenty-four-hour supermarket of scumbags. Harlem, east or west, Spanish or black, it was around-the-clock bargain shopping. Only they were going to use bullets and not dollars for this grocery trip.

The only problem he and the troops had was being white. Worse, they looked like white cops. But that had proved on three previous "calls" to have worked to their advantage. It was all a matter of planning, timing and balls-out execution anyway, as well as fake badges and ID, the cop's eyes and bearing of authority, and the ruse of a special narcotics task force in case a patrolman decided to pull them over and inquire about all the hardware in the van. For the planning phase, it helped to have a police scanner, a few righteous lawmen, warriors in place on the force to pave the way. Not to mention a few parole officers, and a bail bondsman feeding them the intelligence they needed for success.

This night was the big one. If their contact was right, and God help him if he wasn't, the world would be minus at least a dozen scumbags in a short while— some of black Harlem's lowest predators, cracked up, most likely, but who would be smoking in hell real soon.

It had been a short run, but it had seemed like an eternity ago when they had crossed the Brooklyn Bridge, seen and given the Statue of Liberty a salute. They'd proceeded up Fifth Avenue, where the fat citizens dwelled in their posh enclaves, all those fat cats who never got their hands dirty or had an inkling of how ugly or threatening the real world was just a few short blocks north beyond their gleaming six- or seven-figure granite domains. They were liberals who didn't have a clue that a few good men were en route through the concrete jungle to make and thus keep their worlds a little safer place.

Now they were there, forging into the world of scumbags, he thought, ready to put the natives in their place. It was a part of New York City that Stanton naturally hated. The cockroaches were everywhere, selling their crack and their heroin, playing the scumbag game because they despised a system based on character and honor, hard work and discipline. On every corner Stanton saw them, bandanas—or underwear, he called it—wrapped around their heads, baseball caps all screwed on backward, the neck jewelry, the baggy pants, all that gangbanger business. His contempt mounted as their wheelman, ex-Brooklyn detective Bill Scarborough, eased the stolen black Chevy van westbound onto Martin Luther King, Jr., Boulevard.

"Man, stop pokin' along. I wanna get this done and get the hell away from you crazy white—"

From the passenger's seat, Stanton turned and put a stony look on Tyrhee Barkley that drove their confidential informant into nervous silence. Their CI, a

short, scrawny black man, was flanked by two of
Stanton's troops, Al Gurgin and Frank Morrow. Gurgin, a lanky six-foot-six redhead, was cocked and
locked on his Uzi submachine gun, attaching the
sound suppressor. Morrow, big, broad shouldered and
blond, was monitoring the portable police scanner,
earphone in place, ready to update the troops on any
pertinent calls in the area that needed avoiding. Both
former Yonkers homicide detectives ignored Barkley,
who was jumping all over the seat, eyes flickering
around the van as if he were ready to go through the
door any second. No doubt, Stanton knew, the punk
was itching for a fat rock. It was a promise Stanton
had made to the punk he had no intention of keeping.
Three kilos of crack, two of powder cocaine, at least
six ounces of heroin and over a hundred grand in cash
would stay in their war chest in their Brooklyn "station" for future use—the spoils of war, Stanton knew,
earned from his years as a cop, then as a warrior for
Deliverance.

Six-four, two hundred pounds of solid muscle, with
just a hint of some beer pudding around the middle,
Stanton had been a fifteen-year police veteran until
internal affairs grabbed him for extorting drug dealers. Enough allegations, but nothing IA could prove,
so Stanton retired, bitter and angry, right before it
really hit the fan and he was marched to the penitentiary. Like the other troops in the van, he was divorced, paying alimony to ungrateful ex-wives who
never understood a cop's job. He had kids somewhere
out there he hadn't seen, or wasn't allowed to see, in
years.

In the end, he had come to understand that all a
cop, even an ex-cop had, were other cops. And of

course, the real and righteous perspective of just how ugly things really were out there. It was the kind of attitude he'd often found himself defending in a bar fight. His hawkish nose, crooked now, broken more than once from the wrong end of a fist, testified that he would stand up and go the distance for what he believed in. He could also pride himself that he had never lost a physical confrontation with any man, white or black. To this day, he was still known as the "Badass Badge of Queens." It was only one reason, though, the organization had honored him with the position as watch commander for the New York division of Deliverance.

"Just keep your mouth shut, Tyrhee," Stanton warned. "Just relax. Everything's going to work out just fine. There's nothing to be scared of."

"Nothin' to be scared of, shit," the snitch snorted, his nervous gaze wandering over Stanton and his troops.

And Stanton couldn't keep the smile off his lips. He could understand the crackhead's anxiety: four big white former cops, dressed in black, hearts pumped with righteous hate and eyes steely with grim determination; four bona fide tough guys with attitude, toting one Uzi subgun, two mini-Uzis with sound suppressors and likewise armed with silenced Glock 17s in shoulder holsters beneath their windbreakers.

For this call, Stanton had opted for an American Ruger AC-556/556K, also with attached sound suppressor. A little different firepower, 5.56×45 mm, might throw ballistics off some, since the previous targets had all gone down with 9 mm lead through the face. It might throw some confusion onto the crime scene, might not. Hope ran eternal. Either way, it was time for action again. It had been four nights since the last call, near Jefferson Park. Three gang-bangers with sheets that could reach across the East River were caught in their apartment counting their dope money, dead before they could grab up a piece. Their whores had also been executed. No witnesses. In and out, move on to the next call.

Of course, there was growing public suspicion cops were doing the killings. Riots had threatened to erupt in Harlem, but the mayor had come out nearly every day before the cameras, assured all New Yorkers they had leads to prove the killings were done by rival gang members. The mayor was blowing smoke, of course, and Stanton knew the department didn't have the first real lead. Naturally the few warriors Stanton had in place were bound by the code of silence—or else. Still, things were heating up. The organization had a defector. Problems. But it was being handled that very night. Either way, word had come over the fax it was just about time to pull up stakes, regroup with every member of the organization to plan the future. As far as Stanton was concerned, with each minority scumbag they executed, the future could only get brighter.

Barkley wiped some sweat off his brow. "I just want this over, man, that's all."

Stanton narrowed his gaze, fighting back his contempt, an urge to slap Tyrhee silly with the kind of backhand he had often used on a hooker who wanted to get smart.

Barkley had been a small-time dealer, selling to support, naturally, when Stanton had busted him years ago. Then he had decided to extort him for cash, use him as a snitch. Somehow the punk had made it through the years. If nothing else, Stanton gave the guy credit for being a survivor. But Stanton needed Tyrhee to get them to the door, inside. Of course, Stanton could have used a quarter-sized ball of plastique to blow the door, but hitting the targets silent was just as important as seizing the initial moment with swift deadliness. Either way, it had been a long, hard week of leaning on the punk, grooming him, ironing out the logistics, arriving at the numbers. Check, then confirm the targets with their sources inside the department, threaten to put the word out on the street Tyrhee was a snitch if he didn't play ball. He wasn't about to lose his boy now to a bad case of nerves, or a guilty conscience that he was selling out his brothers. Of course, none of them would really know what they were dealing with, the exact layout of the target site or the actual numbers until they were inside.

Stanton put some edge into his voice. "It'll be over soon enough, Tyrhee. And you had damn well better be straight with me."

"It's cool, man. They'll be there, just like I said. I ain't never let you down before."

"I put a thousand bucks in your pocket, so you'd better hope this goes off smooth as silk," Stanton added.

"All that is, is flash money when I get there. You promised me another wad of dead presidents. And when do I get my stuff?"

"When this is wrapped up," Stanton rasped. "You'll get enough rock to either put you on the moon or dump your ass in the emergency room. I don't give a shit. But you're in this until we're home free. We clear on that?"

Barkley grumbled something, then nodded. He took a glass stem from his pocket and rolled it around in his hand.

Stanton nearly went ballistic. "Put that away!"

"I could use one to calm me down, man. Come on, Stanton, I know you're holding."

Why not? Stanton wondered grudgingly. Might keep him under control long enough to pave the way for them. A last request, too. Pathetically enough, Tyrhee most likely suspected as much. Stanton pulled a fifty out of his pocket and tossed it to Barkley. Not wasting one motion, Barkley snapped the rock in two with his fingers, loaded the stem and put his lighter to it. Stanton shook his head in disgust. Crack cocaine was the single most devastating, most ruinous drug he had ever seen, and he had seen them all. The horror stories about what a crack addict would do for a rock were endless.

Facing front, Stanton watched as they proceeded deeper into black Harlem. Everything was brownstone and brick. Dirty, dark, grim. Graffiti covered the buildings. Businesses were now locked down and barred up. Incredible, Stanton thought. Maybe a few honest people lived here, but they were prisoners to the animals, enslaved by their own. There was some kind of poetic justice in that, he decided, but wasn't sure what.

"Better, fellas." Barkley laughed, blowing a cloud of smoke. "Now I can think straight."

"Maybe you can think up some directions now," Scarborough growled.

"Yeah, yeah, this is right," Barkley said, lit up, alive again, feeling good.

Stanton ignored the punk as Barkley told Scarborough to turn, this way, then that. Ghettos all looked the same to Stanton anyway. But he trusted Scarborough to get them back to lower Manhattan when it was done. The backup unit was waiting in an underground garage with the other wheels. No need to wipe anything clean since all four of them wore black leather gloves. Standard operating procedure. When they arrived, the van would be locked down, but if it was stripped or stolen, the backup team could be there in ten to twelve minutes. Either way, they all knew and accepted the risks. Should the heat come down, the call go sour, they would go down to the last man, go out like lions. No one would be taken alive.

"Got something, boss," Morrow announced.

Turning, Stanton met his teammate's laughing eyes.

"Some asshole went berserk with an assault rifle. North in the projects at Macombs." Anger then flared in Morrow's eyes. "Two officers down. It's an all-units. Hostage situation. Means everything in the area will be tied up. Looks like the break we need."

"Too bad about those officers," Scarborough muttered with acid in his voice.

"Yeah," Stanton agreed. "We'll even that score directly, don't you worry."

Seething about the downed officers, Stanton cocked and locked his assault rifle. It wasn't much longer before Tyrhee informed them they were there. Slowly Scarborough rolled them down an alley. It was dark and looked deserted, but the shadows could be hiding any form of predator, Stanton knew. If there was even a wino who might identify them, he wouldn't see his next bottle of cheap wine. As thick tires crunched over bottles, cans and other debris, Scarborough slid the van into a dark corner of the alley, killed the lights and shut down the engine. Just ahead, there was a vacant lot bathed in hues of ghostly light from a nearby housing project.

"Right around the corner," Barkley stated. "Three brothers by the back door. Carryin'. Looked like they got Glock 9s when I was here last time. Ya know, police issue."

Stanton sensed the punk got a kick out of that fact. "No lookouts on the roof?"

"Not that I know of. Told you, I been here and bought before, just like you asked. Tyrhee got the way paved for you. This the next stop 'fore hell, man. Not even the man comes cruisin' 'round here. Get what I'm sayin'?"

"And down the hall?"

"Two more," Barkley said. "Can we do this now?"

Stanton slipped on the black ski mask, then addressed the troops. "Okay, let's roll, gentlemen. And remember. We all go home."

They knew the drill, all right. Ski masks on, they nodded, giving their watch commander the thumbs-up. Gurgin, the designated snatch trooper, hung the duffel bag around his shoulder. More than likely, there would be something to take home to add to their war chest.

Disgorging, with Morrow hauling Barkley along, they shadowed to the corner of the target building. It was supposedly an abandoned housing project, overrun now by rats and roaches, used as a safe haven for the Big H Crew. According to his source, the Big H Crew ran drugs and guns for half of Harlem, black and Spanish. But they also weren't opposed to the occasional stick-up of a liquor store. Word was that they had killed at least three clerks in the past year during armed robberies. A few of the gangbangers had been brought in, nearly broken to confession by hardball cops. But witnesses to their crimes never made it to court, intimidated into not testifying or weighted down to sink to the bottom of the East River.

Crouching, Stanton peered around the corner. They were right where Tyrhee said they would be. Three of them. One with a cigarette, all three quiet and still, gazes fixed at some point across the lot. Stanton was ready to make his move when he crunched a crack vial underfoot. Alarmed, the gangbangers whirled, grabbing for the Glocks beneath their jackets. The last thing the three bangers saw were four shadows in black, surging around the corner, converging streams of whispering lead death chopping through them and driving them hard to the ground before they could cap off the first round.

A half-dozen swift strides, unleathering his Glock with its customized sound suppressor, and Stanton was through the back door, which Tyrhee claimed was always left open. Down the narrow hall, two more bangers came to life. They were shadows, outlined in the outer limits of a lone naked bulb hanging from a cracked ceiling. One chugging 9 mm round cored through each face, and Stanton was moving on, pumped, smelling blood, tasting victory. Down the hall, Stanton caught the rumbling throb of rap music behind the door to the target lair. So far so good. Drill down pat, Gurgin lagged behind, Uzi fanning the gloom up some steps that led to a second floor. Nothing moved upstairs or down. Could well be, Stanton thought, that Tyrhee's info was clear and straight on. Outstanding.

Moments later, Stanton had Barkley front and center to the steel door at the end of the hall. They took up positions, two on each side as Barkley rapped loudly, in some kind of code on the door. The rapper's anthem stoked Stanton with even more fury and hate. They waited an agonizing few seconds. Finally a slat opened in the door. Barkley was all smiles as he flashed the show money.

"S'up, Bad Dog. Told you Tyrhee be back on top. Make believers out of my homeys yet."

There was a curse, then the sound of dead bolts sliding back. Then it threatened to sour. It was a sixth sense Stanton had developed as an undercover narc when he knew beyond all doubt it was going to hit the fan. The sudden look in Barkley's eyes warned Stanton the punk had cold feet, that he knew he wasn't ever meant to land those dead presidents and enough smoke to send him to the stars.

This wasn't the night to disappoint, so Stanton proved him right. The door cracked open, unleashing the fury of rap music, and Stanton put Barkley's lights out with one 9 mm slug through the head. As soon as blood and brains blew out the other side of Barkley's skull, Stanton leathered the Glock and barreled into the door. A black hulk with shaved head was sent flying down the short foyer, skidding on his back, grabbing for a pistol.

Stanton and his troops got busy. The doorman was easy, his face soaking up a 3-round burst from Stanton's assault rifle. The four men in ski masks seized the few critical opening moments, using the shock and hesitation of the bangers to turn the large living room into a slaughter zone. The four men split up, Stanton and Morrow peeling left, Scarborough and Gurgin going right. They held back on the triggers, spraying the room with relentless, coughing sprays of instant death. It was simple enough—if it moved it died.

Stanton found at least a dozen bangers scattered all over the room, jarred quickly from their fear and confusion. Three were jumping from a large black leather couch, grabbing for MAC-10s, one banger seizing an AK-47. A raking burst and Stanton pinned them to the couch, blood, flesh and stuffing hitting the air.

Over by the bar, bottles were shattering as Morrow poured it on with his mini-Uzi, cutting down bangers, spraying a Malcolm X banner with crimson. A ceaseless stuttering of silenced bullets to his right flank, and Stanton glimpsed Gurgin and Scarborough bursting through a beaded curtain, one high, one low, sweeping that room with lead death.

It lasted all of six to ten seconds, but it seemed like an eternity as Stanton and Morrow cracked home fresh clips, then went on hosing flying bodies. Two bangers with shaved skulls near a few triple-beam scales and stacks of cash were popping off with Glocks even as Stanton and Morrow stitched them from crotch to throat. Cracked up, no doubt, the bangers' blood was thick, jetting with an eerie fury as it sprayed the air. Finally those bangers toppled, but it cost Stanton another clip.

Adrenaline racing, slapping a fresh 30-round clip home in his Ruger, Stanton covered their rears. Three bedrooms needed clearing. A shotgun suddenly boomed, shearing off a strip of doorjamb just above Gurgin's head. Crouched, Gurgin sprayed around the corner with 3-round bursts while Morrow went in. A giant black man with a goatee suddenly came roaring out of another room, pistol flaming in his hand. Stanton and Scarborough unloaded on him, shredding his chest apart, hurling him back into the room. A quick pivot, and Stanton turned the huge stereo system into smoking, crackling junk. Silence was followed by the heavy thud of bodies, then shrill female screams were killed in the next instant when Gurgin followed Morrow into the shotgun room.

"Clear?" Stanton called out. "Anyone hit?"

Gurgin and Morrow emerged, giving the thumbs-up. Stanton checked his watch. Just a little over two minutes had elapsed since leaving the van. Not bad.

Suddenly Stanton caught muffled sobs, coming from the third bedroom. A curt nod to Scarborough, while Gurgin went to the triple beams to rake in the spoils of war, and Stanton hit the door. Peering inside, he saw only the banger he'd just wasted, stretched out, eyes wide, leaking blood all over the bare floor. In the far corner of the room, Stanton saw them. The black woman was cringing behind a bed, cradling a scrawny half-naked form to her chest.

After Scarborough informed him they were all clear, Stanton stepped into the room. Right away he spotted the rocks and stems on the nighttable. The bleary, bloodshot eyes told Stanton all he needed to know. The woman was emaciated, a crackhead, with a kid, doing whatever it took to ingratiate herself to the bangers for another night of smoke. Stanton felt revulsion at the sight of her. There was no option here, never had been. Stanton didn't have to think twice about what he would do next.

"Please," the woman sobbed. "Take whatever you want, just don't hurt me or my baby."

The child, no more than five or six, started bawling. Stanton turned a little and met Scarborough's uncertain gaze. It was the part of the job none of them liked, but it was necessary. The way Stanton saw it, he was saving the taxpayers a few more dollars. The kid would probably grow up, just another banger with a gun and attitude, in and out of jail.

Scarborough muttered a curse as Stanton took out the Glock.

"I'll wait outside."

"Grab whatever you see in cash and dope on the way out. And make sure you get our money back from the punk. We're bailing."

The woman's pleading turned to wailing as Stanton sighted down the Glock. "Sorry, baby, but believe me when I tell you, you and the kid will be better off."

Unblinking, Stanton pulled the trigger. This was what he considered real welfare reform.

IT WAS LAWYER NIGHT. More specifically they were gunning for defense attorneys. And it was going to prove some of the sweetest revenge former Harlem homicide detective Mike Garner had ever tasted. Only he was light-years from the Thirty-second Precinct in West Harlem. Long Island was the happy hunting ground this night. Here, in Southhampton, existed one of the last bastions of civilization, Garner thought, for whites only. It was a shame, he decided, to stain the playgrounds of the rich and the exclusive with blood, but the target was a snot-ass rich Jewish mouthpiece who had made a large part of his fortune ruining the careers of good cops. For damn sure, Ben Mortstein had been the knife in Garner's back, his the final blow that had knocked him off the force, into retirement, disgraced.

Sitting on the passenger's side of the black Chevy Caprice, Garner screwed the sound suppressor on the threaded Glock 17, then fixed the suppressor on his Uzi submachine gun. Peering beyond the iron gate, up the dark driveway at the gabled Tudor-style mansion, Garner had plenty of time to chew on the past, get himself in the proper killing mood for this call. And he could feel the prestrike tension in the car, understood the anxiety of the troops on this mission.

Over beers at the Gold Shield Tavern the previous night in Brooklyn, he had discussed it in no uncertain terms with Pete Tappani, George Mahoney and Tom O'Malley. They were to see it as just another call for Deliverance. It didn't matter if the marks were prominent, taxpaying citizens or not. A scumbag was still a scumbag, and defense lawyers were some of the worst predators in society. Having got that squared away, they were ready to pick up the torch, do some righteous cleansing.

Two of the other three troops on this call were former New York's finest. But Mahoney was one of the new breed of the organization, a right-winger from out St. Louis way who had a love of guns and a fierce hate for all nonwhites and liberal government. The stocky, crew-cut Mahoney had proved his mettle on a previous call in the Bronx when they'd hit a ring of bangers who had been extorting local businessmen. This was different. This night they were claiming the heads of white people. If their informant, their setup girl was right, the divorced Mortstein was right now, inside his domain, throwing a little party for a few close lawyer pals—complete with coke, both powder and rock, and a half-dozen two-grand-a-night call girls.

Garner counted nine vehicles in the circular driveway, all luxury cars. It bolstered his confidence that out here in Long Island there was little need for tight security. No gateman, no alarms, not even a pit bull on the grounds. Mortstein was fat and complacent, thinking he was beyond the reach of the ugly, harsh realities most New Yorkers stayed on guard against every day in the Big Apple.

Garner watched as a blonde in fox fur and black leather miniskirt slid out of her Mercedes, strutted up the marble steps to the big double doors. Cindy Miller was a high-priced call girl from the Upper East Side. Known to vice cops, she also worked off-Broadway plays, with big ambitions to make it as an actress. Giving out the occasional freebie to a vice detective was the only thing that kept her from getting busted, but Garner had promised her not even that would save her from doing time. Garner only hoped she gave the target a first-class, Oscar-winning performance tonight. Big busted and long legged, she was exactly the kind of Nordic goddess Mortstein lusted for. Well, in just a few short minutes, she would prove some bitter poison for Mortstein to swallow, the whore Eve for the lawyer Adam.

The wheelman, Tappani, voiced some concern. "Hope our little fox doesn't decide to get a conscience on us."

Intent, Garner watched as the mansion's big door opened, a tall figure in a robe emerging. Mortstein, Garner knew, was glad to see his girl. Moments later, she was inside. Garner checked his watch. Three minutes and counting. The drill was for their girl to excuse herself, explaining she had forgotten something in her car. She would leave the front door ajar, give them the enemy numbers, where they were, what was happening.

Garner mulled over Tappani's words. "She knows what to do. I've been working her for a month. She's Mort's number-one piece. Bastard even has the gall to get photographed with her by your local paparazzi over linguini in the Upper East Side. Like everybody's stupid, doesn't know the deal. Oh, she'll be straight on this, don't you worry. I told her if she doesn't cooperate, vice is ready to end her little reign of thousand-dollar outings. All her dreams of becoming the next Marilyn will tumble down right before her eyes. She doesn't even like this asshole. The guy has a first-class piece like her, and he's so goddamn stingy he doesn't even throw her a little extra for the finer things in life. The guy whines all the time about how the ex is bleeding him. Seems he has some problems, too, when he gets a nose full of powder, if you know what I mean."

Nervous chuckles sounded all around. It helped, of course, Garner knew, to have put a five-thousand-dollar advance in the woman's greedy hands, with the promise of another five grand when she reemerged from the mansion. Naturally it was a promise Garner couldn't afford to keep.

O'Malley spoke up. "Guess you want to do this asshole yourself, Mike?"

"In the worst way," Garner growled. "What I call pro bono payback."

It took Garner back, memory fueling his hate and

rage. Six years earlier, Garner had busted a dealer named Willie Robinson for two murders. Two white guys had come over from Jersey to score, but Robinson had just stuck his Glock in their BMW, damn near emptied the whole clip into the victims. From the crime scene, Garner didn't take but two minutes and one interview of a bystander to pick up the scent of the bad guy. Robinson was known to him, and Garner had suspected the dealer of another murder he was never able to pin on him. With only his partner in tow, Garner had gone through Robinson's front door, Dirty Harry style. It was a clean bust—he even found the gun, the clothes with the victim's blood on them.

Down at the station, he had beaten a confession out of Robinson. It seemed the punk killed the two white guys because he thought they were cops. Well, Garner had found a gun, a .45 in the victim's car, but he'd gotten rid of it; he didn't want to lose Robinson to questionable circumstances. The problem was that Ben Mortstein flew to the punk's side, claimed on television before the trial even started that it was a clear case of police brutality, that his client was wrongfully accused. He stated he was taking the case pro bono because the city, the country needed to see cops were out of control in New York.

Garner knew better. Mortstein took on clients with ready cash, usually big-time drug dealers, embezzlers, Mob guys. The man wouldn't even look at you unless he was collecting a hundred-twenty-per-hour fee. Garner knew he had problems as the lead detective in case.

In court Mortstein, who had a reputation for putting the police on trial, proved Garner's worst nightmare.

First Mortstein got his all-black jury. Second he started parading a bunch of witnesses to the stand who told the court about how fond Detective Garner was of using the so-called dreaded *n* word. How Garner had often bragged about manufacturing evidence in order to nail black suspects. He even found a reporter for the *Times* who had recorded a conversation Garner had with the man over beers where Garner sounded like he was boasting about kicking the crap out of blacks and Hispanics simply because they were all lowlifes and the world would be a better place if it was all-white.

Incredibly the judge had allowed the tape in as evidence. Unfortunately, though, Garner recalled, a snippy little friend of a cop had overheard Garner say he wasn't about to see Robinson walk for murdering two white guys who in all probability had a future. Worse, any witnesses Garner could find either wouldn't testify or they changed their story under cross examination. Mortstein played the race card, the jury bought it and took all of one hour to come back and turn Robinson loose on society.

While Mortstein followed up with a seven-figure book deal about his career as a crusader for the accused, Garner became the most hated man in America, forced to retire once IA started digging into past cases. Damn right, Garner thought, this night was going to be as sweet as it got. It was going to be one for all the men in blue Ben Mortstein had ruined.

Garner checked the long, deserted street. This time of night, people weren't even out walking the dog. Evergreens and shrubbery ringed all the estates. No one should even spot their stolen vehicle.

"Let's roll," Garner said, slipping on the black ski mask.

They were out the car, over the gate and shadowing up the drive. The call girl was right on cue, coming out, alone, heading for her car. Garner led them out of the shadows.

"Twelve people," she told Garner, "all in the main living room, right down the foyer to the right. Everyone's there, tooting up, like I told you they would be. Hired help is gone for the night. They're pairing off, getting ready to split up for the upstairs." She held her hand out. "Done my part, so let's have it. I want out of here."

She was either stupid or brazen, Garner thought. Either way, it was obvious greed had gotten the better part of her. "Thanks, baby, you're a doll," Garner said, pulling his Glock and pumping a silent 9 mm hole, right between her eyes. They left her where she dropped, swiftly filed up the steps and surged through the open door. Mahoney shut the door behind them.

Garner heard them laughing, having a good time, somewhere beyond the winding marble staircase. For all Mortstein's money, the inside looked Spartan to Garner, but he was more concerned with living objects. Tappani went upstairs, checking, just in case. His rear covered, as O'Malley and Mahoney gave the study a quick search, Garner burst into the living room. Right away, he got their attention. There were six guys, a few of them lawyers he recognized from the ugly past. The six females were now scantily clad in lace and frilly underwear. All of them were grouped tight, lounging on two large divans, the women hunched over the coffee table, huffing up powder, or loading stems with rock, tuned in. Shock and fear erupted into shrill female screams.

"Shut up!" Garner roared. "One more scream, one sound, you're dead. Everyone do as you're told, and you'll be fine." Give them some hope the good times could soon keep rolling.

"What is this? Who are you?" Mortstein cried, taking charge. "Is it money you want? I've got fifty thousand in the wall safe in my study."

Uzi trained on Mortstein, Garner closed on the group. The lawyer thought this was a straight home invasion. Run with it for the moment, wait to spring the awful truth, Garner decided. Fifty grand for the war chest was an unexpected gift. The guy didn't even ask about his girl, either, concerned only with saving his own butt. As far as Garner was concerned, he wouldn't have any problem with this. All of Mortstein's gathered playmates had been marked for extermination as soon as they had accepted an evening of the lawyer's hospitality. Everyone, he thought, was guilty of something in the past, had gotten away with some crime, some sin that always demanded future accounting. Better late than never. These people were indulging in criminal activity, after all, right? Thinking they couldn't be touched by the law because of their money and status as respectable members of the community. It would be nice to read tomorrow's headline: Prominent Lawyer Crusader Killed In Obvious Coke-and-Call-Girl Scandal. Well, Mortstein's public image would literally be shot all to hell. Talk about some sweet justice.

Garner waited for his troops, got the all-clear from Mahoney.

"Says he has money in the safe," he told Tappani. "Take him and get it."

Tappani snatched Mortstein by his silk threads. Garner waited another few minutes, helped himself to some whiskey by the wet bar. It was a beautiful sight, a wonderful feeling of power, he decided. They were shaking in terror. He could have anything he wanted right then, and there wasn't a damn thing they could do about it. It took him back some to his years on the force. A cop's job was all about power. It was "us" and "them." If a man had a badge and a gun, he could get away with anything, even murder, as long as he did it clean and smart, covered his tracks.

Tappani returned and announced he had the money. When Tappani slung Mortstein on the couch, Garner took aim with his Uzi.

"Oh, Jesus, no!" one of the men yelled.

They cut loose together, four streams of chugging 9 mm lead ending screams, chopping through flesh, raking back and forth. They spun, dropped, pitched over the divans. Blood and flesh sprayed Mortstein, who slumped to his knees, eyes screwed shut. When the last victim was pounded to the floor, Mortstein looked up, quaking. A little hope flared in the lawyer's dark eyes as he scoured the black ski masks. Everyone else was laid out, twitching in death throes in growing pools of blood, and he was still breathing.

Garner pulled his Glock, then slowly removed his ski mask.

Rage and horror bulged Mortstein's eyes. "You?"

"This is for all good cops everywhere, asshole, who are out there putting their lives on the line so you can sit here and talk liberal shit and put that garbage up your nose." Garner sighted down the Glock.

"You won't ruin any more cops. Court's adjourned, Counselor."

"No!"

Garner wanted it to last a few seconds, so he drilled a coughing 9 mm round into Mortstein's groin. The lawyer grabbed his mangled testicles, starting to scream when Garner finished it with two chugging Glock rounds through the lawyer's face. The ex-cop stood over the dead lawyer, savoring the moment. He felt better than he had in years.

Justice, long overdue, was finally served.

THREE OF L.A.'s former finest sat in the stolen Monte Carlo. For the past three nights, Buzz Macklin, Bull Moran and Jim Nelson had staked out the Korean-owned check-cashing and liquor store near the corner of Washington and Rosemead. Six times in the past two years, Harry Lee had been held up by bangers. One time, Lee had sent two of them out in rubber bags with the 9 mm Beretta he kept behind the counter. A few other times, the cops had nabbed the suspects, but Lee had never testified. Too scared, Macklin knew, of gang retaliation.

Through a hooded gaze, Macklin's green eyes glittered like emeralds as he scoured the street. Shadows roved up and down the block, but no one paid the three of them any attention. And Macklin couldn't find any citizen with a video camera. This was South Central L.A., after all, he thought bitterly. These days, people toted video hardware just in case they could catch a cop getting in some stick time on a punk. Film at eleven. For the moment, Macklin felt secure, their vehicle parked in the vacant lot that ran toward an adjacent alley. They knew how to take the action, if and when it showed, and had their evacuation down. Lightning deadly force, in and out, leave the scene. Ditch the wheels. Get the backup four-door sedan, head north, then east, put California behind with nothing but good memories of a job well done.

"This is a long shot, you know that, don't you, Buzz?" Nelson said. "We should have blown this town last night. They want us to head east. New things for the organization on the horizon."

Macklin turned his shaved head a little and met Nelson's icy blue eyes. "I have a feeling tonight's the night. Past two nights we saw the same black van, the homeboys eyeing Harry's store like it was a piece of juicy steak. Stick with me on this."

"It's gotten too hot in the City of Angels," said their wheelman, the big, square-jawed Moran. "The last call hitting that crackhouse in Watts was too close a shave. Cops could be out looking for anything. Especially three white men sitting in a car in South Central. They see this hardware, and we've got a problem. What happens if we have to shoot one of our own?"

It was a question Macklin didn't want to think about, much less answer. But they had the hardware, all right, to solve any problem. Nelson and Moran carried mini-Uzis in shoulder rigging beneath their windbreakers. Since Macklin was the shotgun lover in the group, an Ithaca 37 5-shot with handgrip, rested on the seat beside him. There was no need for silencers. Backup pieces were standard Glock 17s, tucked in their waistbands.

"Take it as it comes," was the only thing Macklin could think of to say. "Solve each problem as it shows. When this is done, we leave. But we need to take out a few more natives. You know, make the world a little better place. If it doesn't happen tonight, we'll leave either way. Call it cop instinct. I feel lucky tonight.''

Ten minutes later they got lucky. The black van slid to a stop, right in front of Harry Lee's store. The side door opened, and out hopped the three black males they had seen sizing up the store the previous nights. Ski masks and all, armed with pistols. Bingo. There would be a wheelman, and he would have to go first.

"The night's shaping up, fellas," Macklin said, adrenaline firing through his veins. "Three male basics, kiss your asses goodbye."

Quickly, as Moran fired up the engine, they slipped on their ski masks. Before the wheelman of the van knew it, Moran had the Monte Carlo slicing in front of the vehicle, cutting him off. As blindingly fast as the cobra strikes, the three ex-cops were out of the car. Just as the driver threw the van into reverse, his windshield was obliterated by short bursts of mini-Uzi fire. Shards of glass washed over the wheelman's face as it was pulped to crimson meat by deadly precise autofire.

Macklin let his troops take care of that piece of business. The first one through the door, he caught the three armed robbers cursing Harry Lee, telling him to empty the drawer or they'd waste him.

The three bangers saw Macklin coming, but for one of them it was too late. The ex-cop triggered some lead thunder and caught the banger closest to him full in the chest. The deadly force lifted the banger off his feet, sending him sailing, then crashing into a row of bottles. His friends started capping off rounds, but they were hasty, panicked shots. Their return fire went wild, shattering the plate-glass window behind Macklin, who jacked the pump action, tracking on.

Behind the counter, Harry Lee dived for cover. Macklin hoped the Korean didn't decide to join the fight but would opt to let these unknown avengers do their righteous job, and get the hell out of there. Either way, if Lee tried to play hero with his Beretta, Macklin would take him out, too, shrug it off to the Korean's ingratitude. Immigrants were proving themselves a blight on American society anyway, sucking up resources, grabbing up the good jobs from decent white people.

Macklin cannoned off another round, but the 12-gauge explosion missed the second banger, blasting bottles all over the first row. The two targets were scattering, moving as fast as rabbits. Moran and Nelson split up. The targets were scurrying, but there was no way out for them.

Jacking another round into place, Macklin wheeled around the corner. A 12-gauge round caught the target at point-blank range, nearly sawing him in two.

Still one bad guy, he knew, crouched and ran for the end of a row of liquor bottles, feet stomping, one aisle over. They had him pinched in, cut off, doomed. There was a crack of pistol shots as Macklin came around the corner. Macklin saw the terrified banger pivot, a 9 mm Glock swinging around. Glass was suddenly exploding by his target's head, showering the banger with shards, bathing him in flying liquor. The guy flinched, and it was all Macklin and his troops needed. A stream of autofire was chattering from Moran, behind Macklin, as he opened the banger's stomach with an Ithaca blast. Blood, guts and gore flew everywhere. Twin mini-Uzi bursts added overkill, some vicious impetus that helped kick the banger along, sent him crashing through a cooler. Even though their targets had managed to cap off a few rounds, it suddenly felt too easy to Macklin.

He found Harry Lee pointing his Beretta at them as they backtracked for the front door.

"No more rob Harry Lee, no more rob!" the Korean businessman shouted.

"Put it down, Harry," Macklin snarled. "We're cops. We don't want to hurt you. We're just leaving."

Flanked by Moran and Nelson, Macklin led the way past Lee.

"Don't do it, Harry. I told you we're policemen," Macklin warned, Ithaca pumped and ready to blast Lee into a thousand bloody pieces if the guy didn't get that Beretta off him.

Finally the Beretta lowered in Lee's hand. "Just go. Go!"

They went. Outside, though, the worst-case scenario roared up in Macklin's face. Out of nowhere, the black-and-whites were already sluicing to a stop, curbside, nose to nose with the getaway Monte Carlo. At least three units had come off Rosemead, uniformed patrolmen with shotguns and pistols drawn, bursting out of their squad cars. Not good, Macklin thought, knowing already it was over. The cursing that ripped from the mouths of Moran and Nelson had an edge of despair behind the rage. For a moment, Macklin was amazed that the black-and-whites had come onto the scene so quickly. The only thing he could figure was that Lee had hit a silent alarm. They had no choice. To be taken alive by brother officers meant a fate worse than death. A long vacation in San Quentin was the worst alternative for former policemen convicted of executing South Central's home-boys. Moran and Nelson knew it, too.

Macklin cannoned his Ithaca, decapitating the first uniformed officer in his sights. Nothing but head shots would do, since Macklin was certain the officers were wearing Kevlar. But no sooner did Macklin, Moran and Nelson start unleashing their weapons than two more squad cars flew in from the west on Washington. The din of weapons fire was deafening in Macklin's ears as he pulled his Glock, triggering the weapon as fast as he could, one-handed. He angled for the Monte Carlo, glass razoring everywhere, catching at least one more uniformed cop with a 9 mm round. Macklin knew none of them would make it.

They didn't. Macklin glimpsed Moran's head bursting open like a ripe melon, blood and brains going in so many different directions he knew the shots were coming from all points of the compass. Then Nelson cried out and went down, blood spurting from at least a half-dozen holes in his chest.

Macklin whirled, popping off several wild rounds. Even though it was beyond hope, he still had the urge to scream at the officers, "Don't you know who we are? We're one of you. Don't you know we're doing this for you? To save America?" He wanted to, but never did. Buzz Macklin felt hot lead core through his skull a microsecond before the lights went out.

CHAPTER FIVE

Hal Brognola snapped off the tape recorder with an angry jab. Obviously the big Fed had heard enough of another roll call, ex-cops and militant right-wingers from splinter extremist groups planning their next night of murder, laying it out, complete with racial slurs, ugly jokes, chuckles rife with contempt for anyone who wasn't one of them or like them. Brognola was sitting across the large dining-room table from Bolan, with the darkest look in the man's eyes the Executioner had seen in distant memory. Not only that, but the Justice man looked exhausted, troubled. Bolan could well sympathize.

It had been a long grueling night for the big Fed—first dealing with Greenbelt and Prince George's County police at both crime scenes. Then the Maryland State Police, the man from Justice clearing Bolan, both men walking on but not without catching an earful from a state police colonel. Whatever muscle was flexed, the warrior hadn't asked, but he knew the kind of clout Brognola carried. And, if necessary, that muscle could reach all the way to the President of the United States, the chief executive both knowing about and giving unofficial support to the Stony Man operations.

Things had gotten squared away, and that was all that mattered. Next Brognola had secured a safehouse off Crain Highway in Glen Burnie, a suburb just outside Baltimore. They were now bunkered in a secluded, wood-ringed, split-level family home that had been up for sale and that Brognola had snapped up with one call.

It was early morning. During most of the night, Brognola and Bolan had pored over what Westman had, while a team of heavily armed Justice Department special agents secured the safehouse, which would also double as a command center. Computers, teletypes, fax machines and banks of phones were brought in.

Bolan and Brognola had grilled Westman, sifted through a portion of the guy's stolen evidence. So far, what the rogue ex-detective had seized from his former comrades spoke for itself. On the surface, it looked as if the truth was every bit as ominous as Westman had promised.

Westman, sitting at the other end of the table, fired up a cigarette, sipped his coffee. "Before you two get all self-righteous on me, ask yourselves something. Is it the society that makes a cop, or does the cop make the society?"

Cold fury set in the big Fed's eyes.

"I think I've heard enough hate and mindless rage on those tapes to last me ten lifetimes," Brognola said. "You guys aren't any heroes, not even close."

Westman exhaled a thick cloud of smoke. "You miss the whole point, Fed. The only thing that's holding this society together, that keeps the animals from overrunning the rest of us, is a few good men. A man whose heart is right and strong knows the deal. He can't very well sit on the sidelines and watch evil triumph.''

"I tend to agree with that," Bolan said. "Only you and your pals aren't it.''

"It's a matter of perspective," Westman growled. "You blew away or blew up five men last night. Instead of sitting behind bars, sleeping with one eye open for the high hard one, you're still out here on the streets, running around, armed to the teeth. Something's wrong with that picture. What's more, if I'm reading this right, I'm not going to be witness to a damn thing. I've given you names of the cops and right-wingers involved. Something tells me they'll never see their day in court.''

Neither Bolan nor Brognola said anything. If nothing else, Bolan knew Westman was right on that count. It was something the Executioner would have to discuss, iron out in some detail with Brognola. In private.

Long moments of hard silence passed. Teletypes and faxes clacked from the basement, muffled voices of agents working around the clock on special hotlines wired in to various police departments, struck Bolan's grim thoughts, it seemed, from a great distance. The soldier moved to the kitchen and poured himself some coffee. Through the bay window, he looked at the two agents in windbreakers, standing watch on the balcony, surveying the woods. Shadows beyond the agents were turning to light as the sun broke over the safehouse. Agents patrolling the grounds had been issued M-16s by Brognola, with Glock 17s as backup pieces. It was plenty of firepower to tackle head-on almost any threat, the soldier knew. Still, he didn't know quite why, but instinct was warning him the safehouse wasn't nearly as safe as it looked. Somehow both Westman and his lawyer had been hunted down by the enemy. It was a mystery Bolan would have to solve, hoping Westman might have a clue how he was tracked.

"All right, let's get to the bottom line here, gentlemen," Westman said gruffly as Bolan sat back down at the table. "What am I getting out of this besides grief and a bunch of lip?"

"It all depends on where this leads," Brognola replied.

"That answer hardly fills me with a warm, cozy feeling," Westman said. "I gave you the names of those men cowboy here killed. You told me you IDed them through the FBI's state-of-the-art fingerprint network. Got names, precincts, why they were thrown off the force, the whole nine yards of every pertinent fact you need. So far, everything's checked out, right?"

"We're still working on a few items," Brognola said. "It takes time, and you're not going anywhere. As we speak, I've got a team of agents I flew out last night to New York, Miami, Los Angeles and Chicago to pick up any crime reports in person that may or may not relate to the activities of your 'organization,' as you call it."

"Deliverance," Westman said. "We call ourselves Deliverance."

"Somehow that doesn't surprise me," Brognola declared. "What I need from you is the exact location and address of the last known safehouse your buddies worked out of." The big Fed slid a pen and paper at Westman. "Do it. Then we talk about your future. Right now, the best I can promise is to keep you breathing, and maybe out of prison. Your cooperation, or lack of, will make the difference for you.''

Westman smoked, nodded, but started writing. ''I suppose that will have to do—for now.''

''Second,'' Brognola went on, ''I need every detail you can think of about this group's operations.''

''It's all on disk, Fed, six fat boxes of their SOP, from coast to coast. I decoded some of the operations for you, but before we go any further I want you to start thinking about your star songbird here. I give you something concrete. I want more than the run-around.''

''Believe me, guy,'' Brognola growled, ''you're in my thoughts. Why don't you tell us a little more about this Deliverance?''

''What's to tell? You're dealing with former cops, for the most part. Meaning they still think like cops, act like cops, badasses down to a man, who will fight and die for what they believe in—and that's the salvation of America. The reason no one can point to motive or suspects is because these guys cover their asses or get a guiding hand. You've got at least two parole officers I know of, one bail bondsman, a few cops scattered in precincts around New York who feed these guys what they need to know about skips, or assholes who just got out and are likely to resume their good old ways. Bottom line, and I've told you already, Deliverance is huge. It's nationwide.''

''Well, you're right about that, it would appear.'' The fury crept back into Brognola's stare. ''My team is keeping me up to speed. They've been on the phone, on the fax all night to a dozen different police forces around the country. In case you're wondering, I'm getting full cooperation, especially from New

York, because no police chief or commissioner wants to see the Justice Department swoop down and start hauling out their dirty laundry.

"Seems you heroes were real busy last night. A crackhouse in Harlem was wiped out, along with a woman and her young child. A prominent defense attorney who nailed a buddy of yours, Mike Garner, during a much publicized trial, got a client off for murder because of this cop's misconduct and brutality, was executed along with a dozen other citizens in his Long Island estate. There were other execution-style killings of gang members and drug dealers in Kansas City, Cleveland, Chicago and Denver that occurred last night. But here's the hardest fact yet for you to chew on. In South Central Los Angeles, units responded to a holdup of a liquor store. Three men in ski masks emerged and opened fire on the responding officers. The suspects killed four policemen before they went down in their final blaze of 'dishonor.' Thirty minutes later, the suspects, who murdered those cops and who had gone into that liquor store to apparently ambush three black males who were holding the place up, were positively IDed as former Los Angeles policemen. Seems one of the officers on the scene knew one of the shooters from his days at the Wilshire Division." Brognola gave Westman the names, but the ex-cop shrugged. He didn't know them. "So, now you heroes have become cop killers. This what you people consider to protect and to serve?"

Westman turned philosophical. "You don't get it, do you? When society is out of control, why should the police be any different? Fight fire with fire, basic survival of the fittest. I said it before. Just because

I'm rolling, doesn't necessarily mean I don't think they're not right.''

"Let's take a walk, Hal," Bolan said. "I could use some fresh air.''

Brognola shot Westman one last, murderous look. "Likewise.''

The big Fed rose and joined Bolan, heading for the living room.

"Wait a second." Bolan and Brognola turned as Westman told them, "Something you might want to know. It's a major item. I wasn't privy to all the details, since I bolted while it was in the works. But from what I could gather, all the cells in the country are set to link up, real soon. I don't know the location of this big rendezvous, but I gather it'll be far outside any city. Sounded like the organization had something major in the wings.''

Bolan nodded. "We'll talk later.''

WES CANNON COCKED and locked his M-16. The former New York policeman had no illusions as he gave the troops a scathing search for any signs of wavering commitment to the task ahead. They were the suicide squad. But that was fine with Cannon, a man who saw himself with a clearly defined and righteous mission for God, country and the white race. After all, the organization was bigger than any one man, its ultimate goal to rid the country of hopefully any and all minority criminals, eventually throw America into a police state where the right white ideas and decent Christian living could reign supreme once again. Here, personal ambition far outweighed the hopes and dreams of any one individual. Disgracefully so, however, there was a traitor among their ranks. It was a situation that needed righting no matter how much, or whose blood was spilled so long as the Judas bastard was silenced forever.

Standing beside his black Chevy Caprice, dressed in a gray sweater and matching running pants, a commando knife sheathed on one hip, a Glock 21 .45 automatic holstered on the other side, Cannon waited as John Turner strode out of the woods to get him up to speed. Six-four, two hundred pounds of solid muscle with a crew cut and coal black eyes, Cannon used his silence to command a grim respect from the others. He had brought down nineteen warriors of Deliverance, from both Brooklyn and Queens. It was a half-and-half group, he thought, fifty percent ex-cops, the other fifty right-wingers who had been recruited by Deliverance, specifically for just such a call. The wingers were little more than cannon fodder, as far as the ex-cop, who had done time on Rykers for manslaughter, was concerned. The organization was constantly recruiting all good Christian warriors, cop or not. If a man had the right perspective, hated liberal government, gutless media and anything nonwhite, could handle a weapon, he was in.

Cannon gave the warriors of Deliverance, grouped on the dirt road by the woods just off Crain Highway, an approving eye. They were all dressed in gray, toting a variety of hardware, itching, it looked, to cut loose with their weapons. They were like caged tigers, pacing slowly around five vehicles.

"There's a road about a quarter mile east of the safehouse," Turner informed them. "Half of us will move in from there, while the rest of us make a full-frontal assault. I counted six agents on the perimeter. Ten vehicles, could be as many as twenty to twenty-five we're looking at, though. Looks like we got lucky, Wes, tracking the turncoat here.''

''Wasn't luck,'' Cannon said. ''Dumb bastard had no idea a homer was planted in one of those disk boxes, just in case exactly the kind of situation we now face arose. With a range of two hundred miles, he practically told us where he would be. Westman was the one who got lucky, ducking us for two weeks.''

''His lawyer wasn't too smart, either,'' Turner said. ''The guy knew we're on to him. We could have wired his car with enough plastique to have blown him into Rhode Island. Instead we snap on a homer and he leads our guys straight into the arms of the Justice Department. Just a damn shame we lost seven good men last night. What a fiasco,'' Turner added.

It was something Cannon didn't want to think about but had to address. They had been designated as backup by their New York watch commander. One team had been assigned to take out the lawyer while the five-man hit squad went in search of the traitor. If it had hit the fan, Cannon and his team were to move in, bail out the others, use all necessary deadly force, even if it meant an all-out firefight with brother officers. Backup, they had waited in the wings, monitoring police frequencies with their scanners. Well, something had gone terribly wrong last night. Cannon and his team had been forced to ride it out, wait for some other opportunity. With all the cops flying up and down the parkway last night, there was no way they could have gotten close to their targets.

''You think the Justice Department is on to us?'' Turner asked. ''I mean we caught a vague description eyewitnesses gave the police about the shooter who took out our guys. I can't believe one man did all that damage.''

Neither could Cannon. "I only hope the shooter is here. I have a message for him I intend to deliver myself. A guy like that has to be something special. Believe me, if he's here, I'll know the man the second I lay eyes on him.'' Cannon started barking out the orders, designating the teams. "Check your watches. I want the rear team in position in thirty minutes. I'll give one word over the radio. 'Go.' If you can't get close enough to them to use your knives, select your targets around the perimeter and take them out with your side arms, silencers fixed, of course. Head shots. Take no prisoners on this one, gentlemen. We fail to nail, we're fucked. Good luck. And remember. This one is for your country first, for God second and for yourselves last. Keep that in its proper perspective, we'll be going home with a job well done.''

Cannon liked the grim determination he saw on their faces. One of these days, he thought, America would stand up and salute them for helping to make things right again. God save democracy, he prayed in silence, from the savages.

IN THE FEW SHORT HOURS he had spent with a bad ex-cop, Hal Brognola seemed to have aged ten more years to Bolan. The big Fed had dark circles under bleary eyes, his broad shoulders were sagging, his face pinched, and everything seemed wilted and shrunken with grim worry.

The two men walked down a narrow path, away from the safehouse. Bolan surveyed the woods. With full daylight washing over the grounds, there were no more shadows that could hide an advancing enemy.

Still, there were plenty of trees, bushes and shrubbery that could conceal stealthy movement, and the woods ran straight to the highway. Something was nagging Bolan, more and more, about the setup. Somewhere in the distance, to the east, the soldier thought he detected the low grumble of a powerful engine, but the highway wasn't that far.

Brognola unwrapped a cigar and stuck it unlit into a corner of his mouth. "You're on your own on this one, Striker. Able Team has an assignment in New Mexico. Tell me why I feel like throwing up, why I feel the need to kill a fifth of whiskey. What we just heard from Westman, it would look like we are facing the worst possible scenario for a democracy, with the potential for an eruption, particularly among the minority communities, that could well see the worst riots in the history of this country. Time has run out on this one. I've been working on this for several weeks, playing hunches and suspicions, using my contacts, working with the FBI, trying like hell to keep it all in the closet. It would appear, as our pigeon indicated, this organization called Deliverance is on the move. I've tracked the killings from the crime reports I've been gathering. Soon as these executions, all with like MO, start they stop. New Orleans, Miami, Houston, Atlanta. Start again in St. Louis, Richmond, Washington, then stop. There does seem to be a pattern, moving north. Only the killings continue in New York, Chicago, Philadelphia. It tells me this Deliverance is well armed, well financed, and the different cells are in communication with each other. The major cells would appear to be entrenched in the three latter cities. I don't know how many numbers we're looking at. I don't even think Westman knows."

"Well, there's at least seven less enemy guns out there I'll have to face. And at least now I've got names and locations. I leave for Brooklyn ASAP."

"Well, one problem on this is that you can't walk into a New York precinct and go on the muscle. Cops are protective of their own, even if they're dirty, especially if they've gone bad. I'll do everything I can to see you stay mobile if it hits the fan with any law. I'll either be here or downtown in my office. I'll give you a cellular you can take with you. You know you can reach me twenty-four hours a day."

"You know how I feel about gunning for cops, even bad ones. This time out, it's different. We're not talking about one renegade or even a few corrupt policemen. We're looking at perhaps a small army of cold-blooded killers. Hate can be infectious, just like a virus, Hal. I've seen too many times where it starts out with 'them,' then it becomes 'us.' Meaning hatred is hate for all life, any life.

"These soldiers of Deliverance have started out killing citizens who have committed a crime, just because they don't look the same. Soon they'll be taking out some Wall Street broker who's cheated on his taxes, or a little old lady they feel is just taking up space in the world. To answer your question, I won't just stroll into the Thirty-second Precinct in Harlem and flash my badge and ID. I'll hunt down any current policemen helping or covering for this organization. We'll have a little chat about the facts of life, and I'll give him the choice—turn himself in, or…"

Bolan let it hang, and the big Fed nodded in solemn approval.

"Something that bothers me," Bolan said, "is that Westman and his lawyer were tracked here."

"Well, since Westman is interested in number one, I can't see the guy leading them here. He's looking for an all-expense-paid lifetime vacation, and Justice is supposed to foot the tab. It makes me sick to my stomach. The guy has pulled the trigger, I can be sure, on some of their calls. I have to deal him something, if nothing else, string him along. Sometimes a man has to hold hands with the devil."

They were walking back, each man consumed in hard silence by the ugly truth, when Bolan caught the faint sound of a twig snapping. A second later, the soldier discovered his instincts for trouble proved right.

Snapping a burning gaze to their rear, searching the deep recesses of the woods, Bolan caught sight of at least six figures in gray, advancing on the safehouse, armed with assault rifles and submachine guns. And they were tracking Bolan and Brognola's way.

No sooner was Bolan unleathering the Desert Eagle than he was forced to barrel into Brognola, as silent rounds from chugging handguns sprayed the air, flinging chips of tree bark in the Executioner's face.

CHAPTER SIX

Pour it on with relentless lead, a jackrabbit run for the front porch, then charge through the front door—clearly that was the only way into the safehouse for the attackers. From a quick look out of the corner of his eye, Bolan knew the storm troopers had the drill down. Pros who had most likely gone through more than one front door on a bust, the hitters had seized the advantage of surprise. The Executioner glimpsed the fallen bodies of agents along the edge of the woods and near the front stoop of the safehouse. They were bloody, sprawled forms, limbs jerking in convulsions, good men taken out by bad men who had put quiet but instant lead death through their skulls. Their objective to Bolan was obvious, but how they had found the safehouse was something that would need answers, and maybe, accounting for by someone later. If it ever got that far. Either way, Bolan determined, they might invade the safehouse, even take out Westman, but there would be no way out for any of the enemy. Unless, of course, it was feetfirst in a rubber bag.

Even as Brognola toppled from the soldier's unexpected shove, bark erupted from a tree close to where the big Fed's face had been just heartbeats ago.

Bolan got busy putting it back on the enemy. He angled for the cover of a thick oak tree and cannoned off a .44 round, missing his target but drawing autofire from two gray-clad figures. Sprinting to the other side of the tree, their range and position in mind, the Executioner triggered two slugs that kicked both gunmen off their feet. A third thunderous round from the Executioner all but decapitated a gunman with an M-16. A sweeping glance at the gray figures advancing through the woods, and Bolan figured his first head count was off by at least a half dozen, minus three now.

Brognola leaped to his feet and drew his Colt .380, cracking off 9 mm rounds at the hardmen swarming the safehouse. Sporadic return fire peppered the trees around Bolan and Brognola, but both men were already on the move, off the path, bolting from tree to tree.

Several of the enemy vaulted the railing at one end of the front porch, their Uzis stuttering in unison as two agents rolled out the front door. The Justice men were dropped by the gale force of 9 mm lead before they ever got off the first M-16 round. A moment later, Bolan saw at least four gunmen burst through the front door. Two hitters were left on the front porch to guard the rear, their H&K MP-5 subguns stammering, tracking for Bolan and Brognola. Twin lines of 9 mm slugs ate up earth behind the two men as they made cover behind a four-door Ford. The other vehicles of Justice agents were strung out in a line, down the dirt driveway. Bolan's Plymouth Fury was three cars down, and the soldier knew he needed the heavier firepower of his M-16, stowed in the trunk. In the distance, he saw several figures sweeping for the rear of the safehouse, beyond an ivy-covered trellis, coming from the east. It looked to the Executioner as if the enemy striking the safehouse rear had either gained entrance or was already inside. Either way, Bolan knew it looked bad for Justice.

Crouched behind the Ford, triggering the Desert Eagle one-handed, Bolan handed the Plymouth's keys to Brognola.

"Trunk, Hal, key with the square head," he told the big Justice man, the din of autofire assaulting the soldier's ears with near deafening force. "I'll take the M-16, three clips, one grenade for the launcher. You grab the Mossberg in the back seat."

Brognola took the keys. Without hesitation, as Bolan cannoned one round after another from the Desert Eagle, the big Fed raced up the other side of the Ford. Bolan followed his old friend, crouched and on Brognola's tail as autofire blasted out every window of the Ford. Lead-jacketed hornets tracked the two men, whining off the metal of a four-door sedan, more glass shattering, erupting in volcanic sprays of slivers and shards. Suddenly there was silence from the porch. A quick look, while Brognola reached the Plymouth Fury, keyed open the trunk, showed Bolan the two gunmen swinging behind wooden pillars to change clips.

He leathered the Desert Eagle, took the M-16 from Brognola, loaded a 40 mm grenade into the M-203 and stuffed three spare clips into his waistband. A second later, twin storms of lead began thudding into the open trunk. Hitting a knee, Bolan swung around the Plymouth's rear and triggered the 40 mm hellbomb. A few seconds later, the two flaming muzzles of the MP-5s were lost in a thundering cloud of smoke and fire. Through the white blaze, the soldier made out the mangled shapes of the enemy launched through the bay window.

When Brognola seized the Mossberg from the back seat, Bolan informing him it was loaded and ready, the Executioner led the way toward the front porch, alert for any movement on his flanks. All around him, though, Bolan found nothing but the dead. From inside the safehouse, the ceaseless racket of weapons fire told Bolan it was all-out war. He glanced at Brognola, read the cold rage in the big Fed's eyes as he gave his dead agents who had died in the line of duty a look that told the soldier everything he needed to know, but already did.

Brognola was steeled to dish out some ugly payback.

CANNON GAVE the Feds on watch around back of the safehouse begrudging credit. As soon as his troops took out the four agents on the ground with 9 mm rounds coughing from silenced Glocks in near perfect unison, the two agents on the balcony came alive, didn't run, didn't take cover. Their training showed, and their guts took over. If nothing else, it told Cannon those guys had been briefed, knew they were sitting on one time bomb of a witness and were ordered to guard Westman down to a man.

From above, one agent started spraying the woods with his M-16, alerting the Feds inside they were under attack. The other Fed was suddenly riddled with autofire, spinning, then flipping over the balcony rail in a twitching swan dive.

Before he was even three steps out of the woods and running for the sliding glass door he suspected led to a basement, Cannon saw them pouring out of the house, cutting loose with M-16s. From the front, Cannon caught the hellish noise of weapons fire, a distorted mix of automatic weapons chattering away and something that sounded like rolling thunder.

There was no turning back now. If the wingers balked, Cannon would shoot them dead just as easily as he'd gun down these Feds. It helped that he had promised each man a ten-grand bonus upon successful completion of the hit. Since most of the wingers were pretty much just angry rednecks who'd never seen a serious dollar in their hillbilly lives, ten thousand bucks would seem like heaven on earth to them, he knew. Depending on how this mission panned out, it was something he would have to discuss with the New York watch commander later, maybe take it straight to the national commander. Cannon had always wanted to keep it cops anyway.

Greed, though, appeared to urge his wingers on, Cannon saw. His M-16 on full-auto, Cannon ripped a long 5.56 mm barrage into the first three agents out the basement door. Just as his overkill burst tore into them, launched them in a tripled-up tangle of arms and legs, Cannon glimpsed the skull of Fed number two on the balcony burst apart.

Shadows popped up beyond the glass shards. But Cannon and his troops were through the door, blazing away with autofire, taking on any and all comers with unflinching fury. Lead was scorching the air around his head, slugs from chattering M-16s so close to his ear Cannon could feel their hot slipstream. This close an engagement, with no cover, there would be casualties on his force.

At least three of his people went down with bloody

holes marching up their chests as soon as they were inside. Pumped on adrenaline, though, grimly aware it was kill or be killed, that there was only one way in, one way out, Cannon swiftly split off from the others. It looked to him as if the Feds had set up a command center—computer terminals, fax machines, phone banks and a wall map of the U.S. It told Cannon that Westman had been busy squealing. The Feds either knew something about Deliverance, or they were gathering intelligence.

Hot fury stoked Cannon's determination. Disloyalty of a white man toward his own was inexcusable, punishable only by death. White people selling out their own, he thought, was part of what was wrong with America. It was hard-lesson time.

The din of autofire and the brief but sharp screams of men dying in agony ripped the air. Cannon caught two Feds, leaping from behind faxes and going for M-16s canted against the wall, in the face with a quick burst. Clip spent, Cannon ducked, reached the cover of the basement steps, bullets tracking him, spitting wood splinters at the back of his head. Cracking home a fresh magazine, he whirled around the corner. Agents were toppling all around the room, smoke and sparks taking to the air as machines were pulped by deadweight or flying lead. Cannon chopped up one last Fed with a 3-round burst to the face. After a lightning sweep of weapon and eyes, Cannon found they'd cleared the room. Behind him, he discovered he was down to five troops. Tough luck. No ex-cops, though, just wingers biting the big worm.

The only thought locked in his mind was to find and execute Westman. Cannon moved up the steps, sights fixed on the closed door above. Then it felt as if the whole house would come crashing down on his head. What the hell? he thought, staggered by the powerful vibrations beneath his feet. It sounded like an explosion out front somewhere. Grenade? The only way to find out what was happening was to keep moving, keep killing.

Cannon got his wish. The door opened and two faces poked around the corner. The M-16s in the hands of the Feds flamed for a heartbeat, but Cannon raked the doorway with autofire, pulping the faces into scarlet ruin with an extended burst. Topping the stairs, he crouched, his troops strung out behind him. Heart racing, the hellacious pounding of weapons fire right around the corner, Cannon made his move to clear the way. Propelling himself through the doorway, he went airborne, hitting the floor on his side. Skidding to a stop against the wall, he picked out two Feds down the short hallway that appeared to lead to the living room. With their backs to him, the men were engaged in a point-blank firefight with the troops who had gone through the front door.

Cannon gave his men the nod. As they surged out the basement door, he drilled bursts in the backs of the two Feds, filling the air around the agents with blood and shredded cloth. Up and running, Cannon hit the corner wall of the hallway. The air in the barren living room was choked with cordite and smoke, littered with dead men, Feds and his own people. To his left flank, he caught some scuffling, heard an angry voice yell, "Get on the floor and stay down, Westman!"

It was all Cannon needed to hear. A short, ten-foot run through the archway to his left and he would strike paydirt. One last nod to his men, then at the

Feds to his right, and Cannon made his move. Just before he reached the archway, something boiled up in the corner of his eye. Twin flames of weapons fire suddenly parted the front door. Two guys, it seemed, were mowing down his men, Deliverance warriors looking like rag-doll figures, all chopped up to bloody meat. One stuttering assault rifle was paired with another figure thundering onto the scene with a shotgun.

On the fly, Cannon glimpsed a tall figure with an M-16 emerge from a pall of smoke drifting from a gaping hole in the front wall. He didn't know how or why, but one fleeting glimpse at the tall murky figure with blazing M-16 and that icy cold look in the eyes told Cannon they'd just stumbled across the hero who snuffed seven of their own the previous night.

Something hot and sick was all of a sudden clutching at Cannon's gut, and something dark and primal told him he wasn't going to make it. Well, if he wasn't walking away from this, neither was the Judas bastard who was responsible for this fiasco in the first place.

Two swift strides through the archway, and Cannon discovered he had his man. In an eye blink, he read the picture. Westman stood beside a dining-room table, looming over a Fed he'd just dropped with a right. Cannon met Westman's astonished look. Bullets tattooed the archway beside Cannon, forcing him to bolt to the side. It gave the agent on the floor a critical split second to regroup, haul in his M-16.

Only the man never made it to his feet. Holding back on the trigger, Cannon tore the agent apart with scything lead. Incredibly Westman just stood there, looking at Cannon as if he were resigned to his fate.

"How?" Westman asked.

"A homing device, asshole. In one of our disk boxes you made off with."

Westman started to sprint for the kitchen, his back turned. Cannon's M-16 flamed, stitching a line of 5.56 mm lead that caught Westman in the lower back and sent him on a nosedive to the floor. The guy might or might not be dead, but Cannon had a feeling he'd better turn his attention toward the living room. From out there came the relentless stammer of an assault rifle and the seemingly endless and ear-shattering rolling thunder of a shotgun.

Before his focus was fixed on the raging battle and his M-16 could swing around, Cannon glimpsed the tall figure with the icy blue eyes of doom roll up on his flank. That ugly feeling that it was over hit Cannon. He already knew it was too late.

The big man with the icy eyes proved him right.

M-16 POISED and tracking, Bolan led Brognola through the front door. The living room was large but it was barren, with no furniture, no cover. Tough going, close shaves all around.

Surging through the choking cordite, dust and falling plaster from the 40 mm grenade blast, the Executioner cranked up the killing heat, way past scorching. The floor was littered with the bodies of enemy gunmen, but many more federal agents were stretched out, wide-eyed and bullet riddled. Everywhere the floor was slick with running blood, the walls pocked and dripping crimson.

The Executioner peeled to his right, cutting loose on the first two gray-clad hitters in his sights. Brognola came in low, went left and started to fire the Mossberg. Only the fastest and most unflinching gun would prevail. Brognola was no slouch when it came to this kind of fighting in the field. The big Fed might have sat behind a desk, directing Stony Man operations, far away from the killing grounds, but Bolan knew Brognola had been baptized in hellfire in the past, more than once.

Through the drifting tendrils of smoke, Bolan glimpsed a big guy with a crew cut and eyes so obsidian they looked more suited for a pit viper. He would have dropped Crew Cut before he gained entry to the dining room, but five hitmen came roaring around the corner on his heels. Still, one horribly wounded Fed sprayed a quick burst after Crew Cut, driving the bit hitter around the corner of the archway. Unfortunately for that Fed, his ensuing death bought Bolan and Brognola a heartbeat's respite to seek out and destroy.

Five enemy guns opened up on the lone agent, nailing him to the floor. Single-minded blood lust proved the enemy's fatal problem.

Together Bolan and Brognola unleashed a barrage of bullets and buckshot. The targets went down hard, triggering wild bursts of autofire in their final breaths.

Brognola jacked the shotgun's pump action three times, cannoned three rounds that flung erupting scarecrow figures in all directions. Bolan held back on the M-16's trigger, hosing the dead, the dying and the falling, driving them into each other. The clip spent, Bolan was slapping home a fresh 30-round magazine, moving for the dining room, when he saw Westman go down near the kitchen entrance.

Bolan wheeled around the corner, the big hitter's position given up now, found Crew Cut and triggered his M-16. It was a quick burst, and the 5.56 mm rounds ripped across Crew Cut's stomach, the M-16 flying from the enemy's grasp as he toppled. Horrible-sounding groans, a wheezing rasp that told Bolan Westman's lungs had been punctured, knifed the silence.

Moments later, Brognola came up on Bolan's rear, the big Fed jacking the Mossberg's action.

Suddenly there was quick movement in the corner of Bolan's eye. Pivoting, he found Crew Cut reaching for a pistol in an ankle holster.

"Don't do it," Bolan snarled, wanting a prisoner.

"Fuck you!" Crew Cut rasped.

So be it. The Mossberg boomed, and Bolan's M-16 stammered out a lightning burst.

Wes Cannon exploded, was nearly sawed in two by the combined double punch of sizzling lead and 12-gauge buckshot.

Bolan reached Westman and rolled him over. Blood spilled from the ex-cop's mouth as he coughed. "You're one...tough SOB. Brooklyn cop...Paul Daly...wrote address...they murdered his wife...he was good cop...knows them...where to find...bad guys. Started a list...it's in the kitchen."

Bolan looked up at Brognola, who briefly shook his head. Westman was beyond hope.

A strange choked laugh sounded from Westman. "This is...what they call a...deathbed conversion? I was wrong. Get this...homing device...they put it...disk box...God...have mercy..."

Westman's head lolled to the side as the life left his mouth in a long death rattle.

Standing, Bolan met the Justice man's hard stare.

"Let's get you on the road," Brognola said.

The Executioner couldn't agree more.

CHAPTER SEVEN

It was just about time to go. Eight months and three days after his whole world was ripped apart, Paul Daly was ready to make the move. This night, he would break from his six-month self-imposed exile, interrupt his daily ritual and go hunting for the men responsible for his grief and rage.

There was nothing left, either in his life or in the home. Nothing but nightmare remembrance, ugly truth and unquenched vengeance. His small, two-story brownstone off Flatbush Avenue, their home for twenty years, was now cluttered with boxes and crates. Some boxes were stuffed with his ribbons, awards, plaques, clothes, family albums. Other boxes held his son's belongings, or the few meager possessions his wife had managed to bring to America a few months before Saigon fell, six months after the Communists had murdered her entire family before her eyes. All his Medals of Honor and Valor, though, all the Purple Hearts and commendations wouldn't change what had happened. All of his heroes were dead anyway.

It was time to act, hit and run. Whether or not he would put everything in storage before he did it, then just up and disappear into some remote corner of

Southeast Asia, return to the beginning, he didn't know. However the night would unfold, it would be some sort of beginning of the end, he decided. Or would it be the end of the beginning?

Sitting in the leather recliner, the only piece of furniture left in the home, Daly poured himself another glass of whiskey and drew on his cigarette. Evening was falling over Brooklyn, but with the blinds drawn and only the soft yellow glow of a lone lamp on the stand beside him, the living room was bathed in deep shadows. Every night he endured this ritual—sitting alone in the dark, a few smokes and two, maybe three drinks, thinking, remembering, hating. Soon, ripped with agony, he'd feel the cold emptiness all around him and want to bawl like a baby. Then the buzz would settle in, shadowy ghosts from the past come alive. There'd be nothing but heavy silence all around him, nothing but the beating of his angry heart.

"No suspects, no motive, no leads. Sorry, Paul." How many times had he heard that over the past few endless months? Well, the cops had nothing solid, but Paul Daly, a former homicide detective lieutenant, gold shield, knew different. He knew who had murdered Yuen and their son, Christopher.

And the worst thing in the world to Paul Daly was to know the truth, to know when he was right and strong in his heart. To know he was faced with the evil of other men. To know what had to be done in order to make wrong right. In combat, he knew, the worst thing on God's earth was to make the right man wrong, to turn a civilized man into a savage.

As the ritual of his evening loneliness progressed, it welled from the core of his soul, swelled straight from the heart, burned up his throat until the fire raced in his brain, dammed up the acid rush behind his eyes. God Almighty, why? his mind screamed. She should have been there, right now, preparing dinner, her quiet and warm and gentle way filling the home, a purity of spirit, the cleansing flame of love. And Christopher should have been in his second year at Syracuse, home soon for the holidays. Should have been, would have been.

Never would be.

He took her picture from his pocket, wanting to nurse the ache in his heart in some perverse way. Or was he seeking to fuel his righteous fury and determination? God, she was beautiful, he thought, a vision of heaven on earth, an angel sent to make sense out of a life of war, suffering and misery. Those liquid almond eyes, clear ivory skin and silky raven hair cascading down her petite body. That smile of genuine and real love for him on those full lips. How happy she had been to put behind the horror of Vietnam, of losing everything and everyone, but clinging anew to the hope and the promise of starting over, of finding life again in a new world. How she fretted and worried, over the years, but in her quiet way. Staying up and waiting in their bed, reading American books, struggling with the English language, wanting to know always what this word meant, or how to correctly pronounce that word. A soldier's real and only love in a world gone mad, then a cop's wife, only wanting her husband to come home, safe and unharmed, into her arms. He couldn't stand it any longer.

He put her picture in his pocket. Suddenly he caught his reflection, staring back at him from across the room. Not more than forty, twenty years on the force and he looked like an old, tired, bitter man. His hair had turned shock white in the past six months, the blue eyes having long since lost their luster for life, dull now but simmering with rage and hate, the fury of the righteous man driven to act against his nature. He despised what he saw—a once handsome face now sagging at the jowls, deep lines etched into his high forehead, around the eyes. Before he was aware of it, a deep primal-sounding growl of rage erupted from his mouth. Before he knew it, he was standing and hurling the bottle across the room. The mirror shattered, his image ruined, tumbling in shards to the barren floor, a thousand broken pieces, jagged reflection everywhere.

Quickly he opened the duffel bag beside his chair. He strapped on the shoulder holster, checked the load on the Beretta 92-F and filled the holster. He did the same thing with his backup piece, a Para-Ordnance P-12 in .45ACP, tucked it in a hip holster. From the bag, he pulled and flipped open the switchblade, six inches of razor-sharp steel. He folded the blade, then slid the weapon into an ankle holster. Finally he shrugged on a black windbreaker, spare clips going into the pockets.

And Paul Daly strode for the front door, knowing who they were, exactly where to find them.

Either way, it was time to go.

In a world where honor and truth were near impossible to find, Paul Daly would get his moment of justice. Even if it meant oblivion.

God have mercy, he thought as he opened the door and stepped outside into the future, on the men who murdered his soul.

Jake "Lucky" Weller was feeling pretty good about life as he put the fat brown envelope in the wall safe, shut it, spun the dial and dropped the U.S. board map over the built-in vault. Two fat lines of Peruvian blow, a shot of whiskey and, of course, another twenty-grand delivery—his contribution to them to help rid society of unredeemable lowlifes—always put him in the mood to drop a few hundred on his favorite hooker before the night was over. Life was, indeed, sweet for Brooklyn's top bail bondsman. Whoever said crime didn't pay? he thought, chuckling to himself.

The short, stocky, balding Weller waddled on tree-trunk legs to his desk. Plopping into a chair, he poured another shot, huffed up another line. The day was done, all his skip tracers gone off in search of scumbags he'd bailed but who were on the fly. Turning, he ran a smug gaze over the flyers on the wall behind him. Smiling, he picked up his Smith & Wesson 29, "Dirty Harry" .44 Magnum, drew a bead on each face, mostly black, staring back at him from the Wanted posters.

In his day, when he'd been out there, running down skips, he had brought more than a few back dead. He had kicked in his fair share of doors, dodged a few bullets, felt the swish of some punk's knife sweeping past his throat. He had scars all over his torso from old bullet wounds, his nose crooked, broken on several runs when he'd cornered and gone toe-to-toe with a skip. He'd never lost a man, always brought him back, one way or the other. Around Brooklyn he was known as either "Lucky" or "Dirty Lucky." In his business, reputation was everything. Fuck with the bull, you get the horns. That was a nice little phrase he often used, sounded tough, something Clint or Bronson might say before he whacked a punk.

Well, the good old days were behind him. Now he sent his skip tracers out to do the dirty work, to gore or be gored. A good businessman needed to supervise the troops anyway, call the shots from behind the lines, keep things organized, running smooth. And it helped to get paid for "sidework."

Laying the .44 Magnum on the desk, he scanned the bond list in front of him. Mentally he put together the ones due in court soon, just out on his help and generosity, but who were high probables for flight. He had a midlevel crack dealer, a gunrunner, a Middle Eastern businessman from Queens who had been arrested for sexual assault of a female minor, Caucasian girl. A guy like that, a no-bacon raghead, he thought, ought to be strung up by his nuts. He came to America, put a few bucks in his pocket and started running around, hot and out of control for white women. The man deserved the worst.

A lot of money was out there on the line, a quarter million to be exact. Of course, if they never made it to court, he didn't lose anything. With any losses incurred, the organization always covered him, plus the big man dropped off the twenty grand, every other week, like clockwork. All the big man wanted were names and addresses. A successful bondsman, he thought, sipping his whiskey, operated much like a cop. Tips from informants, surveillance, kicking down the bad guy's door, manhandling a scumbag, slapping the crap out of him until he confessed.

Weller stared out the window, past the Lucky Bail Bond lettering. His office was just east of the Brooklyn-Queens Expressway, right at the edge of the park in Brooklyn Heights Promenade. It was close to the East River, with a nice view of the Brooklyn Bridge, the Manhattan skyline. Gulls and tugboats, the ferry district—he didn't want an office tucked in among the clutter of the courthouse scene. Here, sometimes, he could take a walk in the park, feed the gulls, feel blessed he had cop and ex-cop contacts. There were former NYPD cops who were out there, making the world a little better place for decent, law-abiding citizens. They operated from the shadows, of course, unofficial but getting the job done. A bunch of real take-no-shit tough white men. Euro-Americans, he thought, the kind of hero caliber that's made the world, America, what it was, and would be again.

He was thinking about hopping in his '79 Pontiac Formula and heading over to the Gold Shield for a nightcap before he called his brown-skinned Thai girl. They would be there about now, with happy hour winding down, glowing with booze and the righteous knowledge they'd taken out a few more scumbags, planning the next call on some crack-dealing affirmative-action whiners. He was putting the toot in his drawer, locking it up, ready to drop a new list of high probables on the big man, when the front door suddenly opened. A big white guy in a black leather trench coat and the most icy blue eyes Weller had ever seen strolled right in, all business, as grim as hell and acting like he owned the place.

"I understand they call you Lucky," the big man said in a cold voice that seemed to come from the bottom of a tomb.

It took only one glance for Weller to realize there was something about the guy he didn't trust, something in his attitude that warned the bail bondsman this stranger was looking for a problem.

A moment later, he was sure of it.

"Can I do something for you?" Weller growled, hand dropping over his .44 Magnum pistol.

"We alone?"

"Just me and my .44, pal. I asked you a question."

"I believe you can do something for me."

Weller couldn't believe it. The guy was as cool as an autumn breeze, acting like he was untouchable, coming in, taking charge. He actually locked and bolted the front door, then dropped the blinds.

"That's it, asshole, you just grabbed the bull by the horns," Weller snarled, rising, scooping up the Magnum and figuring he could fix the mess later. There was a lot of money lying around. He could make it look like the guy was trying to rob him. He had friends on the force, after all.

But before he knew it, before the Dirty Harry special was a mere few inches off the desk, the big man with the ice eyes pulled a pistol from inside his coat, a wink of lightning. Weller thought it was a Beretta, but couldn't be sure; it all happened so fast. What he was certain of was the sound suppressor fixed to the end of the weapon drawing a bead, a soft chugging sound following up, then a fire racing down his side. The next thing Weller knew he was on his back, a burning hole in his shoulder, the Magnum pistol nowhere to be found. He looked up, teeth gritted, and found those icy eyes boring into him, the face of doom.

"Looks like your luck just ran out."

"What the hell do you want?"

"To put you out of business. But I'm prepared to

give you a choice. Turn yourself in, or I can turn you out.''

The big guy strolled away, back turned, keeping the Beretta low by his side, everything under control. Weller struggled to his feet. The hand cannon was still on the desk. Hope was fading but fear took over. No way was Weller going to lose all he had worked so hard to get because some mystery badass with no name walked out of the blue, went on the muscle for reasons unknown.

''I understand, Lucky, that you've been feeding information to some bad people, ex-cops, to be exact. Seems you don't think the courts in this town are capable or worthy enough to take care of society's problems. You want to tell me about it?''

Weller's mind was racing. Who was he? How did he know?

As if reading his thoughts, the stranger said, ''Who I am isn't important. How I know is even less important. You're running out of time. Are they close enough right now for me to reach out and touch them?''

One guy, Weller figured, against a small army. Stall him or lead him right into the guns? Or bargain his way out?

Weller glanced at the hole in his shoulder. Damn, there was a lot of blood. Surprisingly, though, there was very little pain.

''It'll help pull you together,'' the stranger said, nodding at the bottle of whiskey. ''Feel free.''

Weller went to work on the bottle.

Defiance filled the bondsman as the burning glow hit his stomach. ''If you think you got all the answers, you should know where they are. Gold Shield Tavern. They're there every night, this time.''

"Planning the night's work, I assume.''

"No. Getting geared up to make the world a little better place.''

"For whom?''

"All of us who love this country and want to be able to walk safely down any city street again. You been in a coma for a few years, or what?''

"Skip the end-of-free-civilization routine—I've already heard it. A man named Westman bought the philosophy. He's gone. But not before he made some sort of penance.''

"You mean he squawked, told you about me.''

"And a few of the others.'' The stranger nodded at the phone on the desk. "How about that call to your local police? What I know, you've got quite a lot to talk to them about. Last chance to save yourself.''

Suddenly there was a change in those icy eyes, something that turned even harder, more unforgiving, something that told Weller he had no hope unless he made that call. Either way, Weller knew he was a dead man. Deliverance would make sure he never sang to the real law.

Deal time.

"Listen, I didn't get your name...''

The stranger flashed a graveyard smile. "Reaper. John G. Reaper.''

Weller couldn't hold back a bitter chuckle. "Okay, wiseguy, Mr. Reaper, I got almost a hundred grand in a wall safe. It's yours. No one but you and me needs to know you came here. What do you say?''

A hard pause. Weller felt his heart sink, hope evaporating, a wisp of fleeting smoke in the wind. It was those eyes, blue and piercing, eyes that had seen the world, knew all its ugliness and brutality. Eyes that had known triumph over that ugliness, but at some kind of heavy price. Eyes that knew a man's soul and could judge a man on the spot.

"The kind of justice I'm looking for, money can't buy. No sale. The call."

Weller saw the stranger turn away, just a little. The bondsman glanced at the phone, giving it nothing more than a heartbeat's consideration. His blood racing with rage and fear, Weller made his move. But instinct already warned him, as he grabbed the pistol and started to swing it toward the stranger, that he'd never hear the hand cannon's thunder, never see the guy's head erupt like rotten fruit.

The last thing Jake Lucky Weller heard in this world was one final chug from the Executioner's Beretta.

THE BAIL BONDSMAN was merely the first target on Bolan's hit parade. It was quickly proved to him that Westman had provided some hard truth and straight leads. In the soldier's pocket was a hot sheet of names, addresses, precincts and watering holes where the so-called warriors of Deliverance gathered to stoke the fires of their hate.

Bolan's plan was to seek out and engage, then eradicate, swiftly and with all deadly force required. It seemed simple enough on the surface, but he knew he would be faced with a unique and troubling set of problems. This time out, a part of the law was the enemy. How far the tentacles of Deliverance reached remained to be seen. If this organization of former and current cops and right-wing extremists was, in fact, a national paramilitary force as Westman had claimed...

First the Big Apple. And there were plenty of targets in a town of ten million stories. Naturally the soldier's prime objective was to strike at the heart of Deliverance, but he needed leads, more facts. Not to mention shaving the odds. The best course of action would be to start nipping around the edges of the cancer. Tomorrow they would find Weller. Questions would be asked by the police, an investigation launched, or a pretense of one. From what Bolan knew, had seen in the man's office, the cops either knew or suspected the deal with the bail bondsman. Any guilty parties would likely start scrambling to keep their involvement in the dark while also hunting for the suspect who had put a 9 mm hole in Weller's face. And hopefully word would reach the Big Apple division of Deliverance that one of its key providers was erased from the picture. They might or might not start sweating, looking over their shoulders, jumping at the sound of a car backfiring. Either way, Bolan intended to make them nervous before the night was over. Deathly anxious, in fact.

Next stop was the Gold Shield Tavern. Full night had dropped over Brooklyn when the Executioner found the cop bar on Montague Street. It was a commercial area, businesses, shops, taverns, plenty of restaurants, catering to Greek, Polish or Japanese cuisine. At that time of night, the street was clogged with vehicles; people were everywhere, hunting up a good time.

The Gold Shield, a good-sized tavern tucked in on the block, looked fairly new. Bolan couldn't miss it.

A plate-glass window bore a painted badge, with Gold Shield in big gold lettering on the face. It might as well say Cops Only. There didn't seem to be any place to park, so Bolan circled the block, drove past the Church of St. Ann and the Holy Trinity at the northwest corner of Montague and Clinton. Going back, he got lucky when a four-door sedan, a half block from the Gold Shield, pulled out. Sliding in, Bolan killed the engine.

He had names and descriptions of a few of the former cops in question, thanks to Westman's report and Brognola's follow-up. He watched the tavern for twenty minutes, and saw a few men, going in, coming out. No one fit the description of the big guns he was after. He was thinking about the straightforward approach, roll into the cop bar, flash his Justice Department ID, throw out some allegations, make a little noise and let the bad guys know he was in town, when fate dropped an unexpected angle in his lap.

A broad-shouldered, stocky man with white hair was surveying the street, moving on the Gold Shield from the east. From Brognola's follow-up on former homicide detective Paul Daly, the description of the man matched perfectly. And even from a distance, Bolan was getting a hard read, right away, on the ex-cop. One look, and the Executioner knew Paul Daly even without ever having met the ex-Special Forces hero, turned cop hero.

He knew about the man's wife and son, and knew firsthand himself, from a thousand lifetimes ago, it seemed, what it was like to have your world shattered, to taste the bile and the venom of rage and hate put in your mouth by evil men who had robbed you of everything right and good.

Bolan watched the man for a few more moments. Daly was doing something that seemed strange at first. The white-haired man would give the passersby a sideways glance. Then, when he appeared to think he was unnoticed, Daly would make a darting move for the bumper of each obvious cop car in front of the Gold Shield. The man was either planting some sort of homing device—or he was sticking plastique to those vehicles.

The drive for vengeance, Bolan knew, could become an obsession, something that could force a rational man to do things he would have never even dreamed himself capable of.

The Executioner hopped out of his vehicle, moving to intercept Paul Daly for a face-to-face.

CHAPTER EIGHT

Bolan made eye contact with Daly a moment after the man attached another mystery package to a Chevy Caprice. Surprise, then grim resignation narrowed the ex-cop's gaze when Bolan flashed his Justice Department ID.

"Special Agent Mike Belasko, U.S. Department of Justice."

Daly grunted, scouring the ID.

"It's real," Bolan said.

"I believe you. What do you want?"

"To talk about the future."

"Yours or mine?"

"Yours, mine and a bunch of ex-cops who call themselves Deliverance. How about we go sit in my car for a few minutes?" Standing on the walk as citizens passing the two men threw them curious stares, Bolan looked deep into the man's eyes. Up close, the soldier read right away the pain burning in the man's soul. Because he knew what this man had endured, knew Daly was one of the good ones, Bolan found himself taking an instant liking, felt an empathy toward the tortured former soldier and cop. A long measuring of Bolan churned behind Daly's eyes. The man Bolan faced had been around long enough, had seen enough wrong in his life to know when he, too, was looking at another warrior, was honored to share a real moment with another solid, stand-up act. Bolan felt a connection spark between them.

"Lead the way," Daly said.

Quickly Bolan showed Daly to his car. Inside, the two men sat in a reflective silence for several moments. Bolan sensed Daly already knew what he would hear.

"I know what happened to you, Daly. I know what they did to you. I can tell you for a fact that I have been exactly where you are now. I can also tell you vengeance will eat you up like a cancer."

Daly said nothing, staring at the door to the Gold Shield. Out of the corner of his eye, Bolan watched Daly. He smelled the booze on the man, saw the torment flare in Daly's eyes. And the bulge of the weapons beneath Daly's windbreaker didn't escape the Executioner's scrutiny.

"Is this where you tell me to go home and forget whatever it is I'm thinking about doing?"

"What were you going to do? Just walk in there and start shooting up the place? Spend the rest of your life in prison? You don't win a thing that way. In fact, if you do that, they win. And Yuen and Christopher lose the one man who loved them more than life itself."

Resentment darted through Daly's eyes. Bolan knew he was cutting close, deep.

"I told you, I've been there, I've lost everything the same way you did."

Daly nodded, holding Bolan's stare. "I believe you. I get the impression," he said, the ghost of a sad smile crossing his lips, "that somehow, maybe we're two of a kind. So why don't we get to the bottom line here?''

''I would like for you to go home, let me handle this. I know who they are, I know what they've done, what they're about.''

''If you know all that, you know I can't just walk away.''

''I said I would like you to. Since you can't do that, then maybe you can help me. If you help me, you might survive this, and you won't have to deal with the prospect of Attica. If you get what you want, you'll have to live with it.''

A grim smile lit Daly's eyes with the first sign of real life Bolan had seen up to then. ''I'm starting to kind of like you. You telling me two guns are better than one?''

''You're going to have to trust me.''

''If I walk that extra mile with a man, that's the only way.''

''You'll have to go with whatever plan I make. Follow orders. Can you do that?''

''To the letter. No problem. I was a solder. Follow orders from the right man, nine times out of ten, a soldier succeeds, and lives.''

''Let's not make this that tenth time. What was that you were putting on the vehicles?''

''Homing devices I built myself. Effective range of three hundred miles. Just in case a few of them get away.''

''So, they're in there?'' Bolan asked.

''They're in there, I've been tracking the bastards for two months.''

''Sharpening the blade?''

''Something like that.''

The Executioner was thinking ahead, mentally piecing together a battle strategy. "Wheels?"

"Two blocks over. A 1968 Barracuda. Restored it myself," the man said, an undercurrent of pride in his voice.

"Mind if I see what you're carrying?"

Daly showed the Beretta, Para-Ordnance, then finally the switchblade in its ankle sheath. "Guess you can see I mean business. With or without you, this was a done deal."

"I can see that. You have anything else? In the car?"

"Yeah. Before I left home, I stowed an AR-18 in the trunk. Four hundred rounds. A Remi 700 sniper rifle in 7.62 mm NATO, effective range 820 meters, the choice long-shooter of the United States Marine Corps. Last, but certainly not least, a SPAS 12. A man on a mission, you had better believe it."

Bolan did, letting out a soft whistle at the mention of the assault and sniper rifles and the pump-action shotgun that could clear a roomful of people in a few eye blinks. Sounded like they could be a team.

"Now, anything else before you let me know if I'm really in the hunt?"

Bolan pulled out the hot sheet and handed it over. "Those names sound familiar? Stanton, Gurgin, Garner?"

"Every last one of these murdering sacks of human garbage. You've done your homework, Belasko, but this list just names a few."

"Okay. We're going to sit here a few minutes. I'm going to lay out a plan. We'll have some give and take, share what we know. I'm going to tell you what I know, what's happened, why I'm here and what I intend to do. I'm every bit as serious, soldier, as you about taking these guys down. Once you're in this thing, there's no turning back. We both take our chances. And once we walk into that bar, it's going to get damn ugly from here on out.''

''Nam?''

''And then some.''

''I'm with you, friend, all the way. Your back will be covered.''

''So be it.''

Another grim smile cut Daly's lips. ''How come I get this feeling you're not here to cuff these bastards and see they get their day in court? How come when I look at you, I see a man who intends to see their so-called civil rights violated to the absolute eye for an eye?''

Bolan looked Daly dead in the face, the warrior all steel, all fire. ''So far, neither one of us has said anything wrong.''

THERE WERE SERIOUS problems they needed to address. In fact, they were faced with a potential crisis that could unravel the organization, maybe even bring everything they had all worked so hard to accomplish crashing down on their heads. All those hopes and dreams of making America strong, moral and Christian once more could be trampled in the dust, leaving nothing but ashes in the mouth. If Deliverance died, Stanton thought, then so did any hope to make America right and white again.

Stanton lined up the cue ball, wondering what the hell had gone wrong in Maryland. He had very little solid information from his source inside the FBI who had a close friend inside the Justice Department. Apparently the FBI and the Justice Department were working together, gathering leads on the execution-style killings that had been happening in cities all over the country. Righteous slayings all, no question in Stanton's mind, cops with no motives, no suspects, no leads, at least that he knew of. Or did the cops know? Right now, there was too much silence in his intelligence pipeline, which wasn't good.

Unfortunately all Stanton really knew was that he was minus twenty-seven men. Three separate hits had gone belly-up, toe tag for his warriors, no burial with full honors for men who sure as hell deserved it. Worse, he couldn't even be sure Westman's poisonous mouth had been silenced. Worse still, he didn't know if the roll-call disks and the coded national information line, complete with fax sheets from other cells of Deliverance in major cities, with more intel about their operations on disks, had been destroyed. If nothing else—and it pained his sense of loyalty to the cause to even think it—at least his men had gone down in the line of duty. Dead men couldn't talk.

Either way, it was an utter fiasco. He now regretted his decision to tape those roll calls, to detail so much about their operations. But he was a leader of men, after all, a crusader, seeking only to make the country he loved so much a better place to live in for the kind of people who had made America the greatest democracy in the history of man. Someday he would make history, and Stanton wanted the people of America he cared about to know that he cared about them. At least none of his men had called him on the mistake of gathering potentially and totally self-destructive evidence because he wanted himself and the soon-to-be glory of Deliverance immortalized in

American history. It was smart, however, to put homers in those disk boxes, just in case they disappeared.

Stanton looked at what he had on the table. Ten ball, a long-shot, six inches, just to the left pocket. Stroke it in, bring the cue off the rail, eight ball perched right near the side pocket. He was bending over, heart pumping with controlled rage, when one of the detective lieutenants on his payroll, Mike Masterson, broke his concentration.

"It's getting hot all over this town, John. I can feel the fire reaching out, getting real close to my butt. I mean, it's radioactive hot all over this town. You got citizens everywhere trusting the cops less than ever. Even the fat cats on Fifth Avenue are grumbling about a police conspiracy over their wine and cheese, media all over the mayor and commanders in every borough, shit in the papers about a Gestapo underground among New York's finest. You got cops who think they know something about the few of us you got on your payroll giving us sideways looks. For all I know, IA is right now circling the cavalry around my desk."

Standing, Stanton clenched his jaw as he looked at the beefy homicide detective from Queens. Enough. The guy wasn't only babbling, he was whining. In every war, Stanton knew, there was always a crisis to confront. Without challenge, a warrior never found out just how good he was. For a long moment, Stanton put a steely eye on Masterson. The Queens cop sat on a stool, working on his third double whiskey, but not even the booze seemed to calm the man's nerves.

Sinatra was playing on the jukebox, the talk of cops, the clack of balls from the three other pool tables filling Stanton's ears. Stanton knew he was in the right place, standing tall in the only kind of atmosphere he considered civilized, cops getting together with cops, but for some reason he felt very much alone. At least eight of Stanton's troops were there, getting up to speed from their sources inside the department. They came from various precincts around the city—Brooklyn, the Bronx, Staten Island, Manhattan. Almost thirty cops, patrolmen and plainclothes detectives, were clustered around the Gold Shield for happy hour. But the ones Stanton really needed to hear from, his patrolmen who worked out of the Thirty-second Precinct in Harlem, weren't there. It was bothering Stanton that very little information about the investigations of their hits the previous night had come in through his sources. If one guy could roll over, well, it could start a chain reaction.

Stanton looked around the large tavern, trying to steel his own nerves, sucking in a deep breath, then draining his beer. Gurgin and Morrow were having a few beers with the guys from the Bronx. They were getting tips about some gangbangers who specialized in smash-and-grabs of jewelry stores, then dumped the merchandise through a major fencing operation. Damn, but Stanton wanted to go out on one more call before they rolled out of New York. And the seizure of two or three million in hot jewelry could fatten the war chest. Of course, the robbery detectives who put the scent of those scumbags up their nose would have to get their cut. No problem; that was just part of doing business.

Right now, though, the rest of his warriors, a forty-strong force, were pulling up stakes, dismantling fax machines, erasing disks in their various safehouses scattered around the four outer boroughs. Vehicles were being loaded with hardware and the spoils from their war chests. The troops he really trusted were supervising the pulling out. All that cash and dope, no way Stanton would see any of it walk. Later, he would load his own war chest into his car.

"With all the money I've put in your pocket, Mike, I don't think I like hearing this kind of paranoid talk. I don't pay you to be nervous. Lately you haven't given me a damn thing for my money. I can get more for my money out of my bondsman down the street."

Stanton took his anger out on the cue and stroked the ball, a white bullet that banged the ten straight in the pocket. Even though Scarborough saw he was going to lose twenty bucks, as the cue rolled up and stopped in front of the eight, he gave a whistle of admiration. Stanton sank the eight and took the twenty. Leaders were always expected to win anyway, Stanton thought, putting grim focus back on Masterson.

Masterson worked on his drink, firing up a cigarette with a shaky hand. Garner sat on the stool next to the detective. At the moment Garner was looking Masterson up and down through a hooded gaze, his eyes intense with the natural cop's suspicion.

Anger twisted Masterson's expression. "What, you think I'm wired, Garner? You bastard."

Stanton stepped in before things got out of control. "No, we're not thinking that, Mike. Look around you, look where you are. Down to a man in here, they are either with us, or they know about us but can't do anything because we have enough on every man here to cause him a major problem. You know the deal. They take a kickback from a dealer to look the other way. Or maybe they outright lift a key or twenty grand during a bust, then wink at each other, turn around and sell it back to the next dealer down the street. Or they've busted some asshole up in an alley so bad, violating his rights within an inch of his life, so that if someone wanted to make a few calls, IA would damn sure start snooping around on them, start reviewing all their old caseloads. Or like you, they wasted some black punk in a dark alley when the guy had no piece on him, then planted a backup .38 on him. Knowledge, Mike, is everything, it means power.''

''Look, all I'm saying is that what went down last night in Harlem was one thing. Nobody cares about some burned-out crack dealers. You waste thirty, forty of those types, they're like cockroaches. They breed like them, you can never get them all, and when light hits them, they skitter off into a hole.''

''It just means we've got a lot of bugs to spray, that's all,'' Stanton said, chuckling.

Masterson missed the humor, scowled. ''Damn it, John, the point is, this mess out in Long Island, I mean, when you start rolling into a million-dollar estate and blowing away prominent high-society types, the police have a way of calling out all the troops and getting some answers. You pull something in Queens, that's one thing, but you were a cop. You know I can't tell you anything. Those investigations aren't mine. If I start making calls out to Southhampton or over in Harlem, they're going to want to know why a cop from Queens is so interested. Too many people know what's going on here. It's set to blow.''

Stanton nodded. ''You want out. Is that what you're saying?''

"I'm saying cool your heels for a while. Listen, guys, I'm with you, you know that. I understand we have to do the same dirty shit. We have to steal, lie and then some to keep pace, to beat the animals at their own game. It's the only way. If we are the law, then I understand the unwritten code that we are above the law."

"I hear a 'but' coming up, Mike."

Masterson heaved a breath. "I got a wife and two kids, and I'm two years from putting in for retirement. My dream is to get a cop bar like Tommy here has. You think I'm paranoid, maybe even self-serving, well, I'm not the only one who's getting nervous."

"You with us or not, Masterson?" Garner asked.

There was a long pause, during which Stanton knew it was over in New York. At least for a while. That was fine. At 2100 hours they were pulling out anyway. In time, they would return to this town. The organization had a plan code-named Operation Master Eradication. There were no details yet; the orders were just to link up in Philly with two cells coming north, up the Atlantic Seaboard. Later the national watch commander would tell Stanton what to do, where to head.

"For now," Masterson said, "you're on your own. No one's going to roll on you, if that's what you're worried about. Like you implied, John, one goes down, we all go down. Try to see things my way."

Stanton had the urge to knock Masterson off his stool but somehow controlled himself. "I believe I am, Mike," he said in a quiet but cold voice. "All right, that's it for now. Why don't you give me my time here with my men."

Masterson looked humbled by the abrupt dismissal. "I'm sorry, John."

They said nothing, waiting until Masterson had walked away, the Queens cop making a beeline for the bar.

"How come my gut tells me there just went a problem," Scarborough said.

"Screw him," Stanton replied. "The man's got a dream. He won't do a damn thing to put that at risk."

"What do we know about the mess down south?" Garner asked.

"I know we've got problems," Stanton said. "My source indicates that the Justice Department may be on to us."

"Problem is, we don't know how much Westman's told them, or if he's even dead," Scarborough observed.

"We do know we lost every last single man down there," Garner said. "It won't take much work for the Feds to ID a lot of the men we lost as former cops."

"You know what's really crazy," Stanton said, thinking about what his FBI source had informed him about the first two crime scenes. "I've heard that maybe one guy took out seven of our people at the first two scenes. Even the media is leaking that."

"Who? A Fed?" Scarborough pondered. "No Fed runs around John Wayne-ing the streets."

"That's just it. We don't know what's going on." Stanton paused, then added, "We've got mysteries and no clues. We've got problems staring us in the face or breathing down our necks, and we don't know who or what is coming after us, if they even are."

"We've got another problem," Garner said. "I

know you don't like to think about this, John, but Paul Daly has been seen staking out a couple of our safehouses. I understand he's been asking a lot of questions, hitting a couple of our informants, squeezing them. Same thing he was doing before the, uh, incident.''

Stanton felt his belly freeze. He hadn't thought about Paul Daly in months, hoping the former soldier and cop would have just taken it on the chin, rolled up and faded away.

"Kill a man's wife and son, a cop's family, no less, and you knew you were opening up the gates of hell," Garner said.

It was the first time Stanton had ever heard his authority questioned. Only a few warriors in the New York cell knew what Stanton had done to Paul Daly. What Garner was implying now, that Stanton had quite possibly made a fatal move, needed to be addressed, and in no uncertain terms.

Stanton injected steel into his look, his voice. "I gave that guy every chance to join us. Hell, I liked Daly, I wanted him on the team. Know what he told me? He told me that myself and the rest of us were no better, in fact, we were worse than the criminal scum we wanted to kill."

"How the hell did he even know what we were about?" Scarborough said.

"He just knew," Stanton growled. "He's a cop, with a cop's mind and a cop's instincts. All it takes is a little asking around, and he could put two and two together. Anyway, I should have known better. A guy like that, Vietnam hero, brings home an Asian woman, well, I must have been crazy to think he would have ever joined."

"Is that why you did it?" Garner probed.

Stanton's gaze narrowed, his heart beating with fury. "I can't say I care for your tone, Mike. We all know I lost a brother in that war. If what I did was a little bit of payback, was my way of getting some kind of justice, then that's the way it is. What's more, Daly looked me in the eye, told me he knew I was dirty when I was on the force, that he was going to expose us and bring down our group, no matter what it took. I don't need some crusader on my ass."

"So, why didn't you just take care of him, too?" Garner challenged.

Stanton balked. "I think you know why, Mike."

"Because he was a cop?"

"Yeah, because he was a cop. Because I wanted him to live with a hard lesson. You don't betray a brother officer, no matter what you think of him. Look, if I was going down for that thing, which happened eight months back, I might add, it would have happened before now. It was a clean hit. It's a done deal. He might think he knows something, but he doesn't know for certain."

"He knows, John," Scarborough said. "He may not have the first piece of solid evidence, but I was there when you put the facts of life to him. Play ball or else... The worst thing in the world to face is a man who has nothing left to lose."

"Look," Stanton stated, "what's done is done. I did what I felt was necessary to ensure our survival. If I want Daly dead, he's dead. I hope this isn't brought up again for discussion."

Garner and Scarborough fell silent, appearing to accept Stanton's argument.

"I don't have a problem with what you did, John,"

Garner said. "Like our fat boy over there sucking down whiskey said, maybe it's best to leave town."

"We are. But we'll return, gentlemen. And when we do, we'll declare a righteous war to end all righteous wars on the lower elements of free society when we come back. Now that we've got that squared away, why don't we shoot a few more games? In a little while, I'll call to make sure our force is saddled up. Then, we're out of here. The future is ours to make and to take."

He saw the conviction return to their eyes. Just like that, Stanton felt strong, in charge again. He was cueing up his stick, Scarborough racking it up for another game, when Stanton saw Garner's face turn dark with fear.

"Do you believe this?" Garner said, nearly choking on his beer.

Following Garner's stare, Stanton saw them rolling through the front door.

For what felt like an agonizing eternity, Stanton locked eyes with the man whose wife and son he had killed. Breaking Daly's gaze, Stanton then couldn't help but notice the big guy in the black leather trench coat beside Daly. In the next fleeting moment, it struck Stanton, with all his years of cop instinct for trouble meshing together like a ticking time bomb in his gut, that the stranger was staring straight and deep into his soul.

Something cold, icy and terrible inside Stanton was warning him that the stranger knew just what the score was. He could actually see the man's steely blue eyes, and Stanton read it all, loud and clear.

What he saw was knowledge, then judgment.

And finally death.

THE EXECUTIONER FELT the freeze go through the Gold Shield as soon as he stepped in with his new-found ally. A hard wall of bitter silence hit and surrounded Bolan and Daly, telling Bolan all he needed to know.

The soldier had arrived in the right den of vipers, and it was surely, as far as he was concerned, the beginning of the end for Deliverance.

Of course, getting it done was up for grabs.

Right away, in the crowd of cops he guessed was thirty-strong, he picked out John Stanton. The bad cop in question was easy to spot. Even without a description from Brognola, then from Daly outside, Bolan knew the type of man Stanton and the others were, knew what they were all about, had seen the face of hate and rage to devour all life countless times on his hellfire trail. In the few short moments Bolan locked a hard stare with Stanton, the soldier realised that the big ex-cop "knew." No, Bolan wasn't there for a field interrogation.

Trailing Daly, Bolan sat next to his ally at the end of the bar where the next-closest occupant was five stools down.

A stocky bald bartender with a liver-spotted face made his way to the end of the bar. He sized Bolan up with mean eyes, then told Daly, "This isn't too smart, Paul. I don't like what I'm seeing. You're not a cop anymore. I see you're holding, so either put it out, or walk on."

"Kiss my ass, Tommy," Daly growled. "I know enough about you, well, just for starters, one call to the IRS might shut you down by week's end. Word is, you're doing some moonlighting as a bookie out of the back room."

Bolan stepped in, flashed his ID to the bartender, then stood. "Special Agent Belasko, United States Department of Justice."

To a man, they stopped shooting pool, throwing darts, drinking. The Executioner had center stage.

"No one leaves," Bolan announced. "Tommy here is going to get my friend and me a drink. I'll deal with you directly. I know Tommy doesn't have a problem with that, since he's running a dirty bar that caters to dirty cops who like to take drug money, who like to beat up citizens, who think of themselves as avenging vigilantes who go around murdering anybody they don't feel is good enough to breathe the same air. How about those drinks, Tommy? Pour me a cold one and get my friend whatever he's drinking. On the house, of course."

Bolan saw the bartender look to the pool tables, as if imploring for help from Stanton.

Stanton merely nodded at Tommy and said, "Get the drinks. You've got a big mouth, Mr. Special Agent. For your sake, I hope that mouth didn't just write a check your ass can't cash."

"My mouth's not nearly as big as your boy Westman's," Bolan countered. More freeze, and this time Bolan struck the nerves of fear.

Daly ordered a whiskey and ginger.

While they waited, Bolan told Tommy in a loud voice, "Whatever happens here, stays here. My business is officially unofficial. I came in with my friend, alone. We'll take our chances. Any damage done to your Gold but tarnished Shield, Tommy, comes out of your nest egg. We clear on that?"

Tommy put the drinks down hard in front of Bolan

and Daly, slopping some over the edges. "You're pushing it, pal."

"Are we clear on that?"

"It's your funeral."

Out of the corner of his eye, Bolan watched them. They somehow came out of their paralysis, went back to drinking, made a show of shooting pool, throwing darts or glancing nervously at the big-screen TV with the sound off, in the far corner of the room. No doubt—Bolan read them as predators, ready to strike.

Daly killed half his drink. "You know this might not go the way we talked about."

"That's certainly a possibility."

Daly gave a grim chuckle. "What's life without risk?"

"What's life without justice? You follow my lead, you know the drill we talked over."

Daly nodded, knowing what the warrior intended. They couldn't very well just start shooting. No, the plan was to make Stanton and his troops nervous, let them know a cowboy was in town who knew the score. Bolan would make some noise, do his best to bust them up, toe-to-toe, knuckle-dusting. It would be hit-and-run. And hopefully, Stanton would lead Bolan to the head of Deliverance. It was a straight-ahead battle tactic, the only way to launch his campaign— march in, dig them out, take them down.

Bolan saw a sudden change in Daly's eyes as the liquor fueled the torment in the man's soul.

In a low but choked voice, Daly said, "He had just come home from college on break. Chris and Yuen, they were just walking down the street, going to pick up some food, just a mother and a son. Christ...I got the call not more than an hour later." He clenched his teeth so hard, Bolan saw the veins in the man's forehead stand out. "The bastard told me only three days before to 'play ball, back off or else.'"

Daly threw Bolan a look, then swiveled on his stool and told Stanton, "You! Killer of women and children. I'm here to play ball. You and me need to settle up. I won't kill you—not yet. Consider this just the beginning of payback."

Bolan saw the fury building in Stanton's eyes. The big ex-cop looked at his men, tossed his stick on the table, then said, "Tommy. Lock the front door."

"Look, I don't want any gunplay, damn it!"

"There won't be," Bolan said. "No one in here can risk that, right, Stanton? If the real law comes through the front door, and I dump on them what the Justice Department knows about Deliverance, well, let's just say all your dreams for a new America go straight with you to Attica. Lock the door now, Tommy. If I so much as see you pull a BB gun from behind that bar, the only gunplay you see will be your last."

Muttering a curse, Tommy went and locked the front door.

Bolan and Daly rose off their stools.

CHAPTER NINE

Three long strides from the bar, it became apparent to Bolan who was in, who was out. Eight grim-faced, mean-eyed men drew close to Stanton, then fanned out around the pool tables. With Daly on his left flank, Bolan was closing on the enemy when a plainclothes cop spoke up to break the silence of deadly intent.

"I'm out of this, Stanton. The guy says he's a Fed, and I'm not going to argue with him. You're on your own."

There were murmurs of agreement and nods from other cops in the bar who were bailing out. Somehow, Bolan wasn't convinced they would stay put when it hit the fan. Either way, he would deal with them to a man if they suddenly decided to step in to assist the wrong side.

Stanton showed the cops a dark scowl. "How come that doesn't surprise me? When this is finished, consider your free rides over."

That seemed to be no problem for the other cops, but Bolan needed to make one final point. Moving forward, running a hard gaze over the spectator law, Bolan told them, "I consider every last man in this room dirty. You either know, are involved directly or have covered, or you wouldn't be sitting here. When you leave here, you go back to your precincts and turn yourselves over to internal affairs. Contact the Justice Department. If you don't, I'll come for you, and you can put my word about that on your mother's soul. There's nothing left for any of you men to protect. No place for you to run, no place to hide. You make me come and deal with you my way, then you better be prepared for the truth to set you free forever.''

''I think you need to deal with me first, tough guy,'' Stanton growled.

He turned to address the other cops. ''If I find out any man in here has rolled, I'll personally come for him in the dead of night. I'll take you, your wives, your families. You'll know firsthand what it's like to take a thorough ass-whipping from the Badass Badge of Queens. You men know my rep, you know no man has ever beaten me. I'm not about to let it start now.''

Daly peeled off from Bolan's flank. Nine men, Bolan counted. There was no other way but to move right into the heart of the enemy, tear it out. Sure, they had discussed the strategy in his car, but how it would go down was anyone's guess. The rage of vengeance could well drive Daly past the point of no return. Bolan hoped it didn't come to that. He had explained he needed Stanton busted up, looking over his shoulder, on the run. This was Daly's chance to dish out the beginnings of a hard lesson of Bolan's own final solution to the evil of Deliverance. Still, there was the question of gunplay. No, it wasn't a problem of *if,* but *when* a weapon would come out. But Bolan had to trust Daly to work with him, no matter how it played. If the man proved he couldn't follow orders, then Daly was out of the soldier's plans.

The Executioner and the former soldier hero had two things working to their advantage. First they had the fires of furious and right conviction in their hearts. More often than not, the soldier had seen from first-hand battlefield experience that that alone could defeat the force of wrong. Second they were trained in hand-to-hand combat, thanks to the Special Forces.

Two against nine, though, with all the training in the world, with all the right rage in souls of fire, might not be enough. If Daly had nothing to lose, then certainly Stanton and his savages had even less to lose.

With three men on one side, one more to the left of him, Stanton rolled around the table closest to the bar.

It erupted.

And Bolan and Daly got busy.

Stanton threw a straight right, a blur that Bolan saw at the last split second. A snap of his head sideways, and Bolan felt the flesh graze past his ear. The Executioner drilled a snap kick into the testicles of the big blonde next to Stanton, doubling him up. At the same instant the man went down, Bolan whiplashed an elbow off Stanton's jaw, driving the dirty ex-cop into a gangly redhead. Both Stanton and the redhead toppled, human dominoes, leaving Bolan to deal with the three savages on his left flank.

Two wild looping rights missed Bolan by mere inches. Ducking the intended blows, he exploded upward, a twin volcanic launching of his elbows cracking off each enemy jaw, snapping heads back, hammering two more Deliverance savages to the floor.

A quick look at his flank told Bolan that Daly was

more than holding his own. Daly was taking it on the chin, but the guy was a human cyclone of feet and fists. Enemy heads were snapping as if they were attached to springs, Daly whipping rights and lefts, nearly invisible balled backhand hammer-fists surging back to score before his victims had time to recover a fraction of their senses. One guy came at Daly's blind side with a pool stick. But at the last instant, as if sensing movement to his side, Daly ducked. The stick whistled past his head, smashing in an adversary's nose. Blood took to the air as one more enemy dropped. Wheeling, Daly drove a kick into the cue wielder's gut. When the guy dropped his shattered cue, doubled over, Daly came up with a knee to his face that flipped him over the table, a crimson trail of rain spattering green felt.

Suddenly Bolan heard the animallike bellow of rage. Pivoting, he craned a hook kick off Stanton's jaw, sending the guy reeling into the wall. Picture frames of cops and local celebrities who had passed through the Gold Shield crashed down on Stanton's head.

Pumped on adrenaline and fury, Daly picked up one of the enemy, linking his arm under the guy's shoulder. Pure rage erupting from Daly's mouth, he launched his victim off the floor. Airborne, that guy missiled, headfirst, through the giant-screen TV. As sparks and smoke shot in all directions, cops leaped to their feet in panic, giving a little more room to the combatants.

Bolan took one from the redhead on the chin. Stars blasted in his eyes as the guy banged another one off his jaw. Backing up, the Executioner threw himself under a potentially knockout roundhouse. An uppercut to Red's gut drove the air from the man's lungs. The follow-up was a palm to the jaw, with just enough force behind the blow to further ring his bell but holding back the lethal brutality that would have snapped Red's neck.

Red staggered back as Stanton hauled himself to his feet. Stanton threw a kick for Bolan's head. The soldier caught the leg, put a toe into Stanton's groin, then flung the guy into the wall. One quick look over his shoulder, and Bolan saw the cops staying put, content to ride this one out.

Then it turned serious the way Bolan had feared.

Groans of agony were knifing the air. Bolan noted the ex-cops either laid out or crawling through their own blood, when he saw Daly sight down his Beretta—at Stanton.

The ex-cop struggled to sit up, an insane look in his eyes. He laughed at the sight of Daly closing on him, gun drawn.

"Go on, do it, Daly," Stanton urged. "If I was you, knowing what I know, I'd do it. Or don't you have the stomach for cold-blooded killing?"

"Daly!" Bolan growled. "Don't do it."

If Daly heard him, Bolan wasn't sure. At that moment, he looked to Bolan to be gripped in the same madness as Stanton.

"Put it down, Daly," Bolan said. "That's an order, soldier. You hear me?"

The look of hate faded some in Daly's eyes. A stretched second later, the Beretta lowered.

"Get the hell out of my place!" Tommy hollered from behind the bar. "You did what you came here to do, now get out! Now!"

Bolan checked the destruction, the fruits of their

victory. A couple of the ex-cops tried to get up but fell back down. Outside the sprawled bodies, the cops were staring, wide-eyed with fear but with a new-found respect for Bolan and Daly. Score one for the beginning of his hellfire campaign, Bolan thought. But it was far from being over.

Bolan led Daly to the door. Watching his rear, Bolan waited a moment while Daly killed the beer Bolan hadn't touched.

Moments later, they were through the door, into the bustling night. Inside his car, behind the wheel, Bolan examined the bruises on Daly's face. There was still a distant look of rage and hate in the man's eyes that disturbed Bolan.

"Daly? Look at me."

Daly slowly turned his head and met Bolan's piercing blue eyes.

"That was only round one."

A strange chuckle from Daly. "We did all right, didn't we?"

"It was close. You almost blew it. Let's get this straight. This is no game. I had a good reason for doing what I just did in there. It was a message. They'll run and we follow. Next time, people are going to die. And I'm not doing this for you."

"I could have killed him, but I didn't. That's why I agreed to let you handle Stanton."

Bolan worked his sore jaw, tasted the blood in his mouth.

"Now what?"

The Executioner fired up the engine. "Show me where your car is. Here's the story. We'll go in separate vehicles. You get that tracking box on and don't lose me. As soon as you think you've got something, stop and let me know.''

Daly nodded. ''I think you saw you can count on me.''

''With my life.''

Bolan gave the door to the Gold Shield one last look. It would be a few minutes, if not longer, before Stanton and his pummeled troops picked themselves up to leave.

The Executioner swung his vehicle into the street. The only thing he was sure of right then was that round two was up and coming. Soon.

And for damn sure, people were going to die the hard way before the night was over.

FEAR BROUGHT Stanton to the nauseous surface of a hazy world of pain and distant angry voices. Rage then shame got the man on his feet again.

Shaking out the cobwebs, Stanton found his troops clambering to stand. They were a bloody and bruised mess. Garner's nose was pulpy crimson, mashed like a grape. Tuttlehill's face was swollen and lopsided; there could be a broken jaw there, Stanton knew. In front of Stanton, Morrow rose from the floor, moaning, hands clutching his testicles, tears streaming down the man's face.

The pain Stanton felt himself was white-hot, searing every nerve ending. His own testicles were pulsing, his ears ringing, mouth full of blood, a few teeth loose. Somehow his troops found the floor. To a man, Stanton found them looking at him, full of fear, fury, confusion. It struck him right then they all seemed like cornered animals. Worse, instinct warned him that the big Fed with the icy blue eyes hadn't only dished out one serious butt-kicking, but he'd put on just enough force to not kill them with his bare hands. Even worse, this Belasko wasn't only on to them, but the guy was hunting. This was only the beginning. This was a lesson in pain. Stanton was alive and for a good reason. He suspected he was being used now as bait to get to the others. He hadn't seen the last of this Belasko. The Fed may have won this battle, Stanton thought, but next time out would be different.

Through the ringing in his ears, Stanton heard Tommy barking for all of them to leave.

"Can everyone walk out of here on their own?" Stanton growled at his men. In other words, they knew if they needed serious medical treatment they were beyond a world of hurt; they could quite possibly end up in the East River at this juncture. They nodded, spit blood, massaged jaws, pain and rage burning in eyes, telling Stanton they'd rough it. Still, none of them looked happy at the prospect of venturing outside.

Quickly they donned their windbreakers and bomber jackets, and strapped on their shoulder holsters.

"What about this mess?" Tommy wanted to know. "Who's going to pay for all this damage?"

"Tommy, if you and the rest of you yellow bastards," Stanton snarled, "had gotten off your asses and helped, you might be able to take up a little collection now. What did you guys tell me? You're on your own? That's right. Well, everyone's on their own."

A stocky, dark-haired detective from the Bronx, Turtelli, spoke up as Stanton led his battered troops toward the bar.

"Stanton! Me and the others are going to take you serious about your threat. This thing has gone too far. Our hands may be dirty, but they're not covered in blood. The Feds know now, or know enough, and that scares the hell out of us. If we see you within two blocks of our homes, we'll shoot you on sight. I hope we understand each other."

Stanton put a penetrating stare on each and every cop who was washing his hands of Deliverance. "Okay, I guess we have an understanding, then. There's more where you came from, and from what I've just seen of you men, I know you're not good enough to be either a cop or a white man. Just remember, I know you're worried about your families and your careers, meaning your mouths damn well better stay shut. If you want to save yourselves, that's fine, but if it blows up in my face... Well, I can let it ride for now. But you better believe a day of reckoning is coming. And I won't forget this."

Stanton and his men left the Gold Shield. As they gathered on the sidewalk, Stanton bowled down a citizen, pinning the guy with his murderous stare when the citizen rolled in the gutter. The guy looked like he wanted to get up and fight, then stared at something in Stanton's eyes and seemed to think better of it. The citizen muttered something, stood and scurried off.

Stanton addressed his troops. "Okay, listen up. We know now who we're dealing with. And why."

"The guy's no Fed," Garner said, forcing out the words, wincing in pain.

"Whatever he is," Stanton replied, "he's going to make us deal with him. That's fine. Next time we see him, he's dead."

"One guy," Scarborough said, voicing Stanton's own disbelief.

Right. How could one man, even acting together with another, do so much damage to a bunch of bona fide tough-guy ex-cops? Stanton wondered. The guy was good, trained, probably ex-military. More problems. The list seemed to be growing with each passing minute.

"That's right, one guy, a cowboy," Stanton told them. "I don't know what he's doing with Daly, but if the Feds were serious, if they really thought they knew something, a small army would have come through that door. Now, get in your cars. I'm calling the others. Garner, Morrow, you ride with me. I'm bumping up the rendezvous to one hour from now. Move it out!"

Grimacing, his thoughts consumed with hate, murder in his heart for the big Fed named Belasko, Stanton limped to his vehicle.

As he slid into his Crown Victoria, a scary thought suddenly dawned on Stanton. This was the first time in his life any man had ever beaten him, head-to-head. Who was this Belasko really?

IT WAS BOB MILAN'S twenty-first recruitment call. This run was special; better yet, it was close to home. No flying around in one of the organization's two Lears, landing at private airports, going through the hassle of renting a vehicle, all the paperwork that could leave a trail. This was a straight pickup, face-to-face.

Twenty-one, he thought, pulling up in his Jeep Cherokee at the end of the dirt driveway. There was something magical about that number. Maybe it was destiny, since the requirement age to even get the first foot into the police academy was twenty-one.

There were two of them, the Fullerton twins. They had put themselves through the University of Colorado, four-year degrees in criminal justice. That alone showed initiative, and Milan liked them already, without ever having laid eyes on them. But they had made no attempt to enter the academy. Instead they held down local jobs. Milan imagined the boys, trapped and isolated out here in the Rocky Mountain wilderness, going nowhere fast, wondering what the hell they had gone through college for while nonwhites were out there, grabbing up the good jobs because the government said you had to hire those people, all in the sense of liberal fair play. Quotas, right, the kind of nonsense that was taking the backbone out of the country, where mediocrity was replacing merit and mettle, and at an alarming rate. Well, Bob Milan had his own quotas to fill, but in the name of justice and saving his own people from crime, race mixing, all the ills that were out there, eating up the country like a ravaging virus. He was on a holy mission for the Almighty.

Milan thought some more about his Fullerton recruitment, glowing with the knowledge that he was doing what was right for their future, and the future of America. Their old man, a local ex-sheriff who drank himself out of office, seemed to either need or demand around-the-clock attention ever since the wife had left him for a local. That came straight from the boys, both of them frustrated and angry about their lives, but they had written they felt a sense of duty and loyalty toward their father. That was admirable in a sorry age where families were disintegrating all over the country, kids going off to do their own thing, whatever the hell that was, usually rebelling through drugs and sex. Well, the Fullerton twins wanted to do something important and meaningful with their lives. Best of all, they wanted to be policemen, figuring they could make society a better place, but they needed to be out there, in the trenches, where the action was.

Usually Milan did the recruiting over the Internet. But lately even that had become dangerous, since the FBI and other law-enforcement agencies were looking for guys using the system for criminal purposes, kiddie porn, homos looking to further degrade society. Once again wackos and sick people were fouling it up for guys who, like himself, were only interested in saving civilization, restoring order where there was chaos, in short, returning this land he loved to the hands of decent Christian people.

Now Milan got tips from right-wingers in the organization who knew families with sons who might qualify. Milan would run his own background check, mail out official-looking letters, keep the racist, militant angle toned down. All that would come later when he had the recruits under his wing. Since he was a former Denver policeman, who would question his credentials or intent?

Milan had no doubt he could march the twins down to the Boulder City Courthouse, where they would pass the written test. He had a few buddies still on Boulder PD, one in personnel. But he had bigger plans for the twins. He was thinking about Quantico. Deliverance needed a few good men in the FBI, ATF or the DEA. The only qualifications the young ones needed were to be young, white and angry, backgrounds poor, mostly Midwest, sons of farmers, ranchers. Sons of the earth. Young, stubborn minds were hard to break, of course, but with the right guidance from an older, wiser man with hard-earned experience in an ugly world, they could be molded.

Milan killed the engine and stared at the shabby trailer home nestled in the foothills of the Rockies. He had been driving since morning, a long trek through God's country, wide-open spaces, clean air, snowcapped mountain peaks. The heartland of America, he thought, what this country was meant to be. Beautiful, majestic, rugged.

He stepped out of his Jeep Cherokee, eyes adjusting to the darkness, focusing on the sheen of light coming from behind a curtain in the trailer window. He stretched his six-four frame and adjusted the Stetson hat atop his head. The big stainless-steel .45 Colt felt good beneath his sheepskin coat. Later he might show the twins the fearsome piece, impress them a little. After all, one of them had written that he'd seen *Dirty Harry* a hundred times. The kid said he wanted to be just like that guy, out there, blowing away scumbags. The kid wanted a .44 Magnum, and was itching to say those famous words to some punk at the business end of that piece. It was a little naive, Milan knew, maybe even dangerous. But he could work with the boys back at the compound. There, he could run the twins through the four-hour polygraph test they'd put them through at the academy, grill them how to pass the psych exam.

The brisk mountain air invigorated Milan, but he couldn't stop the sudden queasy tension he felt stir in his belly like a nest of vipers. There were problems back east. Hell, they were faced with a potential crisis, and there were few details coming in. One of their New York people, it seemed, had defected. Right then, he knew the cells were moving north, set to link up. Orders were soon to go out to the various watch commanders on the road.

Besides the troops holding down the compound, the warriors out there doing the dirty work to set America free were to roll west. The national watch commander, Milan's boss, had put together a master plan to launch an all-out assault against the lower elements of America. It would be good for every member of the organization to get together anyway, recharge the batteries, map out the future. Right now the commander was en route by private jet for a face-to-face with the man who essentially funded Deliverance. The war chest needed fattening. One way or another, Milan knew his boss would get what he wanted. He always did. The boss knew people, knew how to pinpoint their strengths, weaknesses or prey on their dark side. The bottom line was simply getting the job done. All it took was the will to commit to the cause, then act.

Milan was striding for the trailer when the front door opened. A burly man in a red flannel shirt and blue jeans staggered into the doorway. Even from twenty feet away, Milan caught the strong whiff of booze.

"You Milan?"

"Yes. Mr. Fullerton?"

"Right. You got it?"

The old drunk was surly and right to the point. Milan stepped up to the father, pulled out the envelope and handed it to him. The old man riffled through the bills, satisfied the two thousand dollars was all there. He was a disgusting sight to Milan, a former lawman reduced to human waste, no better than some back-alley wino. The old man was only interested in money for more booze and didn't give a damn about ideology or the future of his flesh and blood. That was another problem with America, Milan decided. There was no sense of honor there.

"Mind if I come in now and see your sons, Mr. Fullerton?"

Fullerton stumbled back, allowing Milan to pass. He found the twins in the middle of the small, squalid living room. The inside was pretty much what Milan expected—very little furniture, a TV, two rifles mounted on the wall. There were empty beer cans and bottles strewn in the kitchen, which looked as if it hadn't been cleaned in years. The place reeked of slow death to Milan. It would be good to get those boys out of there, put some hope in their hearts, steel in their spines.

"Mr. Milan, sir, good to meet you. I'm Josh Fullerton."

Milan like what he saw already. First Josh held out his hand, and Milan took it. Nice strong grip, sincerity in the grasp. Then Martin Fullerton introduced himself. They were polite but firm, a hard, determined look in their blue eyes, hunger to do something important all over those lean faces. They were both big and broad shouldered, with short blond hair, neatly trimmed and combed. Perfect Aryan specimens. Milan couldn't wait to get to work, shaping their characters.

"We're ready to go, sir, whenever you are."

Milan saw the large duffel bags at their feet, nodded and showed the boys a warm and reassuring smile.

"Yeah," the old man said gruffly, then plopped down on the couch, putting a bottle of whiskey to his lips, sucking down a long swallow. "Maybe you can make something out of them, Milan, being a former big-city cop and all. Me, I was just a small-town sheriff. Maybe you can make men out of them yet."

Milan glanced at the twins, read the shame in their eyes and knew both of them would later apologize for their father.

"You needn't worry about them, Mr. Fullerton. You've got a fine couple of sons here."

They picked their bags up and were following Milan to the door when the old man barked, "Hey, you said they'd be gone a month."

"That's right, sir. I hope that's not a problem. It's what we agreed on."

"My only problem is money. If they're gone longer, think you could send another couple grand?"

"I'll see what I can do, sir."

"Yeah, you do that."

"Let's go, gentlemen," Milan told the twins.

Outside, Milan shut the door, glad to put that place of misery and slow death behind. What a sorry waste of life the old man was, he thought. Anyone else but a brother law officer in there, and he would have just as soon put a .45ACP round through the guy's face.

CHAPTER TEN

For a good hour after their brutal pummeling of the enemy at the Gold Shield, Bolan had followed Daly over what he figured was half of Brooklyn. It was tough driving through all the narrow residential streets, everything packed and crowded with people, cars, cabs. But this was New York, after all. Space was a luxury, privacy even tougher to find. Despite the slow pace, the tailgaters, the bump and jerk of heavy traffic, the clenched fists and middle fingers of impatient New York drivers, Daly made sure Bolan's vehicle stayed near his bumper, no pushing yellow lights, no quick turns.

Either way, Bolan was running out of patience, but he trusted Daly. He had to. Sure, the man had a personal vendetta going on this, but he was a trained professional, and he had shown Bolan he was willing to hang it all out there. Whether Daly's resolve to continue to cooperate would crack was something the Executioner felt he had no choice but to gamble on. If nothing else, two warriors could do twice the damage. And Bolan didn't need some lone crusader out there, in the cross fire, mucking up his campaign. Besides, Bolan liked Daly, and he wanted to see the man come out the other side of this war. Survival, though, was something else altogether. Bolan's prime and only objective was to fight to his last breath to utterly and completely destroy the organization that called itself Deliverance.

At one point, somewhere in Brooklyn Heights, maybe forty-five minutes earlier, Daly had flagged him over. It seemed the man had three different signals on his tracking box, all going in separate directions, one going as far south as Flatbush. Daly wasn't sure whom exactly he was following, but two of the signals were loud and clear, telling him their quarry was close. He informed Bolan the flashing signals would stop for maybe ten minutes, then resume, seemed to be heading in a southwesterly direction, the one from Flatbush now moving due northwest.

From his own surveillance of Stanton, Daly explained the bad guys had several different safehouse locations. To go into a residential neighborhood, start blasting away was too risky, and Bolan told Daly just that. They were to keep following. Something would give, an opening where they could attack, far from innocents on crowded city streets. Daly's hunch was that Stanton was rounding up his people, had a designated rendezvous site, somewhere along the East River. Stanton was putting New York behind, Daly suspected; it was too hot in the Big Apple. Bolan's instinct told him Daly was right.

So Bolan now made his way toward the East River, the ferry district, with warehouses and docked tugs and freighters, tight alleyways and thruways leading to the wharves and piers. As he drove, Bolan left the window down, breathing in the brisk night air through his nose. Red had smacked him a couple of beauts, nothing too damaging, but Bolan's head was spinning a little, his mouth sore and bruised. Either way, he and Daly had given far more than they'd taken.

Deliverance was on the run, or at least Bolan could feel the New York cell within striking distance.

When they were west of the elevated Brooklyn-Queens Expressway, Bolan followed Daly around the corner of what appeared to be a large warehouse. Ahead, through the dim and ominous glow of lamplights hanging from the sides of black warehouses, Bolan spotted the mammoth steel suspension bridge that marked the Brooklyn Bridge. Across the East River, the lit skyline of Manhattan jutted into the dark heavens. The Brooklyn-Battery Tunnel would be southwest. Beyond there was the Statue of Liberty, the very first thing that immigrants had seen when they had arrived at Ellis Island, in search of freedom and the promise of a better way of life. As he thought about the lady with the torch, it sickened Bolan to know what Deliverance was all about. Oppression, domination and subjugation were the only goals of the enemy. It was their will and their way, or complete annihilation of anyone who stood in their path.

The Executioner was geared up to give them exactly what they craved.

Total war.

Daly's red Barracuda rolled about halfway down the narrow approach to the pier, then pulled off into a dark corner between two storehouses. Bolan slid in beside the vehicle, killed his lights and engine and got out.

Daly was already in the trunk, hauling out the AR-18, the big SPAS 12. The assault rifle went around Daly's shoulder, telling Bolan the man was looking for an in-close engagement where the shotgun would take no prisoners.

"They're right on top of us, right around the corner, on the wharf," Daly said, his eyes wild again with that all-consuming look of hunger for vengeance.

"You sure?"

"Positive. I had to kill the volume on the box. I was practically in their trunks. Not only that, a block down, I caught a glimpse of two four-doors. Chevys or Fords, I'm not sure, but it's them."

"All right, slow down a second. Daly, look at me and listen up. You forgotten already what we talked about earlier?"

Daly cracked a magazine into his assault rifle and filled his pockets with spare clips. "I haven't forgotten."

"We need to recon, assess the numbers, put a plan together. Worst thing to do is just bull our way in."

"What's the plan?"

Bolan looked up at the storehouse. "Is there a way to the roof?"

"Has to be a skylight, window, something."

"You have a flashlight?"

Daly dug a flashlight out of the trunk, and Bolan took it.

"We need to move quick," Daly said as Bolan went to the trunk of his vehicle and opened it. "Nervous as Stanton must be, he's liable to start rolling out with the troops any second."

Quickly Bolan pulled out his M-16 and slung the satchel with spare clips and 40 mm grenades for the M-203 around his shoulder. He had beefed up on his firepower before leaving Maryland. An additional satchel was stuffed with thirty grenades, a half-and-half bag of thermite and incendiary steel eggs. Depending on where the campaign led, he might have to call Brognola. One word, and Bolan knew the big Fed could have a man at a preselected site ASAP, fly him in, set him down on a remote field, if necessary, to deliver whatever hardware and equipment the soldier would need to carry on.

For now the Executioner had plenty on hand to lower doomsday on the New York cell of Deliverance.

Bolan handed Daly two fragmentation grenades. "Get your sniper rifle. We're going to hit them hard, but it's hit-and-run. I need a prisoner out of this. Think you can bag me one?" When Daly nodded, took his Remington 700 from the trunk and slung it around his other shoulder, Bolan injected a grim touch to his next words. "One last thing. I don't want Stanton killed. Can you deliver on your word you won't kill him?"

Daly clenched his jaw. "I'll do my damnedest, Belasko, you have my word. But give me something in return. When the time comes, whenever and wherever, I want your word that I'll be the one to check that bastard out of here."

"And I'll do my damnedest to deliver on that score."

The Executioner stared deep and hard into Daly's eyes, holding the moment, making sure there was no wavering in the man. Believing they had reached an understanding, Bolan led the man around the corner and melted into the darkness.

BOLAN FOUND a small army out on the wharf. Crouched, peering around the warehouse corner, the soldier was looking at an unmarked-car convention, a smorgasbord of assault-rifle-toting savages. With Daly at his rear, looking over his shoulder, Bolan assessed the numbers. There were at least fifty hardmen, rolling around close to twenty vehicles. There were Crown Victories, Chevy Caprices, Ford and Mercury four-doors, with the only distinguished vehicles a black Trans-Am and an older-model Mustang. Trunks were open, and guys were checking whatever was inside. Thanks to the light spilling from the sides of warehouses and the piers, there was no mistaking the tall figure of Stanton as the so-called New York watch commander inspected what Bolan guessed was the spoils of war his men had brought to the rendezvous. Fruits of their venom, no doubt, the dark treasures they had confiscated on what Bolan intended to be for them their march to hell.

Beginning soon.

From their position, Bolan found the enemy grouped, maybe forty yards, north. They were strung out around the vehicles, but man and machine were packed tight. Front ends of vehicles pointed Bolan's way, telling the soldier they had come in from the north. That was something of a plus. Once his rooftop vantage point was established, he could cut them off from the north, flush them toward Daly.

The soldier gave the wharf and the piers another hard surveillance. Dark hulls of freighters and tugs were berthed pierside, north to south, but Bolan couldn't find any activity in either direction other than the enemy. There were crates, forklifts, other machinery near the enemy convoy. Once he unleashed the opening salvo of battle, Bolan figured a good number of them could reach cover—or they would make a fighting withdrawal by car.

He figured there was a night watchman somewhere who would be alerted to the riverfront firefight. But from what Bolan knew and had seen of Stanton, the man had either flashed a phony badge and ID, paid him off or outright killed him. To a savage like Stanton, what would one more murder mean in a city that saw almost two thousand homicides a year? At all costs, Bolan wanted to stop Stanton. Of course, the plan was to shave the odds here, grab a prisoner for interrogation. Stanton would be chased out of New York, and hopefully he would lead Bolan to the rendezvous with other cells the late Ron Westman had alluded to. That was the way Bolan wanted it to go down, but he knew once the shooting started, all bets were off.

Bolan strained his ears to hear what the enemy was saying. All he caught was some cursing, angry voices, words distorted by distance or the pent-up, low-toned conversation of men keeping it down out of fear and paranoia.

He pulled back, checked his watch and said to Daly, "Give me ten minutes to reach the roof. I'll hit them from the north, drive them toward you." He looked across the wharf, nodding at a stack of crates. "You might want to take cover over there, but stay put until it begins. Remember I need a prisoner. Try and make your first shot one that cripples. You'll know when it starts. If it looks like they're going to pull out before I make my move, start the show without me. Good luck. We need this round under the belt. By the numbers, soldier."

Silent and swift, the Executioner made his way

back up the side of the warehouse, the doomsday
numbers tumbling down hard in his head. He rounded
the corner and padded down a narrow back alley.
Midway down, he found a door, padlocked, drew his
silenced Beretta and shot his way inside. He closed
the door, leathered the pistol and snapped on the
flashlight. A quick surveillance of the large store-
room, packed with crates and boxes and machinery,
revealed a short flight of steps that led to an upstairs
office. Right above the steps, he found a skylight.

Straining his ears for the sounds of engines firing
to life, or shots, he climbed the steps. Once again he
used the Beretta to blast off the lock on the skylight.
From the office, Bolan grabbed a chair and placed it
under the skylight. A moment later, he was through
and on the roof. On the move, angling for the south
end, he glanced at his watch. Six minutes had passed
since he'd left Daly, who would most likely feel each
few seconds crawl by like an eternity. Once again
Bolan was counting on the man to come through, attempt to leave Stanton in one piece, beaten again and
on the run. But with the numbers they were facing,
some of the enemy would escape. And Bolan didn't
intend to get bogged down in a standoff, blue-and-
whites flying onto the scene.

Almost as soon as Stanton bolted, the Executioner
would be right on his heels. That was provided, of
course, Stanton survived, but Bolan was counting on
the man's tenacity and determination to see him
through the coming battle. Bolan also had descriptions of the vehicles Daly had tagged with homers.
He would select his targets carefully, leave their
tracker vehicles unscathed. Easier said than done, perhaps, but in the hands of the skilled and ultimate war-

rior like Bolan, success was simple execution of a plan, riding it out.

As he neared the edge of the roof, the soldier felt the chill wind hitting him off the East River. Aboveground now, it looked as if the Manhattan skyline were right in his face. He spotted the tugs and ferries, south in the Upper Bay, the tall lady with torch out there, guarding the night.

Bolan hit the edge, kneeled and stared down. They were all down there, Stanton still inspecting his spoils, addressing his men.

The Executioner opened the satchel and loaded a 40 mm grenade into the M-203's breech. A moment later, he sighted down, drew target acquisition on the rear vehicle, a Chevy Caprice, right below. He was a few minutes early, but there was no better time than the present to start the fireworks, to unleash the battle for freedom.

Bolan curled his finger around the trigger, drew a breath and squeezed.

INSPECTING THE SPOILS of war each of his troops had brought to the rendezvous, Stanton couldn't decide if he was angry at his men or grateful. Almost to the vehicle, each trunk held either drugs or cash, or both, as well as a couple of guys with sacks of hot jewels. For damn sure, some of these guys had been holding out on him, building their own little nest eggs over time. Put together all the bricks of coke and smack, all the wrapped bundles of cash, and Stanton figured his own war chest was nickel-and-dime compared with what he found. The big, the only plus, actually, was that every man had shown up when he could have walked. Loyalty to the cause had proved stronger than greed. It was something Stanton had to address.

Of course, none of them knew what had happened at the Gold Shield. Beaten and battered, Stanton could well understand the looks of fear and confusion surrounding him. And for the first time he could ever remember, he, too, was more than a little afraid. Instinct warned him he was being hounded, that maybe even the Feds were now closing in. It was time to leave, but he needed to clear the air first. A few more minutes wouldn't hurt. He'd already put some silenced Glock rounds through the faces of the night watchmen. He could have paid them off, but some uncontrollable rage had compelled him to kill. Oh, well, he figured. If it was all meant to go to hell, he would damn sure take as many men with him as he could. Something of a message to leave behind. But he was far from giving up.

Philly was a hundred-mile drive. All these vehicles rolling down I-95 might or might not draw attention, but with two exceptions they all looked like unmarked units. Each man also had a forged NYPD badge and ID, that might or might not hold up to scrutiny if a state trooper pulled them over. If worse came to worst, the orders were to smoke any lawman who wanted to push his luck. The original plan was to head out, two, three vehicles at a time. But the heat from Belasko had all but screwed that plan. They needed to get to the City of Brotherly Love fast, and together.

"Okay, listen up," Stanton said, running a penetrating stare over the gathered troops, hoisting the MP-5 submachine gun a little higher up on his shoulder. "As you can see, we've had some problems.

There was a run-in with what we were told was the Justice Department earlier.'' It wouldn't help morale to tell the ones who weren't there that it was only two men who busted them up like it was nothing more than stick time on a punk in a back alley. ''We're all here now, and what you brought with you tells me I cannot overlook your integrity or your loyalty, nor will it go unrewarded. From the beginning, we all knew we were in this together, we swore an oath and a man is only as good as his word. One goes down, we all go down.

''Now, I'll take the point when we head out. Only Garner and a few others know the exact linkup site in Philly, but that's our immediate destination. From here on, do not, I repeat, do not let anything or any man stand in your way, law or otherwise. We are facing a crisis, gentlemen. I expect, no, I demand nothing less than for you to fight to the last man. We are a major link in the organization's chain, and it's counting on us. At some later point in time, I'll fill you in on a need-to-know basis about the present crisis, but for the moment all you need to know is that the situation is under control—''

No sooner had Stanton uttered those last words than the night exploded in his face.

Pure terror ripped through Stanton as he glimpsed the rear vehicle, a Chevy Caprice, vaporized into flying scrap by a blinding fireball. Before he knew it, men were screaming and dropping all around him. Wheeling, he saw two men topple, clutching at their legs, blood spurting like a red fountain from those wounds. He was pulling the MP-5 subgun off his shoulder, trying to pinpoint where the attack was coming from, when he saw Tuttlehill's swollen face explode right before his eyes. With all that blood splattering his face, Stanton couldn't be sure if he was hit or not.

When he discovered he was still whole, the headless corpse of Tuttlehill crumpling at his feet, Stanton started barking orders for his troops to bail.

Then another thunderous blast shook the wharf. The second vehicle from the rear was launched down the pier into countless warped sheets. A moment later, as slugs began tattooing the vehicles and at least three more of his men went down, Stanton made out the shadow at the edge of the warehouse roof.

There was no doubt in Stanton's mind who was up there, raining hell on them.

Belasko.

VENGEANCE UNQUENCHED almost got the best of Daly. Somehow he fought back the hate and the fury, and waited for Belasko to unload.

They were all there. It could have been a shooting gallery for Daly, easy pickings. But Belasko's orders were explicit, and Daly intended to honor them. If it didn't happen here, he had no doubt Belasko would let him have his chance to kill Stanton at some point. Belasko was a man of honor, and Daly felt some divine wind of fate had blessed him with the man's presence, not to mention his skill and help.

At the moment, Daly was nothing more than a hunched shadow, having chanced it on impulse, raced across the short stretch of no-man's-land when they were too busy listening to Stanton, most of them with their backs turned. Had Belasko seen that stunt, well, first there had to be some butt left to chew. Nothing in life was ever guaranteed, he knew, especially in combat. No, the good guys didn't always win.

Daly was perched between two crates, had Stanton's face lined up in the crosshairs of his scope. One shot, and he could blow the man's head off. Right there, larger than life in the Redfield 3×9 telescopic sight. Damn, but the waiting was agonizing.

Then it happened—and Belasko was right that he would know when it started.

The blast turned night into day. Before the first explosion even obliterated the last vehicle in line, Daly forced himself to adjust his aim, squeeze the trigger, ride the recoil. Downrange, his first target, a guy on the periphery of the group, went down with a 7.62 mm slug that all but tore off his knee. Working the bolt action, Daly dropped one more of the enemy with a leg shot, just in case. For some reason, none of Stanton's people moved right away; instead they seemed like frozen puppets, shocked, no doubt, by the sudden fury of the attack.

At least, Daly decided, he could make Stanton feel pure terror, cut it close. Daly did. Lining up a lopsided face he remembered from the Gold Shield, the guy right in front of Stanton, he triggered a round that all but decapitated that victim and put him out of his misery for good.

The enemy started scrambling, some seeking cover behind the crates, while others fired up at the roof when two more explosions tore through their rear.

For a fleeting and haunting moment, Daly imagined he felt the ghosts of Yuen and Christopher hovering around him. They wanted to take him back to Vietnam, where he had fought and survived more than one jungle hit-and-run like this. His wife and son were gone, though; he was there. Nothing was left for him but to avenge their murders.

If this was vengeance, he decided, then it was sweet.

Daly grabbed up his assault rifle. Engines were gunning to life. A Ford four-door tried to reverse it out of there, but Belasko blew the vehicle off the wharf with another 40 mm fiery cloud of doom. When Stanton and what was left of his troops saw their rear was cut off, Daly braced himself as they came roaring at him.

Autofire then split the air around him, slugs drilling wood, sparking off the forklift behind him. Guys were hosing down his position with screaming lead, or leaning out the windows of vehicles barreling at him, weapons flaming.

Hitting the end of the crates closest to the warehouse, their escape route, Daly armed a frag grenade and let it fly. The hellbomb found a bouncing intercept point, right in front of a Mercury. At the last split second before the grenade blew, Daly saw Stanton wasn't an occupant in the fiery hearse.

Daly stepped out, unleashing the thundering wrath of his SPAS 12. The windshield of another Chevy Caprice blew in from the hurricane force of 12 gauge annihilation. Combat senses electrified, Daly caught sight of the wheelman's head exploding, a water balloon that looked as if it were dropped to concrete from a hundred feet up. The Chevy careened, slamming into the side of the warehouse. Before the three other guys could pile out, Daly shredded them where they sat, pounded out the rest of the shotgun's 7-shot magazine. Daly was so pumped on righteous fury and adrenaline, it took a dangerous moment for him to realize slugs were whizzing inches past his head.

Just before he was chased to cover, Daly spotted the screeching line of vehicles, tearing out of there. They whiplashed in all directions, reversed, two vehicles quickly ramming through flaming wreckage. He couldn't be sure, but he believed Stanton's Crown Victoria was one of the first vehicles to flee the scene, hit the north corner on smoking rubber and vanish.

There were still a half-dozen vehicles, reversing, metal banging off metal as wheelmen fought with the wild desperation of the damned to get off the wharf.

While Daly hauled in his AR-18, poured it on their rear, he saw Belasko oblige at least one more carload hell-bent on exit.

Only they were launched into the East River, a couple of sizzling stick figures lit up by fire, riding the crests of bloody burial.

THE EXECUTIONER interspersed the first three 40 mm death knells with several quick 3-round bursts from his M-16. In the firelight from the first two explosions, he picked out Stanton but opted to mow down the man's troops instead. Bolan's brief but scorching lines of 5.56 mm lead kicked enemy figures over hoods, or hammered them beneath showering blood to the wharf. No sooner was one pair of victims scythed down than Bolan would load the M-203, send another grenade sizzling down at seventy-one meters per second.

Impact and detonation. Bodies cartwheeling. Flaming wreckage going all over the wharf.

It didn't take but a few moments for the enemy to discover his overhead killing position. In the wavering firelight, as the enemy scrambled pell-mell, hopped into vehicles or held its ground, Bolan locked a heartbeat's stare with Stanton.

Then autofire started chewing the roof's edge, driving Bolan back. All hell had broken loose down there, guys screaming in pain, cursing the night, dying in agony.

Suddenly rubber was screeching.

Downrange Bolan heard the chatter of autofire, then an explosion rocked the roof beneath his feet. The slick flames of the blast shot up into the air, from the south. Daly was hard at work. A moment later, the familiar cannon peals of the man's shotgun shattered the air.

Bolan returned to his own killing business.

Back at the north edge, he pumped out another 40 mm grenade, this time into a Ford. Metal and severed parts of men flew everywhere in at least a thirty-yard radius.

Sporadic return fire punched up edges of the roof, but it was nowhere close. Right then, the savages were more concerned with a hasty exit, plowing through wreckage, even mowing down their own.

One slow group of four almost made it to a Ford Taurus.

Bolan held back on the M-16's trigger, blasting open exposed skulls. He was tracking on when he realized Daly was hard at gruesome work, cutting through the other two with his AR-18.

Quickly Bolan scanned the carnage. Bodies were sprawled all over the wharf. At first look, he had to guess they had cut Stanton's force by at least half, men and vehicles. Down there, the soldier found two guys crawling through their leaking juices, snaking away from the scorching heat of crackling flames. It looked like he had his prisoners. Judging the way they grabbed their legs, Bolan saw Daly had come through.

Another sweep of the killzone, and Bolan didn't find any sign of Stanton. Only moments earlier, he had glimpsed the marked Crown Victoria, Stanton's wheels. Still, Bolan couldn't be sure the dirty ex-cop had survived.

There was only one way to find out the score.

Familiar now with the warehouse layout, Bolan made his way down and outside in short order. As he rounded the corner from the warehouse, Bolan was tuned in for the faintest wail of a distant siren. At the moment, he heard nothing but the hungry lapping of flames. That would soon change. No matter what, a long night in jail, waiting for Brognola to straighten out this mess, would mean critical time lost. Unacceptable without question.

Weapon tracking, the warrior strode onto the hellzone. SPAS 12 slung around his shoulder, the AR-18 fisted, Daly was grim faced, waiting near the wounded.

There were two of them, one of whom Bolan recognized from the Gold Shield.

A jagged piece of smoking wreckage banged the wharf beside the Executioner as he slipped his arm through the M-16's strap and drew the silenced Beretta. There wasn't a second to waste. Looming over the casualties, Bolan put it to them.

He chose the one he didn't recognize first. "You," he growled at the man, aiming the Beretta at the guy's face. "Where are they going?"

The guy got defiant, cursed Bolan and made a motion toward a nearby Glock pistol. The Executioner stroked the Beretta's trigger, one whispering 9 mm round drilling through the guy's forehead.

He had the other man's complete attention. The fear in that guy's expression told Bolan he had a chance to learn something.

"What's your name?"

"Garner."

"Okay, Garner, you don't even need to think about your answer. You get one chance to make it through this. Where is Stanton headed?"

Garner seemed to think about it anyway, but fear washed away some of the pain in his eyes. Just then, Bolan caught the distant but growing bleat of sirens.

"Philadelphia."

"That's a big town. You can do better than that," the Executioner warned. "Last chance. Where?"

Garner gave Bolan a street name, said it was somewhere in the heart of Philly. The linkup was set to go down in an underground parking garage. Stanton would contact the watch commander of the cell in Philly when he was en route.

The sirens wailed closer.

"Let's go," Bolan told Daly, then walked away without another word to Garner.

"Hey, you just can't leave me like this."

Bolan stopped, turned and pinned Garner with a death's-head stare. "The law will be here in a minute. One call to my boss about you, and I suggest you be prepared to do some hard and painful time in the joint."

"You bastard, I was a cop. I'm a dead man in prison!"

"You should have thought about that long before now."

While keeping an eye on Garner, the two men quit the scene.

The City of Brotherly Love was next on Bolan's hit parade.

CHAPTER ELEVEN

Roger Masters was the people's choice to be the next governor of Texas. Already the polls indicated they were flocking in droves to his Independent Conservative Party. They liked their tough-talking Texan who wanted to dump more money into law enforcement, expand the death-penalty law in the state to include major narcotics traffickers and felony three-timers. They wanted to hear how he would tighten the borders to all the illegals pouring into the Lone Star State, create more jobs for homegrown Texans, balance the budget, put Texas back on the map as a national economic power. But they really seemed to love hearing about beefing up the Border Patrol and expanding their power to keep all those Mexicans from invading the state like swarms of locusts.

Texans, he knew, wanted to keep Texas for Texans, like any real American. This was frontier country, after all, land of the Alamo, home of the cowboy. It was still the Wild West out here, only the color of the gunslingers had changed. As far as Masters was concerned, he would like to see a law passed that would give the Border Patrol free rein to shoot on sight any brown-skins slithering across the Rio

Grande. Maybe that day would come sooner than anyone expected.

A business mogul who was stepping into the political arena for the first time in his life, Masters found himself watching what he said in public and on the record, something he wasn't sure he cared to do. Out there on the campaign trail, on camera, on the radio, his every word and move scrutinized, well, it was hardly like sitting in a saloon where the boys got together over beer and whiskey and kicked around the minorities, the homos, the women's libbers. Living in mean-spirited times helped, though, since they were sick and tired of the professional politicians out here in the Bible Belt, fed up with all those broken promises and failed contracts coming out of Washington.

Glowing from his fourth whiskey and cola, he listened to his team of campaign managers. They reviewed a brief history of his life, talking in his living room, around him, as if he weren't there, planning a series of TV ads to be aired all over Texas in the next two months. There were six of them, three lawyers, three accountants, handpicked by Masters for their legal and financial expertise. Longtime friends of the family, they were worthy of his trust. And there were no skeletons in any of their closets. They were clean living, hardworking, honest men with good families, Christian gentlemen, men to ride the rivers with, as the saying went down here in Texas. If they knew the real Roger Masters, he thought, they would sprint out of his ranch-style mansion, flee his four-hundred-acre estate like it was Sodom and Gomorrah set to perish in a cloud of God's fire. He had his own skeletons, to be damn sure, but all that was yesterday—he hoped. Right now the future was all that mattered, and he liked what they were saying about him.

Masters was fifty-five, handsome with the sort of rugged outdoors look a true Texan loved. Image was everything in politics, and these boys knew they had a winner. A multibillionaire, he had created jobs in computers, textiles and steel for hundreds of thousands of Texans through Masters Enterprises, and right after the oil bust of the mid-1980s. He poured millions into charity and had built the Holy Trinity Hospital, which even catered to the uninsured. Play that up for the "disadvantaged," Robin Hood stuff, Masters heard one of his lawyers, John Barnestorm, say while pulling on his foot-long Havana. He had a solid marriage to the same woman for almost thirty-five years, said Blake Turner, another lawyer, one son and a daughter, five grandchildren, both son and daughter with traditional stable families, went to church every Sunday, active in the community.

As they discussed the strategy for the campaign trail, Masters went to the bar and got another drink. They had their papers, the itinerary on the mahogany coffee table, all the numbers, facts and figures that gave him a headache to even glance at unless he had half a bellyful of whiskey. So Masters left the details, paperwork and money juggling of the campaign to his associates. They laid it out, set up the interviews and speeches, kept the campaign running smooth. All Masters had to do was go out there and be himself.

"Get you gentlemen something?" he asked, but all of them declined. They were busy paving his future.

Masters heard about traditional family values. They wanted to play the moral Christian angle; Texans loved core beliefs of simple right and wrong. Texans also loved the tough-on-crime soundbites. It was a major plus that the Fraternal Order of Police was backing him. Tomorrow he would get his endorsement from the fine Texas senator on local Houston television, which would then be aired across the state.

As he sipped his drink, Masters looked around the large, polished-mahogany-and-oak room. Suddenly something dark and icy stirred in his belly, wanted to sour his mood. Up to a point, a lot of what his team said was true, but there were many things they didn't know about Roger Masters. If it ever hit the fan... Well, he didn't want to think about it. He had a good wife, who knew her place was beside her man, a solid family, who honored and respected their father and mother, a big future as the maverick tycoon and soon-to-be governor. Image, you bet.

He stared at the oil painting of his father. He was almost the spitting image of Tom "Big Daddy" Masters. Tall, whip lean, rawboned, iron in the square jaw and gray eyes. Full head of white hair, aquiline nose. Everyone knew that Tom Masters had built the family fortune, during the oil boom of the thirties. The sole offspring, young Roger, had inherited that fortune after his father died from liver failure, more than enough money for him to have squandered a small fortune that no one would miss. No, Roger Masters wasn't exactly the self-made rugged individualist, but no one could ever say that Roger Masters hadn't made good use of his fortune. Two decades ago he saw the future, knew the Masters oil fields would dry up. So, he'd invested in small companies, made deals, built fledgling industries from the ground up until he'd nearly doubled the old man's billions. With his own twenty-story tower in downtown Houston, he'd made his mark. Now it was time for something bigger, no, something huge that would put the new calling in his life. Hell, who knew, he thought, first the governor's mansion, next the White House.

"Okay, that about wraps it up for tonight, Roger," Barnestorm announced, putting his papers together in his briefcase. "It's getting late. We've got a big day tomorrow. I suggest you go to bed, Roger, get some shut-eye."

Turner said, "Eight sharp, I'll be by to pick you up. You're going to be on the Milt Braun show—you know what that means."

Masters knew, all right. Braun was a conservative radio talk-show host. His popularity was enormous, and his was the highest-rated radio show in both Texas and Oklahoma and was about to go national. For two days, Masters's team had been grilling him, briefing him about how to field the calls he would get on the Braun show.

"Then we're scheduled to meet with the senator for lunch," Marty Benson said. "That will be a turning point for the party, Roger. We nail down the senator's endorsement, the sky's the limit. I can see the Republicans practically folding their hand when that happens. Plus we're sure to win over a majority of conservative Democrats. It's all up to you, big guy."

They stood, gathering their briefcases.

"Why don't you review these notes before turning in, Roger?" Jim McLaughlin suggested. "Covers everything we can think of you might be asked by Braun or his callers. Just remember, be gentle with the ones who come at you with both fists."

Masters showed them a big grin. There was a pause as he noticed the frown on Barnestorm's face, the big, stocky lawyer grinding out his Havana with nervous jabs.

"One thing, Roger, and this is serious business," Barnestorm said, grim. "Try and watch those comments about the Oklahoma City incident. You know what I'm talking about? You said if something like that ever happened in Texas, you'd march the murdering yellow bastards to the nearest lamppost and string 'em up by the neck until dead, leave 'em there for the buzzards to pick clean."

"I remember. The thing is, I meant it."

Barnestorm looked uncomfortable. "Well, I played hell getting that reporter to keep it out of the papers. We don't want to blow this because of one off-the-cuff remark, even if you meant it, even if we and others share your sentiments."

"Understood. You know me, fellas. Sometimes what a man feels in his heart just has a way of coming right out of his mouth. If the truth hurts some folks, well, maybe then they need to look at themselves. What I say, well, it looks like they're standing right beside me, according to the polls. Just the same, warning heard, loud and clear."

"Mr. Masters, sir, sorry to interrupt."

Lyle Morton, six-six and 240 pounds of granite, bulging muscle, filled the archway that led to the foyer. He was part of Masters's security force. Morton's size alone got every man on the Masters's campaign team's immediate attention. But it was the shoulder-holstered .357 Magnum pistol that put unease on the faces of his lawyers and accountants. More than once, his team had mentioned they didn't like the idea of Masters parading around downtown Houston with a few gun-toting gorillas. Masters had simply explained there were a lot of nuts out there who wouldn't think twice about gunning down the next governor of this great state; celebrities and men of power and means were targets all the time. They had agreed begrudgingly, but asked Masters to keep the gunmen in the background as much as possible, make sure they kept the hardware under jackets a couple of sizes too big. No problem.

"What is it, Lyle?"

"Got a call from down the gate, sir. A man showed up and said he's an old friend. Told me to tell you he just flew in from Wyoming. He said it's urgent, but didn't give a name."

Masters felt the freeze in his belly, fought to keep the anxiety off his expression. He saw his people staring at him, wondering.

"Is there a problem, Roger?" Turner asked.

There was a problem, all right, but one Masters couldn't tell them about. Not if he wanted to be governor.

Masters forced a smile. "No problem. Probably just like Lyle said. Used to do a lot of hunting up in Wyoming, and I met some good people there. Tell the gate to let him in, Lyle, show the man to my study."

The campaign team didn't look convinced it was all so innocent, but Masters gave them a reassuring smile, said he'd be up and ready for the big day tomorrow. When they said they'd show themselves out, and left the living room, Masters killed his drink, then poured another whiskey, no cola this time.

Just like that, he felt the ghosts of the past coming out of the closet. It felt as if ice went down his spine, locking him up. Paralyzed. He had dreaded a day like this ever since he publicly announced he was running for governor, knew it was inevitable, given all that was now at stake.

Roger Masters knew he had no choice. He had to see the man from Deliverance. Or else.

WHEN THEY HAD PASSED Trenton, crossed the Delaware River, Stanton had them pull into a truck stop to refuel. While gassing up, he took stock of their casualties. The damage was severe.

Now, back on I-95, with Morrow driving the Crown Victoria, southbound for Philly, Stanton mentally assessed his losses. Nine vehicles and twenty-six men were unaccounted for. Factor in the loss of anywhere between a quarter to a half million in spoils, and Stanton knew he'd suffered a major defeat, a severe setback. Of course, there was also the nagging problem of potential wounded having been left behind in New York, hauled in by either Belasko or the cops, the problem of guys singing to save their own butts. Garner was missing, either dead or captured, and at least five other top warriors weren't among the convoy. Garner knew exactly where the force was headed. Stanton couldn't be positive, but he believed he'd seen Garner go down with a leg wound during the opening eruption of bullets and rockets. If Belasko got his hands on Garner, forced their destination out of him, Stanton knew he had serious problems ahead.

Seething, Stanton had sudden mental flashes of the chaos and destruction wreaked on his force. Rage burned hot through his veins, his temples throbbing with racing blood pressure and adrenaline. All those explosions, guys going down, blood everywhere, paralyzed himself by the lightning attack; vehicles being blown out into the East River, his people shot up; the frenetic scramble, under fire, to beat a hasty withdrawal; feeling pure terror, doubting for a moment his courage, especially after the thrashing he'd taken in the Gold Shield. But they didn't have the kind of firepower Belasko did. How could he be called on cowardice? Bullets couldn't defeat rockets dropping on them from out of the sky. Better to retreat, regroup, living to fight another battle than to take suicide on the chin.

Then there was the problem of Daly, a trained Special Forces killer and former hero cop, fueled by vengeance. Stanton knew the organization had plenty of ex-military guys, Vietnam vets turned cops, but he wasn't one of them. He was facing all-out war with this stranger who claimed he was from the Justice Department, a type of guerrilla warfare Stanton had no experience with. Belasko. Probably a friend of Daly's from Vietnam. The guys had teamed up, headhunting, crusaders. If nothing else, Stanton knew he wasn't meant to be taken in alive.

But he also knew beyond any doubt that Belasko wanted him to keep breathing a little longer. Hell, the guy could have killed him with the first round from the roof. No, Belasko was saving him, Stanton knew, wanted to be led to the other cells. There was no other reasonable conclusion. Well, that was fine with Stanton. Next time out, Belasko and Daly would find themselves staring down a beefed-up and stone-cold ready force of forty guns, once they linked up with the Philly boys.

Morrow voiced his concern. "John, we've got problems."

"Tell me something I don't know."

Stanton watched the night pass by, sleepy little towns cropping up here and there.

"If we were made leaving New York, we'd have flashing lights in the rearview by now. Just keep driving," he told Morrow, "keep it together."

Morrow started to glance in the rearview mirror.

Stanton became irritated with the man's paranoia. "Stop doing that. They're all there. You think any of our people are going to bail now? There's nothing in New York for us but trouble. There's nothing for any of us but us."

"What do you know about our Philly contact?"

"Molanski, big Pole, former homicide and robbery, worked north Philly, the black side of town. He's just like us. I've met him personally. He quit the force in disgust. I was told to contact him about a year ago by someone in the organization." Stanton cracked a mean grin. "First thing he said to me was the day they bombed that neighborhood should become a national holiday every year. He's a Vietnam vet, Army Rangers. What I'm thinking is that he must have some contacts, guys who have some serious hardware."

"You mean the kind of firepower that just kicked our butts?"

"And then some."

Stanton picked up the cellular phone and punched in a number. When Molanski's gruff voice came through with a guarded "Yeah," Stanton sucked in a long breath to steel his nerves.

He hoped he sounded strong, confident when he said, "NY Force One. We're coming in. ETA twenty minutes."

Molanski paused before saying, "How come I get the feeling there's a situation on your end?"

"We'll talk when I get there. Out."

Stanton killed the connection and felt Morrow's paranoia drilling into the side of his head. For a long moment, Stanton checked the side-view mirror, infected by his partner's fear. They were all there, but it wasn't his men he was worried about. Visions of his vehicle suddenly blown off the road were racing through his mind.

FRANK SHYROCK PUT it to the man point-blank. "We've got some problems, Roger. We need to have a serious face-to-face about the future."

"You mean you've got problems, Frank."

"My problems are your problems. I wanted to keep this sociable and hoped we could iron out a few things like gentlemen. Since you didn't see fit to return my calls, I felt it necessary to fly down from Wyoming in my private jet. You know what a hassle that is?"

Shyrock waited while Masters shut the double doors to the massive study. Shyrock kept his bomber jacket on, concealing the Colt Python .357 Magnum pistol. Even though Masters was fighting to keep his fear and anger under control, Shyrock had seen a half-dozen goons on the way in, all armed with big pieces. Masters had a bright future, after all, and might call in the goon squad on a whim, have him bounced off the estate.

Shyrock was no slouch when it came to handling trouble. He was six-two, over two hundred pounds, with long arms and big hands, lightning reflexes that had served him well in prison. There wasn't an ounce of fat on him, thanks to five long years in Menard prison, pumping weights, doing push-ups and sit-ups in his cell, sometimes three hundred in a row just to work off the rage and hate.

Masters went and sat behind his large oak desk, scowling. Shyrock looked around the study with an approving eye. American and state flags stood in one corner. A bookcase lined one wall, holding what looked like a lot of leather-bound classics. But knowing the man the way he did, Shyrock suspected the main attraction was the wet bar in the other corner.

For a long moment, while walking slowly toward the desk, Shyrock looked at the animal heads mounted around the room. Deer and elk, a grizzly head, a mountain lion and a bighorn sheep. There was a rifle rack on the wall, just behind the desk. Shyrock knew Masters was a skilled rifleman. Twice they'd hunted together in Wyoming. He remembered the day Masters downed that grizzly, put a .300 Winchester Magnum slug right through its brain, a hundred yards out.

"Don't get nostalgic on me, Frank. I know we go back a ways. I know you didn't come here to talk about the old hunting days neither." Suddenly Masters slid open the top desk drawer. Slowly he pulled out a .44 Magnum revolver and laid it on the desktop.

"What the hell, Roger? You going to get tough with me?"

"Just want you to know I can still take care of myself."

Shyrock shook his head. "Then maybe we need to analyze our relationship. I did five years in Menard for a drug beef. You have any idea what it's like to be a cop in the joint? That's where the real tough guys are, guys in for life without a chance of seeing the outside again, guys who don't give a shit if they live or die. Guys who want a cop's blood or his ass to wear as a trophy around the cell block.''

"Skip the prison war stories, Frank. I've heard them all. More than once."

Shyrock closed on the desk, putting all the hate and rage he had earned while in Menard into his eyes and voice. "What I'm saying, Roger, is that old habits die hard. You are looking at the last of a breed. In fact I'm a fucking dinosaur in this age of double-talking, dishonorable, so-called political correctness, where a guy has to go through sensitivity training to even wait tables. I'm a white warrior who is prepared to sacrifice his own life to take this country back from all the assholes out there. More than once I beat some black guy in the joint half to death with my bare hands. I was never punked. I got respect, I got a rep on the inside.

"This thing of ours, it all started in the joint. That's why I'm standing here having to refresh your memory. I made friends in there with the Aryan Brotherhood. They knew people on the outside, knew cops who later became part of our organization. Whether you like it or not, we're together in this, all the way. Need I remind you of that day I met you in Chicago? Remember? Yeah, wince all you want. You were up there, working some deal. Sucking down whiskey, we met, started talking. You found out I was a former cop and started spilling your guts, damn near started bawling in my arms—you, the hard-drinking, womanizing, two-fisted, maverick Texas billionaire. Is it all coming back now? You told me your daughter was raped by a couple of illegals, 'greasers,' to use your exact words. How crime was out of control in this country and a few good men should stand up and do something about it. Looks like you need another drink, Roger. Allow me.''

While Shyrock went to the bar and poured two whiskeys, Masters said, ''I never thought it would get this big.''

''You mean go this far?'' He handed Masters his whiskey, then took a chair in front of the desk. ''You're a lock to be the next governor. The way I see it, that's a major plus, a golden opportunity for us, the organization. I know, who would have ever dreamed a day like this would come? Governor of Texas who was the genesis for a secret paramilitary organization. You got the ball rolling, Roger. I'm a general, but I'm also a soldier, and you, whether you like it or not, are commander in chief of Deliverance.

''That same day we met, you remember how you offered to pay me a hundred grand to find the bastards who raped your daughter? You wanted them castrated first, then I was to cut their throats. It never happened, because for once the cops got the guilty parties, and even more rare the courts did their job. I told you I had a better idea. That I knew plenty of cops, ex-cops, soldiers, Vietnam and Gulf War vets who felt the same way we did about the mess this country has become. I said I needed a war chest, a quarter million and some real estate where we could start the business of freeing America.

''So, I set you up with some hookers, and we got chummy. Nothing wrong with that, man of power and means, I understand he needs to let off some steam. If I recall right, you also liked to do a little freebasing before you got naked with some teenaged whore. The way I remember, you came to love Chicago so much, you flew up once every couple of months just to be with your buddy. Now, don't get me wrong, Roger, I'm not here to blackmail you. I want you in that governor's mansion—we need you in that mansion. If you're worried about extortion, I can assure you, any hooker starts turning up from your past, causing you any unnecessary stress, I will handle it person- ally.''

Masters killed half his drink. ''Bottom line, what is it you want from me?''

''I've got some problems back east. All my people are heading west, as we speak. I'm sure you read the papers. We've tallied quite the body count of scum- bags these past couple of months. But the heat is on. I don't have concrete details yet, but I expect some answers soon. In about forty-eight hours, my entire organization, our organization, will be amassed at the compound in Wyoming, that piece of real estate your money bought. I've got something major in the works, but I need to fatten the war chest.''

''How much?''

''Two million, in cash, within the next two days.''

Masters snorted, then polished off his drink. ''You expect I can just stroll into a bank and take that kind of money out?''

''You've got it, and don't tell me you don't. Or you can get it. Figure a way. I'll leave a number you can reach me in Wyoming. I don't expect you to hand-deliver two mil. Send one of your goons, but get it to me, Roger.''

''And if I don't, or can't?''

''I'd hoped you wouldn't say something like that. We're friends, or so I want to think.'' He paused, then added, ''You'll have to pardon me all to hell for just walking in here like this and pissing all over your parade, but I think now you know just how serious things are.''

Shyrock saw the man glance at the pistol, weighing his options. There were none, and they both knew it.

"I'll call you tomorrow," Masters said.

Shyrock stood. "I'll be waiting to hear from you. Make sure you fit me into your schedule."

"I'll call you."

The ex-cop nodded, giving the man his penitentiary stare, cold and unforgiving, sizing him up, letting him know with just that look he'd better come through. Masters couldn't hold the stare, so he went to the bar and made another drink.

Frank Shyrock left the tycoon to ponder the future.

CHAPTER TWELVE

It was time to turn the killing heat up, way past scorching. Bolan needed this third strike to incinerate, produce even harder fatal results for the enemy, but he also wanted concrete leads on the enemy's ultimate destination. Without solid intel about the home base of Deliverance, the Executioner knew he could be chasing Stanton clear across the country. Time was sure to run out before the real law intervened, knocked out some cogs in Bolan's juggernaut.

Putting the carnage behind in New York had either been due to luck or a slow response from blue-and-whites. Either way, they cleared the Big Apple.

So had Stanton, judging the way Daly had driven, hard, pushing a little past the speed limit on the interstate.

The short drive down I-95 had given Bolan time to plan ahead. Soon he needed to contact Brognola. He wanted to add a few things to his arsenal, such as a mortar and one hundred pounds of C-4 plastique. The mental list also included a garrote, night-vision goggles and combat knife. They were necessities to carry on the campaign, but they were items he didn't particularly need for the initial launch of his urban warfare on Deliverance. But if his hunch was right, if the hit-and-run continued with success—meaning the soldier and his ally survived this engagement in Philadelphia—they would be tracking Stanton and the other cells far outside any city. Bolan bet the Deliverance compound was most likely secreted in some remote wilderness region.

To be sure, the future was on hold, since there was no guarantee tomorrow would even arrive. Right now the City of Brotherly Love was about to erupt from the Bolan blitz.

Only a few minutes earlier, Bolan had tailed Daly's Barracuda off the Delaware Expressway, into the heart of Philly via the Vine Street exit. Slowly he now followed Daly along Christopher Columbus Boulevard, then past Penn's Landing and the Delaware River waterfront, with the marina choked with all manner of pleasure boats.

Steeled with grim resolve, Bolan was hardly in the mood for sight-seeing, but he had to survey his surroundings, anticipating a patrol car or the enemy. Philly was an odd but understandable mix of modern twentieth-century and old Colonial structures. Steel, glass and concrete behemoths loomed over smaller buildings with redbrick pathways leading to marble-columned, mahogany-fronted structures, a wrought-iron gate next to the First Bank of the United States, an eagle perched on the gateway. Oak and maple stood tall in the night, here and there—old but new, same thing but different, just like the eternal nature of savage man, Bolan reflected.

Two car lengths ahead, he could almost feel the tension crackling from the Barracuda, Daly's shadow turning both ways, searching as Bolan kept following

the man, west on Walnut Street. He sensed they were
getting close to their next engagement.

This time of night, Bolan found very little traffic
and even fewer pedestrians. Shadows roved the streets
or huddled in alleyways. The night, he knew, belonged to the predators, drug dealers, marauding
thieves on the prowl for easy targets that might stagger out of the local watering holes. Despite being
called the City of Brotherly Love, Philly, known as
the cradle of the nation where the Constitution was
approved, where the Declaration of Independence was
drawn up, was as crime ridden and dangerous as any
big city.

Several blocks later they found the garage.

Right away, it looked and felt wrong to Bolan. Two
situations turned up on the street. First he saw the
attendant in the mouth of the garage, pacing, checking
the street. Surprisingly there were only a few shadows
out and about, only one parked vehicle. And Bolan
made the parked car as an unmarked unit, down on
the corner of Samson and Seventh.

Two silhouettes were in the vehicle, watching the
garage. The attendant shot a thumbs-up to the driver
of the unmarked car, then disappeared somewhere
down the mouth of the garage. Was the enemy in the
garage staked out, set to be pounced on by Philly's
finest? Bolan didn't think so. He slowly rolled past
the unmarked vehicle, feeling the eyes of the shadows
in the Crown Victoria boring into the side of his head.
Once again the soldier believed Deliverance was being protected by those who had thrown away their
sworn oath of office. For money or warped ideology,
it didn't matter to Bolan. A bad cop deserved the
worst possible fate. What he had learned and expe-

rienced so far on this campaign now sent an icy wave of unease down his spine. When the law resorted to unlawful extremes of violence, then anarchy was just around the corner. Democracy would cease to exist, would in fact give way to a police state.

Fleetingly Bolan considered that the members of Deliverance might compare themselves to the unofficially sanctioned Stony Man operations. If Stanton had the first clue that the Justice Department mounted clandestine operations against homegrown and international terrorists and criminals, Bolan could hear Stanton plead his case that the Executioner was just like Deliverance.

Only there was no comparison whatsoever. There was no hate in Bolan's heart for humankind, no agenda for imposing his will, no desire for the destruction and oppression of any society, any people. Man was created in the image of the Divine. To judge the creation spit on the Creator, and no man had the wisdom to understand the universe, why one existed, nor was it wise to even attempt to make sense of the great scheme. Naturally any man's actions, his life would speak for itself, and one was judged on those acts. Bolan's war was a fight for any and every man who honored and respected both the written law of man and the unwritten law of the heart. His never ending war was meant to save the innocent from just the kind of savages Deliverance had proved themselves to be.

Daly had to have had the same hunch about the setup Bolan spotted, as he drove on, putting distance to the garage and the unmarked car. West on Walnut, past Washington Square, Bolan followed Daly into a narrow alley. Midway down, they stopped. The Ex-

ecutioner got out and approached the Barracuda as
Daly rolled down the window.

"You read that the way I do, Belasko? A couple
of Philly detectives in our boys' pockets, watching
the store."

"The attendant's a lookout," Bolan said.

The Executioner put together a plan of attack. Up
to now, he hadn't been forced to shoot a lawman. In
the next few minutes, that might change. Back in New
York, he had aborted his original plan to shake down
any bad cops on the Deliverance payroll. Brognola
had the names of any legit law players, and the Executioner and Daly had let any tainted badge in the
Gold Shield know the score. Any and all bad cops
feeding the Deliverance scourge were going down,
one way or another. Whether they were right then
rolling in New York precincts, throwing themselves
on bended knee to internal affairs, was a matter Bolan
would leave to Brognola. The big Fed had names
and precincts, enough evidence—circumstantial, of
course—to begin toppling any bad cops in the Big
Apple. The bail bondsman was simply a hard message
left behind for the enemy. Stanton wouldn't have executed his prime source of information on potential
targets. Or at least that was the way Bolan hoped
homicide detectives read it when they hit the crime
scene. A ripple effect of fear and anxiety would
crackle through the ranks of any dirty cops left standing in New York who knew about Stanton's bondsman and Deliverance. If they didn't turn themselves
in on their own, Bolan could be positive Brognola
could initiate a domino effect.

"Here's the story," Bolan told Daly. "First I need

to take out those two in the unmarked car. Quick and quiet.''

Daly turned somber. ''If they're a stakeout team, legitimate detectives, well, we turn into cop killers and we're no better than Stanton.''

''Believe me, I won't let it come to that.''

''What's the plan?''

A wry grin ghosted across Bolan's lips. ''The plan is to give our adversaries a little more sensitivity training.''

WHEN THE BARRACUDA slid in front of the unmarked car, Bolan rolled out of the shadows, the silenced Beretta drawn. The cops knew there was a problem, and the doors opened, two plainclothes shadows disgorging, digging for hardware beneath their coats. Daly was out of his vehicle, hands up, giving the cops an innocent routine, keeping their attention off the big shadow surging up on their rear.

On the march down the sidewalk, Bolan gave the street, then the garage, a hard look. At the moment, the four of them were alone.

Bolan moved quick and hard, chopping the cop on the passenger's side over the head with his Beretta. While his victim crumpled and the soldier shoved him inside the vehicle, Daly's Para-Ordnance pistol was out and in the other cop's face in the blink of an eye. Bolan opened the back door, then shut the passenger's door. Hopping in as Daly's stunned detective was thrown behind the wheel, Bolan chugged a 9 mm round into the radio console. The cop flinched, starting to growl an oath, but Bolan cut him off, sticking the end of the Beretta's sound suppressor in his ear.

''Clock's ticking on your life,'' the Executioner

said as Daly jumped in beside him and closed the door. "You lie to me, and I'll know, and the next round puts your lights out. Are they down there?"

The cop's dark eyes burned with anger. There was enough flicker in the man's gaze to warn Bolan he was searching for some lie to get him clear. But the cop stared into Bolan's unforgiving eyes and had to have figured he had no choice. He answered, "They're down there."

"How many?"

"Figure at least forty. You mind telling me who you are?"

"I'm with the Justice Department."

"Bullshit."

"Don't call me on it, and you'll get through the night. You're their lookout?"

The cop clenched his jaw. "Yeah."

"You chose the losing team. How about the attendant?" Bolan asked.

"Same deal," the cop said.

"One attendant?"

"Right."

"Where in the garage?" Bolan asked. "And what's your role?"

"Bottom level. I'm to keep the block monitored for any patrol cars. If something doesn't look right, I call."

"How long?"

"Maybe ten minutes they're down there. When they're finished, I'm supposed to escort them to the turnpike."

Bolan put the Beretta away. It was a plus that he'd just learned the enemy was planning to head west.

"Give my friend here any trouble, having to deal

with internal affairs tomorrow will be the least of your problems.

"Hustle up," Bolan told Daly.

Disgorging, the Executioner moved swiftly. Gaze fixed on the garage, he settled in behind the Barracuda's wheel. Behind him, Daly was forcing the cop to swing around, head back for the alley where Bolan's wheels were parked. There, as planned, Daly would cold-cock the detective with his weapon, then cuff both cops.

It almost blew up before he even entered the garage. Cutting across the street, Bolan filled the tight entrance to the garage with the Barracuda. The tall skinny attendant saw Bolan jump out, Beretta drawn, and was already darting for the booth. The soldier swept over the guy, glimpsing the walkie-talkie in the booth right before he slammed a short right off the attendant's jaw. No sooner was the guy dropping than Bolan ripped the attendant's shirt off, stuffed a wadded sleeve in his mouth, then bound his hands behind his back with another section of shirt.

Waiting for Daly to return, Bolan stared down the ramp. Silence.

Less than two minutes later, Daly eased Bolan's vehicle into the garage. The Executioner looked up to the first-level ramp, indicating they should stow their wheels up there, make their way down on foot. Daly nodded.

The Executioner settled in behind the Barracuda's wheel.

In short order, he knew both of them would be descending into the bowels of hell for round three.

The only unanswered question was whether they would rise from the flames.

STANTON AND HIS TROOPS weren't even out of their vehicles before he found Molanski all over them, a snarling human pit bull.

"Before I hand the store over to you people, I want to know what the hell is going on, Stanton. Straight, point-blank, no bullshit because my bullshit detector is geared up."

Surrounded by his force of twenty-five hardmen, Stanton locked a hard gaze with Molanski. Up close, Stanton found the big man, all six-seven and 260 pounds of him, staring down at him, the wrath of God in the former Philly cop's eyes. Those biceps looked like bowling balls to Stanton as Molanski thrust ham-sized hands on his hips. Worse, Molanski's brown bomber jacket with the American flag on the back fell open just enough to show Stanton the shoulder-holstered .357 Colt Python. A lot of hardware was displayed as the Philly cell strung out, face-to-face with Stanton's people. There were enough Uzis, M-16s and MP-5s on both sides to field a small army. Stanton was suddenly glad he had his own MP-5 sub-gun slung across his shoulder, the rest of his force likewise toting assault rifles and subguns.

Molanski wasn't going to like the report, but Stanton didn't think the big man was crazy or stupid enough to give the word to just cut loose, rid himself of an unexpected New York fiasco that could show up in Philly and drag them all down. A human disaster, no, a goddamn wrecking machine called Belasko with his Special Forces hardball-cop sidekick could well be in their face before they left Philly.

Before answering, Stanton ran a look over Molanski's troops. He counted maybe fifteen grim faces that could have been chiseled out of granite. A few of the

Philly guys kept eyes hidden behind dark aviator shades, every last expression blank. But the wall of hard silence in the garage spoke volumes of suspicion and mounting anger. The Philly cell knew there was a problem, and Stanton knew they already knew he was the problem.

Stanton laid it out for Molanski. The big man listened in a terrible silence, weighing, judging, Stanton knew, every single word that came out of his mouth, just like a cop hearing out the confession of a suspect. He didn't leave anything out, but gave it strictly on a need-to-know basis. He covered Westman's defection, played down some the Gold Shield incident, pride getting the best of him, then the hit on the wharf, finally the havoc and destruction wreaked by an alleged Justice Department agent and Daly, but filled Molanski in on only what he wanted the man to know about the former Brooklyn cop. There was no point in fueling the fires of the big man's simmering anger with the truth about Daly's personal crusade.

When he was finished, Stanton stood his ground in the long moments of agonizing silence. He wished to hell the guys would take those shades off so he could read their eyes.

For a second, Stanton felt some hope, saw Molanski's expression soften, then the big man growled, "Sounds to me like you people really fucked up. Any chance you were followed?"

"Not that I know of."

"Not exactly what I wanted to hear." Molanski shook his head, then ran that piercing gaze over Stanton's troops. "Two guys. Unbelievable. Whoever they are, they're good, and they've got the scent. Not only that, they've got the kind of hardware to blow us off the face of the earth.''

"Something maybe I was thinking you could even the odds on," Stanton said.

"Yeah, I know people with that kind of firepower. But it's going to take a few calls. Right now we don't have the time. When we get to Chicago, I can do something. Let me tell you, if it was up to me, I'd cut you loose, but that's too damn dangerous, knowing what I know.''

Molanski paused, seeming to dredge up iron will to compose himself. "I'm one of the few in the organization who knows the big man personally. He likes the work you've done in New York, Stanton. That's maybe the only reason I'm going to ride this out with you. Last thing any of us needs is to be looking over our shoulders for shadows with the heavy artillery. We need to wrap this up and get moving. If it hits the fan, we hit and git. If we get tied up or pinned down, it's over. Running's not my way, but the other two cells have been ordered to link up in Chicago. From there, on to Denver, where the boys from the Southwest and West will meet us.''

"We're covered here, right?"

"The kid let you in, didn't he? I've also got two detectives on my payroll watching the street. When we leave here, they'll escort us to the turnpike, where I'll pay them off and cut them loose. I'm not trying to smear it in your face a little more, but the ones I've got in my pocket here sound a lot more dependable than what you were dealing with in your town.''

"Can we get on with this?"

"Don't get cute with me. From here on, this kick-ass Belasko is running the show. You got a problem with that, speak up now.''

Seething but silent, Stanton braced himself for the big man to take a swing at him, was ready to start throwing punches himself. Baring his teeth, Molanski took a step toward Stanton, hesitated, then turned but stopped and faced him again. Rage was still there in Molanski's eyes, but it was dulled with something that Stanton believed was conviction.

Molanski heaved a deep breath, as if relieving himself of some titanic weight on his shoulders. After a long eyeballing of Stanton and his troops, Molanski told the New York watch commander, ''I want to get the facts of life straight between us, Stanton, before we head out, before me and you have a problem. I'm pissed about this situation, but we'll deal with it. I'm with you, not against you. Later, when we get this squared away, we'll have a few beers, trade some war stories. I know you've been hard at it, cleaning up the garbage. I want to tell you, though, right here and now, I'm damn proud of my own men. To a man they are stand-up, no-shit guys who will sacrifice their lives to make this country we love and care so much about free from crime, and a worthless, whining, spineless minority that's gotten its way too long because of white guilt and misplaced compassion and handouts from Uncle Sam.

''Two days ago, we tracked down three carjackers, tips from our own who didn't want to see a couple of blacks keep on breathing, since they shot and killed a nice young white couple for the guy's Beemer. We've practically taken out a major crew of bangers in north Philly who were moving enough crack and guns through this town...well, let's just say our brother officers are unofficially tipping back a few to us.

"Some of my guys, they were with me over there. I did three, count them, three tours of duty. I fought and damn near died a half-dozen times for this country. Killed more VC, screwed more Saigon hookers than I can remember. All that doesn't mean shit, my blood or my manhood, if we don't succeed in carrying on the good and righteous fight to take back this country. Now. All that said, you want to shake hands and get together on this?"

Stanton couldn't believe it. The guy was a marvel of righteous manhood. Tough but compassionate. One moment ready to kick ass but realizing—hell, forgiving one of his own for screwing up, ready to go the extra mile to make it right. Were those tears Stanton saw misting in the corners of the big man's eyes? He was extending the olive branch. To refuse would be, quite simply, dishonorable. Stanton held out his hand, felt it disappear into Molanski's giant paw. The big guy then grabbed Stanton in a bear hug. Stanton felt his heart skip a beat, thinking the big man had set him up, was going to crush him in those massive arms. Instead, Stanton found himself embraced, patted on the back, sensed nothing but warmth, sincerity and understanding. Molanski released Stanton, showed a warm smile, then moved for his Chevy Caprice. There, Molanski keyed open the trunk. He opened a large duffel bag and handed Stanton a small stack of computer printouts. He caught a glimpse of the cash in that duffel, the M-16 right beside the bag. Philly was tight on its own war chest.

For a few moments, Stanton saw Molanski giving the garage a hard surveillance. What the building was, what the hours were for the garage to stay open, Stanton didn't know, didn't care to ask. All that mattered was they were there, getting down to business. Still, he couldn't help but scour the next level up. There were a few vehicles up there, scattered the length of the garage. One exit, one entrance, each on opposite ends, they were three levels down from the ground entrance. It felt too quiet, too still. Or was he being overly paranoid? Stanton wondered.

"All right," Molanski gruffed, "the big man sent those yesterday by courier. Those are maps with directions to where we're going. One main route, the interstate, with alternate roads. There are also phone numbers to reach our Chicago and Denver cells, to be used only in either an emergency while en route, or to let them know we're coming in when we're close. Hand them out to six of your people, Stanton. Memorize what's on there, then burn them. Let's roll."

Stanton was glancing down at the printout map with phone numbers, handing them out, feeling relief when he heard one of Molanski's people yell, "Up there!"

Autofire ripped the air, Stanton looking up to the next level. Fear tearing through him, he spotted the lone shadow a moment before the rocket sizzled from above, a flaming zigzag finger of doom he'd seen less than two hours earlier. Before he knew it, the explosion thundered, just beyond the scrambling pack of Philly troops.

Stanton wasn't sure if he was knocked to ground by the blast or if he was diving for cover. Either way, his worst nightmare was shattering their world again.

CHAPTER THIRTEEN

Crouched and shadowing parallel down the next level
above the enemy, the Executioner picked a spot to
launch his attack. On the move, deep now in the bowels of the garage, he discovered he was coming in on
the tail end of a tense confrontation between Stanton
and a giant man with an American flag on the back
of his bomber jacket.

The savages sounded ready to devour each other.
Given the headache Bolan and Daly had caused Stanton so far, the soldier could well understand the New
York and Philly cells locked in an angry push and
shove of wills, all of them nervous and paranoid,
ready to blame any and everybody for the looming
crisis that had dropped on them out of nowhere. No
doubt, they would be on high alert, pumped with the
suicidal fever pitch of cornered animals who wouldn't
be taken alive. That was fine with the Executioner.
Their lesson in grief had only just begun.

His M-16 in hand, the M-203 loaded with a 40 mm
grenade, satchel with spare clips and warheads slung
across his shoulder, Bolan settled in between two
parked vehicles. He gave his vantage point a quick
sweep. A Lexus was parked near the end of the level,
beside the exit mouth that led to the ramp. Two other

vehicles were down there, near a door that led into the building. Critical points of cover lay in that direction, he decided, intercept areas to hit them from the blind side. Once the battle started, that was one of two avenues of escape for the enemy.

Then Bolan checked on his ally. On his left flank, near the entrance opening, Daly took up position behind a thick support column. The AR-18 was in Daly's hands, Bolan having handed over two frag grenades to give the man a little more edge to burn down enemy numbers.

Up top, Bolan had laid it out for Daly. The plan was to hit them with another classic pincer attack, but he also told Daly he needed a prisoner, had to establish exactly where the cells were going, and wanted it done on this strike. And if at all possible, let Stanton keep breathing, keep them running, track them to wherever the next stop was scheduled by the enemy. They were to hit them hard, pour on as much devastation as possible, then saddle up, fall in on their slipstream as the joint cells bolted Philly.

Bolan found at least fifteen vehicles down there, figured forty enemy numbers just as the bought-and-paid-for Philly cop had said. Vehicles were strung out haphazardly, backed against the concrete wall. Man and machine were packed tight. Sweet.

Then Bolan got the break he needed. He heard about maps with emergency phone numbers to Chicago and Denver cells, about the main and alternate routes, saw Stanton take the papers from the giant and begin to distribute them to his men. Deliverance was headed due and far west.

Bolan needed that intel, intact.

He swung his aim, away from the cluster of Stan-

ton's people. His finger was curled around the
M-203's trigger when he was spotted. Autofire suddenly punctured the air around Bolan as he pumped
a 40 mm hellbomb into the core of the Philly cell's
heart. The blast erupted, dead center, in the trunk of
a Chevy Impala. Metal sheets razored the air, scything
down four enemy numbers while the roaring firestorm
gobbled up another three hardmen, burning scarecrow
figures hitting the air on that shooting tongue of fire.

But the members of Deliverance showed themselves far more tenacious here than back in Brooklyn.
They were ready and willing to fight, knowing now
who and what they were up against.

For a good number of them, it didn't matter.

Right away, Daly went to work, opening up with
the AR-18, mowing down a few of Stanton's gunmen
before they got the assault rifles off their shoulders.

Braving the slugs shattering glass over his head and
thudding into the front ends of his twin vehicle cover,
Bolan loaded the M-203, popped up and chugged
loose another warhead.

A split second before the enemy pinpointed Daly's
position, Bolan glimpsed his ally hurl an armed frag
grenade.

On the heels of the Executioner's second thundering fireball, which blew apart a Ford four-door,
slammed the flaming hull into the concrete wall,
Daly's steel egg erupted.

At ground zero, Bolan saw only pain, terror and
hard dying happening for Deliverance.

Retreating from tracking fire, the Executioner hit
the other side of his cover, unleashing a relentless
lead storm, his M-16 chattering on full-auto. Guys

were scrambling or falling from fatal wounds. Other figures were nosediving for whatever cover could be found, or they were hopping into vehicles while those who sought to hold their ground, fight to the death, were vaulting trunks or skidding over hoods. Covered then on the other side of vehicles, the enemy came up, screaming and cursing, blazing away with automatic weapons like there was no tomorrow.

Again searching return fire hammered Bolan's position, also forcing Daly to throw himself behind the pillar. Both of them were pinned down for the moment.

The Executioner chanced it, came up and hit them with another 40 mm grenade. His third bomb knocked out two vehicles, launched at least a half-dozen hardmen in various states of dismemberment. Then he was driven to ground by a follow-up barrage of lead streams chewing up metal, blasting out more windows. With all the chaos, boiling smoke and the din of autofire, it was impossible for Bolan to determine what targets had gone down. Swarms of flying lead went on tracking him, hordes of slugs sparking and whining in wild ricochets all around him.

Rubber began screeching a moment later.

A brief lull in return fire gave Bolan a stretched second of opportunity to hose down a Mercury Cougar that was the first vehicle to attempt flight. From above the target car, he blew in the windshield, and saw heads exploding from behind the wheel and passenger's side. Manned only by a corpse, the Cougar plowed into the wall below Bolan, shock waves from that impact jarring the soldier.

Once again, the ultimate destination, their linkup

with the other cells, overrode any final consideration for the head honchos to declare a last-stand war here.

Bolan wasn't about to let them withdraw without inflicting heavy casualties.

Cracking home a fresh 30-round mag in the M-16, then filling the M-203, Bolan sprinted for the exit. He came around the concrete pillar, as a red Camaro roared up the ramp, one gunman leaning out the window, an Uzi flaming in his hands. Bolan hit a crouch as slugs ricocheted off stone, and took that hardman out of play with a 3-round burst from the M-16. Next a Chevy Caprice hit the ramp. One gunman with an M-16 was craned out the passenger's side, while an MP-5 subgunner was extended out the side window, nearly on the roof behind the wheelman. Both of those weapons stuttered in unison, driving Bolan to cover.

The Camaro streaked past the Executioner—only Bolan wheeled around the corner and delivered an explosive surprise into the trailing Caprice. As the Caprice blew by him, slugs screaming off the pillar above his head, Bolan slammed a 40 mm grenade into the front end of that vehicle. The explosion all but incinerated the four occupants, but the fireball was close enough to force Bolan to nosedive to the ground, fiery metal bats flying inches above his head.

Looking up, Bolan found Daly pitching his second grenade around the corner of his pillar. It bounced right in the path of a fleeing vehicle, and the soldier glimpsed the flaming fingers of autofire from the back window of a Ford Taurus an instant before the grenade detonated.

Pivoting, the roar of engines and shriek of rubber grabbing concrete in his ears, Bolan fired at a Crown

Victoria. Return fire cut him off, slugs whistling past his ear, shaving it damn close. Throwing himself up against the pillar, he managed a heartbeat's glance at the gunner. It was the big man who sported the American flag, his M-16 autofire chasing Bolan to ground behind the Lexus. The Philly leader kept on firing, even as his wheelman plowed their vehicle through the burning and still rolling hearse that was the Chevy Caprice.

More vehicles blurred by the soldier, metal rending as they bulled their way through wreckage. The enemy had his position marked, and Bolan knew only a suicidal fool would stand up and fire away in the relentless tracking volleys hurled in his direction.

The Executioner was forced to ride it out, crouched low on the far side of the Lexus. At the other end, he found Daly also driven to concealment behind the pillar. Enemy weapons roared, on and on, until the last vehicle had burned rubber out of there.

Quickly Bolan moved to the edge of the level. Below, bodies were sprawled everywhere among wreckage, strewed on the outer limits of hungry fire.

The soldier leaped over the rail, came down with catlike grace on the roof of the Cougar. He spotted the hard intel he needed. The papers were scattered on the ground, but the Executioner found a bloody figure, scrabbling hard to reach the intel. A crimson-soaked hand raked in those papers, pulled a lighter and flicked it. The fire reached out to torch the critical information Bolan needed.

Suddenly autofire split the air. Wheeling, Bolan saw Daly nail two wounded gunmen to the concrete wall with extended bursts of 5.56 mm lead manglers. Bolan leaped off the Cougar and drew a bead on the enemy who was making his last statement on earth to save the scourge of Deliverance. The flame started to touch the maps when Bolan took the guy out with a 3-round burst. Swiftly fanning the killzone with his M-16 but finding nothing but dead men, Bolan reached the intel and stomped out the flames.

One look at the maps with the phone numbers and he knew their final destination. They might as well have walked him there by hand. There was no mistaking the computer graphics of the United States. Lines were drawn, cutting through Pennsylvania, Ohio, Indiana, with Chicago circled. West through that state, Iowa, Nebraska then another circle around Denver. Finally the line ended north in Wyoming.

They had just delivered the noose for Bolan to tighten around their necks.

"That Stanton?"

Bolan saw Daly nod at the corpse at Bolan's feet. With the muzzle of his M-16, the soldier turned the lifeless face his way. He recognized the big blonde from the Gold Shield.

"No," Bolan said, then showed Daly the treasure trove to lower doomsday on the main Deliverance stronghold.

Daly gave the map one look and said, "It's a long way to Wyoming. Anything can happen between here and there."

"All it means is we pick it up a notch."

"Now that you've got what you need, what about my boy?"

"It's open season."

THE CONVOY ROLLED at a snail's pace, west through Philly, toward the Schuylkill River. Agitated and frightened, Stanton couldn't wait to get on the Schuylkill Expressway, twenty miles to the interchange near Valley Forge, he figured, on the turnpike. Ahead he saw Molanski's Crown Victoria, leading the way through the dark streets of Philly. Stanton kept his MP-5 subgun close at hand,

He looked at Scarborough, who was checking their rear. Stanton had lost more people back at the garage—worse, Molanski had felt the lightning fury of the hit. There had been no time to assess the casualties, not yet anyway. But at some point, Stanton figured he would have to deal with the big man's wrath.

"I saw Morrow go down, John. I hate leaving our guys behind. There's something wrong with that."

"No choice in the matter." Stanton cursed, searched the car but already knew it was in vain. "I left the maps back there."

Scarborough swore. The disaster was now compounded. On top of more lost men, the enemy now had their route, numbers to the other cells.

"Molanski's going to want to know how we were tailed so quickly to the linkup. What are you going to tell him?"

Stanton gave his trailing vehicles a look in the sideview mirror. "The truth. I don't have a clue. All I can figure, maybe Belasko got it out of one of our people back in Brooklyn."

The cellular phone rang. Stanton dreaded answering, felt the ice lodge in his belly and let it ring two more times. He picked it up. "Yeah."

Molanski didn't sound pleased, but Stanton noted right away the level tone in the big man's voice as he said, "Okay, we're coming up to the Schuylkill. We don't have time to jack around with this situation.

My gut tells me those two guys are going to follow. Something also tells me in all the chaos of the fight back there, you might have left behind what I gave you.''

Silence. Molanski obviously wasn't concerned with their frequency getting picked up by a CB. No code, just the hard facts. It told Stanton the man was looking to go all the way, end the fiasco that was Belasko and Daly on the turnpike. Even if that meant a few state cruisers getting into the act.

"Forget it, I don't want to know," Molanski growled. "I said I'm with you, and I'm going to prove it. I'm going to show you a spot to hang back near the on-ramp. I'll leave one of my crew behind. Once we get past the toll, on the turnpike, we slow it down. You come in from behind. I'll leave two crews on the shoulder of the turnpike to fall in when they show, one behind, one in front of them. I figure if it happens it'll be sometime in the next thirty minutes. What are they driving?"

Stanton told Molanski, who said, "Shouldn't be hard to tag our boys then. Listen up. I want them finished for good once we hit the turnpike. We throw everything we've got at them. This could be it, but I'm far from tossing in the towel. Use anything on the highway you can, and don't stop for a state boy. In fact, if we get some smokies on our tail, they have to go. You game for that kind of action?"

"I don't see there's a choice."

"You're damn right there's no choice. I'm helping you fix your mess. No way could we get pinned down back there. Out on the open highway, we can do something. Stay on, I'll tell you what to do."

"And after?"

"We'll worry about that once we take care of your problem, which goes without saying is now my problem. After we clean this up, you owe me."

Stanton didn't like the sound of that. At least Molanski was holding up, making battlefield decisions. Silently Stanton cursed Belasko. Everything had been running smooth, on target and on course. Now this. It didn't seem right. The cellular phone felt like a great weight in his hand, then he flinched when Molanski came back on, started issuing orders.

No need in telling him—Stanton already knew the drill.

Problem was, would Belasko and Daly take the bait? There was only one way to find out. Stanton had the same hunch as Molanski.

It wouldn't be long now before the two crusaders would be on their trunks, guns blazing. The only thing Stanton could be positive of was that the Pennsylvania Turnpike was about to become a highway of death. For somebody, the end was in sight.

But for whom? Stanton wondered.

THE PHILLY SKYLINE faded fast. Bolan stayed on Daly's rear as they cruised northwest on the expressway, putting distance quickly to the outer suburbs. The soldier figured the enemy had no more than a ten-minute jump. It wouldn't be long.

The M-16/M-203 combo lay on the seat next to Bolan, loaded. When they caught up to the Deliverance convoy, Bolan knew they would most likely engage in a high-speed gun battle on the open road.

It would be both tricky and dangerous. At that time of night, traffic was moderate in all three lanes of the Schuylkill Expressway. Keeping innocent travelers out of the line of fire was going to require every bit of the soldier's skill and experience, but he would judge the situation on the spot. He hoped the enemy would take an exit, or stop, disgorge where Bolan could unload autofire and 40 mm death knells.

However it played, he had to be ready for a worst-case scenario. He counted on any noncombatants on the turnpike to pull over or fall back once they caught up with the enemy vehicles and the highway battle started. At this juncture, Bolan could see no other way than to kick it up into high gear, finish Stanton and the New York and Philly cells before they got any closer to the Ohio state line.

Then there was the problem of the state police. So far, Bolan didn't see any flashing lights in his rear-view. But there was a high probability that would soon change.

Before he knew it, Bolan found himself on the turnpike. They were in Valley Forge country, where George Washington's Continental Army had been thrashed at Brandywine, Germantown and White Horse, if Bolan recalled right. Somehow Washington and his troops had survived the harsh winter. Disease, blizzards and little or no food had still claimed two thousand American soldiers. There was something to be said, Bolan concluded, for the will of the fighting man, engaged in the good fight.

For some reason, he saw Daly slow down, slide the Barracuda onto the shoulder, then stop.

Bolan got out of his vehicle and walked up to Daly, who leaned out the window and said, "I didn't know what to make of this, so I didn't stop right away. We've got a problem coming up on our rear. One signal was going due west, the other was at a standstill back where we got on the expressway. I figured they abandoned the car, but it's moving hard and fast now.''

Bolan searched the highway, east. Headlights cut the night a mile back, closing but coming toward them, below the speed limit. A behemoth eighteen-wheeled gas tanker thundered past them.

''The signal I got due west has slowed. You know what it means, Belasko. They're ready and waiting. They want to finish it here.''

''Get your windows down and your guns ready. We keep rolling. They don't intend for us to get off this highway in one piece. Well, let's give them a problem they won't walk away from this time. You lead—I'll keep trailing, unless I make a move to take the point. This is one we can't do by the numbers. Get creative.''

Heading back to his vehicle, Bolan caught a pair of headlights cutting the gap. He malingered a good half minute, standing by the road, waiting. The headlights stopped coming forward. It was the enemy down there; he could feel them.

Finally the soldier hopped in, patched out behind Daly, rolled down the driver's and passenger's windows. Then he unleathered the Desert Eagle, glancing from the Barracuda, the arrow-straight stretch of highway ahead, to the side-view mirror. He gave it some gas and came up hard on Daly's bumper. His ally got the message, put some rev in his vehicle's engine and shot ahead. They were going to hit them from the rear, while the spearhead slowed it up, pinning them in from the front.

Bolan saw the headlights loom up in his side-view mirror even as he cranked it up to 80 mph. Two vehicles, it looked like. One peeled off from the lead car and swung over into the passing lane. He hit his high beams to alert Daly.

Then it happened.

A glimpse of the muzzle-flash winking in his rearview, a shadow craning out the window of the Crown Victoria on his bumper, and Bolan ducked. The back window was blown in by the tracking leadstorm, slugs thunking into the seat, hurling stuffing around the interior. They were coming up even harder now on his rear, the Chevy Caprice racing up to cut Bolan off in the left lane. Wind gusting and glass flying around the interior, the soldier floored the pedal, swung over into the left lane and lurched ahead of Daly. The soldier's vehicle shot down the highway, a metallic rocket clipping the speedometer at 100 mph.

A shadow in the corner of his eye darted past, pulling off the shoulder. In his rearview mirror, Bolan saw the dark hull rolling quickly away, then, fall in with the enemy on his rear. Daly was already giving the Barracuda's engine more thunder, tailing Bolan in the left lane.

Another silhouette of a vehicle shot up in the distance, cutting out onto the highway, launching ahead of the Executioner. A gunman leaned out the back window of that intercept vehicle, an assault rifle flaming in his hands.

Bolan had to act quickly and decisively or the both of them would be sealed in, front to rear, doomed by converging streams of autofire.

The soldier ducked a fraction of a second before the windshield shattered in spiderweb holes, then glass washed over Bolan's head. A look in the rearview revealed three vehicles on the Executioner's rear. Flying up on the Barracuda, he counted four assault rifles or subguns blazing away on Daly. The ex-cop ducked as the vehicle's windshield erupted.

Swinging in behind the intercept vehicle, Bolan saw the gunman fight to hold his balance, his tracking autofire thrown off mark by Bolan's sudden weave.

Bolan drew a bead on the hardman ahead with the Desert Eagle. Squinting against the furious rush of cold wind, Bolan triggered the hand cannon. The hardman's face took the first round, his assault rifle flying away a heartbeat before he was airborne out the vehicle.

Charging the rear of the intercept vehicle, Bolan thundered on with the mammoth Desert Eagle. The back window of his targeted vehicle blew apart. Ahead a shadow popped up on the passenger's side, muzzle-flashes from an assault rifle sparking the dark interior beside the wheelman.

Daly's vehicle was a blur as he roared past Bolan, anticipating the oncoming disaster.

Bolan's gun shattered the head of the wheelman. Sparks marching down the hood of his vehicle, Bolan hit the wheel, rocketed into the left lane as the unmanned intercept car slammed into the guardrail. Like a crushed toy, that vehicle flipped past Bolan's bumper. Suddenly two of the three trailing enemy vehicles were hitting brakes, sliding all over the road.

The third vehicle, the Chevy Caprice, caught the full and terrible collision of the unmanned car. A rending of metal exploded to Bolan's rear as both vehicles looked fused by the impact. Bodies tumbled down the road, then a fireball shattered the night. As wreckage was hurled in all directions, Bolan saw the other two vehicles burst past the thunder and fire.

Ahead, he spotted the twin lines of vehicles, two in each lane. Shadows with weapons leaned out the rear windows. Daly was closing hard on the intercept line. A solitary pencil-tip flame illuminated the vehicle's interior as Daly fired away with the Para-Ordnance. Just ahead of Daly, the gas tanker was blasting its horn, the trucker impatient or afraid, Bolan wasn't sure. But the tanker made no attempt to fall back or pull over. Other than the enemy and the 18-wheeler, Bolan found no carloads of unsuspecting noncombatants. It was as good as it was going to get.

The Executioner made a risky decision, hoping the trucker's skill lent him the edge he was looking for.

Shooting up the right lane, Bolan gave Daly a quick look, then cut in front of the Barracuda. Rocketing ahead, the soldier weaved in front of the tanker, autofire erupting from the intercept vehicles. Letting off the gas, Bolan slid up the shoulder, letting the tanker pass. The tanker's gale-force slipstream nearly threw Bolan into the guardrail, but he grasped the wheel tight. A split second of lost nerve, one uneven stretch of concrete and the end would come at Bolan in a flash.

The wheel wanted to rip itself out of Bolan's fists as he felt his vehicle falling behind the tanker. Then the Executioner sliced out onto the highway, roaring up behind the enemy.

Ahead, Daly cut in behind the tanker, anticipating Bolan's play.

The Executioner lifted the Desert Eagle and drew a bead on the driver of the Crown Victoria.

MOLANSKI HAD TO END IT, quick, no matter what. He'd seen the fireball boil across the turnpike and was enraged that he'd lost more men. Whoever these two guys were, they were good. Field a small army like those two, and Molanski figured he could take the Pentagon down.

No such luck, he thought, leaning out the window, sighting down on the tanker's front tires. Their problem had to disappear, then Molanski needed to find the nearest exit, ditch their wheels, figure a plan. No way they could stay on the turnpike after this kind of carnage. Less than a minute ago, Molanski had called Stanton, told him to get past their hellhounds, get beyond the tanker. No details, just do it.

Molanski saw one guy make his move, hit the shoulder, drop back. The guy thought he had it made, roaring up on Stanton's rear.

With the rush of wind in his ears, the chatter of autofire beside him, Molanski shot out the tanker's tires. The trucker hit the brakes, and Molanski went for the windshield, just to make sure. A long burst of autofire blew the windshield in, and Molanski caught a glimpse of the trucker's shock and terror before a spurt of blood went through the cab.

Molanski watched in grim satisfaction. It was a done deal.

Like some lumbering behemoth dying a slow and painful death, the tanker twisted slowly, toppling, back end coming around, whiplashing across the highway, the fin of some great fish.

Paydirt erupted a moment later when the giant rig proved it was topped out with a full load of fuel.

Stanton and his crew just cleared the titanic fireball that turned darkness into blinding light. A wall of fire boiled in both directions. Anything in the wake of that inferno would be incinerated.

Molanski settled back in his seat.

DALY LET off the gas and moved into the left lane to get beside his ally's vehicle. Enemy vehicles surged past the passenger's side, and Daly ducked the auto-fire. Slugs then suddenly stopped pounding the 'Cuda's bodywork. Popping up, he was lining up Stanton's face when his hated enemy's wheelman cut him off and shot ahead, out of range.

A moment later, Daly saw why the Crown Victoria was blowing away from him. The tanker was going down, the rear end, falling out of the sky, it seemed, set to crush the Barracuda. When it slammed to the highway, Daly lost control of the wheel, felt his side plow into the concrete barrier. The wheel wrenched from his hands, Daly saw he cleared the toppling hulk but the thunder of the ensuing fireball shattered his senses. The world was erupting in his eyes, a blinding supernova. An impenetrable wall of darkness then shrouded his vision. Suddenly it was bitter cold, a gale-force wind lashing him in the face, tearing at his flesh. He didn't know how he knew, but he was flying through the night.

A horrible gut feeling told him it was over. All he could do was brace himself for impact, for a bone-crushing slam into a hard object that would shatter him, break him in two.

Dead. Stanton gone. Vengeance never tasted.

He was flying through the air, eyes shut, when he felt something hard but soft whipping into him. Was he slowing down? Crunching, snapping noises flailed his senses.

He rode the flight, a human missile, but one that was slowing, fast.

Daly steeled himself for sudden impact.

THE EXECUTIONER SAW it coming even before it happened.

One second he was right behind the enemy, and the next they were past Daly, streaking up the side of the tanker. The maneuver had cost Bolan distance, speed. Now he found himself staring doom, dead ahead, in the form of the 18-wheeler.

His foot floored the gas pedal when he saw the autofire directed at the tanker's tires. Then the unmistakable shape of the big Philly leader opened up on the driver, his M-16 going for broke.

The tanker was going down. Crushing impact at high speed would erupt the tanker's load, create an inferno that would vaporize him, Bolan knew, unless he cleared the blast.

The Barracuda was a whiplashing blur ahead of Bolan as Daly lost control of the wheel, vanishing beyond the toppling tanker.

Bolan braced himself, then heard the deafening whoosh of the thundering explosion, the searing heat reaching out for his face and neck.

Surging past the outer wall of the ground-zero blast, the shock waves pounding him, Bolan fought the wheel. He tapped the brakes and found he was lurching uncontrollably from one lane to the other. Suddenly the crushed hull of the Barracuda tore in front of his path, looked nearly sawed in two in the next instant when it bounced off the concrete barrier.

Bolan hit the brakes, riding out the long slide. Any second he expected to hit the guardrail, bounce, flip, crash and burn.

The night and the wind rushed at Bolan, hammering him in the face with invisible fists. Finally the prolonged screech of rubber ended. Heart pounding in his ears, cold sweat coursing down his face, Bolan sat there for a long moment. Somehow he made it. Daly, he was sure, hadn't been so fortunate.

The soldier unfolded from the vehicle and watched the enemy vanish, far down the turnpike.

Anger and grief ripped through the soldier as he turned and jogged toward the pulped ruins of the Barracuda. He smelled the fumes of leaking gas, then the smoking wreckage exploded.

Beyond the dazzling wall of fire, a good mile east, Bolan made out the oncoming strobing lights.

Slowly the Executioner walked east, down the middle of the highway. Daly was gone, a damn good soldier, a man worthy of his grief, Bolan thought. Then he braced himself for a confrontation with the state police.

For this night it was over. For Daly it was done for good. Bolan felt a piece of himself collapse inside. Daly had been there with him, gone the extra mile. Whatever the man's motivation, Bolan knew he wouldn't forget that soldier. Deliverance had merely strengthened his resolve to crush the life out of them.

A groan from the shoulder of the road snared Bolan's attention. The shadow limped toward him. In the glow of firelight, Bolan locked a stare with Daly. The man's face was cut and bleeding, his jacket torn to shreds. A quick look to the woods flanking the turnpike, and Bolan knew the man's flight from the Barracuda had been cushioned by branches and thick brush. A sense of relief, but tainted with the bitter knowledge the enemy was escaping, filled Bolan.

In the distance, a trio of cruisers squeezed past the

strewed wreckage, raced past the flaming sea the downed tanker had washed over the turnpike.

Bolan was already digging out his Justice Department ID, for all the good that would do.

Either way, he knew it was going to be a long tough night. They weren't even out of their cruisers, and Bolan and Daly found themselves staring down the shotguns and pistols of Pennsylvania's finest.

CHAPTER FOURTEEN

They put close to an hour's drive from the highway
carnage when Molanski had them pull off the turnpike. The convoy then headed maybe a half mile
down a dark road, winding through rolling hill country. Stanton had been too busy chewing on his fear
and paranoia to note the exit, pay any more attention
to his surroundings than necessary.

Necessary, at this point, meant survival. Road-
blocks would go up all over the state. Cruisers would
clog the turnpike as they roared out of every barracks
from all directions. Choppers would take to the skies,
searchlights soon to be sweeping over the Pennsylvania countryside. Alerts would go out to the state
police in the surrounding states, and any suspicious-
looking vehicles would give the smokies enough
probable cause to pull them over, demand ID and reg-
istration, then a search of their person and vehicle. A
rolling convoy of six vehicles with bullet-scarred
frames sure as hell classified all of them as suspicious,
Stanton knew.

He feared the worst was yet to come. This disaster
was his fault, now their problem. He was sure Molanski would deliver a serious butt-chewing. Or
worse.

Before they turned onto a dark narrow road that cut through a heavily wooded area, Stanton noted the large truck stop. The lot was full of 18-wheelers, pickup trucks and other vehicles. Lights were on in the diner, shadows, moving in and out, of the large dining building. Stanton suspected Molanski had a plan to get them out of the state.

When they were deeper off the main road that led from the turnpike, lights started dying, with several vehicles angling into the woods, engines killed from behind the brush seconds later. Stanton waited, watched as Molanski disgorged, started giving orders to the New York troops. More vehicles were soon buried in the woods. Moments later Molanski rolled up on Stanton's Crown Victoria.

The window rolled down, Stanton watched the dark shape of Molanski loom over him. The big man calmly told him they were in Amish country, as if he were about to give a tour guide through the Dutch countryside in a horse-drawn buggy. Stanton broke Molanski's penetrating stare and saw what remained of their force step out of the brush and woods after they ditched their vehicles into deeper cover.

"I've got a plan, Stanton. Why don't me and you take a walk to that truck stop. You got money?"

"I got a war chest."

Molanski nodded; he knew the deal. "Bring twenty grand. I'll explain while we walk and talk. Get this vehicle hidden in those woods, then tell your men to get their gear together, be ready to roll."

There was no point in arguing about a mere twenty thousand, Stanton decided, not when their lives were on the line. Molanski had an idea; he had to go with it.

Sliding out of the vehicle, Stanton gave Scarborough the nod, went to the trunk and used his spare key to open it. From his war chest, he took enough stacks of hundreds to equal twenty grand. Stanton passed on Molanski's order, then followed the big man up the dirt road. Fear coursing through him like electrical charges, he cast a somber look over his shoulder. They were less than twenty guns, he figured, including himself and Molanski.

"Yeah, Stanton, I read the fear in our eyes. I count eighteen men altogether. When we get to Chicago, we'll beef up both the numbers and the hardware. A few things I've neglected to mention to you. Two cells who were supposed to link up with us in Philly were ordered at the last minute by me through the big man to go to Chicago. The cell from Detroit has been ordered to go to Cleveland, get with our people there. Cleveland is our rearguard. They've been ordered to hang back. After what's happened, it looked like a damn smart move to keep the troops spread."

Stanton tried to hide his resentment but heard the edge in his voice as he asked Molanski, "How come the watch commander of the top cell in the organization is all of a sudden getting filled in on this need-to-know basis?"

"You've got to ask why?" Molanski growled, leading Stanton up the shoulder of the main road back toward the turnpike, the lights of the truck stop the only sign of life in the black heart of the Dutch countryside. "As far as numbers go, yeah, you New York boys were the biggest. That's obviously proved to be a knife in our backs now. It's set to blow up, mister, unless we get this situation under control, beginning now. Already what I gave you has fallen into enemy hands. Right?''

Stanton checked the road in both directions. Judging the way Molanski was also surveying the road, he knew they would bolt off the shoulder into brush at the first sign of headlights.

Molanski repeated the question, and Stanton answered, ''It happened, yeah.''

''That's why only I've got the code when we contact our people once we're close to Chicago. Something else. The watch commander in Chicago has lined up a major deal for three hundred keys of flake from some Cali boys he's schmoozed up to the past few months. The organization has a major plan in the works, but we won't get the full details until we reach Wyoming. We need this deal in Chicago. It's set to go down tomorrow night. Of course, he won't buy the coke. It's a setup. We grab the coke, waste the Colombians, then trade some of it to a major arms dealer for some of that heavy hardware you've been itching to get your hands on. The rest we can sell back to another major distributor down the road.'' He paused, then said, ''Kind of ironic, don't you think? Former cops fighting to clean up the country of crime and dope, in bed with major narcotics traffickers. The way I see it, though, we can only beat the scumbags by using their own game against them. Same kind of fight-fire-with-fire thinking I know landed you and your people a sweet war chest, I can be sure.''

Stanton scowled, impatient to know what Molanski had in mind to get them clear and free of the state. Philosophy damn sure wasn't going to save their butts at this point.

''I know, you don't like it, being left in the dark

like this. But all the cloak-and-dagger, only a few of us knowing the real score, has kept us going. Called, uh, keeping hope alive. Called covering our butts, you want to get even more specific.

"You've met me once. I've met a good number of the others at a secret roundup eighteen months ago. A couple of your men were there, I recall. Some of us know each other on sight, some of us don't. We were each given assignments from the national watch commander who has seen the future. The future is now. We did what we did in each of our respective cities, as ordered. Now we're pulling in all the troops. Feeling I get is Deliverance is about to launch its own vision of D day against this fucked-up society that was once the greatest country on earth."

They cut across the road and began to descend a grassy slope for the truck stop.

Instead of listening to Molanski, Stanton was dwelling on the savage running gun battle back on the turnpike, the close shave of that tanker almost crushing his Crown Victoria.

"You worked real close back there," Stanton told Molanski.

"I called you before I did it, didn't I? Maybe that fireball jolted you into reality of just how serious I am."

"He made it."

"Who? The Fed?"

"I saw him clear the blast. The other one hit the guardrail. I figure they're scraping what's left of him off the road with a spoon. Must've hit that rail at eighty, maybe ninety."

"You sure about that?"

"I saw him. The Fed stopped and got out to check on his buddy."

"That guy's proved himself a major pain in the ass, and he isn't a Fed."

"Meaning we'll see him again."

"Especially since you left behind an arrow that damn near points the way. Now, I don't think we left behind any wounded in the garage. At least I know any men I've got unaccounted for won't talk."

"You can be sure mine won't, either."

"Well, they got to Philly damn quick, Stanton. How do you explain that?"

"I can't."

"Right, you can't. That's why I'm in charge from here on."

Molanski fell silent, and Stanton didn't bother defending himself. They perched near some brush at the edge of the lot. They waited a good ten minutes before they saw a lone shadow walking for an 18-wheeler. Stanton followed Molanski across the lot. When they were closing on the trucker, the man saw them coming and froze.

Molanski pulled his phony badge and ID. The trucker was a beefy guy, with bloodshot eyes narrowing with suspicion.

"Special narcotics task force, Philadelphia. I've got a proposition for you. You want to make an easy twenty thousand dollars, cash?"

Stanton showed the trucker the money.

"What do I have to do?" the trucker asked.

The man's reaction didn't surprise Stanton. In this day and age, they were out there, everywhere, hungry for a buck. Greed was just another sign of the times. Money was God, character next to nothing. You

couldn't feed yourself on honor and integrity, or grab
the finer things in life through honest hard work, discipline and family values. The working-class hero
was a thing of the distant past. Whatever happened to
America? he wondered.

"What are you hauling?" Molanski asked.

Stanton noted the Oregon tags as the trucker told
them he had just come from New York, dropping off
a load of salmon and trout.

"We'll give you half now, the rest when you get
us to Chicago," Molanski said, then asked about the
custom cab, and was told there was a bed behind the
driver's seat, partitioned off. Stanton knew Molanski
was thinking ahead. He would ride with the trucker,
settle in the sectioned-off compartment if something
turned up on the road, the .357 Magnum ready to blast
away. The rest of them would stow away in the
trailer. It was dicey, but there was no other alternative. Stanton knew the SOP. If smokies pulled the rig
over, decided to inspect the load, they would find
Stanton and the others blazing away with autofire, in
the law's face.

Stanton handed the trucker his advance. The guy
took it quick, eager for an easy twenty thousand. Molanski warned the trucker to do as he was told and
not ask questions. There might be a little bonus in it
for him when they got to Chicago.

Stanton knew better. The only bonus this trucker
would see was a bullet through the head at the end
of the line.

COLONEL WAYNE DANFORTH was seething as he
handed the phone to Bolan. On the other end, Brognola didn't sound too happy, either.

Bolan and Daly had been cuffed on the highway, hauled back to the barracks and thrown into lockup. His Justice Department credentials had been handed over to Danforth, who said he'd check it out. Bolan had given the colonel the direct number to Brognola's office at the Justice Department. The normal booking procedure had been postponed, the soldier kept separated from Daly while Danforth had checked out Bolan's story. Critical time had been lost, weapons and his vehicle impounded, red tape now threatening to put a stranglehold on the Executioner's campaign.

For two hours, Bolan's war against Deliverance had been suspended while he waited to hear about his fate. Brognola certainly had the clout to get him moving again, but there had been delays, problems smoothing out official ruffled feathers, no doubt. The only advantage to the unforeseen interlude had been Bolan catching ninety solid minutes of much needed sleep. Rested, recharged and more determined than ever to bring down Deliverance, he was still in the barracks, in Danforth's office, catching more heat.

"I don't need to tell you, Striker, this is not good," Brognola said over the phone. "This is the second time I've taken an earful from the good colonel there, but I sympathize with his predicament, as I'm sure you can, too. He didn't want to cut you loose. I had to call the governor, who called the colonel and gave him the order to cooperate with you. Meaning you're free to go. Whatever he's impounded, the governor ordered him to hand it back."

Bolan saw Danforth drilling an angry stare into him.

"He's got a mess on the turnpike," Brognola went on. "Bodies all over the road. I understand a trucker was killed. It's no fault of your own, but the colonel's having a tough time swallowing what he's facing. There are now local and state authorities combing through a garage in Philly heaped with a thousand pieces of dead men and wreckage blown all to hell. All the earmarks of your work. You know me, Striker, and I'm not criticizing, but this thing could go public. That would be a worst-case scenario if the media gets solid evidence about this conspiracy...well, we've already discussed it.''

Bolan could sympathize with both the colonel's and Brognola's official burden. The big Fed had been on this around the clock, probably hadn't been out of his office unless it was a quick trip to the rest room. The strain was clear in Brognola's voice as he heard the Justice man heave a long breath.

''The targets you tracked from New York to Philly,'' Brognola went on, ''seemed to have just disappeared into thin air, according to Danforth. Of course, they'll comb every inch of the state, but something tells me the enemy has found a way to vanish. You're back in operation once I hang up. Bottom line, Danforth doesn't know what we're up against. Go easy on him. If he starts asking a lot of questions, well, you know the drill. Give him only what you feel is necessary.''

Bolan then told Brognola what he needed. The mention of the additional combat gear and hardware, complete with mortar launcher and C-4, and Bolan was treated to a long suspicious look from Danforth.

''I'll bring it to you personally,'' Brognola said. ''We need to get up to speed on this, and I need to get out of this office anyway.'' Brognola gave Bolan the location of a small airport east of Pittsburgh. An agent had checked the rendezvous site and informed Brognola of a small all-night diner nearby. He gave Bolan specific directions to the meet site.

"I'll be bringing a friend," Bolan informed the Justice Man.

"I know about Daly. If you've brought him aboard, I can only trust your judgment on that."

"So far, it's worked out, other than this snag."

"There's a major plus that's come out of this. I'll fill you in when I see you."

"One other thing," Bolan said. He was thinking about the maps with the phone numbers, knew Brognola could trace the locations, using the area code and numbers, via either his own sophisticated computer network and connections and clout or have the wizards at Stony Man Farm pinpoint the safehouses of the other cells. "Before you catch your flight, I need to touch base with you again but after I leave here."

"Twenty minutes." Brognola gave Bolan a number, then hung up. The soldier handed the phone back to the colonel.

Danforth fired up a cigarette, scowling at Bolan. "You people down in Washington sure seem to operate a little different than your conventional law enforcement. I'm not the smartest man in the world, but you aren't your average Justice Department agent. Somebody down there has launched a secret war that's blown through my state. I got bodies and wreckage all over the turnpike, and I've been informed they're scraping guys off a wall in a parking garage in Philly that looks like a war zone." Danforth worked out his anger on his cigarette. "Whatever the hell is going on, whoever you really are, well, I've got my orders. When you leave, I'm going to do my damnedest to forget this night ever happened." Danforth paused, seeming to age right before Bolan's eyes. "I look at you, and something tells me you're on the right side."

Bolan kept his tone level with respect. "And Daly?"

"You want him, he's yours. The both of you get the hell out of here before I change my mind and throw my stripes and pension out the window. Anything else? Maybe you need a vehicle?"

"I was just about to ask you for a loaner."

"A loaner. I've seen what happens when you get behind the wheel, Belasko. What the hell, I might as well go all the way, since I'm being so damn cooperative with Washington. I'll have one of my men round you up a Crown Victoria from the lot."

Bolan stood, was turning to leave when Danforth said, "Tell me something, Belasko, give me a little clue anyway what this is all about."

"I don't think you'd believe me if I told you, Colonel."

"Try me."

A weary grin fleeted over the Executioner's lips. "All right. What I've done, what I'm going to do, Colonel, I'm doing it for you and all the men and women across this country who wear a badge and risk their lives every day to uphold the law."

For the ghost of a fleeting moment, Bolan saw Danforth start to smile. The man didn't know Bolan was fighting to save the country from a paramilitary force of trained lawmen taking the law into their own hands. But he knew something was different about Bolan, something major and potentially devastating was going on, that his state had just been unfortunate enough to get a taste of a clandestine war launched against an unknown menace. Danforth's silence and look told the Executioner that maybe someday he would look back on this encounter and thank himself for cutting loose one special agent and his friend.

At least, that was how Bolan perceived the moment. And his instincts about men, both the good and the bad, had never failed him before.

As for the bad, the soldier intended to make final and ultimate believers out of Deliverance. And from beyond the grave.

BROGNOLA WAS THERE and waiting when Bolan led Daly into the diner. It never failed to amaze the soldier how quick and efficient the big Fed would respond to an emergency. But it didn't surprise him to find the man, front and center, ready to deliver what the Executioner needed to track and burn down Deliverance. This time out, they were faced with a national crisis of nightmare dimensions. Bolan could well understand Brognola's personal touch.

Before leaving the lot of the state police barracks in the Crown Victoria, Bolan had put the call into Brognola, gave him the crucial phone numbers, also told the big Fed he needed the maps of the states he would be hitting. Brognola vowed to get the soldier the exact locations, ASAP, and deliver the maps when he saw him. Their weapons returned, along with everything else that had been impounded and logged as evidence, Bolan had then taken the wheel.

The Executioner found Brognola had taken the last booth against the far wall, out of earshot from any other customers. When he saw Bolan and Daly head his way, he flagged down the waitress, and ordered coffee and breakfast specials, all around. Then he dropped quarters into the jukebox and started pushing buttons at random. Bolan knew a hit parade would keep their conversation thoroughly muted from outside listeners.

Bolan's intro between Daly and Brognola was brief. No handshake, just a nod between the Justice man and Bolan's ally, then they got down to business after the waitress brought coffee. Bolan laid out his confiscated findings, explained how he came about them.

Brognola gave the maps one glance, seemed dubious. "You seized the mother lode, Striker, but what's to keep the hunted from calling the other cells in these locations to alert them to their hunters? If they're not waiting for you on the other end, they could well just pull up stakes."

"I don't think so. We've got them running scared. From what I've seen and what I've heard so far, I'm betting the rest of Deliverance will hold their ground to the last man. If they figure I walked away from the wreckage back on the turnpike, I'm counting on them looking for me. These guys don't care who they kill, even if it's their own 'brother' officers. What they did to that oil-tank trucker proves they consider anyone fair game—they intend to go out with a roar. We've hit them hard, shaved down their numbers considerably. At this point, my strong hunch is they're itching to pay us back."

"And you and Daly are going to hit each of these locations?"

"That's the idea."

Brognola handed Bolan a small stack of maps. "I ran down the phone numbers with the help of our people." Obviously Brognola was still leery of Daly's involvement. "Our people," Bolan knew, meant Stony Man Farm. "The addresses correspond to each phone number in those cities. Chicago looks to have three different safehouses, Denver two. There was one for Cleveland."

Bolan looked at the map and figured the best and fastest route was to hop onto Interstate 80. Cleveland was a short drive, northwest of Pittsburgh, the city along Lake Erie the obvious choice to relaunch his war. Then I-80 shot a straight line for Chicago, through Iowa, then south on I-35 to Kansas City, a straight roll for Denver, west on I-70.

"The upshot of this crisis I earlier alluded to," Brognola stated, "is I just got a call from my agents in New York. One detective, a Mike Masterson, and two other homicide detectives from the Bronx handed themselves over to internal affairs. Looks like you got the ball rolling. It's only a matter of time before whoever Stanton's people are in New York fall. Classic domino effect."

A fleeting sense of relief washed through Bolan. He wouldn't have to return to New York, make those "house calls" on any lawmen. So far, he hadn't been forced to gun down any current but dirty badges connected to Deliverance. Maybe they had found the bail bondsman already. The message.

"All the items you requested are in my rental," Brognola told Bolan, then glanced at Daly. "Including ten spare magazines for an AR-18, three dozen 12-gauge shells for a SPAS 12. As usual, I trust you to know what you're doing, Striker."

"Daly's been a valuable asset," Bolan told Brognola quietly.

"Two final items," Bolan stated. "Factor in at least three different target sites along the way, takedowns in each city. I'm figuring forty-eight hours to get to Wyoming, and I need the exact location of the stronghold. It'll be dawn soon. If it goes according to plan, we'll be in Wyoming two days from now. We strike, put the last sunrise on these guys they'll ever see."

"I can use a couple of our people for aerial recon to locate the compound," Brognola said. "Another factor here. We don't know the numbers at the compound, but I'm offering to mobilize a team of eight special agents, heavily armed with orders to shoot to kill. The strike team will be under your command."

Bolan nodded. "That was my second item."

"As usual we're in sync," Brognola said.

Daly looked from Brognola to Bolan. "How come I get the feeling I might be sitting at the Last Supper?"

Brognola lifted his fork and got to work on his scrambled eggs. "Let's eat, then get out of here. You two men have a lot of work to do."

He looked at Daly, added, "Enjoy, soldier. I've got the tab."

THE PHONE RANG five times before Marty Peters roused himself from slumber, unfolded his beefy six-foot frame from the couch, stood and crossed the living room of the safehouse to pick up the receiver. His legs felt like rubber, the phone like a siren in his brain, thanks to the twelve beers and four bourbons of the previous night.

Only one individual had the number to the Cleveland safehouse in the heart of downtown. Peters had been waiting half the night for an update. When it didn't come, he had drank himself into a haze before passing out.

The Detroit boys were there in the three-bedroom apartment, showing up just after 2400 hours. Unfortunately problems had followed them from Motor City. The Detroit cell was minus two men. Peters discovered they'd gone out on a call before blowing Detroit. Seemed the Detroit warriors snuffed out some bangers in their crackhouse, but two of their own had been hit when the punks shot back with Glocks and a mini-Uzi. Valuable time for the Cleveland linkup had been lost as they came down I-75, blood all over the interior as their men were dying before finally breathing their last. It turned out Curt Daniels, the Detroit watch commander, at least had the good sense to weight the bodies down and dump them in Lake Erie, then scrub the vehicle free of blood. Cop instincts and experience still worked overtime in Daniels, but Peters wouldn't have expected any less.

One look around the living room revealed two of the five Detroit warriors watching the morning news, one asleep on the couch, the other two in the kitchen brewing coffee. Peters's force of six were in bed, a few of them sleeping off hangovers. Peters, a former Cleveland vice cop, was reassured by all the firepower they kept close at hand. There was trouble back east, and Peters worried New York's problems might find their way to Cleveland.

He cradled the receiver to his ear. He was the only one allowed to answer the phone, the only member of the cell who knew the password the big man from back east would use. Peters heard silence on the other end but sensed a presence there.

"Yeah?"

"Consider this your final wake-up call. You're going to be hit in ten minutes."

That sure as hell wasn't the password, nor did Peters recognize the voice on the other end. It was a voice that was all ice, sounding like it was coming from the grave. The dial tone in his ear sounded a million miles away. Who the hell knew they were there? The cops? That was the only logical conclusion. No, he corrected himself, there was something else in the voice. Something final. Like impending doom incarnate announcing a death sentence. No, that voice didn't belong to any cop.

Peters banged the phone down, growled at the Detroit men, "Look alive. Barker, check the hall. Moran, get the others in here." He read their expressions of fear and confusion as the rest of the Detroit troops leaped to their feet, poured out of the kitchen, clawing for holstered side arms. Something was definitely wrong, and they knew it. "I was just told we're going to be hit in ten minutes. Something tells me this isn't any bust."

It was confirmation of their worst fear. Barker worked the action on his Uzi and strode for the door. Moran went to get the others front and center, cocked and locked.

The nauseous swirl from the previous night's heavy drinking was suddenly gone as Peters moved for the window. Adrenaline clearing his head, he pulled back the curtain and gave the street a hard search in both directions. Their safehouse occupied one of the larger units on the top floor. The building was an old, run-down complex with no security. The place was infested with drug dealers and bloodsucking welfare leeches. Security here came from the barrel of a gun.

Nothing on the street looked out of the ordinary to Peters, but there was a fire escape that led to a back alley. The raid could come from that direction, but something clicking in the back of his head again warned Peters it wasn't a bust. No, a hit was going down, a hardball take-no-prisoners situation.

Dawn had just broken over the city. From his vantage point, Peters could see Cleveland Stadium, just north of Memorial Shoreway, which was now choked with vehicles of countless citizens going to work, nine-to-fivers who didn't have a clue eleven stand-up white men were hanging it all out there to save the American dream of home, happiness and security. The eternal gray smog hung over Lake Erie. Smokestacks from steel mills, oil refineries and auto factories were already belching so much poison into the sky, Peters couldn't tell what kind of day it was going to be, sunny or cloudy, not that the weather really mattered. He wasn't sure why, but all of a sudden he felt compelled to look at his hometown as if he were seeing it for the last time.

He was reaching for his hip-holstered Glock, the fear mounting, searching the street but unable to find any unmarked units, when he thought he heard a soft chugging noise from behind. Terror then gripped his heart. That quiet sneeze he heard was all too familiar. More than once, he'd used a sound-suppressed weapon himself, knew the final and sudden ugliness of silent death, an unmistakable noise a man never forgot.

They were being hit, and some awful dark instinct

told him they weren't meant to be taken in, hand-cuffed and Mirandaized.

Wheeling, seeing Barker topple from the doorway with blood spurting from his shattered skull, Peters found his worst fear confirmed. A hundred questions wanted to tear through his mind. The voice on the phone had said ten minutes, but the voice had lied, set them up. Who? Certainly not cops, any doubt about official law involvement gone with the blood he saw taking to the air. Their own people, he wondered, suddenly figuring the Cleveland and Detroit cells were too much a liability?

Whatever, Peters knew the answer would never come. He glimpsed his men scrambling from the bed-rooms, weapons drawn, trying to get it in gear.

Then Peters saw a big shadow swing low around the doorway, pitch something into the living room, then vanish as gunfire started chewing the jamb. That "something" rolled up, smack in the middle of his people.

The world shattered around Marty Peters in one horrific explosion.

CHAPTER FIFTEEN

The hard truth was that Mack Bolan was ten feet away from the target site, not ten minutes.

With his cellular phone, the soldier had put the call through on the way up the elevator. It was risky, going public this early, two men with shotguns, ready to blow the early-morning inner-city Cleveland quiet all to hell with frag grenades before unleashing the rolling thunder of 12-gauge doom.

An in-close engagement like this called for the two of them to go through the front door, Mossberg and SPAS 12 thundering away, making sure what they hit stayed down for good.

Two factors confirmed Bolan's hunch that they were square on target. First the voice on the other end of the call sounded edged with suspicion and paranoia, a white man in a bad part of town poised for it to hit the fan. Ten minutes was a smoke job, of course, meant to scramble the troops, get them to show themselves.

It worked. Factor number two showed to begin to seal enemy doom. When the big white man with the Uzi submachine gun stepped through the doorway, out into the reeking hallway of the tough-luck apartment building near Lake Erie, Bolan put one silenced

9 mm round from his Beretta through the guy's temple. It wasn't only the weapon Bolan's target wielded that made final confirmation they had arrived at the right ground zero.

No, the soldier had also become all too familiar with that feral look of hate, rage and fear, the warped emotional ticking time bombs behind the eyes of Deliverance cannibals.

Daly was already crouched on the other side of the door down the hallway. Once again Bolan had gone over the plan of attack. Once again Daly proved himself up to the gruesome task at hand.

No sooner was the hardman toppling through the doorway than Bolan lobbed an armed frag bomb into the living room. He caught a glimpse of maybe eight figures, armed to the teeth. They were rolling up, tight, around a small cluttered area, when the grenade bounced into the middle of the savages. Gunfire erupted, spraying the doorway, then the thunder of the blast filled Bolan's ears as he braced himself against the wall. All the racket was sure to alarm someone in the building. They had to move fast, end it quick. He was counting on any witnesses falling into the I-didn't-see-anything syndrome once the law showed up.

Bolan intended to be long gone before then, on the interstate, en route for Chicago.

First things first, and that meant burning down the Cleveland cell.

The bitter taint of cordite, smoke and blood choking his senses, the Executioner went in low, firing the Mossberg. Daly was on his heels, the ex-cop slipping off Bolan's flank, the massive SPAS 12 already busy. Together, both men started blasting apart anything that stood, crawled or groaned inside the boiling cloud of smoke.

It was a no-mercy, take-no-prisoners deal.

Bolan found there were a few still among the living, but mauled and mangled by the frag blast. Two of the enemy shrieked in pain. Blood was streaming off hardmen's faces from where their eyeballs had been ripped out by countless flying steel bits of shrapnel.

Mercy rounds sent them to the hereafter.

Rolling on, tall and grim faced, Bolan took out two gunners, triggering and racking the Mossberg's action in lightning succession.

Gunfire split the hallway leading from the living room. On the fly, the two soldiers triggered their weapons. Twin shotgun explosions chewed up plaster, gouged basketball-sized holes in the wall downrange. From that direction, two Uzi shooters ducked into a room. There wasn't a second to malinger.

Both Bolan and Daly sent grenades through the doorway of the enemy's cover, then threw themselves against the wall. A second later, the walls shook with the deafening blast. A look down the hall, and Bolan found a hole in the bedroom wall that could have been bulldozed. Through all the smoke and cordite, he spotted smears of blood, top to bottom.

Two more doors remained to check, but they found nothing in either bedroom. All clear.

On the way out, Bolan saw Daly make a brief stop at the hall closet. Bolan knew the man had lost his coat back at the turnpike battle. Daly took a black leather bomber jacket from the closet and slipped it on.

"I don't think anybody here will be needing this,"

he said to Bolan. "It's cold this time of year in the Windy City."

As cold as death, the Executioner thought, and led Daly out of the slaughterhouse.

SHYROCK COULDN'T RESIST putting in the call to the Milt Braun show. The fact was Shyrock had been itching all night to hear how his boy was going to make things better than ever in the Lone Star State.

"You're on the Milt Braun show, the last defender of the free and the brave in this great land we call America. What's your question for Mr. Masters, the people's bet to be the next governor of this great State of Texas?"

Sitting in his Ford rental on the shoulder of I-45, the Houston skyline right in his face, Shyrock waited while his call to the Braun show was placed in order behind the other callers who wanted to talk to the tycoon who would be governor.

Early-morning traffic congestion along the interstate bumped and jerked on its snarled crawl into the downtown area. The ex-cop con wondered how many nine-to-fivers were right then making their way to the Masters building to keep the empire growing, unaware they slaved for a liar and a cheat, alcoholic and sometime cocaine binger who lusted for black hookers. Their tycoon hero, church-going, God-fearing man of the people who said all the right things and always got what he wanted was as racist as any white-sheeted Klansman Shyrock had ever seen. Funny, he thought, how a man with money and power *could* fool all the people all of the time. Well, almost all of the people, at least the ones who deserved to be snowed and fleeced the worst. Like all those liberals with their naive and silly ideas about how we should all just get along.

Laughing out loud, Shyrock recalled how he had neglected to mention a couple of details when he'd seen Masters the previous night. First he'd had no intention of flying straight back to Wyoming, even though he knew trouble was coming west, right on the tails of his troops linking up in Chicago and Denver. He should be at the compound, calling the shots. But the trouble would still be there, waiting, when he flew back, later in the morning. Right now he needed to drive home a message.

The second item Masters was unaware of was Shyrock had left two of his top and trusted soldiers in the Ritz Carlton, put them up in a suite that ran two grand a night. Of course, he'd send the bill to Masters. But two grand wasn't going to cut it. Shyrock needed the two million and he was going to get it, tonight or tomorrow morning at the latest.

Or Michaelson and Travers were going to start showing up wherever Masters went on his campaign trail. If Masters didn't come through, he would be getting more bar tabs, more phone calls, enough headaches and stress coming at him from shadows in every direction, it would push him over the edge. Hell, Shyrock could see the guy crack, go on a week-long bender that would land him in a rehab clinic. Career ruined, he'd be another public spectacle of an American icon, sniveling before the cameras, telling all he'd disappointed how sorry he was, how this was a time of healing, for understanding and forgiveness.

Cradling the cellular phone, Shyrock turned the radio up a little, listening.

The caller said, "Mornin' Mr. Braun, Mr. Masters."

Braun was curt with the woman who started to ramble about her situation, a black mother of four who wanted to get off welfare, she was looking for a job but she had children to feed, no man. Braun nearly demanded the woman to ask Mr. Masters her question. Shyrock could only imagine what Masters really thought about a black woman on welfare.

When the woman didn't get right to the question, Braun sounded a little huffy.

Masters handled Braun's indignation with a gentle brush-off and told the woman he was there, with her, anxious to know her point of view, always the one willing to learn from others, ma'am. Shyrock heard himself growl about the stupidity and naïveté of the average citizen. Couldn't anybody out there spot a con man anymore, besides a cop and the bad guys?

The woman told Masters he was a rich and powerful man in a society she felt cut off from, why should he care about someone in her situation? All the money he wanted to dump into law enforcement, what about the average citizen, decent schools where children could get a good education and have the chance to make something of themselves? Jobs for people like herself who were struggling to survive, and who weren't on crack, abusing welfare dollars, but who were merely concerned about the future of their children? Caught in tough situations, often through no real fault of their own, they weren't looking for a handout, but for some hope they could be part of the American dream. And could he define the American dream, because she was having a hard time seeing it.

There it was, Shyrock thought, the blame game, the abuse excuse. But from what he heard in the caller's voice, Shyrock begrudged the woman her due character. There was no defensive attitude, rife with resentment, that entitlement "gimme" business behind the words. Just a straight and solid concerned mother, trying to get through the day. One exception in a million, of course, Shyrock decided, then wondered where the hell the old man or fathers were. He already suspected the worst. Out there, drinking, doping or carousing, bringing more welfare kids, soon-to-be gangbangers, into the world. There was a solution to all that, lady.

Hope through Deliverance.

And change was coming, to be sure. A year from now, two tops, Shyrock figured he could give the woman a choice for a better tomorrow. His maid or his whore. Either way, those kids she wanted to feed and educate so bad would be initiated, all right, into the American dream.

Masters didn't give a damn about this woman or anything other than his next drink, next million, more power, Shyrock knew. But that smooth Texas drawl he heard was tinged with just the right amount of compassion.

"Ma'am, the fact is I do care. That's part of what's wrong with not only our state but the country today. People turn away too quick from those who genuinely need help. Help is here, and my track record proves I'm more than willing to give it. My whole point has been we need to get back to the family, start the help within the community, making strong again the basic structure of home, school and church, so our children can grow up in a stable environment with two parents.''

That was the thing about Masters, Shyrock thought, listening to the guy pour it on the woman. No real specifics, but feed them what they thought they wanted to hear. Everyone wanted to hear about hope, the promise of a brighter tomorrow, especially where children and the so-called disenfranchised were concerned. It certainly helped the Masters campaign he had at least a billion to throw away on this drive for the governorship. Money was going to buy the guy the mansion. Politics as usual in America, Shyrock decided, where the one with the most money won.

After Masters spoke at length about his agenda for getting back to basics, defined the American dream in general terms, the woman thanked the man for giving her the time to hear her out. It sounded to Shyrock like Masters had won over at least one minority vote.

Another call, this time a guy dripping with schmooze, ingratiating himself all over the airwaves. The caller loved Milt Braun, said Roger Masters was the greatest Texan, hell, the greatest American since Sam Houston.

Finally Shyrock got lucky.

''Yes, you're on the Milt Braun show. What's your question for Roger Masters?''

Shyrock went for the good-old-boy angle. ''Well, hey, how you doin', Milt?''

''Just fine, sir. Your question, please?''

''Just wanted to say, Milt, love your show, listen every morning. Just bought your book. Man, do you know the deal, or what?''

''Thank you, sir. Your question?''

''Well, it's not really a question, Milt. Just wanted

to say hi to Roger. Maybe he recognizes my voice, maybe not. Roger, we used to do some hunting up in Wyoming. I was in town, leaving this morning. Through I'd take this chance to tell you I wish you the best in your run for governor.''

Silence on the other end. Shyrock smiled. He could almost feel the freeze go through Masters over the airwaves.

''Uh, you'll have to pardon me, sir. I can't say I recognize you. Say Wyoming, we did some hunting?''

''What's your name, sir?'' Braun asked.

Shyrock detected the note of fear in Masters's voice, his boy trying to play it off, big shot with old buddies suddenly crawling out of the holes.

''Name? Why, the name is J. T. Deliverance. That's right. Deliverance, just like the Burt movie, you know, where old Ned is made to—''

''Uh, yes, sir,'' Braun interrupted with a nervous chuckle. ''Know the movie, we got the picture. You're an old buddy who just wanted to call and say hello to the next governor of this great state. No questions?''

He was ready to cut him off, Shyrock knew, condescension in the voice. What he wouldn't give for two minutes alone with Braun, show him the hard facts of life.

''Well, I'm leaving town this morning, headin' back to Wyoming. Just want to say, Roger, keep up the good work. You're exactly what we need in the governor's mansion. Hey, before you cut me off, Milt, I want to tell Roger I know a couple mutual hunting buddies of ours from Wyoming are going to be in Houston for a few days. When you see them, Roger,

I'm sure you'll remember them. Hell, they told me they'd like to buy you a few rounds, catch up on old times. Sound all right to you?''

"Well, if I see them," Masters said, forcing a good-natured chuckle, one of the boys now, "I might recognize them. Tell them the drinks are on me. It's the least I can do for some old hunting buddies."

"Hey, that sounds nice, Roger. Maybe someday soon I can catch up to you, talk about that grizzly you downed. Man, that was a sweet shot, seemed like a quarter mile out, you dropped that—"

"Well, thank you, sir, for calling. Candidate Masters always appreciates the support," Braun cut in.

The line went dead.

A snub from the fat man, but Shyrock's face was lit up by a smile he felt glowing, straight from the heart. Message received.

He pulled out into traffic, confident about the future.

THEY HAD BEEN WAITING thirty minutes for Molanski to return. The rig was parked just beyond an industrial park in Calumet City, east of 94. Downtown Chicago was maybe a short twenty-minute drive north, according to the trucker, depending on traffic.

Smoking, Stanton was waiting with the trucker. They stood on the driver's side of the cab, shoes locked in mud and other chemical slime. If the trucker was nervous, then Stanton was ready to jump out of his skin with paranoia and agitation.

The sun was well beyond the noonday point in a cloudless blue sky, but the cold air was choked with the stench of chemicals and other pollutants belching from nearby smokestacks. Time was killing them,

Stanton thought. So far so good, but how long could their luck hold out? Belasko was still out there. And unlike what Molanski had said, the man wasn't a pain in the ass; he was death in human skin. Stanton could feel the guy breathing fire down his neck. Or about to.

Whatever was ahead, Stanton gained some confidence that their numbers would be beefed up at any rate. One cell, the combined Miami and New Orleans crews, the other from St. Louis and Kansas City. But how many men altogether? If Philly was the second-largest force, then he suspected those two linkup cells didn't number more than ten troops each. Then there was this drug business, a major three-hundred-brick deal with some cutthroat Colombians, guys known to murder entire families, down to infants, at the mere hint of a perceived problem. However Molanski and the Chicago crew were going to play that out...well, it was damn risky.

Stanton paced around the trucker. He had been the only one let out while Molanski went to find a phone, put in the call for the Chicago boys to come and round them up. There was no point in making the trucker any more frightened than he was, seeing all that hardware, wielded by a bunch of guys who clearly looked more like cold-blooded killers than cops. Stanton suspected the trucker already knew as much. Greed, though, had him by the shorts, made him risk it all. Greed was going to get him killed.

Stanton checked his watch. It was well into the afternoon. It had been a long, nerve-racking haul to Illinois in the dark, chilly, fish-stinking confines of the trailer. More waiting, more fear and paranoia. Stanton felt himself cracking from the strain and told himself to tighten up. Molanski was holding hard, and he damn sure expected the same from everybody else. The only difference was Molanski hadn't stared into Belasko's graveyard eyes of doom.

The trucker was chain-smoking, looking in the direction of the store and warehouses behind which Molanski had disappeared.

"Where the hell is he? I don't like this. Why don't you just pay me and you guys can be on your way?"

The trucker's impatience was edging toward anger.

"He'll be back, my friend. Relax. Ask the big man about that bonus when you see him, think about that while you're chewing on your nerves." Show the trucker a reassuring smile, keeping it light. "I'm sure he'll be happy to give it to you."

A few more tense minutes dragged by, then Stanton saw the big man rolling toward them.

"About time," the trucker grumbled, tossing his smoke away.

"You pay him yet?" Molanski growled, closing on the trucker.

Stanton listened to the crank and grind of machinery in the distance. Cover noise.

"Not yet. Was going to leave the honor to you. Everything all right?"

"On the way. Any minute. Get the others out here," Molanski ordered.

Stanton turned away, walking down the side of the rig. A moment later, he heard the trucker demand his money, plus a little extra for his time and trouble. Then there were two peals of .357 Magnum thunder. Bonus plan delivered, as promised. All Stanton had to do now was go pluck his ten grand off the body.

IT WAS APPROXIMATELY 340 miles from Cleveland to Chicago. Either way, it had been a grueling seven-hour haul from Cleveland, due in large part to traffic getting out of that town. During the run, Bolan and Daly had switched off with wheel duty. Each man had taken his turn catching a quick catnap while the endless stretch of Ohio then Indiana countryside rolled by on I-80.

Fifty miles from Chicago, Bolan had mapped out their course, drawn in their route from safehouse to safehouse. With three possible target sites, Bolan opted for the one closest off the drive north up I-94 for the heart of downtown Chicago. It appeared all three safehouses were spread around the South Side of the Windy City.

Bolan found it somewhat ironic that a group of racist killers kept holing up in black sections of each city. Then again, the savages of Deliverance had the look and bearing of cops, since a good number of them were, in fact, former lawmen. Most likely the enemy figured they would be held in suspicion by the largely black neighborhoods, but left alone since they looked like the law.

Though he was familiar with Chicago, America's third-largest city, it was still tough going and hard tracking for Bolan. The metropolis was choked with suburbs that sprawled more than sixty-two miles along the banks of Lake Michigan. It was a town crammed with bustling neighborhoods, each with its own ethnic enclave. With the Windy City claiming O'Hare International as one of the busiest airports on earth, where the world's tallest skyscraper, the Sears Tower, now loomed north in Bolan's sight, it was understandable, though agonizing, that traffic congestion and sprawling neighborhoods would slow the hunt.

In a way, the Executioner decided, the stop here fit, coffin tight.

And it was all reaching critical mass. After all, Chicago was a town infamous for the St. Valentine's Day Massacre, its crooked cops, its gangsters like Dillinger and Capone, long since dead and gone, but who were a mirror image of the former badge-wielding killers and thugs of Deliverance. The more something changes, Bolan thought, then began giving Daly directions to the first target site.

Somewhere off South Jefferson, they found the address of the apartment complex.

"How do you want to play it?" Daly asked.

Bolan gave the street a hard search, saw the suspicious and hostile groups of young black men up and down the street. An unmarked Crown Victoria was undoubtedly the universal neon sign—Cop.

The Executioner put a grim eye on Daly. "Right through the front door. Just like Cleveland."

He took two frag grenades, handing one to Daly. With all the eyewitnesses on the street, Bolan opted against any hardware that would be visible. He told Daly their side arms would have to do.

Make it count.

The Executioner and his ally disgorged from the vehicle.

CHAPTER SIXTEEN

No call this time to rattle the enemy, just shake the hardmen from their cage. This hit would be through the front door again, with the Executioner the first one through as before, leading the two-man death force. One high, one low, weapons blazing.

Only something felt wrong as soon as Bolan made the door of the targeted apartment unit.

Right away, he had a bad feeling about what was beyond the door when he heard the utter silence inside from beyond his position. They were either gone, or they were waiting with automatic weapons aimed at the door.

Bolan gave Daly a glance and a nod. For a second, Bolan was leery about something he spotted in Daly's eyes. Was it a wild, suicidal impulse he glimpsed? Reckless abandon? Bolan let it ride, putting his mind to the task.

The mammoth Desert Eagle drawn, the soldier gave the hall a look, both ways. He heard nothing, except the sound of a child crying from somewhere down the hall, the angry voice of a man yelling for someone—maybe the kid—to shut up. A second later, as he reared back and drove a thunderous kick into the door, splintering rotted wood like matchsticks, he found his first suspicion confirmed.

Bursting inside, low and ready just the same, Bolan found the living room bare. A quick search of the bedrooms, and he discovered the same thing. Absolutely nothing, except a lone fax machine. The enemy had abandoned its lair.

Daly didn't look so convinced to Bolan.

The soldier watched as the ex-cop seemed ready to fire his weapon if even a cockroach skittered across the naked floor. There was a strange glow in the man's eyes that Bolan had seen growing more intense during the drive to Chicago. It was crystal clear to Bolan that Daly was feeling the strain of his vengeance, hungrier than ever to kill or be killed. In short, the man was out of control.

Bolan holstered the Desert Eagle as Daly swept in silent rage through the rooms again. Sweat coursed down the man's bruised and scratched face, his lips mouthing a stream of silent curses as he ripped open closet doors, checked under the beds. Bolan followed the man with caution. Watching this dangerous spectacle, he saw Daly was out there in his own world.

The Executioner knew all about the post trauma syndrome other Vietnam veterans often talked about. He had never lapsed into flashbacks himself, going through the readjustment period when returning to the States. He'd never had time to settle back into normal civilian life. The Mafia had seen to that.

Bolan risked it, grabbing Daly and pinning him to the wall. "Daly?" He stared into eyes he wasn't sure recognized him. "Daly, listen to me. They're not here. Get yourself under control or I'm cutting you loose. You hear me?" The light of insanity dimmed some in Daly's eyes, the gun lowering in Daly's trembling hand. Bolan listened to the man's labored breathing for long moments. "Pull yourself together, Daly."

"I...I'm...all right, I'm okay now. Forget...forget this happened, Belasko."

"I'm afraid I can't do that. If I see you're not in control, you're gone. We understand each other?"

Daly nodded. "Yeah."

"Hey, what the hell is going on here?"

The Desert Eagle was out in an eye blink. Bolan whirled toward the source of the outraged voice, saw Daly's Para-Ordnance jutting beyond the corner of his eye. The skinny guy in the overcoat threw up his hands, looked set to topple from pure terror.

"Hey, hey, come on," the guy sputtered. "I'm just the owner of this building."

Bolan noted the bulge beneath the man's coat. Swiftly he rolled up on the guy, who was in his early fifties, bald on top with long tufts of iron gray locks flowing down the sides. Bolan saw the black dots of hair implants on his scalp, glimpsed the gold Rolex watch, wrist and neck jewelry that looked 14K, the Italian loafers. This was one slumlord who was living fat and pretty. One look at the utter disrepair and neglect of the building, and Bolan suspected this guy was cutting all kinds of corners to stretch the rent dollars of his tenants. The soldier wasn't about to altogether bet, though, this guy was the building's owner.

Desert Eagle in the guy's face, Bolan reached inside the man's coat and pulled out a Charter Arms .357 Magnum pistol. He tucked the weapon in his waistband.

"Who are you?" Bolan demanded, hauling the guy away from the door, pinning him to the wall.

"I told you, I'm the landlord."

"Try again."

"I'm telling you the truth, I swear. Maybe I should be asking you who are, kicking in my door, armed to the damn teeth."

"I'm with the Justice Department."

"And I'm the President."

Bolan shoved his ID in the slumlord's face.

"Yeah, well, they had badges, too. But something tells me they weren't any cops."

"The men who were living here?"

"That's right. I came down to throw their asses out, cops or not. Can you get that cannon out of my face?" When Bolan didn't move the Desert Eagle, the man said, "Look, you don't believe I say who I am, you can check it."

Bolan believed the slumlord was exactly who he said he was. The guy was too scared to lie, and Bolan smelled the greed, the apathy toward his tenants and the human race at large, all over him.

"What's the piece for?" Daly asked. "Make sure you get the rent?"

"And to keep it, pal. You take a good look at this neighborhood. Need I say more?" When Bolan put his Desert Eagle away, the slumlord's relief turned quickly to bigoted anger. "I hate coming here to this side of town, but sometimes I have to. These blacks down here are all either cracked out or carryin' serious firepower themselves. Sometimes I have to make a house call, make sure I get my rent."

"Even if you need to pull out a little persuasion?" Bolan said.

"Hey, you walk in my shoes for one day, you see the shit I got to put up with from these people, you wouldn't be standing there, all high and mighty."

Bolan took one look around the apartment: cracked ceilings, peeling paint; cockroaches crawling everywhere; holes in the base of walls where rodents had probably gnawed through, exposed frayed electrical wiring. The entire building was a firetrap.

"Oh, I can see your tenants," Bolan said, an icy edge in his voice, "wouldn't dream of trading all this for a condo up Lake Shore Drive." A pause, then Bolan asked, "How long were they here?"

"Four months. They're two months behind on rent. I came over last week to tell them to pay the sixteen hundred they owe. Swore up and down they would this week. Figure they're white, they'd come through on their word."

"How many?" Bolan growled.

"Four. I didn't like them right away, and should've known better."

"But they were the right color," Bolan said.

"Hey, look, I'm being straight with you. I don't give a damn what you think of me. I'll tell you this, too. From the door you kicked in, I saw enough guns to field a small army. They started throwing badges in my face, told me to mind my own business. I know cops, and they weren't cops. Made a lot of my tenants nervous, having a bunch of mean-looking white guys living here."

"Well, I'm sure your tenants will breathe easier now they're gone and you're back in charge," Bolan told the guy, then nodded at Daly for them to go.

"Hey, what about my door? What about the rent

they owe me? I'm out some serious dough here. What about my gun?''

Bolan stopped and put a cold eye on the man. He could only imagine the abuse and bigotry the tenants here suffered at the hands of this man. Despite what this human cockroach said, Bolan knew not everyone in this building was cracked out, involved in criminal activity. Fully aware nothing in life was ever that clearly confined to broad brushstrokes, the soldier strongly suspected a lot of these tenants were just tough-luck people. Citizens trying to survive another day in the desperate hell of poverty, working mothers and fathers worried about their small children dodging bullets from a drive-by.

Bolan was looking at another shade of Deliverance in the slumlord. Put everyone in the same box of contempt or hatred, at worst, and men who lived in fear could rationalize the wrong in their hearts.

''Life's tough all over,'' the Executioner said. ''If I make a few calls and get the right people down here, you might find yourself in a new home. Right here with your tenants. Have a nice day.''

Bolan left the slumlord muttering to himself. Some things could never be made right.

But there was a wrong in the Windy City that the Executioner could stomp out. Safehouse number two was next on the hit list. Next time around, he intended to score, and heavy.

SHYROCK GOT UP from the big oak desk. It was good to be back among the troops at the compound.

Striding past the large American flag draped from the wall, he went to the window, inspected the base. Beyond his command center, he saw Milan putting

the young recruits through PT. North of the obstacle
course, there was the war-planning and rec lodge,
complete with sauna rooms, an exercise facility and
bar. A low-level wood structure housed the main
troops who manned the compound, while another
small structure served as the munitions and fuel depot.
A large plain to the south had been turned into an
airfield. The building where their young warriors were
bivouacked was well outside the perimeter of the
base. Shyrock wanted their young minds untainted by
any harsh language from some of his redneck wingers
who might think they could impress or intimidate the
young men with hate-filled or tough-guy talk. Shyrock didn't want any of his young and future law-
enforcement officers thinking everything here wasn't
quite as it seemed—at least not until he was ready to
let them know personally what he expected from
them. Milan had informed him they had some good
ones. Young and tough, white and angry and disillusioned, they were ready and willing to be trained,
groomed with the Deliverance philosophy, then
placed in various police academies across the country.

Situated west of the foothills of the Laramie Mountains, the stronghold was isolated in the rugged wilderness of the nation's least-populated state. Satellite
dishes were tucked near the edges of the thick woods
that ringed the compound. Dozens of vehicles were
hidden from view down a trail that led to the south
edge. Even though the closest major city, Laramie,
was a good hundred miles south, Shyrock never felt
secure about the setup. Orders were for none of the
men to patrol the compound with automatic weapons
in plain sight. He never knew when some hunters
from the city might traipse through in search of big-

horn sheep, disregarding all Private Property, No Trespassing signs around the outskirts of his three-thousand-acre compound.

He often considered laying booby traps down the trails, around the perimeter. But he risked one of the wingers going on a binge, stumbling off into the night, drunk, and getting his leg snapped in two by a bear trap or blown up the mountainside by a Claymore mine. More casualties he didn't need, could much less afford. The fax messages and the tip he'd gotten from his FBI source in New York indicated there was a strong possibility the compound was going to be found eventually, and hit. Shyrock wasn't ready to leave Wyoming yet. Not until he got the two million from Masters.

He shot an angry look back at his desk, silently urging the phone to ring. It was well into the afternoon. Banks would have already closed in Houston. Why the hell hadn't the guy called?

Shyrock stepped outside into brisk mountain air, walked down the stoop, his snakeskin boots crunching softly into the thin crust of snow. He called to Milan, "Bob, why don't you give them a lunch break, then come back. Some things we need to talk about."

Milan said to give him twenty minutes, and Shyrock went back into the command post. He was thinking ahead. If they were going to be hit, he would need every available gun. If government agents were going to raid the compound, there would be shooting, and Shyrock intended to win any firefight between his people and anything Uncle Sam threw at them. There was no other way. Too much was at stake. Too much time, trouble and blood had been spilled to not see his master plan through to its righteous conclusion.

Once he launched an all-out war against the lower elements of society, he was certain all good white people everywhere would finally see that it was indeed "us" and "them." It would be a call to arms for the white race that could change American society forever, and certainly for the better.

But there were problems back east that had arisen out of nowhere. Whoever these guys were, hounding his people back east and inflicting casualties like his men were cherries fresh on the cell block, they were good, determined and they were taking no prisoners. His hunch was that a major engagement was just ahead.

Shyrock intended to deal with it, whatever it took. It was good to know that the Seattle and Portland crews were back on base. Ten men, former law and ex-military, well trained, backed by front line experience and fortified with steely determination that white was right, they had just rolled in from their West Coast assignments.

It was tough to lose Macklin down in L.A., but Los Angeles had only been a three-man cell. War always meant casualties, the cost of winning more often than not measured in the number of lives lost. Macklin and his guys had gone down in the line of duty, even if they'd killed a few brother officers. All along Shyrock had expected some of the men in blue on the other side to go down if they cornered his people. He could only hope the ones in uniform his men took out were minorities the department was letting on the force at an alarming rate all over the country.

Seated behind his desk, he opened a drawer and pulled out a large manila envelope. It had been a long time since he'd seen what was inside, but he opened the envelope, started looking at the dozens of eight-by-ten pictures. There, in close-up color, he saw the next governor of Texas in a seedy hotel room in downtown Chicago. At least a dozen photos caught the people's choice for governor rocking up in his birthday suit.

It had been a sweet setup, planned from the very first moment he'd met Masters in the bar, guy boo-hooing about his violated daughter and offering a hundred thousand to a perfect stranger to kill the rapists. Once Shyrock made positive ID on Masters, he rounded up a few of his hooker friends from the old days. One did the real dirty work on Masters, while the other hid in a special compartment behind the wall, clicking away with her camera. Nice shots all, clearly Masters—the tycoon, sitting on the bed with his hooker, lips locked on the crack pipe. At least a dozen other shots could possibly find their way into the hands of Mrs. Masters. If that happened, the good wife would undoubtedly land herself a huge divorce settlement. That alone might prove interesting, seeing if the lady really would stand by her man.

Of course, Shyrock didn't want to resort to extortion. Without the tycoon, Deliverance would have been nothing more than a bunch of angry ex-cops and vets sitting on barstools somewhere, talking about how they were going to do something when they sobered up. The Masters fortune had launched the organization. Masters knew it, but now that he was going respectable he suddenly seemed to have forgotten who really loved and cared about him.

And Shyrock had plans for the future. Once Masters was in the governor's mansion, Shyrock could move the operation to Texas. He wanted to be close to that kind of power, knew Masters could provide a new home base, throw more money around. Maybe even some kind of compound, out in the Texas hills, burrowed deep in the earth. Not only that, but the Border Patrol could use some extra help keeping the greasers in Mexico where they belonged—floating facedown across the Rio Grande with a bullet in the face.

The phone suddenly rang. The man had to have ESP, Shyrock thought, smiling. He picked up the phone, said, ''Yeah.''

''What the hell was the idea with the crazy stunt you pulled this morning?''

''Sounds like I got your full attention.''

''It was an asshole move.''

''Hey, relax. Maybe I meant what I told you and Milt. Just a caller out there in the heartland, a small voice of one of your voters, wanting to pump you up with a job well done.''

''Cut the crap. We both know why you did it. So, what do you have? A couple of goons you left behind, ready to turn up in my office or at my home, go on the muscle?''

''Nothing so blunt. I told you the story. Let's get down to business. Did you get it?''

There was hesitation on the other end, and Shyrock felt his blood boil.

''I, uh, I managed to get one quarter.''

''Five hundred thousand's not going to make it.''

''I told you this wasn't going to be so easy. A man like me, it's going to draw attention, walking out of my bank with two million. Plus I've got to bury that amount of cash off the books. People don't understand about vast sums of wealth. It's tied up in a paper trail of—"

"Stop whining. Have your bookkeepers move some numbers. It went toward your campaign."

"You make it sound so easy, but it isn't."

"You're fucking with me, Roger."

"Goddamn it, no names."

"I don't give a shit if this line's secure or not. I've got major problems. The Feds know. I may need to bail, and it may not be pretty if I end up facing the kind of problem I suspect is headed my way. I want the rest of that money in two days from when I hang up the phone. Don't make me send some pictures of your glory days in Chicago to the local Houston newspapers."

There was shock on the other end. "What did you say?"

"I've got pictures that could have the Missus and some slick lawyers clean out your fortune. I don't think I need to go into specifics."

"You bastard."

"Hey, I was merely protecting the future. We already discussed these things. I hate having to repeat myself. Tell you what. If you get the rest of the money together, we'll shake hands and you can put the torch to the pics yourself. Negatives, the whole sordid mess. I understand your shock and anger, but I was trying to work this out between us like gentlemen."

"I can have what I got flown up to you tonight."

"Skeleton crew, four men altogether you would trust with your daughter's life. They'll be staying with me. You get the rest, call. We'll arrange something where I fly back with your men to pick it up."

"I don't see where I have a choice."

"You never did. You sold yourself to the cause the first day we met. By the way, did you get your endorsement from Senator—"

When he heard Masters slam the phone down on the other end, Shyrock laughed and hung up. He took one last look at the pictures, chuckling. The good times always cost a heavy price, and often far beyond mere money. Well, the tab had come due. Shyrock had the billionaire right where he wanted him.

He was tucking the photos back in the envelope, away in the drawer, when Milan entered the command post. Standing, Shyrock went to the wet bar, built them both a Scotch whiskey and soda. Shyrock took his seat behind his desk while Milan settled his big frame in a leather recliner. Working on his drink and a cigarette, Shyrock got Milan up to speed on the Masters situation.

"That kind of money will go a long way in helping our cause," Milan commented.

Shyrock took a stack of fax sheets, pushed them toward Milan. "Those are the numbers from each of our cells who have been out there the last year, fighting the good fight."

"I'm impressed. Fifty-five male typicals in New York alone." He reeled off the numbers from the other cities, but Shyrock knew the body count by heart. "I like it, I like it a lot. Looks like it's all paying off. What I'm seeing here...well, let's just say we saved the courts a whole lot of trouble. Most of these assholes would have been out on parole, three, four years, rehabilitated and back at it. World's a far better place without these scumbags in it."

"The best is yet to come, Bob. I haven't told you

or anybody yet the details about my master plan. I'll brief you quickly before our people from back east get here. That two million is going to buy me three helicopter gunships and other heavy artillery. Such as bazookas, C-4, enough firepower to take and hold down an entire city. Connections my watch commander from Philly has from his Vietnam days. In life, it's all who you know anymore.''

"Gunships?"

"What I'll need are about twelve men who are prepared to sacrifice their lives for something that is going to happen in New York City, next month.''

Milan's eyes lit up. "You mean the next Million Man March the Nation of Islam has whined so much to set up?''

"Right. Where they plan to march right to the UN. Bad enough the country had to hear all those lies and all that 'woe is us' sniveling from Washington last time, but now they want to cry to the whole world, and the UN has agreed to let them stage this nonsense. What I'm saying is that my plan is set to go. I've got a big freighter where I can stow the gunships, on deck, hidden, of course, to get them up the East River. All I need is the money to nail the deal down.''

Milan whistled. "Can you imagine that? What's the plan? Three gunships swoop down on the march?''

"Unload everything they've got. Hopefully they'll even blow up half the UN building.''

"Outstanding. Think I'll have another drink.''

"There's more. I've got a list of major Jewish and black leaders across the country I've targeted for cleansing. I've also outlined a plan to hit the main NAACP headquarters with enough C-4 to make the

Oklahoma thing look like a firecracker going off. More to come on that. Want to wait until we get a couple of situations here behind us. But what I see is change coming, Bob, the kind of change that will take this country back. When our warriors hit that march, naturally those people will see it as some sort of government conspiracy. I see full-scale riots in every major city across the country erupting. I see martial law declared. I see every stand-up white man taking up arms and shooting on sight anything that isn't white." Shyrock laughed, lifting his glass. "What can I tell you? I have a dream."

They drank and smoked, chuckled, feeling good about the future. Then Shyrock turned serious.

"Bob, you know we've got some problems headed our way. I can't be sure, but we might get hit by the government. I want the compound on full alert, which brings me to what I really wanted to discuss with you. How are the kids doing?"

"Looks promising. No slackers, not the first indication we've got any deadwood."

"Can you show them the basics of handling an M-16? Do it this afternoon?"

Milan stared at Shyrock with a somber expression. "You're not thinking of putting those kids up against a force of heavily armed and well-trained government agents, are you?"

"I don't want to, but just in case, I need to be ready. Tell them as much as you think they need to know, but let them know they may have to soon fire on live targets."

"And if they balk?"

"Convince them it's for their own good."

"And if I can't convince them?"

"Then they aren't any use to us. They have no place in the future of our organization. They have no right to be part of the new America. Just make sure you bury the bodies someplace they won't be found."

CHAPTER SEVENTEEN

Molanski led Stanton and their force into the living room of the South Side Chicago apartment.

It would be the understatement of the century, Molanski thought, to say things weren't going well. But he could feel the troops about to turn the corner. Hope, Molanski told himself, keep it pumping.

They had left behind a trail of dead bodies and burning wreckage, from New York to Philly to Chicago. And this Belasko pain in the ass was still out there. Something warned Molanski they hadn't seen the last of that guy. It was something he had already discussed with his Chicago contact. And Chicago wasn't happy about the grim possibility of a human hurricane blowing in from the east, ready to burn them down, piss all over their big coke parade.

The pickup at Calumet had been punctual, the transfer of men, hardware and spoils of past victories had gone off without a hitch. The problem was filling in Ross Janson, Chicago's watch commander, and that had eaten up time. It was aggravating—no, it was nerve-racking, maybe even humiliating—having to explain the situation back east, reassuring the stocky, dark-haired ex-vice cop everything was under control. And not getting too far in convincing Janson, for that matter. The man had some serious doubts about the Philly and New York crews. Molanski could sympathize. But, hey, they were all in this together, right? Janson's answer had been a little too long in coming. "We'll see what we see," Janson had said.

Molanski had already been forced to lay the bad news on Shyrock, calling the man from the gas station near the industrial park, catching the organization's commander on his private jet while he was en route back to the Wyoming base. The big Pole was getting tired of explaining other people's screwups. Now he was part of the problem, judging everyone's tones and looks, all the hardball questions, slanted with enough accusation to boil his blood. Well, there would be a solution, and Molanski intended to nip any future looming fiascos in the bud, prove his mettle. If another firestorm was coming, he would stand tall and hold his ground.

He watched Stanton give the Chicago crew a measuring. Looking as if he felt he was a leper, standing in nervous silence in the middle of the room, Stanton was figuring the numbers, Molanski knew. He counted eight guns in the Chicago cell himself. The other two linkup crews had already rolled into the Windy City the previous night, and Janson had put them up in the third safehouse with two more of his guys. He figured that altogether they were beefed up to over forty guns.

Later, according to Janson, they would all rendezvous down by the south branch of the Chicago River, somewhere north of the Stockyard District. Designated hit squads would be within stalking distance of where the deal was set to go down. It sounded as if Janson had a solid plan worked out, but Molanski needed to hear more. The problem was that it looked like Janson was taking his time before divulging any more firm details, wondering, maybe, what the hell had just rolled into town, his own people, bringing trouble to his doorstep like this.

Chicago's fear and paranoia was understandable, given the current crisis. A deal this big was something to protect, and they couldn't just walk away from it now, no matter what.

Janson had already explained this was something he had arranged on his own. It was going to be a major coup. The man was jumping at the chance to take all that flake back to Shyrock, who was a former Chicago cop himself, and a personal pal of Janson's. Not only that, but Janson was looking forward to taking out a bunch of top-level narcotics traffickers. Colombian drug dealers, Janson had said, during the drive up from Calumet, were a scourge on America, a twentieth-century plague. This would be a two-pronged victory for Deliverance. Janson said he saw himself as something of a modern-day Robin Hood. Hell, they were going to put the coke to good use, weren't they? Sell it back, buy weapons, finance the Deliverance crusade well into the next century with this score.

Three hundred kilos. With that much dope, the Colombians would go down to the last man to save it. Molanski figured fifteen to twenty thousand a key, and was putting the math together when Janson interrupted his arithmetic.

"Yeah, this is a multi-million-dollar deal, so don't burn a gasket adding the numbers," Janson told Molanski, his voice hard, but a smile on his lips. "I'm getting wholesale price on this, and it comes out to twelve grand a brick. We chop and step, well, I can figure out the millions we can turn on this once we unload it on some distributors out west I know. After we score here, the organization is set for years to come. More hardware, more dirty or border-line cops in place we can buy into our pockets...I think you can understand the importance of this.

"Why don't your men gather around? I'll go over this one time, and I don't need to tell you this needs to be done tight and by the numbers." He nodded toward three duffel bags in the corner of the room. "There's $250,000 in cash in one bag. I'll show the Colombian, a guy named Salvadore, the money. That's just about every last dollar myself and every man in our cell has earned over the years, on and off the force. It's strictly show money, soften him up for the knockout punch. Then I'll ask to see the stuff. I'll choose one brick at random, do a taste test. I don't need a test kit. I know quality stuff soon as it hits my nose, and I've been assured this stuff is uncut. Little pinch, and I'll be in the ozone. After that, I'll let Salvadore take a look at the other bags." Smiling, Janson told one of his men to open the other two bags.

Molanski watched as the man opened the bags to display wads of newspaper, cut to the size of dollar bills, held together by rubber bands. Janson was loosening up. At least Molanski knew they were in. He just needed their role defined. All that cocaine, he thought. It was going to be one sweet score for the good guys.

"You've certainly got a flare for the dramatic," Molanski acknowledged with an approving smile. "Let the Cali boys know they've been set up to burn, then it hits the fan, I assume. I like your style, Janson.''

"Well, I want you right there with me, big man, when it goes off in their faces."

"Before we start congratulating each other, I've got to tell you I have a couple of problems with this. First they'll make us as cops."

Janson was all confidence. "No, they won't. Most guys involved in major cocaine transactions look just like we do, outside your spaghetti-sucking guys in the Mob, of course. Businessmen brokering a deal to save their company, lawyers acting as middlemen for distribution networks Colombians have established with homegrown Yankees. Or cold-eyed, no-shit career criminals. So they'll check us for wires. I'll put on the slightly offended act, but this is business and we'll get down to it after the macho routine these guys love to front off so much. It's just part of the game. You guys know how to play it. Bullshit and lots of nerve. Now, I want everybody outside the warehouse in sync the second we set foot in there. I'll show you where to move in on the troops they'll have watching the perimeter. You better be there and through the door. Believe me, you'll know when it's started. I'll get to that drill in a minute. To fill you in a little more, I swung this deal through a major distributor here in Chicago, a big man who drives a white Jaguar and calls himself the Crusherman."

"Black guy?" Molanski growled.

"Yeah. Is that a problem?"

"You trust him?"

"Much as I do any black. He'll come through, trust me. Some of Chicago's finest have been helping the guy out, if you know what I mean. He arranged the deal, and I've met with Salvadore already. Sure, he ran a background check on me. I got a trucking business out Denver way. Couple of our guys are on the other end to confirm it. The smoke job will hold. These Cali guys are too hungry for a deal like this. Word is they're kind of hot right now, and they need to dump this load."

Molanski still didn't like the idea of all these new faces arriving on the scene. "This Crush guy have any idea who we really are?"

"Not a clue. He'll bring a few of his boys with him, you can be sure. Sweeten the body count of scumbags before we roll out of Chicago. That's how I'm looking at it. How about you?"

"We're with you."

Two of the Chicago guys were finished pouring whiskey for the troops. Cigarettes were fired up. Side arms showed when they all shed their jackets. Janson took a seat at the large table in the middle of the living room. The ex–Chicago vice cop's twin Auto-Ordnance Thompson M1911A-1s in .45ACP didn't escape a passing scrutiny from Molanski. Those big pieces were shoulder holstered, butt first, for a cross draw.

A map of Chicago was pushed in front of Molanski as he took his drink, thanked the crew-cut, bullet-headed guy he knew as Maulin. Stanton, he then saw, was suddenly by the window, checking the alley, the street. Molanski had left one of Stanton's men and one of his own troops with the four vehicles, loaners from Janson. Both Molanski and Stanton had stowed a lot of automatic weapons plus their war chests in the trunks of the loaners. If something looked wrong outside, Gurgin or Sampson were ordered to call up from the portable radios.

Molanski was unfamiliar with Chicago, but he knew the famous Loop that circled the downtown area. They were south of the Loop, the troops sitting with their new vehicles in a vacant lot beneath the El. In the distance, he caught the clanking thunder of the elevated train.

"If it'll make you feel better, I can send down one of my men to sit with your guys," Janson offered, looking at Stanton's battered face with some uncertainty. "Jack," he told a short blond man with tree-trunk legs and who toted a .44 Magnum pistol, "go on."

The man left the room. Stanton seemed relieved that one of the Chicago guys was going to help guard the store. Finally Stanton sat at the table as Janson killed his drink.

"All right," Janson began, "here's the rest of the story. First, you guys have silencers?"

Molanski nodded. The man wanted this deal bad, and Molanski intended to see they got it done, sewed up in Cali and Crusherman's blood. No screwups, no problems, and no shadows with rockets and automatic weapons on their back this time.

He was looking forward to proving his people were up to taking care of business in Chicago. One of the boys again, right back on top of the situation. He killed the whiskey, then got up to make himself another drink.

THE SHADOW that was Mack Bolan was en route to taking care of business himself—killing business.

The silenced Beretta 93-R in hand, Bolan crouched at the mouth of the alley, weighing the situation.

Lady Luck had seen fit to smile on the soldier the second time out. But he had never given up hope that Deliverance was still in Chicago.

Despite losing time in lockup back in Pennsylvania, he knew the enemy couldn't have gained that much ground, lead time in their flight across three states. Stanton and the others would have had to find some way out of Pennsylvania—other than staying on the turnpike in their vehicles—to get to Chicago, unchecked and unmolested, for the next linkup phase. How they had done it, Bolan didn't know.

But they had.

Evidence of Deliverance's arrival in Chicago from back east was less than a dozen yards away from him.

Maybe five minutes ago, Bolan had left Daly with the Crown Victoria, two blocks south, down Wells, near the Chicago River. Near the South Loop, Bolan had found the address of the second safehouse. When circling the block, he'd also spotted the tall redhead he'd busted up back at the Gold Shield. Another guy he thought he recognized from the garage in Philly was standing outside with the vehicles that were parked in a sprawling, trash-littered lot under the El.

The fact that Bolan found the enemy even still in Chicago warned him that something was in the works. Maybe a deal was being worked to beef up the hardware. These guys were former cops, many of whom were most likely also ex-military. They had connections to the right people who could land them a half-dozen rocket launchers, more automatic weapons, a crate of grenades. These men were dangerous, and they weren't stupid. What had been thrown at them so far—grenades and rockets—had decimated their numbers. Bolan suspected the enemy would be looking to even the odds somehow before moving on farther west.

The only way to find out was to ask the spindly redhead, and in no uncertain terms.

It was risky, moving across open ground, apartments and streets with evening traffic flowing in both directions. The rattling thunder of the elevated train would help muffle his stealthy approach from the rear. It was also a plus that night was quickly falling over the Windy City. Even still, a watching eye from the apartments, maybe a derelict popping up from one of the hulks of junked cars...

No other way but to get it done.

Bolan was moving out, shadowing for the cover of an abandoned Chevy, when he saw a blond guy with barrel legs come up on the left flank of the targets. He came from the direction of an apartment building, around the corner of a support pillar. Bolan didn't recognize the man. He had to be one of the Chicago boys. The Executioner decided to save him for his interrogation. If something was causing a delay in their flight out of town, then Bolan's strong hunch was that Blondie had the answers he needed.

The El rumbled over no-man's-land, and Bolan surged ahead.

The redhead was alerted to the sudden movement of the big shadow rushing his blind side.

They went for hardware, clawing inside their jackets.

One chug from Bolan's Beretta and he turned the redhead's expression of terror-filled recognition into a frozen death mask with a 9 mm slug between the eyes. Tracking on, he shattered the next guy's skull with whispering death.

Blondie almost cleared the .44 Magnum pistol from his jacket. He would have cannoned off a .44 round, but deadweight from the soldier's second victim toppled into him. The guy cursed, then he screamed when Bolan drilled a silent bullet through his hand. Magnum pistol flying, Blondie crumpled to his knees, clutching his mangled appendage.

With the barrel of the Beretta, Bolan cracked the guy in the temple, dropping him on his back. The guy looked up with pain and fear. The Executioner gave his surroundings a quick search and found his movements appeared to have been unobserved.

Bolan put the sound-suppressed muzzle between Blondie's eyes. "I'd bet your life that you used to be a cop in this town. I think we both know the score here, so we can skip the small talk." Defiance stared up at the Executioner. "Okay, you want to go the tough-guy route. Here's the deal. One chance. I want you to answer my questions in order."

"Why should I?" the guy snarled. "You're going to kill me anyway."

"Maybe not. It's your call. Here we go, listen good." Bolan asked his questions. The guy had to have figured where there was life there was hope. The soldier heard Stanton and the others were there in Chicago. A major drug deal with some Colombians was going down, along the South Branch of the Chicago River, somewhere off Archer Avenue. A gentle nudge of the Beretta, and the guy gave up the address of a warehouse that belonged to the Colombians. The deal was set to go ASAP.

Bolan had the picture. They were going to rip off

the Colombians. Bolan was further informed this was
no deal involving just a few kilos. Three hundred
bricks, Blondie told him, untouched by any dilutions
to stretch the weight. Deliverance could buy a lot of
guns, explosives on the street with that much poison
floating around, Bolan knew. Well, he could take out
both sides if he played his cards right.

"Now what?" the guy asked.

"Now I cuff you. You're going the distance with
me on this one." Bolan injected ice into his voice as
a sardonic grin ghosted his lips. "Later, when I dump
you off at a police station, you can maybe use the
'abuse excuse' on your lawyer."

Bolan was pulling back the Beretta and took his
eyes off the guy for just a heartbeat. It was long
enough for Blondie to make his move. Worse, it had
been an oversight for Bolan not to confiscate the discarded pistol.

It was a rare mistake that almost got the Executioner killed.

Before he knew it, a fist came out of nowhere,
smacking him in the side of the jaw. Toppling back,
Bolan glimpsed the Magnum pistol scooped up in
Blondie's hand, the barrel swinging his way. Only
lightning reflexes saved Bolan as he drilled one 9 mm
slug through the guy's skull.

An angry rush of air leaving his mouth, Bolan
stood. He holstered the Beretta and went to work,
putting the bodies upright in the Chevy Caprice.

At this point it didn't matter that he left a message.
Either way, the enemy was going to know something
was deadly wrong. But Bolan was riding out the gamble they wouldn't call off the deal with the Colombians.

Let the enemy be on high alert.

Bolan intended to sour their dream-of-a-lifetime coke deal.

Once the corpses were in position, Bolan closed the doors to the vehicle.

Deliverance would soon know Special Agent Belasko, a.k.a. the Executioner, had arrived in Chicago to further ruin the enemy's sick hopes and twisted dreams.

No doubt, Bolan was about to take the chill out of the Windy City with cleansing hellfire.

STANTON KNEW what they were faced with even before he opened the door and Gurgin's body toppled at his feet. His Glock was out, searching the abandoned lot, the street traffic. But he knew Belasko was gone, or they would have already been hit. Another blitzkrieg would have already scattered them in a million bloody pieces clear to Lake Michigan. Stanton suddenly felt as if he were trapped in a recurring nightmare from which he couldn't wake up.

If Molanski had been angry before about the Belasko situation, he now looked livid to Stanton as the rest of the New York and Philly cells gathered around the Chevy Caprice. Somehow Molanski kept the time bomb of his rage in check, giving the bodies inside a cold look.

Molanski steeled himself, sweeping the lot with his own searching gaze. Then three Crown Victorias rolled up behind them.

Stanton jumped at the sound of tires crunching over glass and other litter. In the next moment, he found himself amazed at how composed Janson kept himself when he discovered the slaughter.

But the look Stanton saw the man drilling into him, then Molanski, said it all. Nothing had changed, but everything was different.

"Leave them and the car," Janson growled. "It's clean, they can't trace it to us. Let's roll. Just keep your eyes peeled for this son of a bitch problem that followed you guys all the way from New York."

Car doors slammed, engines gunned. Stanton heard Molanski bark at him to shake a leg. It took an iron effort of will for Stanton to put his Glock away, take his eyes off the deep shadows of the alleys around the lot. Belasko was out there, somewhere, watching them, planning his next strike. Stanton could feel the bastard even if he couldn't see him.

Janson took a turn to yell, while putting some fury and judgment behind the two words. "Let's go!"

Stanton flinched. He knew he was going to have to make an accounting for this situation at some point. The only way to make it right was to blow Belasko away himself and take the guy's head back to Wyoming.

A trophy.

CHAPTER EIGHTEEN

Molanski now had more than a full plate of problems. To digest those problems meant choking to death— on his own blood. And the trouble had very little to do with the suspicion and hostility that greeted them when they walked into the warehouse.

Their relentless nightmare from back east had pinned them down in Chicago. It was no mystery how Belasko had picked up the scent. That damn Stanton had left behind the maps, the phone numbers to each cell. It wouldn't take much work for the Justice Department's computers to tap into confidential phone company files, pin down the exact locations of each cell. He intended to call Cleveland, just the same. If Cleveland didn't answer, then he knew their rearguard had bought it. If that was the case, then Denver was a wash. He would have to alert the Denver troops, order them to pull out, get to Wyoming ASAP.

Once this deal with the Colombians was nailed down, Molanski knew to be on full alert for Belasko.

Future trouble beyond this deal had to wait. At the moment, Molanski saw they had their hands full.

"Hey, what the hell is this? Who the fuck is the new face, man?"

Crusherman, Molanski saw, was barking at Janson,

his deep bass voice like rolling thunder. Molanski couldn't miss him. He figured the guy was at least seven feet tall, three hundred pounds, all of it bulging muscle. The street name fit. The black dealer was as wide as any of the dozens of huge crates strewed around the large warehouse. And he sure looked like he could lift one of the forklifts there, squeeze it to twisted scrap with his bare hands.

When Crusherman unfolded from his white Jaguar, his knee-length black leather coat fell open, revealing a 12-gauge pump shotgun. The barrel of the weapon had been sawed off, the shotgun hanging down the dealer's side from a special sling, rigged around his massive shoulders. Molanski counted three homeboys around the Jag, all of them displaying hardware tucked in waistbands. He wondered what kind of cut Janson had promised the black middlemen. More problems. In short order, though, all problems would be laid to waste.

Molanski held the two burn bags. He was glad now he'd put a backup piece, a Beretta 92-F, in the waistband at his side. A 6-shot revolver, the .357 Colt Python, wasn't going to make it beyond the first few opening rounds. Already he counted four Colombians, armed with either Uzi or Heckler & Koch MP-5 subguns. The Colombian hardmen were hanging back behind a slender, swarthy guy with a ponytail and decked out in an Armani suit that he assumed was Salvadore. Up on the loft, Molanski glimpsed two more subgun-toting Colombians. It was going to be close, damn close. But they were going for broke. Just beyond the group of Colombians, directly beside Crusherman, Molanski saw two dark blue vans. The back doors were open, revealing the neat stacks of plastic-wrapped white bricks.

Molanski fell behind Janson, who took the point, carrying the show money. Trailing them were two of Janson's guys, Maulin and Williams. He heard the warehouse door roll down behind them, bang the floor with a heavy thud.

Outside, Stanton and the others were right then moving in, sound-suppressed Glocks and Berettas poised to start dropping the hardmen left around the warehouse. Two minutes and counting.

On the way in, Molanski figured there were six Colombians spread around the perimeter, all wielding assault rifles. The area around the warehouse looked like a ghost town. Janson had briefly informed Molanski this was the old Union Stockyard area, the livestock trading long since shut down. Still, some of the packing houses held on even as redevelopment was springing up in bungalows and flats, north, along Archer Avenue, which roughly paralleled the Chicago River. A maze of railroad tracks cut the abandoned pens, storehouses and stockyards. Somehow the Markinson Industrial Machinery complex had seized a tract of land here. It was a front, of course, Molanski knew. Markinson hardly had a Spanish ring to it. The only plus was I-55, the Stevenson Expressway, a short run north once they blasted apart the Colombians, Crusherman and his homeboys.

Again the Belasko problem nagged at Molanski. He had filled Janson in on the fiasco back east. Janson had merely grunted and said they'd deal with it. He wasn't happy about losing one of his men, but he wasn't about to call the deal off, bolt town because one guy was hell-bent on putting them out of business. Molanski wanted to explain putting them out of business meant this so-called special agent of the Justice Department planned to see all of them six feet under. Then he figured if Janson was willing to cut his loss of one man for the sake of this major drug transaction, he was likewise expected to ride it out.

That simply meant taking their chances if Belasko suddenly blazed onto the scene.

Molanski's confidence was bolstered only by the fact that Salvadore's greed would have him thinking this was a straight deal. Or they would have already been dead. Already Salvadore was showing a set of pearly whites, his eyes lit with hunger as he fixed his dark gaze on the bag in Janson's hand.

They were searched for wires by two of the Colombians. Molanski then dreaded their weapons would be seized. But Janson had told him when he'd met with Salvadore the first time, where he'd introduced Maulin and Williams, all three of them had been armed. The guns had stayed. In his arrogance, Salvadore believed his henchmen could handle any situation that went sour. Salvadore would leave them with their weapons as a sign of trust, respect. Or so Janson had said.

That was last time. Now they were looking at several million dollars in uncut coke. And the Colombians and the blacks certainly looked on edge about the hardware on the persons of guys who could pass for cops from four blocks away.

One of the Colombians held open Molanski's coat, displaying his hardware to his boss. Despite Janson's pitch, Molanski felt fear ripple through him when he heard the Colombian growl, ''They're all carrying. What about this?''

Salvadore made a sweeping gesture at his gunmen.
"What about all of this?" The Colombian dealer
laughed. "Leave everything as it is, Miguel. This is
business. I understand the need our amigos here feel
for protection."

Janson addressed Crusherman after the black hulk
growled he'd asked a question and he wanted an answer.

"Relax, big man," Janson told the giant black.
"He's a close associate of mine. He's here, I trust
him and that says enough. Can we do this now?" he
then asked Salvadore.

Janson opened the bag, showing the money, then
handed the duffel to one of Salvadore's henchmen.
Salvadore nodded, looked pleased, told his flunky to
start counting the money.

The gunman who had patted down Molanski
reached for his duffel bags. Molanski tightened his
grip, showing the big Colombian with the Uzi subgun
a tight smile. "Mind if we check the merchandise
first?"

"Miguel," Salvadore snapped, the smile holding,
"your manners. Of course, feel free to check the merchandise."

Molanski felt his heart race, pulsing in his ear-
drums. He looked over his shoulder. One hardman
was standing beside a narrow doorway he left open.
The big ex-cop felt Crusherman's angry gaze boring
into the side of his head. The blacks smelled something. They would have to be the first to go, Molanski
determined. He was itching to give them the final rap
dance on their way to hell, glancing at the foursome
grouped around the Jag. The blacks were looking
from Janson to Salvadore, then at one another through

narrowed gazes, the homeboys, tight and suspicious. Crusherman shoveled some coke up his nose from the end of a sausage-sized finger. That seemed to take some of the mean edge out of the giant black. But Miguel was so close, Molanski could smell the tequila all over the Colombian's breath, his cologne so strong it made Molanski's head spin. Be cool, he told himself, feeling the adrenaline rush through him, burning like electrical charges in his blood. He counted off the ticks in his head, figured they were under a minute.

Janson took one brick at random from each van. He flicked open a switchblade, smiled at Crusherman, then speared the steel into a brick. Janson took one heavy snort on his blade from each of the bricks.

"Sweet, Salvadore," Janson said, turning and showing the Colombian a wide smile. "You came through. You are beautiful."

The Colombian shrugged, all smiles, his ego stroked. "Was there ever any doubt?"

Molanski tossed the burn bags in front of Miguel. The guy scowled, then he bent to open the bags. Molanski glimpsed Janson put the switchblade back in his jacket pocket but only after he licked the edge of the blade clean of powder. Salvadore was still smiling. The blacks were looking at one another, grunting something Molanski couldn't make out. Crusherman did another hoover off his finger.

Then Molanski heard the zipper on the bag open, saw the figure of the hardman by the door move out of sight. He caught the familiar chug of a silenced weapon from beyond the warehouse, heard the thud of deadweight outside. He saw Miguel stare at the newspaper in the bag with a heartbeat's disbelief before it dawned on him what was about to happen.

"What is—?" Miguel was snarling, reaching for his Uzi.

The Colombian never made it.

The Colt Python was out in Molanski's fist and thundering a round that blew open Miguel's head before he could warn his boss it was a rip-off.

All hell broke loose around Molanski.

Gunfire was blazing from all directions. Weapons roared beside him as Maulin and Williams cut loose on the Colombians beyond Salvadore. Flaming Glocks in the hands of Janson's troops put the Colombian goons in front of Molanski down for good. Blood sprayed the air around the Colombian boss in jetting red curtains as his men were dropping, crimson stains marching across their chests, their weapons chattering toward the ceiling. Salvadore screamed his outrage but was already dashing for cover behind a stack of crates. Discretion was the better part of valor there, Molanski thought. Real machismo.

Just before he caught the ugly snout of Crusherman's shotgun swinging up in the corner of his eye, Molanski ducked. A thousand wood fragments were blasted over his head, the shotgun in Crusherman's fists racking home another shell.

Molanski's backup Beretta was out and pumping one round after another into Crusherman's chest.

But it looked like Janson had the homeboy situation under control. Long sprays of crimson were splashing the white Jaguar as twin Thompsons boomed and shattered skulls.

Molanski took cover behind the crates as autofire from the loft opened up.

Then it happened.

One second, he saw the first of their hitters storm into the warehouse, peeling off, fanning out. Autofire was blazing from their weapons as they made the scene to seal doom and seize the mother lode.

Then the whole back end of the warehouse was obliterated by an ear-shattering fireball. A second thunderous blast followed, sending at least another six of their troops flying in all directions, shredded, dead before they hit the floor.

Molanski reached out, hauled in the discarded Uzi submachine gun. Another shotgun blast tore off a section of the crate behind him. Incredibly Molanski saw Crusherman firing away with his shotgun, holding his ground even as Janson pumped slugs into him.

Molanski fixed that situation, hosing the giant black, crotch to sternum with full-auto Uzi fire. Beyond that, he knew it was anyone's guess how it would all turn out.

Trouble from the east had arrived, a badass one-man army called Belasko.

The night was far from over, much less their deal being in the bag, Molanski feared.

IF TIMING WAS everything in life, then Bolan's couldn't have been any more perfect.

The Executioner had just come back from planting six blocks of C-4 along the north face of the warehouse when he spotted the advance of the Deliverance force. The enemy was coming up on the south face of the big structure where the deal was in the works. The invaders angled in from the pen area at the northeast corner, a small army of shadows rolling past dark, abandoned buildings, hopping railroad tracks and skirting empty rail cars.

Togged in skintight blacksuit for night work on this strike, Bolan swiftly retraced his path back to where Daly was crouched at an empty livestock pen. Both of them were armed with their assault rifles. This time around, Bolan had added incendiary grenades to their arsenal. The goal of this hit was twofold: savage the enemy, and burn up the cocaine.

Ahead the Executioner watched the shadows, crouched and creeping on the half dozen guards the drug dealer had left outside. A couple of the sentries were smoking, all of them a little too relaxed. That was about to change.

Give or take a few, Bolan counted at least two dozen hitters. Swift and silent, they were boiling out of the deep shadows of a loading area where a few 18-wheelers with the Markinson logo were parked. Bolan figured whoever was now in charge of the combined Deliverance cells had left behind a few troops to watch their vehicles. The stragglers would provide the quick getaway by car, once the load of coke was seized. But Bolan intended to be front and center to deal with any escape in short order.

First order of grim business was to bring the warehouse crashing down in flames.

The front gate had said Markinson Industrial Machinery. It was a front, of course, a midshipping point, no doubt, for cocaine smuggled into the States to then be moved by truck to other cities. Most likely, any machinery he found in the warehouse was disassembled, the cocaine packed in machine parts, crated up.

Indeed, Bolan was looking forward to blowing this operation all to hell.

Maybe a little more than two minutes earlier, he had seen the big Philly leader roll into the warehouse with three other men. They had carried three duffel bags. Buy money.

But he knew Deliverance was going for a straight rip-off. That alone was a major plus. The savages would start eating each other up, and Bolan and Daly would move in on their blind side, lend them a helping hand.

A moment later, Bolan found the Deliverance enemy was in perfect sync. It went off like clockwork, down to the final second. When the Colombian hardmen began dropping, victims of the swarm of whispering lead, Bolan heard the eruption of gunfire from inside the warehouse.

They were piling through the doorway when Bolan hit them from the rear to begin shredding apart their best-laid plans. He triggered the M-203, and a 40 mm grenade sailed through the night. As soon as the first explosion tore through a pack of Deliverance savages, Daly cut loose with his assault rifle. Screams of terror and pain echoed across a short stretch of no-man's-land between Bolan's cover and the warehouse. Daly chopped down the enemy with long scything bursts of autofire.

Loaded up, the M-203 chugged again. Another fiery hole was blasted into the warehouse. Bodies cartwheeled, torn scarecrow figures hurtled through the jagged, smoking maws in the wall.

Bolan pumped another 40 mm grenade into the next enemy group, surging through the doorway. Some made it inside, and those who didn't rode a saffron fireball into the sky.

Daly broke cover, slapping home a fresh clip into

his AR-18, then started triggering the weapon for all he was worth.

Bolan used one more 40 mm bomb to blow in the rolling door to the warehouse, giving them another point of entry.

Judging what he heard, Bolan knew he would find all-out slaughter inside the warehouse, with guys shooting at anything that moved.

The Executioner then gave them a little more reason to dread the night. Pulling out the detonator box, he thumbed the switch, hit the button.

The sound of thunder that followed from the radio-activated C-4 split the night. A mountain-sized fireball shot up into the sky, the darkness around the warehouse lit up like high noon.

Advancing on the devastated opening, Bolan unleashed two 3-round bursts from his M-16. He dropped two figures that rushed forward with chattering assault rifles beyond the drifting walls of smoke and the crackling tongues of fire.

Right on Daly's flank, the soldier reached the smoking maw, taking in the chaos. They were shooting all over the warehouse. At least three-quarters of the north face had been demolished by the C-4 charges. Huge slabs of debris were still raining over the combatants, the dead and the dying.

As autofire tracked him, Bolan made the cover of piled crates. Then he got lucky. Maybe two dozen yards ahead, he saw them scrambling for two vans, heard someone screaming to save the coke.

The Executioner armed an incendiary grenade, gauged the distance and let it fly.

Their coke dreams were a heartbeat away from being incinerated before their eyes. Merry Christmas, the Executioner thought, and wished the enemy a white one.

The perfect lob had put the incendiary right on top of the bricks. For good measure, the soldier pulled the pin on another grenade and tossed it into the bed of van two.

STANTON KNEW the apocalyptic drill of sudden death and destruction by heart now. The nightmare had arrived, and Belasko was blowing up everything in sight and clear for the Chicago River, it seemed.

Somehow Stanton had made it inside the warehouse after the first explosion. He discovered he wasn't unscathed. Blood was streaming down the side of his face. He was also on the floor, his ears ringing. If the first three blasts that had ripped into their rear were fearsome, then the one he heard and saw in the next few moments was something he imagined they experienced at Hiroshima.

Stanton was dragging himself off the floor as their guys charged across the warehouse. Two Colombians were up on the loft, standing tall, hitting the warehouse with autofire. Uncovered, the Colombians up there held their ground, Spanish machismo sure to get them killed. Just ahead, Stanton spotted Molanski chopping up the massive black by the Jaguar with merciless lead storms from his Uzi. It had to be Crusherman. The shotgun was booming in the giant black's hands even as he staggered forward, chopped up and blood flying everywhere. It took a whole clip from the Uzi jumping around in Molanski's hands to finally drive Crusherman to a twitching and very dead corpse on the warehouse floor. Janson certainly helped the situation Molanski was faced with, the

Chicago watch commander's twin cannons blasting apart Crusherman's homeboys.

Badly wounded, one of the black dealers made a beeline for cover, but Stanton drilled him with a long burst from his MP-5 subgun. A look of dumbfounded horror stared across the distance at Stanton as the dealer was driven into a stack of crates.

Stanton heard Molanski screaming to get the coke out of there, when the whole building felt as if it would come down on their heads. Stanton hit the ground as giant chunks of the loft and north wall were vaporized by a rolling wave of fire that left him deaf and stunned for what seemed an eternity. The series of blasts were so powerful, he saw something sail over his head. A fleeting glimpse and he suspected it was whatever was left of the two Cali guys up top that sailed beyond.

When he hauled himself upright, Stanton glimpsed two of their guys bowled down by autofire where the rolling door had been. On the move, he spotted two figures, all too familiar to him now. He locked a moment's stare with Daly, then the ex-cop hero opened up with his assault rifle, chasing Stanton to cover.

Save the coke—that was all that mattered.

Stanton found deeper cover behind some crates as Daly's tracking line of lead chewed up wood.

Through all the chaos, autofire, screaming and cursing, Stanton heard an engine roar to life somewhere ahead. Crouched, making sure he was covered by crates, he moved toward Molanski and Janson to give them a hand with the vans.

"Get the fucking vans out of here!" Stanton heard Janson screaming at the troops.

Crates suddenly exploded in the distance, ahead of

Stanton. He caught a glimpse of a guy with a ponytail behind the wheel of a Mercedes. One goon was hanging out the passenger's side, an Uzi subgun stuttering lead fingers at the guys racing to get in the vans. Two of their people were taking lead up the spine when Stanton caught something bounce on top of the coke pile of one van.

Stanton already suspected it was too late to save the coke. A second later, it was confirmed beyond any terrifying doubt.

"Grenade!" Stanton heard someone yell, a sound of pure rage and utter terror. Molanski was shrieking for someone to get in the vans, get the grenade out of there. Stanton wanted out of there himself and told Molanski just that, but the big man was consumed in a mindless rage, his Beretta snapping off rounds all over the place.

With the ceiling coming down all around them, he couldn't be sure but Stanton thought Molanski had just thrown one of their guys into the van. Right, someone else get the grenade out of there, even as the big man quickly moved away from ground zero.

Then the first vehicle erupted in a blinding mushroom cloud of white fire.

THE WAREHOUSE WAS going up in flames.

Bolan knew they had to evacuate or risk being burned alive or crushed from falling debris as whole sections of the roof groaned, then came raining down.

They were still screaming at guys to get in the vans, grab what they now knew were grenades meant to blow up their dreams. Bolan had a name now to go with the big guy with the American flag on his jacket. Molanski. Stanton was yelling at Molanski they needed to get the hell out of there.

Molanski, though, wanted to hold his ground, save the coke loads. The big man actually hurled a guy into the van to save their deal, then moved away, the Beretta in his fist spitting flame, hurling lead in all directions.

The first van blew, followed a heartbeat later by the second grenade going off in a thunderclap that was muted by human torches shrieking like banshees. White powder showered all over the warehouse, some of the bricks looking like flying fiery bats. But it was the white phosphorus, spewing out in a thirty-five-yard radius and clinging to guys like glue, that got everyone's undivided and horrified attention. It burned at 2700 degrees centigrade, and Bolan could well appreciate their sudden urge to flee.

The fiery human scarecrows were flaming out in a wild zigzag dance in the corner of Bolan's eye when the soldier was forced to duck flying lead that chewed up wood around their cover. Then he saw Molanski heeding Stanton's advice. Side by side, they were backpedaling, firing weapons, screaming their outrage.

A Mercedes streaked out of nowhere at Bolan's position, barreling through crates, clipping one of the enemy and launching him over the roof on its sudden crazed flight.

Cracking a fresh 30-round magazine into his M-16, Bolan broke cover to intercept the vehicle. One guy was firing away with an Uzi, leaning out the passenger's window. Bolan found Daly right on his flank. Together the soldier and the ex-cop from Brooklyn hosed the Mercedes with twin lines of savaging autofire. The Uzi gunner was kicked from the Mercedes by a half-dozen rounds that erupted his skull. Bolan caught a glimpse of a terrified face with a ponytail behind the wheel. Something told him Ponytail was the guy from Cali who had made all this possible.

The Executioner held back on the M-16's trigger, blowing the windshield in, all over Ponytail's face. The Mercedes slammed into the jagged teeth of the devastated wall, bounced, rolled off into the night.

The enemy gunners were retreating, firing at Bolan as they weaved their way out in the distance, dodging falling slabs of roof.

Daly spent one clip after another, but Bolan knew the enemy survivors would make it out. They couldn't afford the time it would take to chase them for their vehicles.

"Come on," Bolan ordered, grabbing Daly by the shoulder and hauling him out of the warehouse.

Outside, Bolan heard the roar of engines, somewhere around the corner. The deal was done here, the enemy's dreams soured. Bolan was heading back across no-man's-land, in the direction of their Crown Victoria, when he caught the angry look on Daly's face.

"Let's go, Daly."

"You're not going after them?"

"It's done here. We need to put distance, quick."

The mountain of fire behind Daly rose, high into the night. It wouldn't be long before an army of flashing lights would swarm all over the hellzone.

Bolan was forced to repeat the urge to make tracks. Finally Daly fell in beside the Executioner.

"I don't get it, Belasko. We've got them. Why not put the finishing kill on them?"

Bolan put steel into his voice. On the move, melting into the deep shadows of abandoned pens, he growled, ''If the cops take us in again, we might lose them at the finish line. The fact is, I want to give them a good head start to the finish.''

Daly kept pace with Bolan, some of the anger and confusion fading in the man's eyes. Bolan would explain when they were on the interstate, but he was pretty sure Daly already knew the score.

The Executioner wanted all vipers in one nest the next time out.

CHAPTER NINETEEN

The pit stop was off I-80, a hundred miles or so east of Des Moines.

Stanton waited in the Chevy Caprice with Scarborough at the wheel, Downey and Burrows in the back. The sprawling lot ringed a large rest stop, with diner, gas station and convenience store. A few vehicles and several 18-wheelers were parked near their troops. Or, rather, Stanton bitterly thought, what was once again left of the combined cells.

It was well after midnight. For almost seven hours and four hundred miles, cutting across Illinois, crossing the state line and into Iowa, they had ridden fast, in hard silence. The new national speed limit certainly helped their flight. If they weren't cruising at sixty-five or seventy, there were stretches of interstate where they could fly at seventy-five, even push eighty and not worry about smokies.

But so could Belasko.

Some cold and dark instinct that stuck in his belly, to slowly twist and rip like the edge of an invisible knife, was warning Stanton they would see the big bastard again. Soon.

It didn't really seem to matter that distance had been put quickly and safely to the ravages of the in-

cinerated coke deal. A lot of their guys were dead and
left behind again, and there would be no millions in
cocaine to land the cause a major war chest. Stanton
no longer seethed about new disaster, much less the
loss of face once again. He was simply worried about
surviving. All that could have been and should have
been didn't matter a damn if he didn't live to see
tomorrow. There would be other drug deals, other
chances for the big score.

Or so he hoped.

Eight cars, he counted, maybe two dozen guys left
to take back to Wyoming. If that's where they were
even going.

If they would even make it.

Stanton watched as Molanski made his second call
from the pay phone. They were fueled up, ready to
roll, but the big man had been on the phone for a
good ten minutes, making them wait. Stanton felt the
strain of being the hunted when he had always been
the hunter. Worse, the stink of repeated failure was
eroding his confidence, down the final layer of
bruised pride. Rage at fate, and hatred of their hunters, was all that kept him going.

Even from a distance, Stanton could feel the big
man ready to explode into sudden, even senseless violence. Some trucker had come up on Molanski's
back side when Molanski dropped the quarters into
the slot for call two. The trucker was a big, solid guy,
looking as if he thought muscle alone could pressure
Molanski into hustling with his call. The trucker
stared at the big Philly ex-cop, almost in his face, then
started pacing around.

Something bad was about to happen to the trucker.

Stanton hoped Molanski had the good sense to keep gunplay out of the picture.

Stanton got out, telling the others to sit tight. He needed a private word with Molanski anyway. He wanted to be sure he'd seen right back in Chicago. Janson and a few others had been burned alive by the incendiary grenades Belasko had tossed into the vans. Those blinding white waves of fire, eating up their coke loads, formed a vision of hell that had stayed branded in his mind. Not to mention their guys, shrieking all over the warehouse, torched up, burned alive. That alone added a new dimension to an already bone-chilling fear Stanton felt. Taking a bullet through the head was one thing. To be lit up, a human fireball, was something else altogether. If Molanski had thrown one of their guys into the van to snatch up that grenade, well, Stanton needed to clear the air with the big man. All of a sudden, it was no longer one for all.

Slowly Stanton walked toward Molanski. He heard the big man curse, then Molanski slammed the receiver against the phone with such force he shattered it into a dozen or so pieces.

The trucker took his chances. "Goddamn, boy, I needed to use that phone. What the hell's wrong with you? I been waitin' on your big dumb ass for ten minutes. My radio is out—"

Without warning, Molanski dropped a huge paw on the trucker's shoulder, spun and hammered the guy's face into the phone. There was a sickening crack of bone, echoing, it seemed, through the lot. The trucker dropped like a sack of Midwest grain. Stanton couldn't tell if the man was dead or not, but there was a lot of blood pouring off the phone, pooling around the guy's sprawled body.

"So, use it!" Molanski rasped, then strode on.

"I think we need to have a word, just you and me," Stanton said after he begrudged an appreciative glance at the twitching mass on the ground.

"My thoughts exactly," Molanski growled. "This Belasko problem is on the way. Here's what I want you to do."

Stanton listened, feeling his anger mounting the more Molanski kept him relegated to a semiflunky role. Molanski said once they were a little closer to Des Moines, Stanton was to find a spot off the interstate where he could sit on a stakeout for Belasko. The agent was sure to stay on the arrow-straight line of I-80, since that was clearly marked on the maps Stanton had left behind in Philly. Molanski had a pair of infrared binoculars, if that would help the surveillance. Belasko couldn't be far behind.

"Now, what's your problem?"

Stanton squared his shoulders. The moment of courage had come and gone, it seemed. What was he going to do anyway? Even if he heard the truth, could he just pull out his Glock and put one between Molanski's eyes?

In the next moment, Molanski's gaze narrowed. It was as if that piercing search could read his mind, as the big man said, "You're thinking about Chicago. You're thinking maybe you saw something back there you didn't like. You're thinking I'm some kind of asshole for maybe tossing one of our own in the van like I did. You're thinking maybe I should have gone after that grenade." Molanski lit a cigarette, letting the tension thicken. It looked to Stanton as if he were enjoying the possibility of an ultimate confrontation between them.

Molanski blew a thick cloud of smoke over Stanton's head. "You know what that shit was the guy threw at us back there? It was white phosphorus. That stuff will cling to a man like glue, burn the skin off his bones like he's been dipped in acid. He can roll around in a vat of ice water, and he won't put it out. I've seen that stuff before. It's a bad way to die. Those guys had about two seconds to get those grenades out, save that coke, way I figured. Janson was the only one moving, but he was more busy killing blacks. What I did was called motivation. Once again we ate it. I'm getting sick and tired of swallowing a big fat turd, sick and fucking tired of running. We've been fighting on that guy's terms up to now. It stops, here and now, in the heartland of America.

"Look around and breathe the clean air of the average working man who's been shit on by the government, the immigrants, the liberals who whine every day in our face because they're trying to even the odds by dirty underhanded shit when they really know their place is kissing our ass and thanking their lucky stars for being allowed to breathe the same air we do. Since it was us who built this country on our own blood and sweat and pure spine. Listen to me. Out here, among all these farms probably up for sale or snatched up by guys in suits who have never done a hard, honest day's work in their lives but who claim they have ideas and ways to make it right, well, this is what we're fighting to save. America. It doesn't get much more righteous than this." A pause, then he added, "Let me tell you how motivated I am to put this guy out of our misery for good. I'm sending everyone else ahead to the main base. I called Denver, and they're pulling out as we speak. Cleveland was hit."

"How do you know?"

"Because they didn't answer the goddamn phone. I'm sticking with you, Stanton. I'll be with you on the stake. We finish this Belasko problem here, or we don't make it to Wyoming. You up for that?"

Stanton, who felt inspired, growled, "What do you think?"

Molanski grunted, a dangerous glint in his eyes. "I think you were thinking about popping a cap in my ass."

Stanton froze at the sight of the murderous insanity burn into Molanski's eyes. A moment later, the look died and the big Pole laughed.

"That's all right," Molanski said. "You're both right and wrong about the way you read it. But save all that bad energy for Belasko. You're going to need it. You can be damn sure he's hot on our ass."

Molanski brushed past Stanton. Incredible. The man seemed to have all the answers, knew how to say all the right things. The only problem was their nightmare had proved he was in no mood to buy anything the big man was selling.

Stanton headed back for his vehicle, recharged but still uncertain. One way or another, they were going to finish with their problem from back east. So why didn't he feel as good about their chances as Molanski? Why did Stanton think they were about to make their last stand in the middle of Nowhere, U.S.A.?

HANDS TIGHT on the wheel, clipping the speedometer at 70 mph, Bolan drove them on into the dark night, down the endless ribbon of I-80.

They had crossed into Iowa an hour earlier. Chicago was burning, another hit-and-run victory, but a major coup was in their wake. The enemy was once again on the run, reeling, scared, but maybe lying in wait now to ambush their pursuers.

It was far from over, Bolan knew. Deliverance had taken a pummeling of the worst sort, but the fight wouldn't be knocked out of them until every last member of the paramilitary organization was dead.

Bolan had been thinking like the enemy all along, anticipating his adversary's moves, strategy. Instinct now told him they would call ahead to the Denver cell, order them to roll out of the Mile High City, get to the stronghold. There, the enemy could defend its twisted cause to the last man. The right-wingers knew a major headache was on the way, knew he had the scent to dog them down to the square yard of wherever they went.

Forget Denver, they were riding I-80, hard and geared up for the worst, all the way to Wyoming.

Up to now the enemy had scattered, fled before overwhelming firepower. In major cities, across several states, the enemy couldn't risk facing down the real law—not when the organization still believed it had a future. So flight had been their members' only option. Each city was a springboard. Beef up the force, and, as Bolan had seen, try to bless the organization with a few million bucks of cocaine. Well, scratch one major drug transaction, bag up a horde of Colombian narcotics-trafficking parasites for the worms.

Each time the roving cells sought more strength in

numbers, Bolan and his ally had shown them there was no hope in outmatching the kind of artillery that had been unleashed on them. At some point, though, Bolan figured a few of the troops would be waiting ahead, in the night, to try to get the two-man scourge off their backs for good. To stand and fight was the only alternative left for Deliverance.

At a rest stop back in Illinois, Bolan had used a pay phone to call Brognola. The big Fed had mobilized an eight-man force, had them already in place, in a motel in a three-horse town, a few miles north of Medicine Bow. Aerial recon and satellite surveillance had pinpointed the Deliverance stronghold. Brognola told Bolan he would be linking up with the strike force under the guise of Agent X, the code phrase when he met with one Agent M, "X marks the spot." Exactly who or what the members of the strike force were, Bolan didn't know, didn't ask. They could be special agents of the Justice Department or Delta Force commandos, for all he knew. Bottom line was the Executioner trusted Brognola's judgment on the matter, knew the warriors on the other end would help him get the final job done. Agent X was in charge, no questions asked.

So Bolan went with the Justice man's program. Brognola didn't want names put with faces, just in case this thing went public. Of course, Bolan knew public outrage over a clandestine force of killer ex-lawmen was Brognola's last concern. And Bolan's only top priority was getting to Wyoming and eradicating Deliverance.

"Something I've been thinking about."

Bolan glanced at Daly out of the corner of his eye. The man was back, as strong as ever. Just the same,

Bolan kept his guard up in case Daly looked set to blow in mindless rage, finally eaten alive and driven past rational thinking by vengeance.

Daly lit a cigarette. At the rest stop, the ex-cop had purchased a six-pack of beer. He was working on his second bottle. Bolan needed the man's head clear, but had decided to allow the caged tiger his medicine.

To a point, Bolan could overlook this man's one obvious problem. The Executioner had the biggest heart in the world for good people. But he was a realist enough to know all men, good, bad or in between, were flawed in some way. Daly was one of the good ones, but Bolan had suspected as much all along.

Why did he feel like he was going to miss the guy? Why did he feel the urge, burning out of nowhere, to mourn for the man? Why did Bolan suddenly feel a hand of doom settle around Daly? Was it the strain of battles, heaped one after another on the campaign? Was it the weariness, driving bone deep, from countless miles behind the wheel and little sleep and food that was threatening to drop some dark mood on him? Was it the bitter knowledge of having to kill men who were former law officers and who had thrown away their sworn oath to protect and to serve that was eating at his guts?

Daly worked on his beer and smoke, then said, "At the end of the line, I'm betting that somewhere, somebody has financed this thing of theirs they call Deliverance. Somebody big, powerful, with money and clout. There's no way a bunch of ex-lawmen, no matter how much drugs and drug money they've lifted off dealers or extorted or walked out of some evidence lockup with, no matter who they are now connected to in legitimate law enforcement, could have gotten this big without a sizable charitable donation. Someone none of us knows about got this thing launched.''

Daly was working on it, pretty much along the same lines as Bolan. Beyond the main troops, the soldier was betting someone of power and respectability was funneling money to the so-called national watch commander. It was something that had been pricking at the back of Bolan's mind since the beginning. But he had been too caught up in the hit-and-run savaging to give it any serious thought before then.

''A businessman, maybe? A mogul?''

Daly shrugged. ''Or worse.''

Bolan nodded. ''A politician.''

''With a lot of money. A guy with right-wing views, extreme views he tries to play down before what he considers all the little people. But get him on a bar stool with his cronies, and every other word comes out of his mouth would have him stoned to death by his loyal constituents who he has fleeced and holds in complete contempt.''

Daly fell into silence, then Bolan said, ''I'm listening.''

''Well, I know your boss has probably pinned the location of their stronghold down to the square foot by now. Sure, he can tap into their phone records. That's where you find the real big man. These guys have thought they were untouchable, invincible. That is until we showed them they aren't. It all tells me there's someone who got the show started at some point. A Mr. Big, if you will. Phone records will point to the source.''

Bolan had run tracing all past phone calls from the

stronghold by Brognola. The soldier had been informed the computer wizards at Stony Man Farm were already working on it. If there was a major financier in the shadows of Deliverance, the Stony Man team would find him, or them.

Bolan checked the rearview mirror. Nothing behind them. A few lights burned in the distance, out there in the darkness of the flat plains of Iowa. Their weapons were on the floorboard or back seat, close at hand.

Bolan sensed Daly's mood turn grim. With his switchblade, Daly opened the cap on another beer.

"Why don't you get some sleep?" Bolan suggested in a quiet voice.

Daly showed a smile that Bolan didn't like. Behind the expression, he saw the man on the verge of lapsing into depression, maybe despair. Beyond that, even a willingness to commit to his burning for revenge, even if it meant suicide, which wasn't good.

"This is my last one," Daly said.

Something was warning Bolan it was just about the last of anything for Daly.

AFTER THE WARM GLOW of the first few drinks wore off, a wall of dark depression went up, a looming behemoth that wanted to crush the life out of him. All too soon, a voice of thunder would then rumble out of the blackness, tell him it was all just shit anyway, give it up. He couldn't. It was always like that anyway, the only thing about drinking Daly hated.

Still he did it to himself. Hell, he'd come to know the demons so well, they were a second skin he could no longer live without. He even liked the despair that always threatened to follow, a feeling that he was sinking into himself, dragged down, on the verge of being consumed by demons who were laughing at him, taunting him. Before now he could beat those demons, with sheer will. This time he wasn't so sure.

When the despair started to wash over him, Daly would simply have another drink. He would have done just that, right then, if it weren't for Belasko. But he liked the guy, and he understood what needed to be done. More important, he respected the man. Belasko was counting on him, but Daly wasn't even sure he could give the man his due allegiance. The demons had grown too strong.

Despair. Unfulfillment, even in vengeance. That never ending "burning yearning" to know why. Why? Why were they gone? Why had they been taken from him?

It was becoming too much to shoulder.

And Daly would miss Belasko, this big bad cowboy who wasn't any Justice Department special agent, though he was damn special. In some ways, they were alike, only Daly couldn't quite pin down the similarities. What he suspected, though, was theirs was a doomed alliance. Some silent demon was even right then telling Daly it was never meant to be. Happiness, love, a home and a family, a friend like Belasko, that was for other people.

The night rolled by. Daly sipped his beer.

It flared, out of nowhere, from the deepest, most remote part of his being. It rolled over him, a seething hotness that burned from the belly, up through his chest, until he felt the blood pulsing behind his eyes. An outsider who didn't know him would call it self-pity. Modern social thinkers, the pop-cult gurus called it alcoholism.

Daly knew better. What he felt was pure rage at

life. At the utter and cold and unfathomable injustice of the world. Right, whoever said life was fair, and all that crap. Life was a raw deal. The good kept suffering, the bad kept dumping their ill ways all over the rest. It was that simple.

But there was an answer. Only most men, he believed, would never know it, until it was too late.

The answer was called death.

Another deep swallow of his magic elixir, and he heard their names, his voice scream in silent fury through his mind. Yuen. Christopher. They had been his whole world, the only two things in his life that ever made sense. With Yuen, there had been little or no drinking, no rage, no thinking that the world was just shit because he'd seen how unjust and how ugly man was to his fellow man. With Yuen, there'd been peace of mind, a stillness of the soul, a quiet beating of the heart. Funny about the true power of love, he reflected.

Strange, even brutal, how nothing truly good and right in life lasted.

He didn't want to go on without them. There would never be another woman like Yuen. Never. Not in his lifetime.

She had survived the war, but life had ultimately robbed her, cheated her of everything pure and good and simple that could have been. He felt himself clench his teeth so hard, he could have snapped them off. God in heaven, he thought, felt the fire build behind his eyes. Just like that, it was only ten minutes ago. There she was, right in front of him, all beauty, all purity of spirit. He could reach out, touch that soft, beautiful, scared but utterly dignified woman-child on the face, the woman he had saved the day the VC had come to wipe out their village. Never looking, never even thinking about being some hero, some savior, just doing it because it was right. Their platoon saving the whole village from...their own. Down to the last man, woman or child. A lot of the guys under his command went home in a body bag. Damn right, it made no sense.

"Snap out of it, Daly. They're coming up on our rear."

Daly came back and found Belasko staring at him. The guy knew he'd been lost, was right there at the edge, about to throw it all away. But the man understood. He didn't know much about Belasko's past, but Daly knew the man had his own demons. The guy was all right, something about him. Belasko was a man's man. A soldier's soldier.

A warrior.

The problem, Daly found, was racing up on their bumper. One look over his shoulder, and Daly got the picture. Two shadows had burned rubber out of the night, streaked up on their rear out of nowhere. Headlights popped on when their hunters closed.

They had been waiting for them to run down this stretch of highway. Belasko had anticipated their play all along. Logic always dictated a certain course of action anyway. The enemy was scared, but had to finish the two of them before they got any closer to Wyoming.

Daly reached over the seat and hauled in their assault rifles. He found Belasko looking from the rearview mirror, then putting a piercing moment's gaze on him.

"You back together, soldier?"

Daly nodded. "I'm right here, with you all the way."

Bolan hit the gas, streaking for an exit ramp when Daly killed his beer, rolled down the window and threw out the empty.

Daly liked the setup. Just a couple of guys with a real pair, riding it out, ready to take it on the chin.

He showed his ally a hard grin. "I've always wanted to do that. I figure there's an outlaw in all of us." He cracked a clip into his AR-18, doing the same for the M-16. "I like you, Belasko. I'm going to miss you. But you know the deal. I can see it in your eyes. I didn't see him clear, but that's Stanton back there. I can feel the guy. You know, the problem with the devil, Belasko, is that the devil knows he's wrong, but he can't stand it. Only one way to change his thinking. I want Stanton, if it's the last thing I do. I'm in the mood. As far as I'm concerned, the world can kiss my ass."

No, the world could kiss it goodbye, Daly thought.

A heartbeat later, the back window was blown in from a tracking line of autofire.

CHAPTER TWENTY

Bolan knew Daly was one hundred percent gripped by the insanity of reaping his vengeance. It was the moment Bolan had known all along would eventually erupt. The human time bomb was right then about to explode, no matter what. Damn the odds, the consequences, the final outcome. For tomorrow was simply more of the past, the future just a terminal cancer that was going to kill him anyway. Or so went Daly's thinking.

Whether the man proved himself a fatal liability, well, the Executioner had his own and very much life-threatening problems at the moment.

Everyone, friend and foe alike, was on his own.

Ducking the hail of hot bullets sizzling over his head, cracking the windshield into a line of spiderweb holes, Bolan floored the Crown Victoria along the exit ramp. Two vehicles stayed pasted on his bumper, but he put some distance to their hunters as he shot off the ramp, rounded the bend and rocketed down the off road. Still, another burst of autofire from behind blasted out half the windshield. Daly fired back, the AR-18's chatter in Bolan's ear, piercing his senses.

A veil of darkness shrouded the flat plains in both directions. Bolan searched for a suitable battleground,

off the beaten track. He didn't want any more innocent blood shed, as he had seen when the enemy had
blown that tanker all over the turnpike.

It wasn't hard to find a good spot, well off the road.
It was farm country, isolated and remote, but this was
Iowa, after all. It certainly appeared as if they were
in the middle of nowhere, at the end of the world.

A half mile later, Bolan sent his vehicle flying over
the embankment. The wheel tried to tear itself free of
Bolan's grip as he bounded them onto a wide-open
plain. In the distance, a series of windmills loomed.
Beyond the towering steel structures, he saw a corn-
field. Somewhere there would be a farmhouse. Gunfire was sure to alarm any farmer in the area, but the
stretch of plain looked deserted in all directions.

Bolan discovered the plain wasn't as flat as it first
appeared.

A deep rut nearly swallowed the Crown Victoria.
Bolan rode out the vicious jounce, glass bouncing off
his head, his eyelids slitted to mere cracks against the
rush of wind smacking him with angry pinpricks of
glass slivers in his face.

Behind, the enemy roared off the road, two metallic
rockets that quickly grew in Bolan's side mirror.
Autofire sparked from behind, and the glass exploded
to Bolan's side.

He hit the wheel, hard to the left. Tires grabbed at
the soft earth, spewing long funnels of grit and dust
in his wake. He was about to swing the vehicle
around, go right at the enemy when he saw the trench
take care of a Chevy Caprice. One moment the Caprice was coming down hard in the rut, and in the
next the car was flipping on its roof, rolling, out of
control. Glass and strips of metal were taking to the

air as one figure was hurtled from the rolling mass of crushed debris.

There were other survivors, Bolan saw, as he sluiced the Crown Victoria around, three guys scrabbling to clear themselves of the Caprice.

Bolan heard Daly curse and was reaching for his M-16 when the ex-cop did what the soldier least wanted: he flung the door open and threw himself out into the night.

A berserker howl struck Bolan's ears as Daly hit the ground and rolled. Then the man stood and surged into the headlights of a charging enemy Crown Victoria. With his assault rifle swinging up, Daly ran ahead, holding back on the trigger. His first marching line of slugs blasted the windshield in, but the shocked faces behind flying shards ducked out of sight.

Bolan hit the brakes.

The enemy vehicle whiplashed in a long slide. When the vehicle stopped, a dozen yards from Daly's suicide charge, four shadows poured out of the Crown Victoria. They unleashed their weapons, pencil-tip flames parting the cloud of smoke boiling over them from behind.

Bolan had no choice but to cover Daly's charge. It was going to end quick and hard. Consumed only with his drive for vengeance, Daly had shot Bolan's game plan all to hell. The Executioner had intended to make tight circles, have the Crown Victoria's tires kick up a wall of dust, disgorge then cut the enemy down as they choked on grit.

So much for that.

Crouched beside the front driver's side of his vehicle, Bolan cut loose with his M-16, spraying the vehicle side to side, front to back. Return fire hammered his vehicle, slugs thudding into the front end with such force the Crown Victoria was rocked on its chassis. There was no 40 mm grenade loaded in the M-203, nor did Bolan have the time or opportunity to put a bomb in the breech.

He poured it on with full-auto slaughter. In the periphery of their headlights, he saw two shadows topple from the Crown Victoria, his tracking lead eating up their chests and stomachs.

Then Daly went down under savage bursts of autofire.

Bolan smelled the leaking fuel from the crushed hull of the Caprice. They were sliding sideways, firing on the run, away from the wreck. Bolan mowed down another enemy shadow, flinging him to the earth under stuttering bursts of 5.56 mm lead. He caught a glimpse of Stanton as the guy made cover behind the Crown Victoria.

Four left.

One guy opted to stay covered behind the overturned wreckage.

Bolan then saw Daly rise from the ground. The man was drenched in blood, wounded bad, but going for broke. If Bolan didn't do something quick, it would be over for good for Daly.

Reaching into his vehicle, Bolan hauled out the Mossberg.

He saw Daly draw his side arms and forge ahead, into the face of certain death, his handguns booming away. Glass was exploding from the windows of open passenger's and driver's doors, Daly's relentless fire forcing the enemy to duck.

Daly screamed Stanton's name.

Bolan pumped two 12-gauge rounds into the Caprice wreck, going for the fuel tank. Pumping out one more round, the Executioner struck explosive paydirt.

The hull erupted into a fireball. Razoring sheets of metal ripped over the enemy. To a man, enemy survivors hit the ground, as their comrade in hate and murder was launched backward from the roaring cloud of flames.

Daly moved ahead, his weapons jumping in his fists, searching out death and ready to take just the same.

Damn tomorrow. It wasn't going to get there anyway.

Swiftly, moving out and jacking the Mossberg's action, Bolan cannoned another 12-gauge charge into the figure jumping up behind the passenger's door. The guy went down hard.

Molanski and Stanton popped up, both men blazing away with automatic weapons. Whether they scored direct hits on his doomed ally, Bolan couldn't be sure. But Daly rolled on, twitching, cloth and blood spraying the air. Somehow the man stayed on his feet, even managed to fill his guns with fresh clips.

Bolan sent Molanski tumbling back with a 12-gauge burst to his stomach as the big man's autofire tracked his way. The Executioner cocked the pump action, was turning death sights on Stanton when a shadow groaned and staggered to his feet.

He made it all of two steps away from the burning wreckage when the Executioner sawed him in two with a blast from the Mossberg.

One after the other, volcanic eruptions of inhumanity sailed through the night.

Still, Daly fired on, even as Stanton held back on

the trigger of his MP-5 subgun. Both men were screaming at each other, primal sounds of pure agony and hatred penetrating the hellish racket of weapons fire.

Suddenly Bolan saw Daly vault onto the Crown Victoria, triggering his guns at Stanton at point-blank range. The MP-5 kept on flaming in Stanton's fists.

Soaking up Stanton's leadstorm, Daly spun on the roof of the Crown Victoria, then toppled in a headfirst dive over the trunk.

Stanton wobbled, soaked with blood, then also pitched out of sight from Bolan.

A moment later, he heard Stanton snarl, "Yeah, Daly, I killed them both." The voice of rage came from the darkness, choked with agony, but still full of hate, even fueled by a new edge of raw venom. "You could have been one of us, you self-righteous bastard."

Bolan picked it up a notch, drawing his Desert Eagle. They were mere shadows, trying to get up from pools of crimson, spouting around their feet. The Executioner sighted down the Desert Eagle and drew target acquisition on Stanton as the man squeezed the trigger on his Glock.

But Daly got what he wanted.

It cost the ultimate price, either way.

The razor-sharp steel of the switchblade glinted firelight as Daly flicked it open. Both men stumbled at each other. The Glock cracked, and Bolan saw blood explode from the exit wound in Daly's back. Even as the light faded from the ex-cop's eyes, the man was spearing the switchblade into Stanton's throat, then ripped flesh open in one vicious sideways motion before he pitched to the ground.

For a long moment, Stanton stood there, blood streaming down his chest. Gurgling on his own juices, Stanton teetered, turned toward Bolan with a look of profound disbelief.

Then Stanton dropped in a slow-motion crumple, his lifeless form sprawled next to Daly.

The crackling of fire in his ears, Bolan stood over his dead ally. It felt like some eternity had come and gone as he stared down into the unseeing eyes of the man who had fought so valiantly beside him.

A man, a warrior who knew the mission. Dead. A tortured soldier who just couldn't take it any longer.

Bolan clenched his jaw, bent and closed the man's eyelids. It didn't have to end this way, he knew. Daly could have made it. Maybe. Maybe not.

Cold anger and grief welled up in Bolan as he stood. Yeah, the man had gotten what he had so badly craved. The man's ultimate destiny was now out of Bolan's hands. No matter what, he wouldn't forget this warrior. Ever.

Silent mourning could wait. Deliverance was still alive and well.

A hideous groan knifed Bolan's senses. Pivoting, Bolan saw the American flag, nearly glowing, it seemed, beneath the umbrella of dancing firelight.

Molanski sought the shadow that was Bolan with hate-filled eyes. A trembling and bloody hand was reaching out for an Uzi subgun.

"You bastard. You ruined everything. We only wanted to make the country we love strong again."

Even as he was dying, the man held on to his sick belief that he and only he was right, that only his world and his will mattered.

The Executioner loomed over Molanski and sighted

down the Desert Eagle. What was it Daly had said? The problem with the devil was he knew he was wrong, but couldn't stand it. Right. Pride wouldn't let him.

Molanski took his pride with him as Bolan triggered the Desert Eagle.

"IF YOU DON'T HEAR from me in twelve hours, you know what to do. Then do the same to his wife, his children, his grandchildren. If you feel up to it, well, let's just say there's a bonus in it for you if you move on to his top campaign people. I want a statement that will make his loyal followers vomit over their breakfast. I want to read about it in the paper, over a double whiskey and a fat steak. We'll laugh about the job later. Right now, just stick with the orders."

Shyrock paused, as he listened to Travers fill him in. It seemed like their boy had made himself scarce all of a sudden. Speaking engagements had been suddenly postponed. The guy had been caught by his two-man stakeout team at the Houston Civic Center in a heated discussion with his top campaign advisers.

Travers then informed Shyrock they had followed Masters to the W. P. Hobby Airport, watching as the man put his wife on a flight they discovered was bound for Los Angeles. The wife had relatives in California, Shyrock knew, but she would be easy enough to find. When he got to her, he would dump the ugly truth on the uppity rich bitch. While she wept in shock and outrage, he would have some fun with her, penitentiary style. He'd decide how to take her out after a few hours of letting off some steam on her.

That was tomorrow's plan. Right now, it looked like Masters feared the worst and was circling the wagons. Suddenly the orders didn't seem so easy to carry out. Everything was on the line. Masters was scared, desperate, scrambling to save his future. The man was going to hold down the fort, defend his empire even as the walls were crumbling down on his head. Well, if Shyrock was going down, he damn sure wasn't about to go out alone. He wondered if this was how his hero, his idol felt in those final hours when the Russians were rolling through Berlin, looking to skin him alive.

"Okay, just stay on him. I'll get back to you."

Shyrock hung up and looked at Milan.

It was well into the afternoon. Two hours earlier, Shyrock had gotten the call from the cells east. They would be in base before nightfall. Only the Philly and New York watch commanders hadn't been heard from.

More problems on top of problems. Shyrock had been told Molanski and Stanton had dropped back to deal with the crisis that had plagued them from New York. It seemed as if the problem from back east had tailed them all the way to Chicago. Janson had lined up a major cocaine deal with some Cali guys, but the problem Shyrock was informed about—again—was a special Justice Department agent called Belasko who had blown the deal all to hell. Again. His people had been out on the road, taking casualties across half the country, this bastard, Belasko, nailing them wherever they went. Spooky.

A fucking crisis, bet your ass. It made his blood boil, but Shyrock was looking forward to taking care of the problem himself. A guy like that, all balls, nothing but fire in his eyes, well, Shyrock knew the type. He would recognize their problem the second he laid eyes on him.

Shyrock looked at the duffel bag. It was open, revealing neat stacks of rubber-banded hundred-dollar bills. The bag was far from being full.

"You sure?" he asked Milan.

Milan sucked in a deep breath. "I counted it twice. There's only 150 grand there. Our boy only sent two guys with the plane. Direct order number two he disobeyed. I've got some men sitting with them now. I slapped the crap out of our boy's boys. They claim they didn't touch the money."

Shyrock rubbed his face, got up and poured himself a drink. He filled Milan in on the situation he instinctively knew was headed their way.

"How many people you count on base?"

Milan got up and made his own drink. "If the numbers you got from back east are correct, we're looking at sixty, seventy guys tops."

"What about the kids?"

"They're scared, Frank. I showed them the basics of using an M-16. I might have read that situation wrong. The Fullerton kids, well, they're scared the most. All of them know something's wrong. I told them they'd better be ready to use those M-16s. I got a lot of questions, and I blew up. Forget the kids."

"Okay. Here it is, and it doesn't get much simpler than what I'm going to lay out. We're going to be hit. Round up all of our people—the men, that is. Have them ready for me to brief as soon as our east cells get here."

"And the kids?"

Shyrock killed his drink in one long swallow. "If they don't want to fight, well, there'll be others. You tell them what to do. They're your responsibility. If they hesitate, start crying, well, just have your assault rifle on full-auto mode. I hope that's not a problem for you, Bob.''

''No problem. Just seems like a sorry waste of good talent.''

''There'll be more where they came from. Hell, they're everywhere across the country. They go to public schools where blacks are carrying concealed weapons, they're sick and tired of being harassed and intimidated, their women messed with by the animals. Future threatened by liberal-government programs that are just handouts to keep the natives appeased, let the faggots have their version of a nuclear family. Only all the bullshit out of Washington the past three decades has cost good men and women across this country for too damn long. It's hit our pocketbooks, it's ripping our families apart, dirtying up our blood-line with race-mixing because that's the only way a lesser person can upgrade him- or herself to the status of a man, a human being. Shit, I was in prison. You know what I know, seen what I've seen, done what I've done just to survive, keep some guy's pole out of my ass, well, let's just say I'm here, ready to go the distance to save my own.''

Shyrock went to the bar for another drink, shaking his head. ''Why can't the government leave us alone to do our job? To take care of the business of cleaning up the mess they created? I mean, can't people, our own people, see what we're doing is the only way, the only course of action that will save this country? That will save our race? If we don't do it, twenty years from now, there will be no America, at least not one we recognize. At a time like this, I can't help but think of the Founding Fathers. They would shake their heads and wonder just where and what the hell went wrong with their vision. They wouldn't even recognize this country.''

A sudden rage seized Shyrock. He cursed, then flung the glass against the wall. When it shattered, he saw Milan flinch and growled, ''You with me, Bob? Because right here and right now we are weeding out the weak, we are separating the men from the boys. I need you to look me right in the eye and tell me, Bob.''

Milan killed his drink. ''I'm with you, Frank. All the way.''

Shyrock smiled. He believed the man. Milan was a man of honor, after all. No matter what was ahead, he knew the man would defend the cause to make America right, strong and pure again to the last drop of his blood.

Frank Shyrock felt good about dealing with the future. He was there, back and stronger than ever. Deliverance would prevail. Or he would die defending it.

THE BODY WAS COVERED by a blanket and lay in the back seat of the '67 Ford Galaxy.

Nightfall was quickly dropping over the snow-capped mountain range when Bolan drove deeper into Wyoming.

The Executioner felt haunted, angry. At Daly, for one, for throwing his life away in a final moment of utter insanity. But he understood the man's crazed last act of self-fulfilling doom in order to sate his lust for revenge.

Bolan had been there, after all.

It had been what, a good thousand-mile drive? Across Iowa. Then ditching the shot-up Crown Victoria on some little-traveled road near a small town close to the Iowa-Nebraska border. He'd walked into town, purchasing the cream-colored Ford for eight hundred dollars, and a blanket to cover Daly.

Near Omaha, midmorning, the state's welcome sign had read Nebraska…The Good Life.

The good life. The American dream.

Welcome home to the roots of democracy, cornfields and wheat, amber waves of grain.

Bolan felt the ghosts out there in the heartland, the working, struggling toil and the sweat of men forgotten, replaced by the fast and outrageous fame and fortune of modern pop culture, those sports heroes, rap singers and rock and rollers and all the popular so-called beautiful people who made more in one minute than a schoolteacher earned in two or three years. In some ways, he saw what the enemy saw. But there was no hope in making anything better through one group's desire to isolate the rest of humankind, oppress and dominate through fear, intimidation and violence against others as an outlet for that hate and fear.

The dark side of human nature made all the sense in the world to Mack Bolan. That was a large part of the problem, had proved to him to be Daly's final undoing.

So many endless miles. So much blood. Spilled by the damned and, he hoped, by the forgiven. The drive, the loneliness, the anguish of losing someone who might have been a friend, eating at Bolan's guts. Thinking. The past, the present and the future, meshing into one fireball of pain, the bile of anguish in his mouth.

A good thousand miles, and Bolan felt the vehicle continue to drive itself. Brognola's directions to the remote motel were perfect.

In the distance, clearing a four-building town, west of the interstate, the Executioner spotted the two 4×4 pickups.

He could have been there sooner, had Brognola pick him up by jet, somewhere between Daly's last moment on earth and the Laramie Mountain Range.

The soldier stuck to his own game plan, his own timetable.

Let the enemy all gather, ready to defend their so-called cause.

The Executioner pulled in, killing the engine. He was stepping out when the big man in black, all the bearing of a professional military man, stepped through the doorway.

Bolan gave him the password, then said, ''Tell me what you've got, then I'll tell you what I want.''

The Executioner already knew what he wanted, had thought about since he put Daly's body in the Crown Victoria.

Bolan wanted final and ultimate justice.

Justice for all.

CHAPTER TWENTY-ONE

Crouched in the woods, Bolan punched the button on the side of his chronometer. The illuminated dial flashed for a second. He had twenty-five minutes, and counting, to place the blocks of C-4, and take out as many sentries around the compound as possible. From the north and south edges of the perimeter, two four-man teams of black-garbed commandos would storm the complex.

Always easier said than done.

No matter how many times the Executioner had gone into enemy turf on a hard probe, each situation, each time out was different. Anything at anytime could go wrong.

Failure, though, was something he never thought about. Failure simply meant he wouldn't see the sunrise.

From deep cover in the brush and trees, off the side of the trail, the soldier cradled his M-16. He counted several dozen vehicles, strung out in a line, far down the narrow dirt trail. There were cars of all makes and colors. Crown Victorias and Chevy Caprices seemed to be the standard wheels for the ex-lawmen of Deliverance. Here, though, the soldier found more than a few of them liked their vintage hot rods—old Mustangs and Buicks, '55 T-Birds, late fifties Cadillac convertibles, a few Vettes in mint condition. A lot of muscle and style, money and sweat stretched out before Bolan.

It was time once again to incinerate their dreams. One charge of plastic explosive, placed every three vehicles, should do it. There would be no escape for the enemy.

Slipping the M-16 across his shoulder, Bolan drew the commando dagger from the sheath at his side.

The soldier was weighted down with fifty pounds of C-4, but he intended to lighten the load soon. Spare clips for the Desert Eagle rode in a pouch on the hip of his blacksuit, as did extra mags for the M-16, three frag grenades and three 40 mm loads for the M-203. Since this strike at the enemy was coordinated with commandos with no names, to be launched in the middle of the night, Bolan wore a stick-on white star on his chest. When it hit the fan, there would be a lot of chaos, a whole lot of hard dying. There was no sense in getting cut down by friendly fire.

The trail wound off into thicker stands of trees to the north. He counted four men, all armed with automatic weapons, standing sentry duty. Two were positioned at the far end from Bolan, smoking cigarettes. The other two guards were shadows, outlined in the outer reaches of the soft hue of a klieg light that shone on the lead vehicles. They were the closest, and they would be the first to go.

Back at the motel, some thirty miles south, Bolan had gone over the aerial and satellite recon photos. There looked to be four main structures around the complex. If possible, he intended to find out what each building was, and spare anything that looked like a command center.

There was a good reason for that.

He had called Brognola before leaving the motel to touch base. It was as if the ghost of Daly, with his words about a Mr. Big had found their way into the room. Indeed, Bolan had caught rumblings from Brognola that there was someone powerful who was maybe financing the organization. More details were to come, since Brognola was still checking on it, running down phone records. If hard proof of a major player helping Deliverance from the shadows was somewhere on the compound, Bolan intended to find it.

He left the satchel with the C-4 behind and padded out onto the trail. Sentry three moved away, toward the others at the far end. Dagger in hand, Bolan crouched behind a red Corvette. Swiftly he sprinted to the far side of his first victim.

Bolan sprang from between a Monte Carlo and white Cadillac convertible. One hand clamped over the guy's mouth, the soldier hauled the sentry out of sight from the others. One lightning stroke, and the Executioner slashed the sentry's throat with razor-sharp steel. Moments later he laid the corpse in the thin crust of snow, wiped the blade clean on the dead man's pant leg and sheathed the knife.

Hunched low, Bolan drew the Beretta. He needed information about the compound, a name of their so-called national watch commander, positions and numbers of the enemy force. So far, he hadn't seen any signs of booby traps, but he needed that confirmed either way before venturing any deeper into the southern edge of the compound.

Bolan was shadowing up their blind side when it nearly went to hell. One of the sentries became alarmed when he found one of their own missing.

"Benny?"

The guy lifted his assault rifle, moving away from the others.

Bolan made his move. Popping up on the far side of a black '55 T-Bird, he drilled a 9 mm round from the silenced Beretta through the guy's skull. Tracking on, he pumped another slug through the third sentry's forehead.

The fourth sentry was stunned by the sudden attack. It was long enough for Bolan to send the guy's Colt Commando assault rifle flying from a hand that was shattered by another 9 mm round.

In three long strides, Bolan was all over his prisoner. The garrote was out and wrapped around the man's neck before he could bellow a curse or scream a warning.

Bolan pulled the guy off the trail, thin piano wire drawing a line of crimson across the guy's throat.

When he had the man in the brush, on his knees, Bolan quietly growled in his ear, "Three seconds to answer some questions. Tell me everything you know about the compound."

Bolan heard what he needed. There were sixty to seventy heavily armed men. Shyrock, ex–Chicago cop, was the national watch commander. His command center was at the south edge, isolated from the war-planning lodge, fuel and munitions depot. No booby traps ringed the perimeter.

Suddenly Bolan's prisoner fell into hard silence. The guy was holding back. Bolan encouraged him to

talk with just enough force on the piano wire to dig
a little deeper into his throat.

The guy's hands clawed at the wire, as if that
would save him. Bolan tugged a little, and he went
utterly still.

"Okay, okay. Two guys, they flew in today with
some money for Frank. Some big shot from Texas,
Houston, I heard. Frank's got something on him. This
big shot, I don't know his name, don't know who he
is, I swear. Word is he's sort of the founder of Deliverance."

"Anything else?"

"Well, yeah. There's the kids."

Bolan felt his heart skip a beat. "The kids?"

What he heard next sent Bolan's blood racing hot
with rage. He heard the name Milan and heard how
Deliverance had been combing the heartland of
America for young angry men, "their own blood,"
according to the guy. Young guys who wanted to be
in law enforcement were contacted by phone, Internet, in person. Milan was a former cop from the Denver PD, had contacts and connections in the Mile
High City's force. Milan knew the SOP for placement
into and through police academies.

Bolan got the whole sordid picture. Deliverance
had been building for the future. They had targeted
poor and disillusioned young men from small-town
America. They brought them to Wyoming, where
young and impressionable minds were indoctrinated
into the racist hate agenda, to be trained in body and
mind, and sent through various police academies. Being a former cop, this Milan, Bolan knew, could show
the kids the ropes, how to beat the psych tests, pass
written exams with ease. In short, how to lie, cheat

and steal for the organization while out there on the streets of American cities, executing whoever they felt was unworthy of living, at will.

It was an age-old concept, a form of psychological warfare that had led entire nations to declare wholesale slaughter on the rest of mankind. Prey on a man's fears, pump him up with enough arrogance and belief that he or his own kind were the only worthy species, and he would go all the way, march to his own death to prove his own superiority.

Bolan asked exactly where the kids were and heard they were in an isolated lodge at the far north end of the compound. Then he heard Milan was right then at the bivouac, armed with an MP-5 subgun. They all knew they were going to be hit. The kids were expected to pull their weight, or Milan had been ordered to kill them all.

Bolan seethed in silence. If there was any chance of saving those young men, he would. For the most part, he figured they had been unknowingly led into something that was far beyond their comprehension. The deceit and clever lies, mixed with some degree of truth by old and world-wise savages, might have worn thin, since Bolan's prisoner informed him the kids were scared and didn't want to fight. So this Milan was going to execute his dream gone sour.

Bolan had heard more than enough.

Terror suddenly bulged in the guy's eyes. "Okay, I told you what you wanted. How about getting this thing off my throat?"

"Sure thing," Bolan said, releasing the pressure, then smartly rapping the butt of his M-16 against the guy's head and slipping on plastic cuffs.

Quickly Bolan backtracked to the doomsday

satchel. In under a minute, he had the charges in place. All labor of love in the form of vintage wheels would soon go up in flames.

He checked his chronometer. It was going to be cutting it close.

He had to get to those kids.

Their future was now, Bolan knew, in his hands, their only hope of salvation being hauled away from this place of hatred and certain death.

Bolan moved out.

He offered a silent prayer that he wasn't too late.

THE POTENTIAL RESCUE run ate up fifteen minutes. But Bolan had penetrated the compound, made his way to the lodge where the young dream warriors of Deliverance were going to be slaughtered if they didn't do what their recruiter wanted. Which, according to the intel he'd forced out of the sentry, was to wield a weapon and go out in some twisted blaze of glory for the organization against an undetermined, unknown enemy force.

On the way, Bolan had placed the rest of the C-4 at both corners of what he suspected was a main barracks for the enemy. Indeed, he'd seen enough gunmen, inside and outside the big lodge, to know the plastique would decimate their numbers. If all went well.

So far so good. Three more enemy shadows had been put to the final sleep by knife or garrote, then dragged off into the woods. And Bolan had sensed their tension, their alertness before each kill. It told him Shyrock knew they were going to be hit.

It made sense. The savaged cells from the east had most certainly already alerted their national watch commander to the seemingly unending series of disasters that had followed them, like a hurricane, from Brooklyn, west, all the way to Wyoming.

In the distance, Bolan saw a tall bulky figure standing in the doorway of the lodge—Milan, no doubt, an MP-5 subgun in his hands.

The Executioner settled behind an outhouse, taking in the night. Milan was barking at his recruits, then yelling at the young men. The kids were confused, scared to death. This wasn't something they had bargained for, being handed a weapon and ordered to kill or be killed.

Bolan moved out, giving his surroundings one last sweep. The entire compound was nestled in the foothills of the Laramie Mountain Range. It was rugged wilderness, in the middle of nowhere. For Shyrock to maintain a compound of this size, Bolan guessed the sheriff of the local county had been paid off. More players had covered for the enemy, but they would be dealt with in time.

Right now, Bolan was on the verge of scattering half the complex up the mountainside. All he had to do was pull out the detonator box. One flick of the switch, one stab of the button, and one radio signal would activate the C-4.

He checked his chronometer again. The team of commandos would be in place by now.

First he had to save the kids.

"Listen to me, gentlemen!" Bolan heard Milan yell. "This is potentially an hour of crisis. You are being called upon to help save your own futures. You have weapons, and you will follow me and do as I tell you."

Closing on the lodge, Bolan found no other targets

around the structure, other than Milan. South, beyond a thin ring of trees, he saw the buildings of the main compound. Several shadows patrolled the structures from that direction.

Suddenly the soldier heard a frightened voice cry out in protest, "I don't understand, Mr. Milan. Who is it you think is coming to...I don't know, get us? Are we going to be arrested?"

Another scared voice from inside wanted to know, "Is it the FBI? You're telling us we might have to shoot somebody. Who is it? This isn't the way it was supposed to be."

"Yeah. We were told you would help us get into the academy. All we want is to become policemen."

"And you will, if you do exactly what I tell you. First I need an answer from you boys." Milan's voice was mounting with anger, impatience. "I have given you weapons, I have shown you how to use them. Now, are you going to follow me and do exactly as I order?"

"Who are we supposed to be fighting?"

"I can't do it!" Bolan heard another young voice cry out, scared to death. "Something's wrong here."

Other young voices protested their dissent.

Milan's voice fell to a cold level of deadly intent, as Bolan shadowed up to the front door.

The ex-cop lifted the subgun and snarled, "Why, you little punk-ass cowards! It would sure look to me like none of you are good enough to be part of a new America."

Someone started to scream in terror from inside. Milan shouted, "Obviously you're mice and not men. Sorry, gentlemen."

Bolan pulled his Beretta and yelled, "Milan!"

The big guy in the sheepskin coat spun, and Bolan cored two coughing 9 mm rounds through Milan's face.

Then it went south on the Executioner.

He was surging for the doorway when he caught the shadow wheel around the corner of the lodge. The assault rifle was flaming in the shadow's fists. Bullets ate up wood beneath his feet as Bolan cleared the stoop, diving through the doorway.

The Executioner hit the floor. On the roll, he was already swinging the M-16 off his shoulder when he suddenly found the muzzle of another M-16, pointing down toward his face.

Bolan found a big blond kid, with terror and confusion in his eyes, looming over him, on the other end of the weapon.

CHAPTER TWENTY-TWO

There was a good chance the kid was so scared he would trigger the assault rifle out of sheer panic, but Bolan didn't think twice about slapping the muzzle away from his face. He was on his feet, pulling the M-16 out of the blond kid's hands, when he was forced to turn an instant burst of autofire at the shadow barreling through the doorway.

The soldier cut that enemy down with a figure-eight burst, ragged holes spouting crimson as the guy back-pedaled out of there. No sooner was that bullet-riddled scarecrow pitching back, across the stoop, than Bolan pulled out the detonator box.

He didn't hear any footsteps beyond, but made the door, giving the front of the building a hard check just the same.

He found the enemy had been alerted by the gun-fire. Defenders were scrambling through the doorways of the structures of the main complex when Bolan activated the plastique.

Night was turned into day. Two mountainous balls of blinding fire roared skyward. The series of tremen-dous blasts at the far south end sent flaming wreckage soaring high above the trees. Glowing hands of sear-ing fire reached out for maybe fifty yards in all directions from the big lodge, vaporizing anything that moved. Thunder rolled for long moments and the earth shook under Bolan's feet. The fuel and munitions depot then erupted. In the distance, the fuel tanks of sky-bound wreckage from the trail ignited in midair.

It was doomsday for Deliverance.

He saw the commandos break cover to the north edge of the woods. In the distance, four fingers of lead doom parted the night from the south. Packed groups of enemy figures, either running pell-mell across the compound or picking themselves up off the ground, were mowed down where they were.

Bolan walked back into the lodge. He ran a cold eye over the young men. This was no time for sympathy or understanding. They were scared and knew something here was terribly wrong. Someday, perhaps sooner than they liked, they would find out just how wrong it was here.

"Stay here. Do not go outside. I'm with the United States Department of Justice. I am the real and only law you need to obey any longer. Are we clear on what I want?"

They nodded, down to the last young recruit.

Outside, Bolan swiftly forged toward the savage firefight.

Autofire blistered the air in all directions.

The Executioner pumped a 40 mm grenade into a group of five shadows headed his way. The blast scattered them in countless shreds of torn flesh. One guy who had survived the soldier's fireball was groaning, hauling in his weapon, crabbing along. Bolan delivered a mercy round into his skull.

Moving on, the soldier swept long raking bursts of

M-16 autofire over anything ahead that wasn't wearing a white star.

They were dropping, spinning and screaming all over the place, dying hard for the twisted cause of Deliverance.

The Executioner strode, tall and grim, to the outer limits of ground zero. Fire raged in his ears, the heat from the inferno so furious there was no longer even a trace of men's breath in the cold mountain air.

The Executioner rammed a fresh clip into his M-16, then poured on the killing heat, cranking it up another few degrees.

SHYROCK HAD ALERTED his men guarding the Masters people to have his jet fueled up. If it went bad, there was a chance he would have to bolt from the compound, fly directly to Houston. There, he would pick up the rest of his money, in person. Masters could do it the hard way or the easy way. Personally Shyrock wanted the guy to try and get tough with him.

Then it went bad.

The whole compound sounded as if it were being uprooted, blasted clear into the next state. The concussive force was so great, Shyrock found himself knocked to the floor of his command post, windows shattering, glass and other debris flying everywhere. What the hell had just hit them?

Then something came crashing through the ceiling. It bounced, rolled and hammered through the wall. It was on fire, mangled up so bad it took a full three seconds for Shyrock to recognize what was left of somebody's vintage Mustang.

The problem from back east had arrived.

Shyrock grabbed a Colt Commando assault rifle.

He hauled in the duffel bag with the money and slipped it around his shoulder.

Outside, the national watch commander of Deliverance found utter pandemonium. The war-planning and rec lodge was obliterated, nothing but sprawled bodies all around the flaming ruins. Worse, whatever troops had survived the initial explosions were being hosed down by two teams, firing away with assault rifles. Precision bursts from chattering M-16s bowled his people down, gutted them or blasted open their skulls as they scrambled or picked themselves up off the ground.

Shyrock made a beeline for the woods at the west edge of the compound. Beyond was the airfield. The game here was dead. They had been hit hard, and this was a take-no-prisoners deal.

He was thinking he could always regroup, start over. Next time, he would have to begin small, of course, but maybe that was the best way to go. Keep a new organization to a couple dozen men, at least in the starting-over phase.

All he had to do was get to the jet in one piece, with his money.

Then he realized he'd left behind the Masters photos, and cursed. He couldn't go back now. Hell, he'd figure out something later. Maybe dig up one of the hookers from Chicago, have her start showing up on the campaign trail, legs flashing all over the place. Maybe run right up and plant a big sloppy one on the tycoon's mouth, film at six o'clock. "Remember me, Roger, from Chicago?"

Then Shyrock saw him. He was a big shadow, maybe a dozen or so yards away. There was no doubt who that big guy with the M-16 was, as firelight washed over his face and Shyrock took one look at the unforgiving steel in those eyes.

"Shyrock!"

The big guy was calling his name, coming his way. Shyrock triggered the Colt Commando, but the guy moved, as quick as lightning. One second, Shyrock had his autofire tracking him; the next heartbeat, the problem was gone.

With all the flames, smoke, guys screaming and dying, it was hard to tell who was who, or who was doing what exactly.

Somehow, Shyrock made the cover of the trees. He was racing ahead, fanning the gloom with his Colt Commando when he saw something bounce up, right in front of his path. One look at the object, and he knew exactly what it was an eye blink before the grenade erupted.

THE EXECUTIONER'S frag grenade hit a perfect intercept point. It blew up in Shyrock's face a split second after the national watch commander became aware he was in his last moment on earth. Countless pieces of lethal steel bits shredded the man. The duffel bag was sent flying, ripped apart by the explosion. Then tattered pieces of hundred-dollar bills fluttered to the floor of the woods.

Bolan turned toward the hellzone. He ordered two of the commandos to secure the airfield, not to let anyone leave. If any aircraft attempted to take off, they were to blow it out of the sky. The soldier then told another commando to stay with the kids at the lodge, make certain no harm came to them. There was a moment's look of confusion thrown Bolan's way, then the commandos dispersed to carry out his orders.

The C-4 blasts had done most of the gruesome work for Bolan and his commandos, known only to him by letters. Still, he discovered two of the team had been killed in the line of fire. Another commando was down, wounded, and Bolan made his way to Agent Z. The Executioner scythed down a half-dozen racing shadows with short bursts of M-16 fire. If anyone tried to stagger to his feet and raise a weapon, he burned him to the ground.

All that was left was a little mop-up. Dead men littered the compound in all directions. Wreckage was still hammering the earth around Bolan as delayed blasts thundered from the trail. A wall of fire ringed the perimeter. It was a vision of hell on earth, and maybe beyond. At least for the enemy.

Checking his flanks, but finding no enemy left standing, Bolan, after making sure a commando stayed with the wounded man, rolled for the smoking command center. It was the only building left intact, but it had taken a direct hit from some guy's vintage wheels. A tongue of fire was right then lapping at the shattered hole in the back wall.

Cautiously Bolan plunged into the boiling smoke. Inside the building, he crunched over debris as he moved to the desk and opened the top drawer.

In plain view was a stack of sordid photographs. Bingo. He wasn't sure he recognized the older man in the pictures, naked, and smoking crack. A lot of the pictures showed the man in various sexual acts with a woman. Recognition was nagging at him as he heard boot steps crunch over the litter outside. Looking up, he found one of the commandos stepping through the smoke. A moment later, the commando was beside Bolan, scouring the photos.

The commando swore softly. Bolan read the disgust in the man's eyes as the commando asked, "Do you know who that is?"

ONE MORE DRINK to calm the nerves. If only the damn phone would stop ringing. Whoever would be calling that time of night was another headache.

Finally Masters ripped the phone off his desk, extension and all, and flung it across the room.

Lyle entered the study. "Is everything all right, sir?"

"Get my limo. I'm going to the airport."

Lyle, faithful servant, nodded and left Masters alone.

After that drink, Masters dialed open the wall safe. He took fat stacks of hundred-dollar bills, which totaled a quarter million, and stuffed a suitcase. He had lied to Shyrock, but Roger Masters wasn't going to be strong-armed by bad memories he had long since tried to forget. Okay, there'd been a hooker or two along the way. Smoked some crack. Got his knob polished. What was the problem anyway? Yeah, they'd feel cheated, betrayed, those loyal friends and followers who were touting him as the man of the people, the big Texan who was going to make things right. But make what right, anyway? Crime was out of control. The savages owned the city streets; the whole country was on the verge of collapse, anarchy. The only real answer was to start killing people. Deliverance style. That had seemed the perfect, the only solution, long ago. Things had changed since then.

The problem was he had money. Too much money. They all wanted it, or if they couldn't get it, they'd steal it, or they wanted a piece of him. All the time, they came to him with their get-rich-quick deals if only he'd back them with some capital. Or they had their hand out for a loan. Or they hung around, waiting for him to pick up the bar tab. They were jealous and petty, didn't deserve to be in the same room as him. That included his campaign advisers. All day long, nagging the hell out of him. Was there a problem, Roger? He didn't seem himself. Was there something they should know about?

They didn't understand that he needed to get away for a few days.

Of course not.

They'd never understand how a man as rich and powerful as he was should be able to do whatever the hell he wanted and others should just let him be. That included his wife, frigid, nagging and always whining. Spending his money like there was no tomorrow. No wonder he needed a strange piece on the side on occasion. Well, he'd packed her off for her sister's place. She had an unlimited expense account. That should keep her quiet for a few weeks.

Hawaii sounded pretty good. Let things cool off. Maybe call Frank, reason with him.

Masters made another drink, sat at his desk and opened the drawer. He pulled out the .44 Magnum and grabbed a few speed loaders. He was worried about his Wyoming trouble; it was that proverbial dark cloud.

Shyrock was an ex-convict, full of hate and rage, but he could back up his talk. By now, Shyrock would know he'd been lied to. He could have gotten the man's money, but it was all too risky to just start forking over a quarter million. Maybe next the bastard would want a half million. Once something like that started, there was no stopping it.

Why couldn't Frank understand? Roger Masters was going respectable. He had to distance himself from this Deliverance business. What the hell was wrong with people, anyway? Well, the same thing pretty much, he decided, that was wrong with the rest of the country. They were out there, whining all over the place, living only to take, not caring about anything or anybody except their own small world of greed and want. Human nature seemed to have come full circle in the land, at its worst. He wondered if he even wanted to be governor. They would tell him to watch his drinking, watch his mouth. Bunch of do-gooders. The country was full of nothing but lawyers and assholes.

Twenty minutes and two drinks later, Lyle hadn't reappeared. Something was wrong. He'd seen those two around town, half the day. The same cold, dead eyes Frank had. Frank's people, his gunslingers, he was sure of it. They were stalking him, ready to get tough if he didn't deliver the cash. Frank had told him as much on that loudmouthed guy's radio show.

He was reaching for the intercom when the door to his study suddenly opened. Lyle staggered in, blood soaking his shirtfront.

"Who's there?" Masters screamed, grabbing up his .44 Magnum pistol as Lyle crumpled to the carpet.

"We can do this the easy way, Masters. All Frank wants is his money. There are two of us. Your people are dead. Don't do anything stupid, Masters."

They were just outside the door.

"You the two jerks who've been followin' me around all day?"

"Come on, Masters. Let us come in. We can talk this out."

Masters lifted the .44 Magnum. "Okay. That's fine. Show yourselves."

He was crouching behind his desk, sighting down the big cannon, when the first of the two men stepped into the doorway. One of them had his hands up, but the holstered side arm was left exposed by his open jacket.

Masters squeezed the trigger. The sound of the cannon going off shattered the study. He rode the recoil, seeing he'd scored a direct hit.

"Take that back to Frank and tell him he's fucking with the wrong Texan!"

It felt good to see their terror, Masters decided. He was going down with the Alamo. Sam Houston would have been proud.

BOLAN PARKED his rental by the front gate. He was still togged in blacksuit. It had been a short flight down to Houston in the tycoon's own Lear, his pilots in tow. Bolan had called Brognola and filled him in. The phone records checked out to a worst-case scenario, pointing to the Roger Masters office building in downtown Houston, and his estate, twenty miles outside the city proper.

It looked like the soldier was at the end of the line. The man who would be king of Texas had duped and lied to the unknowing followers of whatever his vision was for too long.

The Masters dream was crystal clear to Bolan. It was simply another version of Deliverance, only Masters was slated to most likely grab the reins of power in the governor's mansion.

Armed with the silenced Beretta and Desert Eagle, Bolan slid out of the rental and headed up the driveway and discovered the first of four bodies. Going into this, he was made aware by the pilots of the tycoon's security force. They were simply bodyguards, none of them perhaps knowing whom exactly they protected. If he'd run into them, he would give them a choice.

Flight or fight.

Masters would get a little different option.

Give it up and come clean with the law, or face the Executioner's final and ultimate justice.

The sound of the hand cannon roaring from inside the mansion told Bolan that Masters wanted the hard way.

Crouched, Desert Eagle in hand, the soldier went through the open double doors. He was moving down the foyer when he heard an angry voice snarl, "Not smart, Roger. Frank's not going to like this."

Frank. It was all Bolan needed to hear.

He reached the corner of the hall and saw the figure hunched beside an open doorway that led to a study.

The guy never saw it coming. One squeeze of the Desert Eagle's trigger, and Bolan blew off half the man's head.

The soldier reached the doorway to the study and told Masters he was with the Justice Department.

"Bullshit!" Masters yelled, and pumped two .44 rounds into the doorway, splintering wood above Bolan's head.

"It's over, Masters, Shyrock's dead. I know what he had on you. I've seen it. You don't have to see it end this way."

"If you're really with the Justice Department, show

me a badge. On second thought, skip it. I saw Frank flash enough phony badges, so, you can go to hell."

Bolan knew the voice of insanity all too well. The guy wasn't going to be taken in alive. This was the devil, locked in pride, defending his kingdom to the last vile breath.

So be it. The estate was isolated enough so that gunfire wouldn't alert anyone to call the police. On the flight down, Bolan had the pilots, close associates of Masters, fill him in on the estate, personnel. There were no butlers, maids or hired help. Only the security force, and they were dead.

"Last chance, Masters."

Bolan pinpointed the direction from where that voice of rage bellowed. Dead ahead, maybe fifteen feet away, twelve o'clock. Probably hunkered down behind a desk.

"If you're really with the Justice Department, then you know who I am. I can't let you take me in. I'd be ruined, disgraced. They'd eat me alive in prison."

"At least you'll live."

"Live?" The guy laughed. "You call that living? Talk to Frank for two seconds about life in the penitentiary. It's not my way. I'll tell you what. You want to be reasonable about this, I got a quarter million in cash, right here. It's yours. Just walk away."

"I'm not for sale. You have two seconds."

Masters replied by drilling two more .44 slugs through the doorway. Then Bolan heard the hammer clicking on a dry chamber.

The Executioner made his move. He was through the doorway, darting to the side, when he saw Masters drop six live loads with a speed loader into the .44 Magnum pistol and snap the cylinder shut.

Bolan hit the floor as the hand cannon boomed, blasting a hole in the wall where his head had been a second earlier.

Masters was screaming, swinging the hand cannon toward Bolan.

The Executioner came up, triggering the Desert Eagle. The first hollowpoint round blew open the chest of the tycoon, who spun in a spray of blood and shredded cloth.

Masters staggered, a look of utter disbelief on his face. He tried to track for Bolan, even as he was dying, clinging with desperation and terror to his world.

When Masters finally pitched out of sight, Bolan stood and holstered the Desert Eagle. Heavyhearted, troubled, Bolan turned to leave that place where something of a final justice for all had been proclaimed.

The dawn of the
Fourth Reich...

THE

Destroyer™

#114 Failing Marks
The Fatherland Files Book III

Created by
WARREN MURPHY
and RICHARD SAPIR

From the mountains of Argentina the losers of World War II are
making plans for the Fourth Reich. But when the Destroyer's brain
is downloaded, he almost puts an end to the idea. Adolf Kluge
plans to save the dream with a centuries-old treasure. But then, the
Master of Sinanju may have different plans....

The third in The Fatherland Files, a miniseries based on a secret
fascist organization's attempts to regain the glory of the Third Reich.

Available in February 1999 at your favorite retail outlet.

James Axler

OUTLANDERS™

ICEBLOOD

Kane and his companions race to find a piece of the
Chintamanti Stone, which they believe to have power
over the collective mind of the evil Archons. Their
journey sees them foiled by a Russian mystic named
Zakat in Manhattan, and there is another dangerous
encounter waiting for them in the Kun Lun mountains
of China.

One man's quest for power unleashes a cataclysm in
America's wastelands.

A preview from hell...

JAMES AXLER
DEATH LANDS®
Dark Emblem

After a relatively easy mat-trans jump, Ryan and his companions find themselves in the company of Dr. Silas Jamaisvous, a seemingly pleasant host who appears to understand the mat-trans systems extremely well.

Seeing signs that local inhabitants have been used as guinea pigs for the scientist's ruthless experiments, the group realizes that they have to stop this line of research before it goes too far....